THE STONE COLD THRILLER SERIES - BOOKS 7-9

A STONE COLD THRILLER BOXSET

J. D. WESTON

WESTON MEDIA

STONE GAME

CHAPTER ONE

When the doors of Pentonville Prison closed behind Noah Finn and he smelled the fresh air, he knew that life on the outside would be harder than on the inside. At least when he was locked up, guards could lock him in, and encounters with other inmates who preyed upon men like him could be kept away, as long as Noah played the game and reciprocated the good deed when the time came.

It had only been three years since he walked as a free man and nothing much had changed, except the sky was blue and cars were newer and more modern looking. On the inside, Noah had developed eyes in the back of his head. An almost sixth sense of situational awareness was the result of an extremely difficult first three months. He'd been beaten, raped and forced to do shocking things to other men with the point of a sharpened tool in his ear as motivation.

On the train to his old home in Dunmow, Essex, he sat at the far end of the carriage where he could see the other passengers and anyone who came in from the next carriage. He would be ready. Something else he'd learned; it wasn't good enough just to know where everybody was; he needed to be ready to defend himself whatever way he could.

He sat and watched London slip by and give way to the green fields of the Essex countryside. It was the middle of the day and a few other passengers shared the journey with him. All of them were oblivious to the man who sat at the end of the carriage, and the terrible things he'd done.

Eventually, the train stopped in Chelmsford, where Noah disembarked and made his way to the bus station outside. It seemed an age since he'd been there, and he remembered it well, despite the local council's vain attempts to keep it looking fresh.

Standing waiting for the bus that would pass through his village of Dunmow, he felt vulnerable. He was aware of his appearance; his dirty old running shoes, tracksuit bottoms and an old leather jacket were all the clothes he had. His smarter jeans had been ruined on his first day inside when he'd been accidentally left alone with two other inmates. Maybe it had been a genuine mistake, but Noah thought otherwise. He knew it had been a chance for the guards to size him up, to see if he would be trouble, to see if he would fight back, cry or just take his punishment. Noah Finn had curled into a ball on the floor and taken the beating. He hadn't cried, it had all happened too fast; the tears had come when he was taken to his cell and left alone for the first time.

The bus arrived and Noah stepped on, glad to be somewhere relatively safe. He noted the cameras on the bus; they hadn't been there before he'd been away. It gave him a sense of security. He kept telling himself that he'd paid his penance, and he was now a free man. Yet he couldn't shake the feeling that society hadn't forgotten, and they never would.

The ride took thirty minutes, and Noah allowed himself a smile at the familiar sights. He made a plan. He'd pick up a few things from the store and then go home, where he'd stay for a few days. It would take that long to get his things together and his money sorted. Then he could leave, and go find somewhere he wouldn't be recognised. A new life was what he needed. A fresh start.

The bus stopped at the north end of the village, and Noah stepped onto the pavement. He habitually looked left and right and then behind him before he began walking at a brisk pace towards the big store halfway down the high street. He glanced over his shoulder and avoided eye contact with the few people he passed by looking into the shop windows. Thankfully, nobody recognised him.

He began to feel safer when he turned into his quiet street. His house was the third from the end, a semi-detached three-bedroom house that his parents had left him. A part of Noah was thankful that his parents were dead. They'd be destroyed by the shame. But part of him wished his mum was alive; he always felt safe with her. She had died a few years after his father, and as he walked along his street, he remembered how they'd sit together in the evenings. Noah had often been taunted by the local children for his appearance. He knew he had the look of a dummy; he knew his jaw hung open, and that his eyes were too close together. He knew his clothes weren't fashionable.

The kids had thrown stones at him and called him names. Some of it was because his parents were strict churchgoers and seemed to be stuck in the fifties or sixties. But he knew that he didn't help matters by the way he looked. One time, some boys had found him in the woods at the end of his street. It was the only place he could go to relieve himself when he got the urge. His parents wouldn't allow their son to molest himself in the house, and though he had his own room, their strong belief in God made him feel as if He was there, even though he secretly didn't believe himself. A stone had hit him on the back of his head, and he'd fallen over with his tracksuit bottoms around his ankles. That was when the taunting got really bad.

Noah's father woke up one morning to find the word 'wanker' sprayed across his old Ford Cortina, and people began to cross the street when Noah was walking towards them. Word had apparently gotten around the small village.

Those boys would be adults now, thought Noah, as he pushed the gate of his house open and closed it behind him. He wondered if they would remember him, or if it would all be put down to childhood shenanigans. He wondered if they'd still call him 'Nobby Noah' if they saw him. He didn't know why he cared what they thought or if they'd remember him. None of it would matter in a few days.

But he knew three girls who would never forget. He also knew that three girls meant three families, brothers, fathers and mothers who would all know sooner or later that Noah had been released. If he could keep his head down for a few days until his money came through from the transfer, he would be okay.

He stepped through the overgrown garden to the familiar brown front door, which now had flaky paintwork and abusive insults sprayed across the small glass window at the top. He shut the door behind him and leaned back onto it. Closing his eyes, Noah took deep breaths. He was safe.

He pulled the small security chain across to its locked position and let his eyes wash across the large hallway. The parquet flooring was just as he remembered it, dirty and dusty, but exactly as it had been. The flowery wallpaper his father had hung was peeling in some corners, and a simple wooden statue of Jesus on a cross was fixed to the centre of the wall between the front door and the entrance to the living room.

The house was large with huge bay windows at the front and a great chimney breast in the living room. The journey and his emotions had gotten the better of him and, seeing the couches in the front room, he realised how exhausted he was. He tested the lights; the electricity was still on. The bills had been paid automatically from his account while he had been away.

He sat down on the green couch and gently bounced twice, relishing the comfort. His mother's crocheted blanket hung over the back, just as Noah had left it. The TV wasn't a flash flat screen. It was big and boxy, and he had to stand to turn it on. He'd had a nicer TV in his cell, but not his mum's comfy green couch.

While he was up, he took his small bag of groceries to the kitchen. The huge butler sink stood empty, and his mum's pans and cooking implements hung on the walls all around it. The old gas stove seemed to have an angry face due to the position of the knobs and handles. The pantry door was closed. Noah knew it would be a mess inside. He knew the perishable food would either be stale or already eaten by whatever rodents had got in, but there would be tinned food. With the addition of the few items he had in his bag, he would get by for a few days.

"Just a few days," he told himself, smelling the musty, stale scent of his old home. Beyond the kitchen was the small glass conservatory his father had built when Noah was a boy. He recalled how he wasn't allowed to help in case a piece of glass fell and cut him in half. He also remembered that the conservatory could be looked into from the forest at the end of the garden. He wouldn't go out there.

It was a light summer evening, and he'd had a long day, so Noah ventured upstairs. He was looking forward to changing out of the clothes from the prison. Most inmates had clothes brought in for them. But those who either didn't have anybody or couldn't afford it wore the clothes they came in with or whatever was left behind by previous inmates. Noah had been given a pair of old tracksuit bottoms, which he'd taken to the shower room with him to wash.

The old bath taps gave some resistance, but eventually, after coughing and spluttering, and an initial brown offering, they had produced clean water, and it was hot. He let the water run and walked to his old bedroom. The bed was unmade but everything was as he had left it three years earlier. It was a mess. The police had turned the place upside down. It was as if they had known where to look. They'd found the girls' underwear beneath his drawer inside the cabinet, but had turned the place upside down anyway.

He stepped over the mess and pulled out some clean clothes and a towel from his cupboard. Then he stripped, wrapped the towel around himself and headed back to the bathroom. The bath was halfway full when he stepped in, relishing the clean feel of the water and the hot steam cleansing his body. Showers inside had been sparse and brief or long and painful if he timed it wrong. He was pleased to sit in the water, and a small guilty smile crept onto his face as he laid his head back and put his arms on the bath edge.

That was Noah's mistake.

It was fifteen minutes later when he tried to turn the water off that he realised he couldn't move his arms. They were stuck to the bathtub. He panicked and tried to rip them off, but whatever held him there began to tear his skin. He kicked the tap off with his foot and sat and thought about his predicament. He was confused. His skin was stuck by some kind of adhesive. But it was impossible.

Then he heard the voice outside the door.

CHAPTER TWO

"Isn't it wonderful?" said Melody, staring out the window of their rented camper van as Harvey coaxed it around the tight country lanes. "Don't you miss England?"

Harvey didn't reply at first. He finished taking the bend then straightened the van and selected fourth gear before he glanced across at Melody, who sat doe-eyed at the rolling fields and green trees.

"It's nice, yeah," replied Harvey eventually.

"Just *nice*?" asked Melody with a smile. "I love England at this time of year, the countryside and the rolling hills, the birds. It makes me wonder what life was like when things were simpler."

Harvey didn't reply.

"I love the colours in the grasses and the trees and the blue sky," said Melody. "I love the way the fields seem to join like a patchwork quilt that stretches on forever."

"Have you spoken to Reg?" asked Harvey. "You said you were going to call him to arrange meeting up."

Melody knew the romance of the scenery was beyond

Harvey, and she let the change in conversation go as easily as it had come.

"Yeah, I spoke to him yesterday. I *told* you I did," said Melody. "Don't you remember me saying?"

Harvey didn't reply.

"What *is* wrong with you?" asked Melody.

Harvey glanced across at her.

"Harvey, your silent, sultry demeanour won't work with me. Tell me what's wrong."

"Nothing's wrong, Melody. Tell me about Reg and dinner. Will Jess be there?"

Melody eyed Harvey, who purposely looked away and out of his own window.

"Yes, she'll be there. I'm looking forward to seeing them. It seems weird Reg having a girlfriend, doesn't it?"

"Are you going to give me directions?" asked Harvey.

Melody understood Harvey's tone. She knew not to push for an answer; it would come eventually, maybe when he was ready to talk.

"Just stay on this road and turn right at the end," replied Melody.

They drove on in silence. The glorious countryside around them overshadowed the fractious mood.

By the time they had reached the end of the long and winding lane, some thirty minutes later, the signs for Dunmow began to appear more frequently, and Harvey began to provoke conversation with Melody.

"So, this is where you grew up then, is it?" he said, seemingly impressed.

"Not far from here. We lived in the village, the campsite is close to our old house," said Melody. "I wouldn't mind taking a walk around there at some point to see the place."

Harvey didn't reply.

Instead, he turned a corner near an old cottage with a huge thatched roof. The high street stretched out before them.

"So?" said Melody. "What do you think?"

"It's nice," said Harvey. "I like it."

"It used to be a lot smaller when mum and dad were younger, but it's such a pretty place. I think it still has most of its charm."

"Where are they buried?" asked Harvey.

"Not far, in the next village, we'll go there now."

"The *next village?*"

"Yeah, it's a stunning little place called Little Easton. They got married there too."

Harvey didn't reply.

"That's where I'd like to get married, Harvey, so mum and dad can be there. It's a beautiful church."

Melody watched for a reaction from the corner of her eye. Harvey slowed for a pedestrian crossing and turned to look at her, catching her sly stare.

"If that's what you want," he replied.

"You wouldn't mind?" she asked, surprised at how easy it had been to convince him.

"Why would I mind?"

"I don't know, maybe you had ideas of your own."

"I did," replied Harvey. "My idea was to get out of crime, move to France, ride my motorbike and sit on the beach for the rest of my life. And now look, I'm getting married to an MI6 operative, and we've got a dog and a bloody camper van."

Melody smiled and turned in her seat to see their dog, Boon, laying on his back on the couch at the rear of the camper. His ears pricked up, and he lazily opened an eye. He closed it again and let his ear fall back flat, and Melody turned back to Harvey.

"Didn't think you'd get so lucky, did you?' she said jokingly.

"You *are* happy though, aren't you? You seem it. Turn right here."

Harvey took the turn. "I'm okay, Melody," he said. "I wouldn't change any of it, so don't worry."

"What's been your favourite part of the trip so far? Kent, the Lake District or Norfolk?"

"It's hard to say," replied Harvey. "The Lakes, I think. I have memories of them all, but the Lakes were peaceful and exactly how I remembered it."

A few minutes later, they came to a large church on the right-hand side of the narrow lane.

"Stop here," said Melody. "This is it. Do you see what I mean?"

"It's pretty," said Harvey as he stopped the camper opposite the old church.

Melody wasn't listening. She was already climbing out the van and opening the door for Boon, who was pleased to see the old trees that lined the field.

"You want some time alone? You know, to go see your parents?" asked Harvey. "I'll keep an eye on Boon. We'll be by the lake down there." He gestured at the small lake that sat at the bottom of a hill.

"Thanks," said Melody. "I'll just be ten minutes at the most. Okay?"

"Take your time," Harvey replied.

Harvey watched Melody cross the lane and enter the small churchyard then he took a slow walk to a small road bridge that crossed over the lake beside the church. Boon followed, keen to stretch his legs.

Their trip had been perfect to date. It had been Melody's idea to take some time to see the country, and Harvey had agreed willingly but had wanted to stop at a few places, places he'd been in the past, in a previous life.

They'd spent a few days in Kent, and then a week in the Lake District, just walking and eating glorified pub food. Then they'd driven their camper over to the East Coast, and made their way down to Norfolk for another week, just enjoying the peace and quiet. Little Easton had been their next stop, and Dunmow, the village where Melody had grown up.

He was pleased to see her so relaxed and happy, which in itself, was a strange feeling for Harvey. Enjoying someone else's happiness was an odd sensation for him. He'd never been selfish, and deep down his moral compass was set true, but he'd never been close enough to someone to enjoy their happiness.

He was slowly coming around to the idea of being married. He still needed to officially propose, according to Melody. They'd discussed getting married briefly at the beach by their home in the South of France, and although he hadn't got down on one knee and proposed, Melody had seemed excited at the prospect.

Harvey had thought before about being married, and now for the first time in his life, he didn't have any objections. Married life would offer stability, some semblance of normality, which was a far cry to what Harvey's life been so far. Maybe it was too much to ask, he thought. Maybe he'd done so many bad things that even marriage wouldn't bring a normal life, peace and quiet. It was almost immediately after they had been discussing the idea on the beach in France that they'd been approached by a man neither of them had seen before. The man had been serious when he'd offered Harvey work. He'd said that a man with Harvey's skills was hard to find.

Harvey had turned down the offer. He'd been lucky to live as long as he had, given the situations he'd found himself in. Harvey had spent most of his life taking people out for his criminal foster father. It wasn't something he was proud of but he wasn't ashamed either. He'd killed more people than he remembered, and was grateful for the fact that he couldn't remember them. During his training, Harvey had honed his skills on the lowest members of society, paedophiles and sex offenders mostly. People that wouldn't be missed.

For much of Harvey's life, he'd sought the men that had raped and killed his sister, Hannah, when they'd been young. The sex offenders he murdered were his way of offering some kind closure to Hannah, and the countless other girls that had been assaulted, had their families destroyed and suffered so severely. But once he'd eventually found Hannah's rapists, the need to target society's scum had ceased. Harvey had been able to move on, knowing that Hannah's memory could live in peace, even if she couldn't, and there was no longer a dark shadow hanging over her.

But recently, he'd been having dreams.

That's where the urges used to start, the urge to deliver suffering to those who deserved it. When the dreams started, Harvey would begin his hunt for a target. The internet had made it easier to find them. Offenders leaving prison or awaiting trial were easy targets. Old newspapers online or in libraries would give Harvey their backstories. Once he'd found a target worthy of suffering, he'd spend weeks researching them, following them, identifying their patterns and building a plan.

He stood on the bridge looking over the lake. Large carp swam close to the water's surface, and the geese and ducks swam around them. He didn't want to start killing again, but the dreams were overbearing. They weren't too bad in the early stages, but if he didn't satisfy his urges, the dreams slowly became more intense until it was all he could think about.

He stared down at Boon who was watching the geese with a hunter's eye.

"How am I going to do it, boy?" he asked the dog. "How am I going to lead a normal life?"

Boon didn't respond. He didn't even look up at his master. The geese were far more interesting.

Harvey leaned on the side of the bridge and pulled a piece of wild grass that was growing close to his hand. He rolled it in his fingers mindlessly then flicked the little green ball into the water. The geese and ducks saw the movement and darted across to it, but a fish plucked it from the surface before they reached it. They were all too used to being hand fed, thought Harvey.

"Penny for them," said Melody as she approached the pair on the bridge.

Harvey turned sharply to her, snatched from deep thought.

"They're not worth a penny," he replied.

CHAPTER THREE

"What do you mean you're getting alerts, Tenant?" said Jackson. "You need to slow down and start making sense. You're running operations downstairs, and if the team see you flapping like this, you're going to lose your credibility. You need to stay strong."

Reg Tenant shuffled his feet.

"It was the old team, sir," he began.

"You mean Frank's team?" asked Jackson, long since bored of dealing with the repercussions of a dark ops team that he'd helped bring to a close.

"Yes, well, as you know, we were unofficially dark ops, and well, we did a lot of stuff that was very unofficial and-"

"Not quite legitimate?" suggested Jackson. "Is that what you're trying to say, Tenant? You did things that bent the rules, but it was overlooked because the results were good. Am I right?"

"Yes, sir. We did what we had to."

"Tenant, I have a file on you all as thick as the Yellow Pages. I can assure you that everything you lot got up to was recorded and is safely tucked away. I personally refer to the files quite frequently so I wouldn't worry yourself about the records. But..."

He pointed his index finger upwards. "I think we both know that Harvey Stone bent the rules a little more than most, and if someone *were* to look him up, it would probably raise a few eyebrows and take some explaining on his behalf."

"But, sir," said Reg, "that's just it. I knew the data was stored in a database so I ran some plugins that would send me alerts every time one of our names shows up in a search result."

Jackson cocked his head and began to listen intently.

He was sitting at his desk in his office in the Secret Intelligence Service building on London's Southbank and was responsible for a small covert operations team. He'd been recently promoted, which let Reg step up into Jackson's old role and run the operations as a team leader. Jackson merely steered the ship from the lofty heights of his office.

"I started receiving alerts, sir. Information was being pulled out about Harvey and what he did before he joined the team."

"Ah yes, Frank's data."

"Sir?"

"When your previous boss, Frank Carver, was *'killed in action'* shall we say," Jackson gestured inverted commas to accompany his statement, "we found the information on his laptop to be..." He searched for the right words. "Potentially useful."

"It was *you* who stored it, sir?"

"It *was*, Tenant. It was a department laptop, and the data was taken for analysis when Frank died."

"But now someone has found it, sir," said Reg. "Does that mean that Harvey will-"

"Get into trouble?" asked Jackson. "No, Tenant. Frank wasn't completely inept. He secured full exoneration for your friend Harvey Stone. But I must say, the charges would have been severe. Stone would be looking at something like two to three hundred years imprisonment."

"He's been cleared, sir?"

"Exonerated, Tenant," corrected Jackson. "I dare say some would have called to bring back the death penalty had the knowledge been made public."

"But nothing was proven, sir. Is that right? Besides, he even helped you get your promotion, didn't he?"

Jackson glared at Reg. He sat forward in his chair, raised his finger and lowered his voice.

"If you ever mention that incident again, Tenant," he said, "to me or especially to anybody else, it'll be the last thing you do in this organisation. Just forget any of it ever happened."

Reg took a step back.

"I'm sorry, sir, I didn't mean to bring it up."

"It was all based on Carver's notes," said Jackson, moving the conversation forward. "It was what he used to persuade Stone to join the team in the first place."

"The noose," said Reg under his breath.

"The what, Tenant?"

"Oh, err, nothing, sir. Thank you. Sorry to have troubled you." Reg turned and started towards the door. "One more thing, sir."

"Go on," said Jackson, leaning back in his chair and rolling a pen between his fingers.

"So, who would be looking for Harvey? Why would his name come up in a search? It's a secure database, even I can't access it directly."

Jackson took a deep breath and let it out slowly. "Your friend Stone, Tenant," began Jackson, "upset quite a few people during his time with the force, even as an unofficial member of an unofficial team. He was wreaking havoc, as you know, and behind the scenes, Frank Carver was the puppet master pulling on every string he could find to stop Stone being carted away."

"Frank was *helping* him?" asked Reg.

"He was," said Jackson. "And once the exoneration was in place, there was little anyone could do but wait for him to do something else."

"That's entrapment, isn't it?" asked Reg.

"Not entrapment, Tenant," said Jackson. "He wasn't led into a situation where we knew what crimes he would commit. But we did know he would commit a crime eventually."

"But he's not in any trouble now, sir?"

"You're fond of him, aren't you?"

"He saved my life, sir. He saved all our lives on several occasions. But mostly, it's Melody, his-"

"Ah, Mills, yes," said Jackson. "She's a good friend?"

"She's the best, sir. I just worry for her. If Harvey is being investigated, then she might be in trouble too."

"Reg," said Jackson, "I can assure you that, to my knowledge, Harvey Stone is not being investigated. It's probably just a random result. You're seeing them soon, aren't you? Did I hear you mention that a while ago?"

"Yes, sir. We're having dinner, the four of us."

"That'll be nice. Send my regards, won't you?"

"I will, sir." Reg opened the door and took a step. "Oh, and sir?"

Jackson raised his eyebrows.

"Thank you, sir."

CHAPTER FOUR

"You can't stay in your cell all day, Tyson," said Prison Officer Grant. "Get yourself down to the showers and clean up. You don't want your poor old dear smelling you like that."

"I'm okay, thank you, sir," replied Tyson. "I'd like to carry on reading my book."

"Tyson, I don't think you heard me. Get yourself down for a shower. It wasn't an invitation," said Grant. "How long do you have left?"

"Tomorrow, sir," said Tyson.

"The big day, eh?" said Grant. "Well, until tomorrow, you still need to follow orders. Get yourself down to the showers and clean yourself up. You stink. When was the last time you showered?"

"A few days, sir. But I can wash here in the basin."

"Tyson," began Grant, "look, it's gym time. If you're quick, you can get in and out before they finish."

Shaun Tyson put his book by his side and sat upright. "Okay, sir," he said dejectedly.

He collected his prison-issue towel and a clean t-shirt then stepped gingerly out onto Pentonville Prison's G-wing for vulnerable prisoners.

The showers were at the far end of the wing on the ground floor, so Tyson had to descend the mesh steel staircase, which clattered noisily. It was essentially a dinner bell for G-wing's less pleasant clientele.

Shaun kept as far from the open cell doors as he could as he made his way along the wing. He hated the walk. He hated the time of day, and he hated the prison. It was recreation time, and while others used the time to visit the gym, many didn't. They preferred to sit in their cells out of harm's way, or worse, waiting for someone like Shaun to walk past. Like a spider waiting for a fly.

G-Wing's vulnerable prisoners unit held a mixed bag of prisoners. While some, much like Shaun, were indeed vulnerable, fragile and ready to break at any given moment, other prisoners, more adapted to prison life, had found their way onto the wing and quickly established their place in the hierarchy.

It was these prisoners that Shaun feared.

He walked along the middle of the wing on the ground floor, kept his head down and moved fast. All the cell doors were open, but his peripheral vision kept watch for movement as he passed. He saw no movement. The concrete floor was painted grey with a gloss finish that the prisoners cleaned every day; to become a cleaner was a privilege you had to earn. Shaun had preferred to stay low during his three years inside. The cleaning duties gave prisoners access to all floors and they could ferry messages from prisoner to prisoner, which earned other less-formal privileges. Shaun needed no privileges. Shaun had been counting down the days since his arrival.

The showers consisted of an open wet room with a fixed bench to one side where prisoners could leave their clothes while they showered. Small partitions partially segregated each shower but offered little in the way of privacy.

As Prison Officer Grant had said, and to Shaun's delight, he found the shower room empty.

He gave a quick glance out of the door to make sure nobody was coming then pulled off his shirt and his prison-issue tracksuit bottoms as fast as he could. Then he darted under the shower, keeping his underwear on. In case someone came in and saw him, it offered a barrier of protection against the regular attacks.

The water was freezing at first but it soon became warm. It wasn't hot enough to soak under and relax, not like the shower at his mum's house, but it was just warm enough to wash under.

Shaun didn't particularly care about the temperature. Shower time was when he was at his most vulnerable. Shower time was when the spiders came out and the flies like Shaun found themselves trapped in sticky webs. Shower time was high alert.

He finished washing and pulled the water from his long, unkempt hair then quickly squeezed into his clean t-shirt.

Feeling pleased with himself for being so quick and not getting caught, he picked up his tracksuit bottoms and fumbled with the drawstring. He'd pulled them off in haste without untying them, and now the knot was stuck. He fumbled some more, but with wet hands, the job was frustrating.

"I hear you're leaving us?" said a voice from the door

Shaun's worst fear.

He knew the voice; it was the one voice he'd been dreading to hear and had been so close to avoiding.

"Tyson," the voice said again, "I'm talking to you. It's rude to ignore somebody who's being nice to you. You know that, don't you?"

Pops Little liked to think of himself as the wing's father

figure. The vulnerable prisoners unit needed someone like him for the inmates to go to with their problems. At least, that's the premise he used to befriend the younger and more vulnerable prisoners, like Shaun.

Pops Little was a predator.

Shaun had been caught in his web on his second day. He remembered it well. In fact, he'd never forget it. It had happened while everyone was working and Shaun hadn't been assigned a job yet. He'd been crying in his cell, adjusting to prison life, when Pops had walked by and seen him upset. He'd seemed so nice at first, and somehow, by using some kinds of psychiatric techniques, he'd coaxed a full confession from Shaun. Shaun had even cried on his shoulder. How stupid he'd been.

Shaun had been imprisoned for sex offences with a girl that had approached him while he sat in a park, which had then led to other girls recognising his picture in the local paper and coming forward with their own stories. But there were still more that hadn't come forward, and Shaun had told Pops all of them. It had been one of Shaun's biggest mistakes. Pops had threatened to use the information against Shaun and had forced him to do terrible things.

"Tomorrow," said Shaun, "I'm getting out."

"Good for you," said Pops. He had a thick wave of grey hair and features that one might think of when describing a generic grandfather, soft stubbly cheeks, glasses, a friendly smile, but hands as strong as any man's that Shaun had ever felt. "So, I guess this is goodbye then, Tyson?"

Shaun struggled with his tracksuit bottoms and decided to try to get them on without untying the knot.

"No need for that," said Pops. "Why not just pop them back down on the bench, eh? I think you owe me for helping you through your little spell here, don't you?" He shoved himself off the wall he'd been leaning on and made his way to Shaun.

"No, Pops," said Shaun weakly. "I just showered. I-"

"So, we'll shower again," said Pops smiling, "together."

Pops began to unbutton his jeans. "Come on, Shaun," he said, grinning. "One last time for old Pops. You'll miss me when you're gone." The old man grinned a yellow smirk.

Shaun closed his eyes. He couldn't bear to look at him anymore. He felt Pops grab his hand and pull it towards him.

"No, Pops," cried Shaun. "I don't want-"

"It's not about what *you* don't want, Shauny boy," hissed Pops. "It's about what *I do* want, and what *I know*, so if you want to go and breathe some fresh air tomorrow, if you *want* your freedom, you'll do what I say."

Shaun bit his lip and clenched his mouth shut.

"So get on your pretty little knees and say thank you to old Pops one last time."

"No," whimpered Shaun. "I can't do it." He began to sob. He squeezed his eyes closed but felt Pops forcing his hand open.

"That's it, Shauny," said Pops. He growled into Shaun's ear.

There was a dull thump.

Shaun opened his eyes to find Mr Grant standing with his baton in his hand. Pops fell limply to the floor between their feet. Shaun was terrified. He expected a beating from Grant, but instead, the prison officer nodded at the door.

"Get yourself dressed, Tyson," he said, "and get back to your cell."

"Yes, sir," said Shaun. He hopped on one leg as he pulled the tracksuit bottoms over his feet and squeezed them up to his waist.

"Sir," he called after Grant. "Sir?"

Grant stood at the door, half in and half out of the shower

room. Shaun collected his clothes and towel and stood in front of the much bigger man.

"Thank you, sir," said Shaun. "I just wanted to say thanks."

"Not my doing, Tyson," said Grant. "Warden said to keep an eye on you, so I am."

Pops moaned behind them and rolled onto his back on the wet and puddled floor.

"Get yourself back to your cell, Tyson," said Grant. "See if you can make it through the next twenty-four hours without getting into any more bother, eh?"

CHAPTER FIVE

An old, bearded, drunk man bounced off the sickly, lime-green walls of the short, windowless corridor that led from the three interview rooms to the cells of Chelmsford Police Station.

Detective Chief Inspector Zack Harris stepped to one side to allow the homeless man and the escorting officer to pass. He was being released with no charge, free to go and piss up another shop front window the next night, and hope for another free night's stay in a cell sleeping on a sticky, blue plastic mattress. The whole transaction would cost the British tax-payer a few hundred pounds in labour, paperwork, admin and, of course, the inevitable deep cleanse of the cell once he'd left.

Harris continued along the corridor to the single desk at the end. He leaned over the counter and spoke to the deputy sergeant.

"Any free cells, Malc?" he asked.

"Hey, Zack," replied the officer. "Yeah, three and five are both free. Are you expecting a guest?"

"Probably, you remember Noah Finn?"

"Noah Finn?" said Malcolm. "The name rings a bell, but-"

"Nobby Noah?" said Harris, jogging his colleague's memory.

"Nobby Noah? Yeah, I remember him. Is he out already?"

"Skipped his parole meeting yesterday. Only two days out."

"Can't say I'm sorry, Zack," said Malc. "I'm not sure if society is ready for that nutter just yet."

Harris slapped his hand on the counter.

"I doubt very much that Pentonville is ready to have him back either, Malc." He turned and strode confidently back up the corridor and called back to Malc over his shoulder. "Catch ya later, Malc."

Harris buzzed himself through the thick security door that opened up into the rear car park, and then clicked his BMW unlocked. He'd arranged for a local squad car to meet him outside Finn's house and had told them to wait for him to arrive before knocking. Finn's house wasn't officially in Harris' area. But he'd been the arresting officer three years previously, and the powers that be thought a familiar face and knowledge of the previous case history might help ease any situation. Harris had dealt with skipped paroles before. Typically, the parolee was either adjusting and hadn't realised the penalties or, in the case of long-term vulnerable prisoners, they'd locked themselves away, too fearful to leave their homes.

The journey took twenty-five minutes, and the house was how Harris remembered it, in need of some TLC. There was the addition of abusive graffiti, and the garden that Mrs Finn had so lovingly tended had over-grown, but it still had the terrible brown door and old wooden windows.

Harris pulled up alongside the squad car, wound the window down and flashed his ID.

"Any sign of anyone?" he asked.

"None, sir," replied the officer. "Been here ten minutes now."

"Okay, look lively, boys. Let's get one of you round the back in case he makes a run for it. One of you stay in the car, and I'll take the front."

"Okay, sir," said the younger of the two officers, who was sitting in the passenger seat. He opened the door and made his way towards the footpath that led into the woods three doors down.

Harris parked his car, got out and locked it then headed to Finn's house. He caught the movement of a twitching curtain in the neighbour's house but ignored it, closed the gate behind him and walked to the front door. An old brass knocker took the centre position above an old brass letterbox.

Harris gave three hard knocks on the brass knocker.

He straightened his suit and tie then took a cursory glance through the bay window, keeping his suit jacket from touching the dirty old house. He couldn't see much, just some old tatty net curtains and a grim-looking living room.

He gave another knock then lifted the letterbox flap and bent down to peer inside. There was no sign of anyone, or even that anyone had been there recently. Just an old empty house. He stood back to look up at the upstairs windows and saw the neighbour's curtain twitch once more. This time, he caught the lady's attention and gestured for her to come to the front door.

A few minutes later, long enough for the old lady to don her cardigan and shuffle through the house, the white PVC door opened a crack and her head peered into view.

"It's okay, I'm with the police," said Harris. He flashed her ID. "I'm looking for Mr Finn. Have you seen him recently?"

"Oh, I see," said the old lady. "You can't be too careful these days, you know." She opened up the door and stepped outside very gently onto her own garden path. "You're with the police then, are you?"

"Yes, ma'am," replied Harris. "I'm looking for Mr Finn. Have you seen him recently?"

"Oh, I see, in trouble, is he?"

"No, ma'am, no trouble. Just a few routine questions, that's all. Have you seen him in the past couple of days?"

"Have I seen him? Noah, you mean?"

"Yes, ma'am. I just need to ask him a few questions."

"Well, he hasn't been around for a while now. Poor fellow. I knew his parents, you know? Lovely, there were."

"I'm sure," said Harris. "When was the last time you saw him?"

"Well, that's the funny thing," she said, "I thought I saw him yesterday. Or was it the day before?"

Harris' head cocked to one side. Suddenly, he was getting somewhere. But slowly, very slowly.

"No, it was the day before," said the old lady. "I know because I'd just been to the shops. It's quieter during the week, you see, no children flying around on their bicycles and roller-whatsits."

"Ah, so you have seen him?" asked Harris.

"Seen him?" said the old lady with a confused look.

"Noah, ma'am, Noah Finn."

"Oh, little Noah. He was such a sweet little boy. My husband and I used to watch over him if Jack and Sue went out. He was only so big back then." She held her hand up waist high. "He *was* a pleasant lad though, *never* any trouble."

"And when was it you saw him?" asked Harris.

"I told you, it was the day before yesterday. I was sat watching the box, and well, not many people use this road, only the occasional dog walker going into the forest, so it usually catches my eye if somebody does, you know?" She leaned closer and whispered, "I like to keep an eye on things," then gave Harris a little wink.

"That's great. And what time might that have been?"

"Might what have been?"

"What time did you see Mr Finn, ma'am?"

"Oh, I see. Oh, I don't know, must've been early or late afternoon. Let me see, I watched the news, I always like to watch the news, my Harold used to watch the news, I must have picked it up from him."

"And then what did you do?"

"What did I do?" said the old lady. "Well, I watched the news then I took a little walk to the shop to get a few bits in for the week. I'd like to go to the big supermarket but there's no-one to take me now Harold is gone, and it's too far to walk, you see."

"So what time would you have gotten *back* from the shop?"

"Oh, I don't know. Maybe three o'clock?"

"And you saw Noah on the street?"

"No, I made a sandwich, and I'd just sat down to watch that TV program with the two women, you know the one?"

"When you *saw* him?"

"Yes, dear. He walked up the path. I thought it was odd, but you know, I don't like to be nosy."

"Of course," said Harris with a smile. "Well, thank you, Mrs...?"

"You're welcome, dear," said the old lady. "Are you sure I can't get you a tea while you're waiting?"

"No, thank you, that's very kind. I have a busy day ahead."

Harris got the impression she wasn't going to go back inside her house, so he turned and gave the knocker another three raps before he bid her good day then walked back to the waiting squad car. The officer already had the window rolled down, and he smiled at Harris as he approached.

"She seems nice," he said.

Harris ignored the comment. "How's your mate getting on?"

The officer lowered his head and reached for the push-to-talk button on his radio handset. "One-one-nine, any action?"

The two men waited for him to reply. Harris stood and looked up at the house. It was like time had stood still in one particular spot and life had continued around it. The officer tried his colleague again.

"No reply, sir," said the officer in the car. "Want me to pop round and check on him? He might be in a dead spot."

Harris checked his watch and pushed off the car. "It's okay, I'll go," he said. "I could do with the walk. Keep an eye out here. No-one goes in or out."

The path into the woods was clear, as if the council had kept the route free of forest debris and the trees trimmed. But the bushes either side were thick and tangled. There was a small gap between the back fence of the last house on the street and the bushes, so Harris slid sideways into the space and made his way along, cursing at the damage to his newly polished shoes. The space widened out until it was large enough for him to walk normally, but he still had to duck under low branches and step over debris.

Small was nowhere to be seen. He wasn't in the trees and wasn't on the path. Harris gave Finn's back gate a gentle nudge. It was a six-foot high wooden panel with a curved top and black ironmongery. The gate swung open and Harris stared into the overgrown garden.

An apple tree stood in the centre of what was probably a well-kept lawn back in the day. Harris judged it to be sixty feet in length. A carpet of rotten apples surrounded the base of the old tree. A small garden shed stood immediately to Harris' right; the padlock was intact. The shrubbery and bushes on either side of the stepping stone pathway leading from the gate to an old glass conservatory had grown out and onto the lawn, along with thick weeds.

Harris made his way slowly up the path, careful to step on the flagstones provided to avoid spoiling his shoes further. It wasn't until he was a few metres from the conservatory that he noticed a broken glass panel on the conservatory roof. It hung down precariously and Harris noticed that it was swinging softly as if a breeze was gently trying to wear its last functioning hinge away and bring the glass down with a smash.

Harris took a step onto the crazy-paved patio to have a look inside and then recoiled in shock.

Lying unconscious on the floor of the conservatory was Officer Small.

Harris reached for the conservatory door and wrenched it open, which released a length of string that had been fixed to the inside door handle. The string pinged away on its route around the room, pulled by some unknown force. Harris' eyes followed the string's movement, which finished at the hole in the glass ceiling.

He opened his mouth to call out. But it was too late.

The glass panel swung from its broken hinge for what seemed like a slow-motion eternity. Harris wanted to react. He wanted to move. He wanted to shout, but no words came.

All he could do was watch in horror as the sheet of glass that had been hanging so delicately from a single hinge broke free and fell vertically to the floor, severing Officer Small's head clean from his body.

CHAPTER SIX

Harvey sat bolt upright in bed, which woke Boon and Melody. The camper felt claustrophobic, and Harvey's sweat glistened on his chest. His arms ached as if he had been lifting weights and training, and his jaw hurt from grinding his teeth.

He pushed himself off the edge of the bed and pulled on his cargo pants and boots.

"It's dark," said Melody groggily. "Where are you off to?"

Harvey didn't reply.

He opened the door, let Boon jump down, excited at whatever was happening, and then stepped down onto the grass. He closed the camper door behind him and pulled on his plain white t-shirt.

A small picnic bench stood a few metres away, so he climbed up, sat on the table and put his feet on the wooden seat to tie his laces. Boon sprang from tree to tree to see who had tried to claim his territory while he'd been locked in the camper, occasionally glancing up at Harvey to make sure he was still there.

A short while later, the camper's rear door opened and Melody stepped down holding two cups of coffee. Without saying anything, she walked over to Harvey, handed him a cup, and then plonked herself beside him.

Boon had completed his perimeter check and was idling back to his owners when Melody broke the silence.

"They're getting worse, aren't they?"

Harvey didn't reply.

"Why won't you talk to me, Harvey?"

Harvey looked away.

"I know, you know?"

"You know what, Melody?"

"The dreams, Harvey. I know you've been having dreams, and listen, you don't have to say anything, but if you want to talk about them, I'm here, okay?"

"How do you know about my dreams?"

"I sleep next to you, Harvey," replied Melody. "I know they're getting worse because they're getting more and more aggressive. You growl in your sleep."

Harvey looked across at her. He couldn't help but adore her. He hated her knowing about a weakness, but there was no getting away from it.

She growled playfully and leaned into him, linking her arm through his.

Harvey smiled.

"Thanks," he said.

"So you want to tell me about them? Do you remember them at all?"

"Vividly, Melody."

"Fact or fiction?" she asked.

"The dreams?" replied Harvey. "Fact. Old history, but undeniably, fact."

"You know what I think?"

Harvey didn't reply.

"I think you were exposed to some terrible things, Harvey.

What you saw when you were young would have broken most men. But you're different, you're resilient. What you did for your foster father had an impact on you."

"You don't understand."

"I understand enough to know that those things have a tendency to catch up with you. You killed people for a living, Harvey. No matter what way you paint that picture, it's always going to be ugly. You're a good man, Harvey Stone. Your conscience is dealing with the past. But it's over now. You have to *remember* it's the past."

She stroked the inside of his arm with her thumb and took a sip of the hot coffee.

"That's the old you. You left it all behind," Melody finished.

Harvey didn't reply. He took a sip of his own coffee then took a deep breath.

"I did some terrible things, Melody."

"I know, and the fact that I'm still here with you is a testament to how I feel about you, how everyone feels about you. You're a good man, you always have been, and people love you."

"I dream of the things I did. The faces, the pain. It's all there, it's all so real."

Melody was silent for a moment, then, "How long have you been having them?"

"All my life, Melody."

"I haven't seen you have them before, in your sleep, I mean."

"They come and go, like a calling."

"A calling?" said Melody.

Harvey didn't reply. She thought about his choice of words.

"In the past," she began, "when you had these dreams, you said they come and go. How did you stop them before? Sleeping tablets? Music? I hear listening to music helps distract the mind."

Harvey didn't reply.

"We could try it?" she offered. "I'd be happy to have something classical on while we sleep. It might be soothing."

"It's a calling."

Melody stopped at the abruptness of Harvey's tone.

"You said that before, a calling to what?"

"An outlet. When I got them before, I'd go out and find someone." He stopped himself from saying too much.

"A girl?" said Melody. "You have me for that." She smiled and nudged him.

"No, not a girl," said Harvey. "Not that type of calling."

"Who then?" asked Melody. "Come on, there's nothing you can say that will shock me, Harvey. I've seen what you're capable of. What did you do?"

"The problem isn't what I did," said Harvey, "it's-"

"Go on," coaxed Melody.

Harvey sighed audibly and put his head in his hands.

"It's the way it makes me feel."

"How did it make you feel?"

"It's not normal, Melody," said Harvey. "I can't be right in the head."

"Are you saying you want to see someone? I can arrange it, confidentially I mean, no implications."

"I don't need to see a shrink, Melody."

"There's nothing to be ashamed about, Harvey. It's common. Even if you don't feel like you need to see one, you can go and they just keep you on track."

"Keep me on track?" snapped Harvey.

"Keep you-"

"Sane?" said Harvey. "Is that what you were going to say?"

Melody didn't reply.

"I'm not seeing a shrink."

"Okay, I just-"

"Well, thanks but no thanks. If I'm going to get through this,

I'm going to do it the same way I overcome everything else in my life."

"So what's the problem?" asked Melody. "I mean, that's a great mindset to have, but if you really have such a strong mindset, what do you have to worry about?"

"I told you before."

"Tell me again," said Melody. "I'm trying to understand it. I want to support you."

"How it made me feel. That's the problem. At first, I did it to ease my tension, to feel like I was doing good. I did it because they deserved it."

"Retribution?"

"Yeah," replied Harvey. "I was helping the people that couldn't help themselves."

"But then?"

"But then it became something else."

"Like what?"

Harvey looked her in the eye.

"I enjoyed it, Melody."

CHAPTER SEVEN

"Malc?" said Harris.

"I thought you wanted one of my rooms?"

"That won't be necessary, mate," said Harris. "Things just got a bit lively here."

"Oh, okay. I'll take the reserved sign off the door and put the welcome mat away, shall I? Has he done a runner?"

"The exact opposite, mate, someone got at him," said Harris.

"Beat him up?" asked Malc. "How bad is he?"

"Dead, mate. Glued him to the bathtub with some kind of epoxy cement."

"Glue?"

"Yeah, you know the type that stays wet until it comes in contact with something?"

"What the-"

"I know," said Harris. "But whoever it was wasn't satisfied with that. The sick bastard cut his nuts off."

"They did what?"

"Then stuffed them in his mouth."

Malc took a second to digest the image. "Who'd do that to him?"

"It's a fairly long list, I'd say. There must be a few brothers and fathers out there who were just waiting for their chance."

"I guess you'll be busy interviewing then for a while?" asked Malc.

"I guess so, mate. There's a sicko out there that needs locking up."

"I'm speechless, Zack."

"And the worst thing about it was that Finn had probably learned his lesson but some twisted son of a bitch made him talk, probably wanted to hear him confess before he killed him. Imagine if it was your daughter that had been raped and the police had kept Finn out of your reach? You'd want to hear it from his mouth, right?"

"If I say yes, will you be interviewing *me*?" Malc joked, but immediately realised his insensitivity.

"Whoever our man is, he's disturbed, Malc. Finn's entrails were laying in his lap. His stomach was slit open. Doc reckons he was alive when it happened."

"Oh my-"

"That's not all. You're going to find out, so I might as well tell you," said Harris. "Our man set a trap up around the back of the house."

"A trap?" said Malc. "What for?"

"I took two of the Dunmow uniforms with me. One stayed in the car in case Finn did a runner, the other covered the back of the house."

"I don't like where this is going, Zack," said Malc.

"Sick bastard was there, Malc. He was just waiting for us."

"Go on," said Malc, not really wanting to hear what was next.

"He took out one of the uniforms, an Officer Small, cut his spinal cord and left him lying under a pane of glass."

Malc was silent for a moment, picturing the scene.

"The trap?" he said.

"I opened the door, Malc," said Harris. "It triggered the trap. The glass fell and took his head off."

Neither man spoke. They both knew the dangers of the job but it was rare that anything happened so close to home. In London maybe, but fifty miles out of the city in the countryside, life was tame in comparison.

"Sounds like the public is out for blood, Zack," said Malc.

"How do you mean?"

"There was something similar in Norfolk last week. Different setup but similar. Some guy was awaiting trial, some kiddy-fiddler or something, and the public got to him first. It was brutal, apparently. Took him into the woods and tortured him. Burned him alive eventually."

"Jeez," said Harris.

"You think it's connected?" said Malc.

"No mate, this was personal."

"So why did he kill our boy?" asked Malc.

"I asked myself the same thing," said Harris. "If he hadn't of killed Small, we'd have had to wait another twenty-four hours for the warrant. This guy wanted us to find Finn. Small was just a signpost."

"Somehow that makes it a whole lot worse," said Malc.

Harris didn't reply.

"Shout when you're free, Zack, if you need anything."

"Yeah, cheers, Malc."

Harris hung up the phone and sat back in his chair. He hadn't heard of the Norfolk killing, but then he hadn't really paid much attention to anything outside his own world for a few weeks.

He ran an internet search on the story before looking through the internal files. Often the publically available knowledge told the researcher a few more details that weren't always captured in an official police report, speculative details, opinions. Harris knew they couldn't be relied on as hard fact, but he wasn't looking for hard evidence, he was looking a holistic view of the Norfolk incident.

He was looking for a link.

The internet search produced two pages of potential results, plus a few more details on the victim's backstory. Dennis Strange, a twenty-nine-year-old from King's Lynn in Norfolk on the East Coast of the British Isles, had been found by a dog walker in the early hours. The man had wished to remain anonymous and was being treated for shock.

Strange's body, or what remained of it, had its limbs mostly burned off before being dragged from the thick undergrowth onto the path as if the killer had wanted him to be found.

Strange, who had been awaiting his court appearance, had been reported missing two days previously. Many thought his disappearance had been an admission of guilt, but his parents had been adamant of his innocence. His body had been found on the day of his court appearance.

Harris checked the police report. There were no witnesses; nobody saw anything untoward. No tyre tracks, no fingerprints, no sign at all except a small fire, a pile of Strange's clothes and his ruined body.

"Practised," Harris said aloud to himself. "That isn't the scene of a first-time killer."

He was still waiting for the forensic report on Finn's house, but he knew already. There'd be no substantial evidence, not even the glass that had cut Small in two would be tainted. It was all too calculated.

"Who glues somebody to a bathtub?" said Harris aloud.

The killer had *wanted* the police to find the bodies. The cases were too similar not to be connected. What type of man goes to all the effort of taking someone somewhere private to torture them and then drags them back out to be found?

"Is he boasting?"

He picked up the telephone handset, dialled a three-digit extension and waited for it to be answered.

"Zack?"

"Malc, are you thirsty?"

"Thought you were busy?"

"I am, but I'm thirsty as well."

CHAPTER EIGHT

The Sheep's Head pub stood on the high street and was a busy lunchtime venue for the local businesses. A crowd of car salesmen from the nearby dealership stood at one end of the bar, a few local tradesmen stood at the other end, and many of the tables positioned around the pub were busy with couples and colleagues deep in conversation. The pub did a good lunch, which brought customers in from all over town, and had done for years.

Harris stood with Malc at the centre of the bar and ordered two ales.

"You okay, Zack?" asked Malc. "You seem a bit shaken up."

Harris reached out and took the first pint from the barman. He took a sip and then set the glass down on a cardboard beer mat. He leaned down on his elbows. Then, as if agitated, he stood upright and took another sip of his ale.

"I looked up that Norfolk case," he said quietly.

"Oh right," said Malc. "Gruesome, wasn't it? Burned the victim's arms and legs off in a bonfire. How does someone even think of that?"

"Yeah, it's sick, Malc."

"What's on your mind?"

"Doesn't it seem odd to you that both killers went to extreme lengths, *risky* lengths, in order for the bodies to be found? Finn's killer *killed* a policeman so that we'd find Finn, who was glued to the bathtub, so he probably couldn't place the body anywhere, and Strange's killer dragged him out onto a footpath several hundred feet away."

"What are you saying, Zack?"

Harris leaned with his back against the bar and one foot up on the brass footrest.

"Isn't it also odd that both murders were a little...?"

"A little what, Zack?"

"Out of the ordinary, Malc."

"Out of the ordinary, Zack?"

"Yeah, out of the ordinary," replied Harris. "When did you ever hear about someone being glued to a bathtub and having their entrails pulled out *while the victim was still alive?*"

"Yeah, that *is* a bit weird. But it takes all sorts, right?"

"And how about burning someone's limbs off one by one, again while the victim was still alive?"

"Okay, so they're both a little out of the ordinary, as you put it."

"And Small?" said Harris. "The killer took the time to set a trap for God's sake."

"Have you had the reports back yet?"

"No, they'll take time, but I just find it a little too coincidental. When I first read the Norfolk case, you know the first thing I thought?"

"Go on."

"Practised," said Harris. "Bloody practised. Who is practised at this type of thing?"

"Serial killers?" said Malc, unsure of where his old friend was going with the conversation.

"Yeah, sure, serial killers are one. But you know what struck me? What connected them both?"

"What, Zack?"

"Professional," said Harris. "Not just practised, but bloody professional."

"You mean they were hits? Contracted?"

"Maybe," replied Harris. He'd fallen into deep thought, so Malc left him to think and tried to enjoy his pint while he watched the football highlights on the TV.

A man and a woman entered the pub. Malc caught the eyes of the tradesmen follow the woman across the room. She wore a short, tight-fitting leather jacket with black leggings that showed off her lean figure. The man was of average build, dark hair, and had a dog on a lead, who sat as soon as the pair reached the bar.

"Do you have a lunch menu, please?" asked the woman to the barman. "I hear the food is still good here?"

She spoke clearly and confidently and had no twangs of an accent. Malc tagged her as a local girl.

"I'll take the steak," said the man, without waiting for the menu. "Well done, side salad, mushroom sauce and a water."

"Make that two, please," said the woman, returning the unopened menu. "Shall we get a table?" she asked her companion.

Malc turned back to Harris. "You solved it yet?" he said, as he swallowed the remains of his pint and set the glass down on the wood.

Harris smiled weakly and finished his own pint.

"Let's go. I could stay here all day." He placed his glass on the beer mat, nodded thanks to the barman, and made towards the door. "I'm sure there's a connection, and if there is," said Harris, "he'll strike again."

"Well," said Malc, who was holding the door open, "you go catch him, and I'll lock him up for you."

CHAPTER NINE

Harvey took the table nearest the door and sat with his back to the wall, where he could see the entrance and the rest of the pub. He watched the two men leave and overheard a brief snippet of their conversation, which caught his attention. He continued to watch them walk from the pub door, through the car park and onto the pavement. One wore police-issue shoes, trousers and a white shirt under a long warm coat. The other wore beige pants, brown shoes and a similar long coat to his friend.

"Police?" asked Melody.

"Smell them a mile off," replied Harvey.

"Oy, you were one once."

"Unofficially," he grinned.

"I can't imagine what it would be like to be in the force around here. At least we were kept busy by serious crimes. Can you imagine having to go door to door, or investigating robberies and small crimes?"

"They probably say the same about London police, some people like the quiet life."

Melody smiled. She knew he was referring to himself, and his desire to just stop and relax.

"I was thinking about what you said," began Melody.

"Don't give it too much thought, Melody," replied Harvey. "I should never have told you."

"I *need* to know though, Harvey. I need to know the things that *affect* you. If I understand, I can be there or not. I can do whatever it is I need to do to help you through it. That might be talking or it might just mean I give you space. Whatever it is, I'll do it."

Harvey cut the sides off his steak, four perfectly straight cuts to form a square piece of meat. He cut the square in half and then cut the rectangles in half. He repeated the cuts with the smaller sections until he was left with four rough-edged fatty parts and sixteen smaller squares of meat, each a mouthful, and each of them small enough to fit into the little pot of mushroom sauce.

"The food has always been good here," said Melody, as she watched him prepare his food. "It's just one of those pubs, you know?"

"Yeah, we had a few pubs like that in East Ham back when I worked for John."

"I didn't take you for a *pub* type of guy," said Melody with a smirk.

"I'm not, but we'd have to go in and collect the protection, so we'd have lunch there too sometimes. Julios was a big eater."

"So protection rackets aren't all about beating up the owner and taking his money?"

Harvey grinned at the stereotype. "No, not at all. Most places were happy to pay us. They knew we kept them safe. That was one thing about John; he was fair. If a business paid, they had no trouble at all. He'd send the boys in at the slightest of bar fights. He pretty much owned them all in the end, all the pubs worth having anyway."

"Sounds dull," said Melody. "I mean surely you had better things to be doing?"

"I didn't mind it, nor did Julios. He thought of it as a familiarity check. It was a way to make sure he knew all the faces, and more importantly, to make sure they all knew him. Anyway, that's in the past. When are we meeting Reg?"

"I told him I'd call him. I thought we could leave the camper somewhere and catch the train into London?" replied Melody. "It'll be in Clapham somewhere. He said we could find somewhere to sit outside so Boon could come too."

Melody's phone began to vibrate in her pocket. She took it out, looked at the screen and saw the double zero number that Reg had used before, which meant a secure line. "Speak of the devil," she said.

"Reg?" asked Harvey with a raised brow.

Melody nodded and hit the green *connect* button.

"Hey Miss Mills, or should I say Mrs Stone?"

"Not yet, Reg." Melody smiled and reached across for Harvey's hand. "We were just talking about you."

Harvey stood and indicated silently that he was going to use the washroom, leaving Melody to talk to Reg.

"So how's things? Where are we meeting?" asked Melody.

"All good, thanks. We thought we could go to the pub on the common. They're pretty cool about dogs in the garden, and I guessed you guys have done so much travelling in that old camper that you could do with a nice pub meal?"

"Yeah sure," said Melody. "Sounds good. Haven't had a pub meal for a while."

"Good, you'll love it," said Reg. "Where are you guys camping tonight?"

"Oh, Harvey wanted to go back to Theydon Bois tomorrow night. So we'll find somewhere local tonight. There are plenty of campsites and there's a place near Ongar my dad used to take us fishing. I'd like to go there just for old time's sake."

"Theydon Bois?" said Reg. "Why would Harvey want to go back there after what happened?"

"I'm not sure, Reg. I think he wants to see his parents' graves. We saw mine earlier."

Reg was silent.

"Reg?" said Melody. "What's up?"

"Nothing much probably," said Reg. "Listen, Melody, are you alone?"

"Yeah, Harvey has just gone somewhere. Why?" Melody's voice took on a serious tone.

"I just had an alert come through," said Reg, "from a secure database."

"So what? Surely you get those every day?"

"No, not like this, Melody. Someone's been looking into Harvey."

"What? Why?" she asked.

"I don't know, but listen, don't kill me for telling you this-"

"Reg, what's going on?"

"Apparently, Frank made records."

"Of what?"

"Of Harvey, Melody," said Reg. "He recorded everything he found out about him, everything Harvey told him, all the unsolved crimes that Frank put down to Harvey. Frank had been chasing Harvey for a long time, Melody. He didn't even know the extent of Harvey's crimes until he began to get more information from him."

"And he made this record? On a database?" said Melody, her voice higher than she intended.

"No. Frank's records were private. He stored them on his laptop. I doubt he meant for them to be seen by anyone else. But..." Reg sighed. "He probably didn't know he was going to be investigated and-"

"And what, Reg?" Melody asked. "Shot?"

"Well, I didn't want to go there, Melody, but yes."

"So when the old headquarters was shut down and Frank's laptop was confiscated, all the files were uploaded to a database for anyone with the right level of security to access. Am I hearing that correctly?"

"There's a strong security level, so it's not open to anyone, but yeah, someone with the right pay grade can see everything Frank had on Harvey. Basically, Frank managed to put together a list of unsolved crimes that fit Harvey's style, motivation and methodology."

"His noose?" said Melody. "You're talking about the noose that Frank had on Harvey all that time."

"Exactly, Melody."

"And now someone is accessing his files? Is he in trouble?"

"I don't know," replied Reg. "Jackson doesn't think so, but it's not my database. I don't have access to the SQL server. But I figured one of us might land in it one day, you know? For all the stuff that happened when we were on the team. So I ran a small plugin that would let me know if our names were called up in any searches."

"So it could just be random?" asked Melody. "What is it? A keyword search?"

"Well, not exactly," said Reg. "It's a search for similar cases. Whoever ran the search entered the details of a crime and pulled similar cases. Harvey's name popped up twice."

"And what was the search?" asked Melody. She closed her eyes in anticipation, unsure if she really wanted to know the answer.

"Well, we both know what Harvey did for John Cartwright."

"Reg, don't wrap it in fluff."

"Well, these are different. These are outright murders, Melody. They're not gang-related at all."

CHAPTER TEN

Harris stood at the long wall in his office. He stared at the photos that he'd stuck to his magnetic whiteboard of Noah Finn, Officer Small, and the Norfolk victim, Strange.

There was no apparent direct link between the crimes, save for the location of the Finn and Small murders, and the crimes that Finn and Strange had committed.

He pulled open the middle drawer of his filing cabinet and found a folded and tattered ordinance survey map showing the British Isles. Using a few small magnets, Harris fixed it to one end of the magnetic board. Then, using a black marker, he circled King's Lynn and Dunmow. The two locations weren't too far to travel but were far enough to make the journey purposeful. If it *was* the same killer, the murders would need to be planned.

Harris used a red marker to mark the journey by road using the A10, and a green marker to highlight the public transport journey by bus and train.

He marked the journey times beside each coloured line. The journey by road was fifteen minutes faster, not enough to make a huge difference, which left both methods of travel open.

The door to Harris' office opened, and one of his researchers poked his head inside.

"Those reports you asked for, sir," he said, offering a blue folder.

"Thanks, George," said Harris. "Anything of interest in there?"

George held his gaze. "I think you should take a look, sir."

Harris caught the tension in George's voice. "Come in," he told him. "Take me through it."

A round, four-seater meeting table stood in the centre of the office. Harris cleared the surface of his files and allowed George to begin taking him through his findings.

"So, sir," he began, "let's look at this objectively. We identified that the Finn and Small murders were out of the ordinary, and by that I mean they were not your average gun to the head or throat sliced jobs, right?"

"Right," agreed Harris.

"Okay, so we ran a few searches to begin with to give us a pool of data. Homicides in the last week, month and year. There's a fair amount of data, so we narrowed that down to unsolveds and in progress, which narrowed the data down to a manageable amount."

"Good. How many are we talking about?" asked Harris.

"Still a couple of hundred, sir," replied Harris. "But after that, we removed all the gun crime and knife crime. This had a great result and left us with enough that we could then go through manually and remove any other run-of-the-mill murders. The results speak for themselves, sir."

"Go on," said Harris. "Where does it leave us?"

"Three, sir," said George, "including the King's Lynn burning."

"Three?" said Harris. "In how many years?"

"One, sir," said George, "well, two weeks, actually."

"Two weeks?"

"Do you want to see them?" asked George, tentatively, as if he didn't actually want to see them himself.

Harris looked at the closed file with George's hand laid flat on top. "Open it up," he said.

George reluctantly opened the cardboard folder. Harris was met with a photo of a man who'd had his face peeled off. There had been an incision from the bridge of the nose to the nape of the neck, and the skin had been forced down revealing the skull.

"He has a taste for the extreme this one, George."

"Forensics results are a bit bizarre on this one," said George.

Harris tore his eyes away from the horrific photo and met George's.

"From the tissue they found beneath the guy's fingernails, the angle of the cut and the way the skin had been pulled down, they reckon he did it himself, sir."

"He did this to himself?" asked Harris, his eyebrows raised.

George nodded, unable to reply.

"Where was he found?"

"In a forest, sir. A small village near Canterbury."

"A small village you say?" asked Harris.

George nodded. "Yeah, Queensbridge I think, sir."

Harris turned to his map and found Canterbury.

"East of Canterbury, sir," said George, seeing what his boss was doing. The map of the British Isles was too high level to show small villages, so Harris circled the approximate area.

"Who was he?" asked Harris.

"Rimmell," said George. "Anthony Rimmell."

"Anything on him?" asked Harris.

George sighed. "He's on the list, sir."

"The list, George?"

"The sex offender registry. It-"

"It's okay, I know what that is," said Harris. "Had he served his time?"

"He was released a few years ago," said George. "Reports and statements from his neighbours state that he kept himself to himself, had a council job and lived a quiet life."

Harris pulled four magnets from the top corner of his board and stuck the new image below the Norfolk murder.

"Who's next?" he said to George.

"Elaine Stokes."

"A woman?" asked Harris.

George nodded. "Her body was found in the Lake District, in a-"

"Small village?" finished Harris.

"Little Broadwater, sir."

"On the-"

"Registry?" finished George. "Yes, sir. She served five years. Had a fetish for-"

"Spare me the details, George," said Harris.

"You want to see the photos?" asked George.

Harris nodded slowly.

George revealed the next photo. Elaine Stokes had been tied to a tree, her fingers had been severed, her tongue cut out, and her eyeballs removed.

"Post-mortem report suggests the victim was alive throughout the ordeal," said George.

"How did she die?" asked Harris. "Blood loss?"

"No, sir," said George. "Heart attack."

"I guess it all got too much for her," said Harris. "Any sign of-"

"Sexual interference, sir?" said George. "No."

Harris put the picture on the magnetic wall and marked the village location on the map.

"What dates do we have, George?" said Harris. "Let's see if we can understand this guy's travel patterns."

"Canterbury was ten days ago. Lake District was seven days ago. Norfolk was four days ago, and Dunmow was one day ago."

"Every three days?" said Harris. "Seems weird that the timings are consistent."

"Three days is easily long enough for somebody to get from one to the other by public transport, sir," said George.

"Hotels," said Harris. "Get onto them. I want the names of anyone who stayed in a hotel in those areas at those times cross-checked. Start with a five-mile radius then move out to ten. You know what to do."

"That's not the end of the report, sir," said George, making a note on his pad to check the hotels.

"There's more?" said Harris.

"I ran a search, sir, for similar methodologies, similar victims. You know, scratching at anything I could. I extended the time frame of the search."

"Go on," said Harris.

"Nine years ago, in a small village here in Essex, a dog walker found Roland Dyer dead in a forest."

Harris was intrigued with where George was going with the story and sat on the edge of his desk listening intently.

"He'd peeled his own face off, sir," said George. "'Same cut, same everything."

"He's done it before?" said Harris. "'The killer, I mean?"

"Seventeen years ago, Debbie Taylor was found tied to a tree in the middle of a field in Sussex."

Harris' eyes opened wide. "With her fingers, tongue and eyes removed?"

"Yes, sir, same methodology," said George. "But Elaine Stokes died of a heart attack; Debbie Taylor had to be finished off."

"Is there more?" asked Harris.

"Thirteen years ago, Eric Dove was found in East London with his limbs burned off. Just the charred stumps of his arms and legs and his brutally beaten torso."

"Any convictions for any of these?" said Harris, shaking his head in disgust.

George shook his head. "All of them in the unsolveds, sir. Essex police have a pile of files three feet high, all brutal murders, all victims were sex offenders, or at least on the list, and all of them unsolved."

"All in Essex?" asked Harris.

"Seem to be. Essex and East London anyway, and the surrounding counties."

"But these recent murders span the country?"

"Maybe he just passed his driving test, sir."

"Right," said Harris, ignoring George's poor taste in humour. He pushed himself off the desk. "Let's separate them. Two columns, old murders and new murders."

Harris began to re-arrange the victims on the magnetic board.

"When was the last of the old murders?"

"Two or three years ago," said George. "Some guy was found boiled to death in one of those old copper bathtubs like you see in the films."

"Boiled to death?" said Harris, disgusted at the thought.

George nodded.

"What the bloody hell are we dealing with here?"

"I don't know, sir, some kind of vigilante, I suppose."

"Boiled in a bath, George?" said Harris. "Was the victim on the list? I think I remember reading about that in the paper."

"*He* wasn't actually on the list, sir," said George. "But he was found in a basement with a known sex offender tied up beside him."

"Alive?" asked Harris.

"He's serving his time now," said George. "Pentonville Prison."

"Can we talk to him?' asked Harris.

"Not without a few questions being asked."

"Questions, George?"

"Like what exactly are we doing here? We're not exactly the right people for this job, are we? This is nationwide, sir. Government stuff."

"Yes, but the government aren't looking, are they?" asked Harris. "And *we* are. Right, here's what I want to see, a map beside this one with every one of those unsolveds on."

George nodded. "Easy."

"Then," continued Harris, "beside that, I want to see a list of the murders. Don't worry about the names of the victims. I want to see methodologies."

Harris began to pace. His mind was piecing the information together. "Two columns, new murders, old murders. Got that?"

"Yeah, we can do that," replied George.

"Put Elaine Stokes beside Debbie Taylor, Eric Dove beside the Norfolk guy, and Anthony Rimmell beside Roland Dyer. I think the killer is reliving his past. We should be left with a list of methodologies that he hasn't *re-enacted*."

"Right, sir. A list, sir," said George, making another note. "Got it."

"Then, get someone to do some research on known sex offenders already released, due to be released, or pending trial. Find the official sex offender registry, check the names on that, plus there's about a dozen unofficial lists online. Check the names on each list, discount any that do not contain the names of all the recent murders. Bring me the lists that do contain them. We may find the list that the killer is using to find his victims."

"Right, I get it, sir. So we'll have a map with all the old murders on, a list of methodologies, and a list of potential victims."

"Yeah, that's right," said Harris. "Hold on, George."

"Sir?"

"Noah Finn? Has the methodology been-"

"Edward Constable was found glued to his bathtub with his stomach slit open and his entrails on his lap," said George. He then took a deep breath. "They also found his testicles in his mouth. Eight years ago, sir."

Harris listened to the description and tried to fight the image forming in his mind.

"George, are you up for this?" asked Harris. "It could be quite a sensitive case."

"I'm game, sir," replied George. "But there's one thing I don't understand."

Harris looked across the room at him standing with his hands in his pockets and staring at the photos on the wall.

"Why would somebody be so vicious?" he asked. "I mean why go to these lengths to hurt these people? We're not just talking about murders; these people died slow and painful deaths."

"Easy," said Harris, turning back to the board, "suffering, George. He likes to make them suffer, just like their own victims."

George stood silent then asked, "But why?"

"Because *he's* suffered, George."

CHAPTER ELEVEN

"I used to come here as a kid," said Melody, looking at the lazy river roll past and the trees blowing gently in the soft breeze. "Dad would bring us here for a day of fishing, so we'd wait for him to tire of us being too noisy then we'd head off into the trees. I do miss England, Harvey."

Harvey didn't reply. He stared at the water rolling past.

"You're keen to get back to France, aren't you?"

"I'm keen to get on with my life, Melody."

"Our lives, you mean?"

"Yeah."

"You don't sound so sure about that, Harvey."

"I'm just not used to doing nothing, Melody. I'm adjusting. I feel like I need a run. We've been cooped up in that van for two weeks now."

"We'll be home in a few days. Let's enjoy it while we can, and before you know it, you'll be running along the beach again."

Harvey didn't reply.

"Do you still want to go to Theydon Bois tomorrow? To see your parents' graves?"

Harvey nodded and laid back on the grass. The graves of his parents were unmarked and hidden in an orchard on his foster father's old estate. The visit would awaken many memories for Harvey.

Boon took Harvey's laying down as an invitation for him to move in for some attention, but Harvey held his hand low in a silent command, and Boon simply laid by his side.

"Do you mind if I head into town?" asked Melody, sensing Harvey's need to be alone. "The town centre is just a few miles away. I'll be gone a couple of hours."

"Fine by me," said Harvey. "I might take this dog for a run."

The pair said goodbye, and as Melody steered the big vehicle onto the track that led from the trees to the main road, Harvey began to slow jog along the riverbank.

The run felt good, it always did, and soon, Harvey began to feel more like himself. He sprinted for a long flat stretch then slowed for a short burst between the trees. He found an old stone bridge and crossed over to hit a big hill that lay on the far side of the river.

Boon stayed at his heels the whole time, loving the exercise as much as his master. He would occasionally split off from Harvey to bound through the long grass or run through the shallows of the river, but his eyes never lost sight of Harvey.

With his arms pumping and his breathing in a locomotive-like rhythm, Harvey sprinted up the hill. At the top, he stopped and immediately stretched his muscles, taking in the view below him. A blend of yellow, brown and green fields lay in random patchwork formation across the landscape, broken only by the dark green lines of hedgerow and small pockets of trees. Melody was right; England was a beautiful place, he thought.

But England also held dark memories that Harvey would sooner forget.

The dreams had gotten worse since they had arrived in

Essex. The memories were so much more alive. They had even passed a field the previous day where Harvey had once buried a man alive. The horrors of Harvey's life, the faces of the dead, and the guilty pleasure of killing were coming together at once, and there appeared to be no escape for him.

Harvey sat down at the top of the hill. Boon slunk between his legs and curled up in the space.

"What's it all about, boy?" he asked Boon as if the dog could read his mind.

Boon looked up and nudged him, but Harvey didn't respond.

From where he sat, Harvey's view was unobstructed in almost every direction, save for the forests that ran beside the river. But inside, there were too many obstructions.

He laid back, enjoying the peace and quiet. The birds chirped and the breeze lightly rustled the grasses and the leaves in the trees. Boon curled into him, closed his eyes and soaked up the summer sun that warmed his face. Harvey's tired mind and the serenity of his surroundings soon carried him away into sleep.

Old memories began to come alive once more.

Flashes of visions and the terrible things he'd done were captured as if a bright light had frozen them in time and etched them onto a photographic film in his mind.

The face of the man he'd buried alive flashed once, just as Harvey was covering the last trace of his face with soil. He'd left a hosepipe in the man's mouth, to allow the sick pervert a few more agonising minutes of life while Harvey had filled the hole.

The flashed image of the man's face eased into the sickening memory. Harvey had finished with the shovel and covered all traces then slowly tightened the end of the hose, gradually restricting the man's air. Then he released the hose and heard a lengthy gasp, as the weight of the soil took its toll on the body below.

Harvey had put the excess hose flush in the ground so that passers-by wouldn't find it, and then he'd left the man to die a slow and painful death.

Boon's barking woke Harvey with a start. He sat bolt upright and wiped the sweat from his brow. His shirt was wet, and his breathing heavy from the vivid dreams.

Boon barked once more.

Harvey slowly recovered from his doze and rolled onto his side to find Boon sitting beside the corpse of a man who'd been pinned to the ground with wooden stakes through his wrists and ankles. He was crucified with his arms outstretched, like Jesus but with his throat cut.

Harvey dizzied. He remembered the scene. It was almost identical to one of his dreams, and to a previous kill.

He moved away, scurrying backwards on his hands and feet across the grass. But the ground was sticky. Blades of the fresh and lush green grass stuck to his bloodied hands.

His shirt too was spattered with red. Harvey recognised the spatter. It was horizontal and arced. The result of a sliced throat.

"Boon, come here," called Harvey, as the dog began to sniff the stiffening corpse. But Boon's ears flattened against his head. His tail dropped low, and he looked around him as if confused.

"Boon," said Harvey. "Here, boy."

The dog eyed him with caution.

Harvey stood, but Boon bolted away down the hill. He looked back briefly and saw Harvey chasing after him, so the dog picked up speed.

Harvey tore across the bridge after the panicked Boon and narrowly missed a small family who were out enjoying the sunshine, walking the path along the riverside. Boon was gone, and the family gathered behind the father, who stood like he was protecting them.

Harvey stared at his sticky hands again then back at the family, and down at his bloodied shirt.

"Your phones," said Harvey. "Put your phones on the ground, one at a time."

"Get away from us," said the man, his arms outstretched behind him holding his daughter and his wife.

"Throw your phones on the ground, and I'll leave you alone."

Two phones landed beside each other in the grass.

Harvey stared as if waiting for a third.

"She doesn't have a phone," said the man. "She's too young. Take them and go."

Harvey bent to collect the two phones and then tossed them in the river.

"It's not what it looks like," he said.

"Please leave us alone. We don't care what it looks like."

The sound of Melody arriving in the motorhome and honking the horn distracted Harvey. He turned back to see Boon jumping up at the driver's door to reach Melody.

"Go," he told the family without turning. "Leave, now."

CHAPTER TWELVE

Melody parked the camper in a supermarket car park and sat back in the seat. She pulled her phone from her pocket, found the recently dialled numbers and hit Reg's name.

He answered after one ring.

"Melody," he said, "how did I know you'd be calling?"

"Something's wrong, Reg," she said.

Reg knew that when Melody omitted the pleasantries, trouble was afoot.

"Talk to me, Melody. What's up?"

"He's acting weird. He's quiet, like something's on his mind."

"Isn't he always like that?" asked Reg.

"This is different. Something's very wrong. And I can't help thinking about what you said."

"We've been running our own investigation here," said Reg. "Jess and I-"

"What did you find?" asked Melody, cutting him off. She'd known he wouldn't be able to help himself. He was one of the best researchers she'd ever come across; if there was something to be found, Reg would find it.

"Remember I told you about that search?" he asked.

"Yes, it's all I can think of, Reg."

"So it turns out that some detective in Essex somewhere has entered the information of a few recent murders, brutal killings, Melody, and the search has flagged previous similar murders, all unsolved crimes."

"So?" said Melody.

"Identical murders that were carried out by none other than-"

"Harvey? No, it can't be true, Reg."

"Hey, I'm not making any allegations here. I'm just-"

"I know, I know, but I can prove it wasn't him."

"Have you been with him the entire time, Melody?"

"Well no, of course not, but a lot of the time."

"And where exactly is it you've been?" asked Reg.

"Are you questioning me, Reg?"

"No, Melody, I'm helping you," said Reg. "What route have you taken on your travels in the past couple of weeks?"

"We came from France," said Melody, "into Dover, and then up to the lakes."

"Did you stop along the way?"

"Of course we stopped, we're on holiday, enjoying the peaceful countryside."

"Okay, Melody answer me this, did you stop in a little village called Queensbridge, just outside Canterbury?"

Melody was silent for a few seconds then, "How did you know that?"

"Just a hunch, Melody," he replied. "Then you went to the Lake District?"

"Yes, we stayed for a while. We moved about a little, did some hiking."

"Did you go and stay in the village of Little Broadwater?"

"What are you getting at, Reg? You're scaring me," said Melody.

"Little Broadwater, Melody. Did you stay there or not?"

"Yes, we did. But nobody's ever heard of it. We found a little campsite and parked up. How did you know?"

"And, from there, you drove across to Norfolk?"

"Reg, stop it," snapped Melody. "Just tell me what you know."

Reg took a deep breath of air. "Melody, about ten days ago, a man was found brutally murdered in the village of Queensbridge, outside Canterbury."

"No," said Melody. "*That's* where we were."

"There's more," said Reg.

"Go on then."

"A week ago, a woman was found murdered in a forest in Little Broadwater. A couple of hikers stumbled on her body, what was left of it."

"Reg, stop."

"And last week," Reg continued, "a man was found in King's Lynn, Norfolk, with his arms and legs burned off."

"Reg, no more," cried Melody. "I said stop."

"You need to hear this, Melody. You *need* to know the truth."

"I can't *handle* the truth, Reg. It can't be-"

"Yesterday, a man was found glued to his bathtub in Dunmow. He had his gut slashed open, and his balls cut off and stuffed in his mouth."

Melody began to sob. She couldn't reply.

"Get yourself out of there, Melody."

"It *can't* be him," she said. Her voice whined as she fought to hold back more tears.

"I'm sorry, Melody," said Reg. "The database pulled out unsolved crimes then the results were whittled down to disregard shootings, stabbings, and what you and I might regard as ordinary murders. The data they fed in was matched and every one of the results was nearly identical to the records that Frank made of Harvey's old crimes. Luckily, the database did not match Harvey's name, just the crimes that Frank tagged as potentially his."

"But he was pardoned. He can't be found guilty of those crimes now, surely. Even if they did match his name."

"He was exonerated, Melody, for the older crimes. But these recent crimes?" Reg paused and searched for the words. "They're his style. He might as well have signed them. If Frank was here, he'd called it the methodology. They have Harvey written all over them."

"But why?" asked Melody. "Why would he need to do any of this?"

"Every one of these victims was on the sex-offenders list, Melody."

"The recent victims?" she asked.

"Old and new," said Reg. "They're not just common in methodology. They have the same motivation."

"And Harvey had the means," said Melody.

"Now," said Reg, "what are you going to do?"

"What *can* I do? I'm marrying a *murderer*," said Melody.

"Melody, come on. We all knew he was troubled. Come and stay with us. You'll be safe here."

"Safe?" said Melody. "You think *you're* safe?"

Reg didn't respond.

"*None* of us are safe, Reg," said Melody. "If Harvey knows that we know, that's it, game over for you and game over for me."

"You think he'd go that far?"

"He spoke to me the other night, Reg," said Melody, calmly and with the unemotional, flat tone of acceptance. "He told me he'd been having dreams."

"Dreams?"

"Yeah, but that was it. It's not like he's sleepwalking and doing this. But he woke in the night, he was upset, so we talked."

"And?" prompted Reg.
"He said he..."
"He said what, Melody?"
Melody was silent.
"Melody?"
"He told me he enjoyed it."

CHAPTER THIRTEEN

"George, let's go," said Harris. "There's been another one. Meet me downstairs."

He let the door close and took the two flights of stairs to the ground floor.

"Ground units are already on site, sir," said a female officer behind the central desk of the police station as Harris approached. She handed him a sheet of paper. "One body, male, early twenties. Sounds like he had his throat cut."

"Forensics?" asked Harris.

"En route," came the reply. "Uniforms are already on site closing the crime scene down."

George came bounding down the stairs and joined Harris.

"Ready for this?" Harris asked.

George nodded softly then followed Harris through the door to the station car park.

"If it's him, he's close," said Harris as he pulled his BMW onto the high street, "and if he's close, we can nail him."

"Do we have a description?" asked George, scanning the report Harris had given him. "Who called it in?"

"Some bloke out for a walk with his family made a call about a strange man running after a dog with blood over his shirt and on his hands."

"And who found the body?"

"A couple of kids out playing in the forest." Harris breathed out loudly through his teeth. "They'll need a bit of therapy after this."

"How did he die?" asked George, flicking through his notes.

"He had his throat slit, according to the report."

A cog clicked in George's brain.

"Was he pinned down with stakes through his wrists?" he asked.

"I don't know. Read the report," said Harris.

George began to compare the report against his own notes.

"Jesus, it's the same," he said finally. "Benjamin Green from Southend-on-Sea. Released from prison for sex offences and found three days later pinned to the ground in a forest with stakes through his wrists and ankles. That was five years ago." He continued to flick through the notes. "It says here that his throat was cut and he drowned slowly in his own blood. The killer was never caught."

Harris indicated and put his foot down. The BMW shot past the traffic that had slowed for the traffic lights and into the wide country lane ahead.

They found the crime scene a few minutes later. The road had been cordoned off, and the entry to a small picnic spot was awash with glaring blue flashing lights atop local squad cars.

An officer stood taking statements from a few cars parked to the side of the road, a workman in his unmarked van, a family in a large car, and a woman with her dog in a camper van.

Harris slowed for a police officer to lift the red and white tape over his car as he passed under. He nodded his thanks before stopping on the shoulder of the empty road.

Ten minutes later, they were both stood looking down at the body.

"See how neatly the stakes have been carved?" said Harris. "It's like he selected the branches and took time to carve them."

"So he was planning this?' asked George.

"Either planning or watching and waiting," replied Harris. He looked about him. They were stood at the top of a small hill. A river cut through the ground below them, and a small forest stood to their right. Long grass grew wild and free around the edges of the hill, but the middle was soft, lush grass, recently mowed by the local council.

"There," said Harris, pointing to a spot a few meters from the body. "Something's flattened the grass. It looks as if somebody laid there."

"Why would they lay beside someone they just killed?" asked George.

"Tell me more about the victim," said Harris, ignoring the question. "Was he on the list?"

"Actually, no, sir," said George. "No previous, no history of anything. He was a local boy."

"So why *him*?" asked Harris to himself. "Why change the motivation now?"

The sound of an approaching helicopter drew near then faded as the police chopper flew in concentric circles around the area.

A police photographer stood patiently nearby, waiting to photograph the scene before the body was removed. A hundred yards away, a few locals were being held back by uniformed police. A couple of boys with a football had obviously seen the action and come to see what was happening.

"Are you waiting for us to leave?" called Harris to the photographer.

"Take your time, sir," said the man. "He's not going anywhere fast."

"Can you get a shot of the grass there?" Harris pointed to the flattened spot that lay a few meters away.

"Yeah, no problem," said the man as he came closer.

"Get a tape measure on it too. I want to know how tall the person was who lay there," said Harris. "Let's go digging, George." He walked off towards the few locals that stood behind the red and white tape a hundred yards away.

He was met with a greeting nod from the uniformed policeman and then he approached the boys with the ball.

"Hi boys. Any of you know who that is?" Harris said, pointing up the hill.

"That's Liam, mate," said the boy with the ball, a ginger-haired kid with a face full of freckles.

"Last name?" asked George, making a note on his pad.

"Liam Charlton."

"You knew him?" asked Harris.

"Come on, boss. They're just kids," urged George. He was not keen to get a bunch of underage kids involved in a police investigation without their parents' consent. The backlash would be unbearable.

"It's okay, mate," said the ginger kid. "Yeah we knew him, but he's a bit of a loner."

"Is he okay, mister?" asked another kid beside him, a smaller boy with a mass of shiny brown hair and two missing front teeth.

"No, sonny," said Harris. "He's *far* from okay."

"Right, that's enough," said George. "Thank you, boys, on your way now." He pulled Harris' arm and led him away. "What are you trying to do, land yourself a court case?"

"They're just boys, George," said Harris. "They know more than you think. They've seen worse in films these days."

"That's right, sir, they're just boys, and they don't have their parents with them. So anything they say that you try and use as evidence won't stand up in court anyway."

"Stop fretting, George," said Harris, taking one more glance at the body, the trees and the river. "Why don't you make yourself useful and go find out what the uniforms found out on the roadside."

Harris began to walk down the hill to the river.

"And what about you, sir?" George called after him.

"It's a bit hot, George," said Harris over his shoulder. "I might soak my feet in the river."

CHAPTER FOURTEEN

Melody parked the camper in the picnic area where she'd left Harvey and Boon. Movement in the corner of her eye caught Boon tearing along the path up to the van. He jumped up and pawed at the windows for Melody, so she opened the driver's door and let him in. Instead of jumping across to the passenger seat as he usually did, Boon sat on Melody's lap with his ears pinned down flat as if he'd been naughty.

Melody searched through the windscreen for Harvey and saw him a hundred feet away stood beside the bridge. Even from afar, Melody could see his hands and arms were bloodied and hung loosely by his side. His white t-shirt had a red stripe across the front. The tone of his gaze was the eerie stone cold look that Harvey was known for.

Sirens sounded in the distance, and the whomp of an approaching helicopter grew closer.

Melody's eyes locked onto Harvey's.

She shook her head.

"No," she said disbelievingly. "No, you can't have." Melody looked harder at the blood on his hands and up his arms. It was as if he'd butchered somebody.

The sirens grew louder, and the helicopter began to creep into view from the far fields. Melody chanced a glance up into the sky and behind her to see if the police had arrived. But when she looked back, Harvey had gone.

Melody's mouth hung open. It couldn't be possible. What had he done?

The sirens were fast approaching now, so Melody turned around in the car park. She hovered by the exit for a moment, half expecting to see Harvey run from the trees and climb into the van as he'd done when they worked together. But this time he didn't appear.

"Is this goodbye, Harvey Stone?" she said softly to the rearview mirror, and then slowly pulled out of the car park onto the road.

She was stopped fifty yards later by one of two police cars that had been tearing down the hill from the town centre. The first car drove past, and the second stopped to let an officer out before parking across the road to stop any traffic from passing.

The officer on foot guided Melody to the side of the road, and soon after, stopped a family in their MPV and a man in a plain white van.

Melody knew the game. She'd wait in the camper for the officer to get to her. The others would climb out of their cars and become aggressive with the officer for delaying them. He would then make them wait longer.

Her mind spun at dizzying speeds. What had Harvey done? Was Reg right? Was Harvey was up to his old tricks again? She felt the dull stab of loss in her heart, and her breathing quickened. She cracked the driver's window ajar and rested her head on the steering wheel.

"You okay, miss?" said the officer who stood beside the camper.

Melody didn't react.

The officer tapped on the window, and Boon began a low, menacing growl.

Melody sat up straight. She stared ahead and composed herself. Then she lowered the window.

"I'm afraid I'm going to have to ask you to step out of the vehicle, ma'am," said the officer. He then turned away and spoke into his shoulder-mounted radio.

Melody opened the door, moved Boon off into the passenger seat, and dropped down to the ground. She held onto the door for balance. Her head still spun with the suddenness of it all. Thirty minutes ago, she'd heard that the man she loved might be a serial killer; that news had been bad enough. But she had been able to defend him, even if not wholeheartedly. But now she'd seen the blood on his hands, and how shaken Boon was. Then the look on Harvey's face had confirmed her darkest thoughts.

"Ma'am?" said the officer. "Are you okay? You look shaken."

Melody looked despondently at the officer's uniform, from his polished boots to his immaculately pressed trousers and shirt, to his shiny shoulder IDs.

"Ma'am?" he said again.

"I'm fine. I just need a minute."

"Can I ask you what you're doing out here?" he asked.

Melody heard his voice but was lost in her own world. She imagined Harvey killing a faceless victim, his control and calm making the job seem effortless, his stone cold gaze watching with evident joy at the suffering he was causing.

"I need to know what you're doing here," said the officer.

Melody snapped out of it and focused on the officer once more.

"I'm walking my dog. I *was* walking my dog," Melody corrected herself.

"Have you had some bad news?" asked the officer. "Would you like a female officer to talk to you?"

"No," she said, "no need." She took a deep breath. "What's wrong anyway?"

"Who said anything was wrong?" said the officer.

"I sensed something was wrong when you and your mates came tearing down here and pulled me over," said Melody. "I'm on the force. Well, I used to be anyway." She offered a weak smile.

"You're not anymore?" asked the officer, suddenly interested.

"Special Intelligence," said Melody.

"Oh, I see," said the officer. "Well, if I could just take your details, I'll see about getting you on your way."

Melody gave the young officer her details and waited while he ran a check on her name and the plate number.

While he was gone, Melody watched as two plainclothes detectives arrived in a BMW. Melody knew the look, the car, the authoritative presence.

Were those the men that ran the database search?

She watched with interest as the two men parked, walked across the bridge and up the hill. Melody saw for the first time the red and white taped off area, a body under a sheet, and a few nosy locals who wanted in on the action. She gazed into the trees and wondered if Harvey was watching her, watching them, or had made his escape.

She hoped for one last glimpse of him.

A small part of her hoped that he'd escaped, while another part of her wanted him to be caught and locked up so he could do no more harm. But a large part of her didn't want one or the other. It just wanted them both to be back in the little farmhouse in France, waking up to coffee, making love and spending the day on their little beach.

"What a nightmare," she said aloud without realising.

"What's a nightmare, Miss Mills?" asked the officer who had

returned to the camper. "Are you sure you're okay? I can get you something if you want."

"Am I free to go?" she asked, ignoring his offer of help.

He nodded. "But don't go too far if you don't mind, Miss Mills. We may need some more details."

"I thought you said nothing happened?" she said to the young man. "So what would you question me about?"

"You know how it is, Miss Mills," he replied. "We may uncover a development." He smiled as if his answer had been a smart reply.

Melody climbed back into the van and started the engine. She leaned out of the window. "Let's hope for your sake that whoever is under that sheet up there doesn't need your help, Officer Grey." She winked and pulled onto the road, leaving Officer Grey wondering if she just complimented him or insulted him.

CHAPTER FIFTEEN

Shaun stood and heard the gates of Pentonville Prison close behind him. He clutched a plastic bag with his few possessions and walked timidly away from three years of hell.

He'd been given a small map and directions from the prison administration, but he pocketed the map and chose to just walk. He just wanted to be away from the place.

He felt eyes bore into him, as they had for the past three years. Everything he'd done had been seen, and everything he'd said had been heard. In prison, privacy was a luxury that was forfeited. He felt like the people he passed on the streets all knew where he'd been, and worse, he felt as if they all knew why he'd been sent there in the first place.

He kept his head down and walked.

Shaun found Caledonian Road, a busy street that allowed him to fall in with the other pedestrians, people who ignored him. He relished the feeling of being ignored, of being alone on the outside; it somehow made him feel part of something.

Shaun thought it bizarre how he felt included in something where people ignored him, ignored everyone else around them, and all had places to go in a hurry. He pulled the map from his pocket and studied it as a tourist might. He decided he'd walk to Hornsey Station. From there, he could take a train directly to his mum's house. The walk ended up taking more than an hour, but Shaun didn't mind. By the time he reached the train station, some semblance of normality had kicked in.

Life on the outside.

The train ride to Potters Bar was a welcome break. The carriage had been empty, and the seats were softer than his prison bunk had been.

He lifted his feet up onto the seat in front, only to remove them when somebody else boarded the train at the next stop. It would take a while, he thought, to get over the fear.

He tried to remember his mum's house and wondered if it had changed. He'd told her not to visit him after the first time when she'd broken down. He couldn't face putting her through the agonising turmoil of visiting again. But when he'd earned enough money to pay for his weekly TV privilege and his tea each week, he'd spent whatever else he had on calls to her.

It had been easier that way.

He thought of Pops, who had sat in the visiting room not far away during Shaun's mum's first and only visit, the look in his eye, those thin, cruel lips, and the knowing wink he'd offered as Shaun consoled his crying mum.

Shaun had broken first, and that had set his mum off. It was a common sight in prison, and most prisoners ignored the emotions of others. Everybody felt it, the missing, the shame, the guilt and the heart-wrenching agony of watching a loved one sit across the table wondering why you did what you did. It wasn't just the prisoners that suffered; it was the lives of those around them that were destroyed.

An unexpected and overwhelming feeling of claustrophobia

kicked in when Shaun stepped out of Potters Bar Train Station. He couldn't be sure if it was because of the familiarity of the buildings and the layout of the town, or just plain old paranoia, but the feeling returned with a vengeance. It was as if every person he passed on the street eyed him with suspicion and knowing. Heads turned in the cars that drove by as he crossed the main road into the quiet side streets. But somehow, instead of getting away from the stares, the secluded roads offered the few passers-by more time to study him, to remember him.

The weird kid who fiddled with young girls.

Shaun began to run. He took to the alleyways that ran between the streets behind the rows of houses until he came out onto his mum's road. From there, he dropped his pace to a brisk walk and kept his head down until the sanctuary of his mother's garden path fell into his field of vision. He fumbled with the gate at first, and then the front door key in his sweaty palm, which had been one of his possessions the prison administration had taken.

He failed to notice the light blue Ford parked a few houses down and the man with the digital camera and telephoto lens.

Shaun quickly slammed the front door behind him. He hadn't meant to; it just closed quicker than he expected. He put his back against the door and rested his head on the wood to regain his composure. Then, hearing his mum in the kitchen, he pushed off the wall and opened the kitchen door.

Shaun's mum had been waiting for him. She was sitting at the small square kitchen table with a cup of tea in one hand and a cigarette in the other. An overflowing ashtray on the table mat was evidence of how she'd spent the morning.

There was a long silence as mother and son exchanged looks of mixed emotions.

"Oh, Shaun," said Mrs Tyson, and then burst into tears.

Shaun bent to hug her, and buried his face in her hug.

"I'm home, Mum," he said. "I'm not back there again. I promise."

Mrs Tyson pulled away, composed herself, and wiped her eyes.

"It's good to see you home, Shaun," she said. "Are you hungry?"

"Erm, no, Mum," he replied. "Not really."

"What have you had to eat?"

"Nothing, Mum," said Shaun. "I just couldn't stomach anything."

"Well you *must* eat," said Mrs Tyson. "I've got some bacon and some bread, and later I'll go to the store. What do you want for dinner? My treat."

"Oh, Mum," he said, "you don't have to do that."

"I know I don't *have* to, Shaun, but I *want* to. I want to cook you a nice dinner. What was the food like? Did they feed you well enough? You look like you lost weight."

"I'm okay, Mum, honest."

"Well, I'll do a roast," said Mrs Tyson with finality. "How about a bit of beef with all the trimmings, eh? Then we can sit, and you can tell me all about what you're going to do now you're out. We need to put all this behind us and move on."

She began to dry a dish that was already dry and had been sitting on the draining board beside the kitchen sink.

"Okay, Mum," replied Shaun. "Thanks. Do you mind if I go upstairs? I've been looking forward to nice hot shower."

"Oh, let me run you a bath," his mum began. She set the dish down with the towel and stubbed her cigarette out in the ashtray, spilling ash onto the table. "You can have a nice long soak with bubbles, the way you used to like it."

Shaun smiled. "Thanks, Mum." She gave him another hug but pulled away again as the tears began to well up. She made her way past Shaun and up the stairs to the bathroom.

Shaun plonked himself down at the kitchen table. He wiped away the spilt ash and emptied the ashtray into the bin behind him.

Maybe everything was going to be okay, he thought. Maybe life *would* get back to normal.

CHAPTER SIXTEEN

London's traffic passed by Melody in a blurry haze of headlights.

She was sitting on a bench on London's Southbank, waiting for her old colleague and good friend, Reg, to finish work. Boon sat patiently at her feet and seemed to enjoy the noises and smells that accompanied London.

Reg had done well for himself. He'd started his career in tech by hacking into corporations and wreaking havoc, as kids do. But he'd soon developed skills and escalated his antics to larger and more technically challenging hacks. The MoD had been one of those challenges, and subsequently, he'd been caught. His parents had enrolled him in a rehabilitation program for young offenders, and from there, his talents had been spotted, guided, and moulded into a solid tech research operative. His talents had given him experience with the Serious Organised Crime units, from which he'd been asked to join a team of dark ops specialists, who focused on domestic organised crime.

Melody considered his success while she sat and waited for him to finish work in the Secret Intelligence Service building.

She pondered on how life had a funny way of working out for some but not for others. It was as if life needed balance. There were choices and then there was balance. If Harvey hadn't joined the team, the cases they'd all worked on together would have had very different outcomes. Perhaps they wouldn't have been so successful.

Maybe some friends that had fallen along the way might still be around. Perhaps Frank, their leader, wouldn't have got so involved. Maybe *he'd* still be alive too.

But the scenes *had* played out, and Melody *had* made the choice to leave the force to live with Harvey in their little French farmhouse, while Reg had been picked up by MI6 and was now an operations team leader, which was led by Jackson, another former team member.

Meanwhile, Melody suddenly found herself very alone with nothing to show for any of her hard work. She'd been told a hundred times that her career possibilities would be endless if she continued on the path she was on. But she'd chosen wrong, and now she was out.

She was out and soon to be married to a man she'd just learned was a serial killer. She laughed to herself, not a hearty laugh, just a disappointed exhale of air that summed up her situation.

She'd known Harvey had been a killer, the whole team had known. That was the very reason he'd been brought into the team. He was the man they had all looked to when there was dirty work to be done. When the regulations and restrictions that bound a government employee prevented them from doing something that was necessary, Harvey was the go-to man. He was unofficially attached to the unofficial dark ops team, and in return, he'd been given a clean slate.

But now, he was muddying the slate he'd worked so hard to clean.

"Penny for them?" a voice said, somewhere far away.

It was Reg. His big childish smile filled his face from ear to ear, as he approached the bench. Melody stood and flung her arms around her old friend. Boon jumped up at them, excited to see Reg. She didn't say hello or ask Reg how he was, Melody just buried her head into his shoulder and held on tightly.

"Hey, what's all this?" he said. He pulled Melody away to take a look at her face, but she kept her head down, embarrassed by her tears.

"Melody, come on, sit down," Reg said gently while making a fuss of Boon.

"I've ruined it," said Melody. "My life. You were right, I *saw* him."

"Melody, come, sit down. Tell me what you saw."

Melody dropped down onto the bench beside him and searched for a tissue in her bag.

"*Blood*, Reg, all over him."

"*Blood?*" asked Reg. "So he-"

"He did it again. The police found a body where we were going to camp, and I saw him. I'd been to town to call you and when I got back, I saw him. I saw him, Reg. *I saw the look-*"

"Whoa, slow down, girl," said Reg. "Where were you?"

"In a village near Chelmsford. Oh God, Reg, what have I done?"

"Let's not be hasty. Let's find out what the police know, and we'll go from there."

"There was a body. It was under a sheet. Red and white tape, uniforms holding back the public, a helicopter. A bloody helicopter, Reg."

He lifted his arm and put it around Melody's shoulders. "Listen to me, Melody, we're going to find a cafe with internet, and we're going to understand what's happening here. Okay?"

Melody sat with her head in her hands and didn't respond.

"Melody, right now, you need to be strong. You can get through this. I've seen you pull some seriously crazy stunts, don't let this be the one that breaks you. Come on, let's go." Reg stood and began to walk. "I'm going with or without you, Melody." He shouldered his satchel and began to walk away.

"*Wait*," called Melody.

Reg turned but continued to walk backwards.

"You're right," she said as she stood. "Wait for me."

CHAPTER SEVENTEEN

George stepped away from the magnetic board and snapped the lid back onto the whiteboard marker.

"There," he said. "Queensbridge, Little Broadwater, King's Lynn, Dunmow and now Rettendon."

"He's moving inland," said Harris, "towards London."

"Not necessarily," said George. "I mean, he might be heading that way, but if he's following the historical murders, he won't go into Central London, he'll skirt around the edge of it. I did a heat map, look." George pulled an A3 printed map of South-East England and stuck it to the board beside the old and new murders.

"It's not hard to see that most of the unsolved crimes on our list, if they were indeed carried out by our man, were all in the East London and Essex areas. He ventured further afield for some, but if he was targeting a particular type of offender-"

"Sex offenders, George. Let's just get it out there," said Harris.

"Right, sex offenders, sir," continued George. "Then he may have been running out of targets and therefore *had* to look further afield."

"George, you're right," said Harris.

"Well, the map doesn't really lie, sir."

"Not the map," said Harris, "but what you said. If he had to look further afield, that means something is driving him to do this. Don't you see?"

"Not really, sir."

"Well, let's make it easy. You like steak, right?"

"Of course, sir, doesn't everyone?"

"But if the supermarket where you did your weekly shopping had run out, you wouldn't bother going to a different supermarket, would you? Not just for steak?"

"No, sir," replied George. "I'd buy something else and hope they had it next week. If they still didn't, I'd re-evaluate where I did my weekly shopping."

"Right," said Harris. "So if the killer was just picking off sex offenders as they cropped up in his neck of the woods, kind of a hatred thing, then all the previous unsolved murders on that heat map would all be in one area. But they're not. Most are, yes, but not *all* of them."

George still didn't understand the analogy.

"Let's put it another way," continued Harris. "If this town ran out of petrol, you would drive to the next one to get it, wouldn't you? Because you *need* petrol, you can't go without it. Whereas you *can* go without steak, it's not a *necessity*."

"I think I understand where you're going with this, sir."

"Something's driving him, George. There's a need, a thirst. He needs to satiate some kind of inner..." Harris searched for the word.

"Demon?" offered George.

"Demon," said Harris excitedly. "If he couldn't find a target when the need came, he *had* to look further afield because he *needed* it, just like you need petrol.

Harris stepped over to the magnetic board, took the white-board marker off George and circled the murders that seemed to be away from the huddle.

"George, my friend," said Harris, standing and throwing the marker back at him, "we have ourselves a demon."

CHAPTER EIGHTEEN

Reg and Melody sat in a beer garden outside a pub beside Vauxhall Railway Station. Boon lay under their feet with a small silver bowl that the bartender had kindly provided. Melody had sparkling water and Reg had a pint of diet coke.

Reg flipped open his laptop, connected to his phone's 4G data signal, and flexed his fingers, more for show than anything else.

"Okay," he began, "let's begin with what we know."

"We don't know anything for sure," said Melody. "We know there was another murder, this time in Rettendon. We know that Harvey is involved somehow, and-"

"And that's about all we know, right?" said Reg.

Melody looked slightly dejected but nodded.

"Come on, Melody, we can do this," said Reg. "It's us." He nudged her with his elbow and smiled, giving her a cheeky sideways glance.

"Okay, we also know that more murders happened in the places we've been to," said Melody.

"That-a-girl," replied Reg, happy to see her beginning to get into the research. "So let's just start plotting a map here. You remember the places?" he asked.

"Queensbridge, Little Broadwater, King's Lynn, and Dunmow. But now we'll need to add Rettendon," said Melody.

"Right," said Reg, "so according to Frank's data, Harvey erm-"

"You can say it, Reg," said Melody. "Harvey murdered somebody in each of those areas."

"Yeah, but it wasn't just murder, was it?" said Reg. "It wasn't a random attack on a member of society."

"No, it was a personal vendetta," said Melody. "For his sister, Hannah, and all the other victims of sex crimes."

"Exactly. According to Frank's files here, Harvey researched these sex offenders and carried out precision killings. Harvey told him that he used to treat them as training."

"That's right. It *was* training," said Melody. "It was how he got so good at what he does."

"Killing?" asked Reg.

"And not getting caught," finished Melody.

"And in the meantime, he found peace for Hannah's memory."

"Yeah, but you know what?" began Melody. "I think there was more to it than that."

"How do you mean?" asked Reg.

"Well, just talking to him about it over the past few days-"

"You talk about all this stuff? Like over breakfast or something?"

"No, not like that. But he's been quiet recently like something has been on his mind."

"You mean the silent, brooding serial killer was quiet over breakfast?"

Melody shot him a look.

"Sorry," said Reg. "Bad taste."

"He's been having dreams," said Melody, "violent dreams, and he gets aggressive in his sleep."

"And what did he say about that?"

"He just said that in the past, he'd had them, and that was like his calling. That was when he'd begin to research a new target."

"So the killing wasn't just to bring peace to Hannah?"

"Yeah, it was," said Melody. "But there's more to it than that. They brought him peace too, a kind of therapy."

"And he's been having these dreams again?" asked Reg.

Melody nodded. "Yeah, plus he's been quieter and quieter. At first, I thought it was because of the wedding, you know? It's a big deal for him to be centre stage, not hiding in the shadows."

"Okay, can I say something?"

Melody nodded.

"We need to piece this together, but to do it, we're going to need to assume Harvey is guilty, that he's actively killing again, and-"

"I know, Reg," said Melody. "We need to treat him like a suspect and disassociate ourselves from him."

Reg nodded. "Think you can do that?"

"I think I have to," said Melody.

"So we're *not* trying to find him guilty, we're trying to catch him before the police do, and the only way we're going to catch him is by working out where he's going next."

"Reg, no," said Melody. "You could lose your job, aiding and abetting and all sorts."

"If we can get to him, maybe we can get him out of the country, somewhere safe. I don't have to be involved. But you know what? I want to. We owe him that."

"He's already out of control, Reg. I don't know what he's going to do next."

"So where is he now?" asked Reg. "Where did you leave him?"

"Rettendon, by the murder scene," replied Melody.

"Okay, so let's get down and dirty, Melody. Let's see if he has any targets in the area."

"How are you going to do that?"

"The sex-offenders register," said Reg flatly.

"But that won't show their addresses, will it?"

"No, I'd hope not, but I thought you had a little more faith in your old friend than that," said Reg with a smile.

Within a few moments, Reg had an up-to-date copy of the register on his laptop.

"How's this for a hit list?" he said to Melody, showing her the screen.

"There's so many," she said. "These are all-"

"This is all the UK registered sex offenders," said Reg. "Let's start by focusing on Essex and East London."

Reg ran a few commands in the database to add location filters, and the list shrank but still ran off the screen.

"There're still a lot of names there, Reg."

Reg cleared the filters, and the database populated with the full list of names again.

"So, according to Frank's data," said Reg, "I think I'm right in saying that many of the victims-"

"Targets, Reg," corrected Melody.

"Targets?" said Reg.

"That's what Harvey called them, targets. If we're going to find Harvey, we need to think like him."

Reg nodded.

"And besides, Reg, I still love the guy. I don't like to think of him as having victims. He might still be saveable."

"We need to disassociate, Melody," said Reg. "Remember?"

"I am disassociated, Reg. But a girl can cling to hope, can't she?"

Reg gave her a flat smile and carried on.

"Anyway, many of the *targets* were either due to go to trial or had recently been released from prison when Harvey-"

"Killed them," finished Melody. "Killed them violently in the most horrific manner possible, causing slow and agonising deaths." She returned his stare. "I'm okay with it, Reg."

"I'm not sure *I* am," said Reg.

"So who do we have?" asked Melody.

Reg eyed her quizzically.

"Who do we have that's either due up or due out?" said Melody.

"Oh, I see," said Reg, getting back into the research. "Well the database can't actually name people who are yet to be found guilty, for defamation reasons I imagine, but it will show names of people that have recently been released. Let's start with one month, shall we?"

"No, one week," said Melody. "The list will be smaller. Try one week in the London and Greater London areas."

"If you say so," said Reg. His fingers began to fly across the keyboard and the database shrank with each tap of the *enter* key as the filters cleared out the names until they were left with just one.

Shaun Tyson.

CHAPTER NINETEEN

Harris was sitting at his desk in his office. The magnetic board displayed a clear picture of the killer's movements over the past couple of weeks and historically. Photos of the victims, locations and methodologies all tied into one and other. But it was all reactive. None of it was a clear indication of what was to come, or where.

That bothered Harris.

Catching a serial killer would propel Harris' career from small-town detective hopefully into something bigger and better. Even if the government agencies got hold of the case and took over, he'd be the one to guide them. He had the research, and he'd been close once before, he'd felt it on that hill. The killer had been close by.

His office door opened, and Malc poked his head into the room.

"Thirsty, Zack?" he asked.

Harris shook his head. "No, Malc, not today, mate. This one needs a clear head."

Malc followed Harris' gaze to the magnetic board and stepped inside to get a better look.

"Oh, for God's sake, Zack," he said. "You could have warned me." He turned away from the ghastly photos of dismembered, burnt, and ruined bodies. "Do you *really* need them up on your wall, Zach?"

"It's good for motivation," said Harris.

"Motivation?"

"He's out there somewhere planning another one, and I'm going to stop him." Harris stared unblinkingly at the wall. He was transfixed.

"Are you sure you're cut out for this?" asked Malc. "Try not to wind up on that wall yourself, eh?"

But Harris was lost in thought.

"Alright, mate, I can see you're busy. Don't be a stranger, eh?"

Harris snapped out of his gaze. "Yeah, sorry, Malc. Got a lot on my plate right now, mate."

Malc peeked behind the door again and studied the mass of sickening photos and George's scribbled writing. "What's all this then?" he asked, pointing at the two lists of old murders and new murders.

"He's done it all before," replied Harris. "We think the killer is re-enacting his previous murders."

Malc's face took on a disgusted look. "He's clearly sick, presuming, of course, it *is* a man?"

"I think so," said Harris. "The last one in Rettendon had a flattened patch of grass beside the body like he'd laid down beside it, maybe even savoured the moment. I had the photographer give me a scale. We're looking for a man, six-foot-ish, average build."

"That narrows it down then," said Malc. But Harris didn't crack a smile.

"I remember this one," said Malc, pointing at a photo of an

Eastern European man in what looked like an antique copper bathtub. "Boiled in the bath. I read about that one in the papers."

"Like you said, Malc, he's a sick puppy."

"Yeah but hold on a minute, didn't they find another guy tied up next to the bathtub? It was like the killer had let him go, spared him almost." Malc tapped his forehead trying to think. "Ah, what was his name?"

"Yeah, Shaun Tyson. He's serving time now. George reckons we can't go near him without raising a few unwanted flags, and the last thing I want on this case right now is more attention. It's bad enough that the reporters are hanging around outside, waiting to pounce on me as soon as I step out for a coffee."

"You might want to check that, Zack. This was the guy I was reading about last night. The second guy, Tyson, he was locked up for sex offences, but he's just been released, I'm sure of it. I was round the in-laws last night in Enfield. The guy was from Potters Bar, which is close by, and the local rag did a piece on him. Even had a picture of him at his mum's front door."

"Are you sure it was the same guy?" asked Harris, sitting up from his slouch.

"Yeah, *positive*. The headline was something like 'Boil-in-a-bag Sex Pest Set Free.' You know, imaginative stuff. I doubt he'll make the national papers, but the local one, the Enfield Gazette or something, was having a field day on it. I was surprised they could do that, you know. I mean, the guy is obviously a nonce and needed to be locked up, but the bloke served his time. I said to the missus, when the local boys find out about him, he'll be bloody lynched, he will."

Harris picked up his desk phone and punched a three-digit number.

"George, in here now."

CHAPTER TWENTY

Harvey Stone woke from another horrific vivid dream to find himself under a bridge beside a river. The memory eased slowly into reality and pushed the images of the dead faces from his mind.

He sat upright and clutched his knees to his chest. The cold night had taken hold of his body, and his shirt was damp from the wet ground.

Harvey considered his situation. He was effectively on the run. How had it happened? He'd managed to evade the law his entire life hiding in plain sight, and now he was clean, suddenly he found himself hiding under a bridge. If he was going to make a move, it would need to be now in the early morning light.

He'd watched from the trees as the police had cordoned off the area, and had watched the two plainclothes detectives study the body. He hadn't even had time to study the body himself. He didn't know if the murderer had left clues, but he knew how they'd done it.

Harvey had murdered somebody that way before.

Benjamin Green, Southend-on-Sea. Harvey couldn't remember when exactly he'd done it, but he knew he had. He'd dreamed of the face. He remembered the sharpened sticks that pinned him to the ground, and the tiny nick of the wind-pipe, not enough to sever it completely, but enough to start the clock ticking. Harvey could see Benjamin in his mind's eye, drowning in his own blood.

The victim on the hill had no face, not in Harvey's memory. In his mind, the face was replaced with a morphed composition of his many targets.

And Melody.

Melody's face. Suddenly it was her lying there on the hill beside him, in his mind. They were rolling around, deep in a passionate embrace, and then blood, thick, hot, sticky blood on Harvey's hands, coming from the back of Melody's head.

He kissed her.

But she wasn't kissing back.

She was lifeless.

He tried to roll her over, but she was fixed, her wrists, and her ankles, pinned to the ground by wooden stakes, carved by his own hand.

Her eyes were closed.

He slapped her face.

No response.

"No, Melody," he cried.

He felt her chest.

No movement.

No breath.

"Come on, wake up."

A pool of blood that ran from her sliced throat soaked her mass of thick brown hair as it lay on the sodden ground. Her soft, glowing skin had sunk to a pale white.

Then somebody stood over her.

A shadow.

Harvey lunged out at the shape, but the space was empty.

He fell to the ground and clutched at the small smooth stones beside the river.

Suddenly, he felt as if his chest was being squeezed. He fought for air, but there was none. He rolled back onto his elbows and crawled away from her body, but there was no body, no blood.

Just the shape of a man who stood, unmoving. Watching.

Harvey rolled away and stood in the grass by the side of the bridge. It was daylight now, and the river flowed by noisily over the rocks. Harvey peered tentatively under the bridge then looked all around.

He felt eyes on him like weights that hung heavy from his limbs.

He found the spot where he'd slept, where he'd seen the body, the faces, Melody's face.

It was a dream; it had to have been. All that lay on the ground now was a makeshift bed of leaves and a crumpled up newspaper he'd used to stop the biting wind.

The newspaper.

Boil-in-the-bag sex pest set free.

CHAPTER TWENTY-ONE

"It's here on the right-hand side," said Reg, leaning from the rear of the camper into the front to point at the little house with the wrought iron garden gate and narrow footpath that sat among quiet back streets of Potters Bar.

Melody drove straight past the house without slowing and found a suitable place to turn the camper around. She parked away from the streetlights, one hundred meters away from the house, turned off the engine and then climbed into the back with Reg, who was pulling the little curtains closed.

"Just like old times, Melody," said Reg, as he passed her a set of binoculars from his pack.

"Except we used to have Harvey *on our side*, Reg," said Melody. "I never thought we'd be *hunting him down.*"

"We're not hunting him down, Melody. We're saving the bloke. God knows, *he* saved *us* enough times."

Reg had set up his laptop on the van's small dining table and connected it to his phone's 4G data signal. "You think it's odd that all this is happening at the same time that Shaun Tyson is being let out?" he asked.

Melody lowered the binos.

"Now that you say it, yes."

"But what does that *mean*?" asked Reg. "I mean, who would have known Tyson was being released? And how would Harvey have found out about it?"

"Tons of people would be in the know, Reg," said Melody with a long sigh. "The prison service, family, enemies. Can you imagine how word spreads when somebody like that is set free?"

"Would the media know?" asked Reg.

"I'd hope that they wouldn't, but I guess sometimes information like this is leaked." Melody sat back and took a cursory glance through the binos.

"What if it *was* leaked before your trip and Harvey has been leading up to this all along? Planning it. It is, after all, the one guy he spared."

"Oh my God," said Melody. "It was Harvey who suggested stopping in Queensbridge *and* Little Broadwater."

"What about King's Lynn?" asked Reg.

"King's Lynn and Dunmow were my idea, but they were always part of the trip. He knew we'd go to both places. So if he was researching targets, he could have done that weeks ago."

"Here," said Reg, leaning back from his laptop, "there's an article about Shaun Tyson in the Enfield Gazette yesterday. It says here that-"

"Yesterday?" said Melody. "That can't be it. Check the back issues. If he was planning this all along, he would have had to have known about Shaun a few weeks ago at the very minimum."

"I'm checking the back issues," said Reg. "Doesn't look like anything else has been mentioned about it. So how would he have found out that Tyson was being released?"

Melody gasped. "What about the other targets, the other murders?"

"What about them?" asked Reg.

"When were they released?" said Melody. "If they were already released then maybe Harvey just struck lucky. But-"

"If they had also only just been released, then he definitely has someone on the inside feeding him this information," finished Reg.

"Damn it," said Melody. "I don't know how, but it's somehow worse that all this was premeditated. How could I be so stupid, Reg? He planned this all along."

"Don't beat yourself up about it, Melody. How were you to know?"

"I knew he was a killer, but I thought he was over it. Do you realise how stupid that sounds?"

Reg exhaled through pursed lips. "It doesn't look good, does it?"

Melody sat with her head in her hands.

"You need to make a choice, Melody."

She looked up and peered through her fingers.

"You need to decide if you're going to help him," said Reg, "or stop him."

Melody stared at Reg with raised eyebrows.

"I love the man, Reg," she said. "But now..." She hung on the words, dreading to say them aloud.

"You have to take him down, Melody," said Reg quietly.

A silence fell between them and Melody's eyes began to glisten in the dark of the camper.

"There's another problem, Reg."

He waited for her to finish.

"He's Harvey Stone," said Melody. "He's unstoppable."

CHAPTER TWENTY-TWO

"Are we going to sit here all night?" asked George. "We don't even know if he's going to show up."

"He'll be here alright," replied Harris. "It might be tonight, it could be tomorrow, but he'll be here."

"What makes you so certain?"

"It's all too convenient. Tyson is let out and our man just *happens* to be on a trail of destruction?"

"Yeah, but how would he even know that Tyson has been let out? And even if he did know, he must have known Tyson was being let out-"

"Weeks ago," finished Harris. "The others were just a warm-up."

"A warm up?" said George, incredulous. "You mean like a practice?"

"You saw it yourself, George. The man is good at what he does, but he hasn't struck for a few years. I think he's been honing his skills on whatever scraps he can get and saving himself for this one."

"Tyson?" asked George.

"He's the one guy who got away."

"He let him go though, didn't he?"

"I'm not so sure, George. I mean, why would he let him go?"

"I don't know. This is all just speculation."

"No," said Harris, "we're onto something here. I can feel it. Shaun Tyson was found tied to a wooden beam, while some other guy was boiled to death, right?"

"That's what the reports say," confirmed George.

Harris turned his face away from the headlights of a passing VW camper van that trundled past them.

"The guy that was boiled, what was his name? The Eastern European guy, he was the only one out of all those unsolved murders that wasn't on the sex offenders list, right?"

"Right," said George slowly, trying to see where Harris was going.

"So what if the boiled guy was actually a sex pest, but just hadn't been caught? What if nobody *knew* he was a sex pest apart from our killer? And what if our killer had been looking for this guy all along?"

"I think I'm beginning to see," said George.

"Good, stay with me," said Harris. "So if the killer was hunting the boiled guy all along, it could have taken years, George. Meanwhile, he hunts down known sex offenders, easy targets, to satiate his needs and to hone his skills."

"His demons?" asked George.

"Yeah, you saw the heat map," said Harris. "He stayed local. He only ventured out when the hunger struck and he needed a kill. That's what it is, George. He's got a need, a thirst, and when the need strikes, he kills, but not just anyone, only sex offenders. It's like maybe he was abused or something by the boiled guy? Or maybe someone he was close to was abused, or worse? I don't know. But the boiled guy was the ultimate hit for him, and the killer was angry enough to go vigilante against sex offenders until he found him."

"And that's when the killings stopped," finished George.

"Exactly," continued Harris. "He'd found what he'd been looking for, and his thirst died."

"Only now, his thirst is back," said George.

"And Shaun Tyson is the only man known to have survived this guy."

"So how do you explain the nationwide killing spree in the past two weeks?" asked George.

"Like I said, George, he's reliving the past. He's awakening-"

"The demon?"

"That's right, George," said Harris. His voice lowered, and his eyes focused on the house in front of them. "Tonight, we're going to catch ourselves a demon."

CHAPTER TWENTY-THREE

Panic set in the moment Shaun opened his eyes.

His heart raced, and he searched blindly into the dark corners of the room.

He flung back the covers and stepped onto the soft carpet. His confused mind took a few seconds to understand where he was, but then reality caught up, and he leaned with his elbows on his legs and his head in his hands as his breathing calmed and his heart rate slowed.

It would take a while for Shaun to adjust to life on the outside.

No shrieking drug addicts were filling the night, no howling and torturous cries of repent or begging for mercy. There was just silence.

There was no cold brick wall either, or hard concrete floor that welcomed the icy and stale air. There was just the warmth of the central heating and his mother's soft furnishings that retained the heat.

There *was* dark, but Shaun reached for the lamp that stood beside his bed, a luxury he'd been without for three years. Nobody could dictate lights off to him anymore. He flicked the light on, off, and back on as if reconfirming the power of choice, a luxury of freedom. He then turned it off once more to enjoy the darkness in safety, the safety of his home, a way of pushing his mind to understand that he no longer needed to live in fear.

Not inside the house anyway.

Shaun rose and walked barefoot to the window. The feeling of the warm, soft carpet under his feet brought a smile to his face. He pulled the curtain back and peered through his bedroom window. He'd had a small window in his cell but the bars had obscured the view and the sloping ledge had prevented him from pulling himself up to see out of it. The most he'd ever seen had been of the dull, grey London sky.

A few houses opposite had lights on, and Shaun felt the urge to wait for a careless neighbour to step out of the shower as he'd done many time before. But he tore his eyes away from the houses, battling to keep his perverse habits at bay.

He focused on the dark instead.

Somewhere out there in the darkness was the girl he'd met in the park that time, the girl that had been so keen to see and feel an adult male in all its glory, yet had run when they had finished and told her mother. He wondered if she was okay. He wasn't sure if it was his own remorse, guilt, or if it was a genuine concern for her he felt, but he certainly felt it. He'd thought about her many times over the past three years. It had started the day after they had met, with lustful images of their short time together, but then, once the police had knocked on his door and taken him away, his thoughts of her had turned to spite and hate. He'd remembered her in the darkness of his single cell, bad thoughts, not the soft touches that he'd remembered fondly, but evil, sadistic thoughts of what he could have done to her. What he should have done.

Maybe?

But the emotions that he felt for her as he stood by the

window in the dark, experiencing his freedom for the first time in three years, were kind. He realised that it hadn't been her fault. He should have known better. No matter how hard she had asked, no matter how relentless her hands had been, he should have walked away.

He hoped she was okay.

He'd considered sending her a note but had been advised that his restraining order would see him back inside. He wondered what might happen if they were to meet on the off-chance on the street, if he would have a chance to tell her how sorry he was. He played the scene out in his mind over and over. The first time around, she was friendly. She'd be older now, maybe even old enough, and they'd held hands. She apologised for what he'd been through, and he told her how he felt, how he'd thought of them together and the softness of her skin. But the scene rolled around again in his mind and returned to them meeting on the street. This time, she screamed for help, shouting that she was being attacked. People recognised him. There were angry men all around, towering above him. But between them, he'd seen her, and she smiled cruelly, a devious evil smile as she stood in the background and the blows had rained down on him from above.

He let his forehead rest against the glass. It was cool and refreshing. It pulled him from his imagination but left the images there as a reminder.

He wondered if he *was* actually better. He wondered if the urges would return. His thoughts suggested they were still there somewhere, hanging in the shadows waiting to strike, waiting for the chance when Shaun's mind was weak, and the opportunity arose.

His mother's disappointed face drifted into his thoughts. She was surrounded by a sea of hate and anger. He remembered that feeling of hatred in everybody's eyes that had stabbed him like daggers as he'd stood in the dock, while the judge and the prosecution had painstakingly carried out the legal procedure to the letter. He'd wished that he could have just told them yes. "Yes, it was me. I did those things. She was innocent, and I took advantage. Now please take me away. Take me away from the eyes, the hate."

It had felt like a lifetime. But when the judge had finally brought his hammer down and declared him guilty on all accounts, and he'd been led shamed from the room, he'd turned briefly to see his mum once more. The look in her eyes had pierced him. While those around her sent sharp, hellish looks of hate, they had merely formed the shaft of the arrow. It had been his mother's disappointed eyes that had formed the sharp point. But not of evil, not of hate, they'd carried a look of shame, a shame so deep and gut-wrenching that he'd been unable to shake it from his mind, even as he stood there beside his bedroom window three years later.

The last image that crossed his mind that evening had been of Pops, of the things he had made Shaun do, and the things he had done to Shaun in return. The old man's rough beard had been abrasive against Shaun's stomach, and his calloused hands around him had been rough, not like hers. He'd tried to contain his arousal at the time, but Pops had been smart, evil but smart. He'd sat with Shaun and provoked filthy conversations about the dirty things they'd both done. He'd watched as Shaun had relived his time with the girl. Shaun remembered all of the girls, but it was mostly the last girl he fantasised about, the girl who had cried to her mum. Pops had waited to see Shaun's body react, when there was no turning back. Shaun, in his tight track-suit bottoms, hadn't been able to conceal his arousal and had succumbed to Pop's desires.

Shaun felt sick.

He needed water to wash his mouth of the evil that Pops had put in there. He could feel it. He could taste him.

He began to cry.

But he didn't wail or sob. Prison had taught Shaun to cry quietly. It was best if nobody knew. He wiped the tears from his eyes and reached for the glass of water beside his bed, but movement outside caught his eye. It wasn't much, just a shadow that moved briefly in his mum's back garden. He searched for it again and wiped his eyes with his sleeve to see more clearly. But there was nothing out there except the shed, the greenhouse, and his mum's favourite little apple tree.

CHAPTER TWENTY-FOUR

"I hate sitting here knowing that Harvey could be in there right now doing God knows what," said Melody.

"We could move closer?" suggested Reg.

Melody hovered on her answer. "We might drive him away," she said.

"So what's your plan?" asked Reg. "Wait for him to leave and then nab him? We don't even have weapons."

Melody gave Reg a sideways glance.

"You do have weapons, don't you?" he said. "Melody, have you been driving around with-"

"I've carried a weapon for nearly ten years, Reg. It's not something I like to leave at home if I can help it. It's a hard habit to break."

Reg shook his head. "I'm seriously going to lose my job, you know that?"

"Who's going to find out?" asked Melody.

"The entire street if you starting opening fire in the middle of the bloody night."

"Relax. I have a suppressor," said Melody. "Besides, we won't take him down here, we'll follow him. Find somewhere more suitable."

"You're really going to shoot him?"

Melody took a deep breath and let it out slowly. "I don't see any other option apart from calling it in and watching him be taken away."

"Melody, listen to yourself. You were going to marry this guy and now you're talking about killing him. Maybe we should let-"

"I'm not letting him go to prison, Reg," Melody snapped. "He'd rather be dead that locked up. I know *that* much about him."

"Melody I'm not sure I can be involved," said Reg. "I'm sorry. But I didn't realise we'd be killing anyone, that will just make us as bad as-"

"As bad as him, Reg? No. No, it won't." Melody lifted up the bench seat she had been sat on and pulled out a long black Peli-case.

"Oh no, Melody. I've seen that case before," said Reg.

Melody popped open the two latches and lifted the lid.

"Oh for God's sake," said Reg. "When you said you were carrying, I thought you meant a little SIG handgun or something, Melody."

Melody began to build her Diemaco sniper rifle. She kept her head down and continued to piece the gun together as she spoke.

"Have you ever fired a handgun, Reg?" she asked, as she snapped the stock into place.

"In training, and once or twice in-"

"Did you ever *hit* anything, Reg?" she asked.

"Well, come to think of it, no. No, I didn't."

"Do you know how close you'd need to be to take someone down with a handgun, Reg?" She stopped what she was doing and looked up at her friend.

"Erm, well no," he replied.

"You *could* get lucky. You could hit him in the head. But even from twenty metres away, the odds are against you."

She started to load the magazine with rounds from a brand new box.

"So imagine this," she continued, "you're twenty metres away from someone, a trained man, quick and agile, and you miss your first head shot. Close your eyes and imagine it, Reg. Tell me what happens next. Tell me how it plays out."

Reg took a breath and closed his eyes.

"Erm, I take another shot?"

"Did you even aim? Are you nervous?"

"Yeah, I'm aiming."

"At his head? He's turned. He sees you."

"Yeah."

"He's coming for you, fifteen steps."

"I fire again."

"That's still a tough shot, Reg. You missed. You're shaking with adrenaline and fear."

"I'd go for the body; it's a bigger target."

"Five steps away."

"Even I couldn't miss from there."

"Bang. Too late. He's on top of you. He's wounded, he might even be dying, but he's disarmed you and just put the gun to your head."

Reg was silent for a moment. "It happens that quick?" he asked.

"Now," said Melody, as she snapped the magazine into the rifle's slot, stood it upright on its butt, and closed the lid of the case, "imagine it's Harvey you were firing at."

CHAPTER TWENTY-FIVE

It was a strange feeling for Shaun, as he sat at his mum's kitchen table in the dead of night. His head was thick with the pressure that formed from a whirlwind of emotions, guilt and mostly shame, but also the desire not to be a bad person, not to go back to prison, and not to let shame rain down on his mum. She deserved better.

It was with these words that Shaun finished his note and scrawled his name with an X underneath it.

He told her he loved her and would be back once his head was clear. He hoped she'd understand, and he would, of course, phone, so she would know how he was doing and where he was.

Shaun didn't fold the note. He left it on the table by the ashtray where she would see it as soon as she woke up.

The trip away would do him good. It might even toughen him up a little and teach him to stand on his own two feet. He'd heard a guy in prison talk about how he went travelling when he was younger, and Shaun had marvelled at his courage. At just eighteen, Jason King had jumped on a ferry with barely enough money to get to him through a few weeks of eating poorly and sleeping in hostels or on a beach. But he'd done it and survived with so many wonderful tales.

"Life has a funny way of working out," Shaun remembered him saying.

Shaun recalled how Jason had found buses and trains to get him to the coast, then either walked for miles or scrounged rides where he could to get to the next town or village. He'd ended up joining a few other travellers and picked fruit for a small wage and free board in an old shack. Then, when the season was up and he'd saved enough money for the next stage of his journey, Jason had moved onto another adventure.

Prison life had allowed time for Shaun to think. Often his thoughts felt like they were hideous B-movies that had been cast by the devil himself. But sometimes, a positive thought slipped through and found its way to the front of his mind. Life on the outside, a new beginning, a fresh start. Whichever form they came in, they encouraged the hope that had been suppressed by the evil inside him.

It was hope that now ran freely in his thoughts.

Thoughts of what France might look like, or what it might be like to once more stand amongst peers, and not be *that* guy, to not be avoided. Most of all, Shaun clung to the hope of one day being normal.

He could have listened to Jason talk all day about how beautiful Austria is and what life is like in Amsterdam cafes, about Roman architecture and the treasures to be found in the small villages that dot Europe's countryside. But Jason's audience had been a party of imprisoned perverts who, each time Jason had begun an anecdote, had steered the tales of wonder onto the less pleasant topic of sex and debauchery.

Shaun had quietly considered Jason's stories of the girls that he'd met on his travels, and he'd felt a pang of jealousy at how easily Jason had spoken to them. Jason had said that people are more comfortable approaching a man on his own, whereas they might hesitate before talking to a group of guys. Shaun would like that. For someone to ask if he'd like to join them doing whatever they were doing, dinner, drinks, or even just laying on a beach chatting.

Shaun had a plan, albeit rough and loose. He'd walk through the night, just to get away from Potters Bar; that was the first and most crucial part of his escape. If he tried to leave during the day, his mum would hold him back with her emotional ties.

Then the devil inside would smile at his captivity and creep out from the shadows again. He needed to strike while hope ran freely through his mind.

In the morning, he'd be far away enough to find a train or a bus station, where he'd start his journey south to Dover and wait for the ferry to France. It might take him a day to get there, he didn't even know how far Dover was from Potters Bar, but it didn't matter. He'd get there eventually. There was no time constraint, and freedom truly did lie outside the door.

All he needed to do was strike up the courage to take the first step.

He'd emptied his little savings pot that he had in his bedroom, and then shamefully taken the envelope that his mum kept in an old coffee pot in the kitchen. He knew she would be angry, and he'd tell her as soon he could, once he was far away. She'd understand. It was all to make him better.

He stood and collected his little rucksack from the floor. He hadn't taken much, just a few changes of clothes, his trainers, his passport and the photo of his mum that he'd kept in his prison cell.

Shaun gave the room a final glance and made sure the note was in full view. Then he turned out the light and closed the kitchen door quietly.

A nervous smile crept onto his face when he opened the

front door and stared out at the dark and empty street. Freedom is just a few steps away, he told himself. He zipped up his jacket, stepped out into the night, and closed his mum's front door behind him.

Shaun noticed that since he had begun to prepare for the trip, which had been just an hour, he'd managed to restrain his evil thoughts more easily, and more positivity was being let through.

Things were changing.

Life has a way of working out.

He took a final look up at the house and thought to himself that he'd return a few months or a year from now. Maybe he'd have a girlfriend. Maybe he'd find success as well as growth on his travels. But whatever happened, when he returned, he would be a changed man, of that Shaun was sure.

That was the last positive thought he had that evening.

A strong hand reached from behind him and forced a chloroform-soaked rag to his open mouth.

Shaun struggled, he even kicked out at his assailant, but within a few seconds, his knees buckled and he fell limply to the ground.

CHAPTER TWENTY-SIX

"Whoa, Melody, we have action," said Reg.

Melody jumped up and reached for her binoculars. She saw the limp, unconscious body of Shaun Tyson being dragged into the side door of a black van.

"I see him," she said. "I knew it, Reg."

"Are you going to take him out?" asked Reg.

"No, not here, there'd be too many eyes. Let's tail him and see where he takes him."

Reg loitered, half standing and half crouching in the back of the camper.

"You drive, Reg," said Melody.

"I knew you were going to say that," replied Reg, grumbling as he climbed into the driver's seat. He started the camper's engine but kept the headlights turned off.

"Keep the lights off," said Melody from the back.

"Yeah, I remember," said Reg. "This ain't my first rodeo you know?"

The black van pulled away slowly and its headlights flicked on a few moments later when halfway down the street.

"This ain't his first rodeo either," said Reg quietly. He engaged first gear and pulled out into the quiet road.

The VW camper rode the tarmac smoothly, and Reg waited for the black van to turn out of the street before he gunned the throttle to reach the end of the road, where he saw the van disappear around a bend.

"Keep this distance," said Melody.

"Is it safe to turn the lights on now?" asked Reg.

"I thought you said this weren't your first rodeo?"

"Well, you know," replied Reg, "I don't want to upset my Jedi Master."

Melody didn't smile at the joke. She was focused on the van in front.

Reg clicked the light switch on the dashboard and the headlights flicked on. He followed the black van in front, as it weaved through the maze of backstreets and onto Potters Bar high street.

"He's heading for the motorway," said Melody, seeing the van turn left.

"We can't take him out there," said Reg.

"No, but if he's going where I think he's going, we'll have our chance."

"I can't believe we're actually doing this," said Reg.

"What?" said Melody. "Saving lives?"

"Going after Harvey. He's still one of us."

Melody sat forward.

"That's how I was thinking, Reg," she replied. "But you have to remember that Harvey won't be thinking like that. He's ill, he must be."

"Like mentally?"

"How else would you explain it? You see what he's done, you know what he's been through. It would have broken most men, but Harvey pulled through. On the exterior, he's this tough, no-nonsense guy that's afraid of nothing."

"But on the inside?" asked Reg.

"On the inside, Reg, he's hurting. He knows it's not normal to do this. He knows *he's* not normal. I often wondered if he yearns for normality, or if he even knows what normality *is*."

"You don't think it's some kind of destiny?" asked Reg.

"I doubt he believes it's destiny. In Harvey's mind, things just are, or they're not. Things happen, or they don't. You plan for them, or you don't. You live-"

"Or you die," finished Reg.

"Exactly."

"We're approaching the motorway, Melody."

"Keep your cool and stay well back. The motorway is well lit and he'll spot the camper a mile away."

"Do you think he'll spot that BMW?"

"What BMW?" asked Melody.

"The one that's been following us all the way from Potters Bar."

CHAPTER TWENTY-SEVEN

"You're getting restless, George," said Harris. "Can you try and keep still? The way the car is bouncing around people will think we're up to no good in the back seat."

"I can't help it, sir," replied George. "I need to stretch my legs."

"What are you, a kid? Calm down. We're onto something good here. Just think of the glory, George."

"Glory?" said George. "Do you honestly think he's going to turn up just because-"

"He'll be here, George," interrupted Harris.

"I know, you can feel it your bones, right?" said George. "I just wish I could feel a nice pint of lager in my hand instead of cramp in my legs. Sod the bloody glory."

Harris gave him a sharp look.

"I asked you if you were up for this, George."

"I *am* up for it, sir," replied George. "It's just bloody boring is all. It would help if we could actually see the front of the house. All I can see is that van-"

"Which makes this a perfect position, George. We see everyone who comes and goes, and they don't see us."

"I'm bringing a book next time."

Harris looked across slowly with a frustrated look on his face.

"Here I am, trying to bring you on, help you climb the ladder, George, and yet all I hear is you moaning about cramp and boredom."

"I can't help it, sir."

"Think about that board in my office, George," said Harris. "Think about the faces of those men in the pictures."

"You mean the dead sex-offenders, sir?"

"I mean the faces of human beings, George," said Harris. "There's a man out there with a taste for blood. He's outwitted the police for twenty years. He cuts people to ribbons, burns and boils them alive. He's a twisted man. It doesn't matter if he's a vigilante trying to do good, to me, he's a killer, a madman. He's loose, he's dangerous, and he won't stop until someone stops him."

"And that someone is-"

"That someone is me, George." Harris spat as he said the words. He'd wound himself up. "We're going to take him down, and you can either carry on moaning about cramp and boredom, or you can help me catch him, and just maybe you'll learn enough to get a foot on that ladder."

George listened to his superior's rant with real affection for his positivity.

"You honestly think we can do this?" he asked.

"Yes, George," said Harris. "I honestly think that when, not if, but *when* our man comes walking down this street and gets into that house over there, we'll be on top of him."

A vehicle started its engine somewhere in the quiet street.

"What's that?" asked Harris, turning and looking through the rear window. "Look alive, George. Where's that engine coming from?"

"It's the van, sir," said Harris excitedly. "It's on the move."

Harris spun back to face the front and watched as the large black van pulled slowly from its parked position on the side of the road and began to make its way up the street.

"Aren't we following, sir?" asked George.

"All in good time, Georgy," said Harris. He stared transfixed at the van. "All in good time, my friend."

Harris' hand moved to turn on the car's ignition.

"Hold on, sir," began George. "Look behind, there's another van pulling out."

"That's a camper van," said Harris. "That would explain how he gets about, but who's in the black van then?"

"You think he has help?" asked George.

Harris' eyes widened.

"We never even thought of that," he replied.

"What do we do?" asked George, suddenly sounding nervous.

Harris let the van pass, waited a few seconds, and then started the BMW.

"We let it play, George."

"But there'll be more than one of them."

"And there's more than one of us. What's the problem?"

"Well, what if there's three of them?"

"Then we call in backup, George," said Harris, as he edged the car away from the kerb. "This is a real find. If we need help, we'll ask for it. But if we can handle it, then we'll handle it."

"Righto, sir," said George, sounding unsure.

"Do you feel it George?" asked Harris.

"Feel what, sir?"

"The electricity. Can't you feel it thundering through you?"

"Not really, sir," said George. "But my cramp's going away."

"Well, you might want to forget about your cramp, George, and start to tune yourself into this."

George stared at the van in front and saw the lights turn on once it was away from the house.

"Have you ever done this kind of thing before, sir?"

"Have I ever captured a serial killer, sorry, serial *killers*?" said Harris. "No, George, as it happens, no, I haven't. But you know what? All that is about to change."

"Looks like he's joining the motorway, sir," said George.

"Where's he taking us?" said Harris under his breath.

He reached under his seat and fumbled around, then brought out a small Glock handgun. He hit the little silver button on the left side of the moulded grip and let the magazine fall into his lap.

"There's a box in the glove compartment," he said, handing the empty magazine to George. "Load that."

"A gun?" said George. His voice rose a full tone. "Where the bloody hell-"

"George, load the bloody weapon and stop acting like a kid."

"But, sir, we aren't supposed to-"

"We aren't supposed to do a lot of things, George," snapped Harris. "But we do, don't we? Because it gets the job done, doesn't it? And right now, Georgy, we have two targets, both of which are prime suspects in a serial homicide investigation."

"Two suspects," said George, suddenly grasping something. "The camper, sir. It's the same one."

"Same one as what?"

"Rettendon, sir," said George. "I thought it looked familiar. It was at the crime scene. The uniform was questioning the driver, a girl with a dog. Remember?"

"George, you clever bastard," said Harris. "You're right. That, my friend, is far too much of a coincidence for my liking."

"It's turning off the motorway, sir."

"Where's she going then? Think fast, George."

"Okay, what if the van is an innocent and the killer is in the camper? Maybe Shaun Tyson got in the van without us seeing, and maybe the camper was waiting for him to pull away."

"Or, what if there really are two killers and one's leading us on a little magical mystery tour?"

"Gut feeling, sir?" asked George as he loaded the magazine with the brass rounds from the little cardboard box in the glove compartment.

The atmosphere in the car had grown thick as the drama unfolded, and the decision time had come from out of nowhere.

"Gut feeling, it's the camper van," said Harris. "Are you sure it's the same one?"

"I'm positive, sir," said George. "But I'm sure I can see someone in the back window."

"So how about this?" said Harris. "There's two of them. It's a couple-"

"Like Bonnie and Clyde?"

"They'd blend in everywhere," said Harris.

"And who'd suspect a woman of being capable of doing those things?"

Harris began to pull off the motorway, following the camper at a safe distance. They both watched as the black van continued on its path and then was out of sight.

"I hope you're sure about this, sir," said George.

CHAPTER TWENTY-EIGHT

"I hope you're sure about this, Melody," said Reg, as he pulled the camper off the motorway onto the slip road and watched the black van drive away.

Melody took a deep breath and exhaled through pursed lips.

"Only one way to find out, Reg," she said.

The slip road led down to a roundabout, where the right-hand exit led under the motorway and into London, and the left-hand exit led into Epping Forest and the countryside beyond.

"They're following," said Melody, gazing out the rear window.

"Which way?" asked Reg. "Left or right?"

Melody took a few seconds to look at the options.

"Left," she said. "We need to find a quiet road in the forest."

"What are you planning, Melody?"

"Something Harvey showed me once," she said. "It somehow seems apt right about now."

"Who are they?" asked Reg. "Why do you think they're following us?"

"Police," said Melody flatly. "I'm sure I saw that car in Rettendon with two men in the front."

"That particular car?"

"That particular car, Reg. They were detectives, plain clothes, and if they did their homework just like we did ours, then they must have come to the same conclusion, and knew Harvey was going to strike as soon as Shaun Tyson was released."

"So why's he following us?" asked Reg. "We're not the bloody killer."

"No, but *they* don't know that," said Melody.

"If they think it's us, then we need to either lose them or finish this soon," said Reg. "They could have back up ready to block the roads. All they'd have to do is call it in."

"I don't think we're going to lose them in this camper van, Reg," said Melody, as she armed the rifle. "We're going to have to do this the hard way."

"Just hold on a minute, Melody," said Reg, turning in his seat. "You might be bleeding bonkers enough to shoot a policeman. But you know what? I'm not. I don't want to lose my job. I suddenly don't want any part of this. It's going from bad to worse."

"I thought you were talking earlier about Harvey being one of us?"

"I did, I was, he is, or was," said Reg in a panic. "But there's no way I'm being involved in shooting policemen, or anybody, come to think of it. You've gone nuts, Melody. You've spent far too much time with Harvey."

"And what's that supposed to mean?" snapped Melody. "Too much time? I love the man. Of course I spent time with him."

"And he's rubbed off on you. There's no way you would even consider shooting a policeman a year ago."

"Reg, just calm down and keep your eyes on the road," said

Melody calmly. "Whatever happens, we're not going to let these detectives take Harvey down. If he's going to be stopped, it's going to be me that stops him, not someone who doesn't understand him. He won't deal with that well."

"So...?"

"So I want you to gently slow down, just a fraction, Reg, and I'm going to count down from three. When I say the number one, I want you to brake hard."

Melody crept beneath the rear window and loosened the locks on either side of the clear Perspex. She took a glance and placed the BMW at five hundred yards back.

"Slower, Reg. We need them closer."

"You're crazy, Melody," replied Reg. "I don't like this at all."

"Reg, do you trust me?"

Reg hesitated.

"Reg, I asked if-"

"Of course I trust you. I think you've gone nuts but I trust you. I'm still driving, aren't I?"

"That-a-boy, Reg," she replied quietly. "Now slow down a bit more, just ease off the accelerator a little."

The camper began to slow, just enough to allow the BMW to slowly close the distance.

"Okay, that's good," said Melody. "Now I want you to indicate left as if you're going to pull over."

Reg did as he was instructed, and the BMW grew closer still. Melody watched with a trained eye. She tried to think like the detectives. She had been one for so long, so it came naturally.

"They're going to pretend to pass slowly and then cut us off. Are you ready for the hard brakes?"

Reg shook his head in disbelief. "Yes, Melody," he said. "I'm ready, but this is on you."

"Three."

Reg took a deep breath.

"Two. Easy now, Reg."

"I'm easy," he said, unable to hide his nerves.

"One."

CHAPTER TWENTY-NINE

Panic set in the moment the van took a corner at speed, sending Shaun sliding across the wooden floor into the side panel, waking him from his drug-induced sleep. The bag over his head was rough on his face, like Pop's beard had been, and his wrists were bound with what felt like gaffer tape.

Shaun struggled to control his breathing, trying in vain to see through the bag's material. But the van was dark and offered no indication of size, or even if he was alone.

"Is anyone there?" he whispered.

No reply.

"Hello?" he said, slightly louder.

The rumble of the road noise and the van's diesel engine were the only replies.

He worked his way into a corner by sliding like a worm, and then pushed with his bare feet against the wooden floor and his face against the metal side of the van until he was sitting upright.

Then the tears came again.

Shaun thought of his mum. She wouldn't even know he was in trouble. She would find the note, she'd be upset, but Shaun had hoped she'd be happy that he was off on a quest to better himself, to be a better person, and to finally make a go of life.

Except he wasn't. His quest had ended after just one step. There would be no trip to Europe. No hitch-hiking, no fruit picking, no sleeping rough, no making friends, no meeting girls.

It wasn't the first time Shaun had been tied up and thrown into the back of a van, but he sensed it would be the last. The brutality of the attack flashed across his mind. Strong, practised hands had held him and forced the chemical-soaked cloth onto his mouth and over his nose. He'd tried to move his head away, to gasp at fresh air, but he'd been easily overpowered.

His nose ran, but all he could do was reach up with his shoulder and smear snot across his wretched face inside the bag.

He was helpless.

"Is anybody there?" he called out again, slightly louder than before. But again, no replies were offered. Just the rumble of the road and hum of the van.

The noise was constant. He gauged the speed at motorway speed. He hadn't felt a turn for a while.

Shaun was tired. Emotionally exhausted. The joy of being released from prison after three years had been tainted by the ever-present shame and guilt that had coursed through him as a reminder that he was a sick and twisted man. Then the feeling of control he'd felt in the kitchen had been wonderful, almost uplifting. He was leaving, he was heading off to Europe to better himself, to make his mum proud of him again, and now fear had returned and sunk its bitter teeth into his skin.

He'd taken one step and been cut down.

He began to shiver, from both the fear and cold, so much so that his torso began to ache. With his legs pulled up to his chest, he forced his bound wrists over his knees to hold himself and preserve any body heat he could. In doing so, he felt the gaffer tape stretch, just a little.

But it was enough to spark hope.

Maybe he could escape? Maybe he still had a chance? His bag. Shaun remembered he had a multi-tool in the top pocket. It had been a gift from his mum and he'd never used it.

He felt around with his feet for the bag's soft material. Had he dropped it? Had his assailant taken it? Was it sat on the seat in the front beside him as he drove?

His foot touched something soft.

It felt like his bag.

Shaun pushed himself flat on the floor and shuffled across to it. Elation set in followed closely by desire.

He found the multi-tool.

From memory, he knew that the fold-out blade was on one side with a little groove for his thumbnail to pull at. He fumbled with it and finally felt the blade release stiffly from its folded position.

A few awkward moments later, the tool was in his hand with the blade turned inwards, and he began to cut the tape.

The van slowed and took a long sweeping bend. Shaun steadied himself. His heart began to race. Hope was winning the race of emotions in his mind, but the van's movements meant the driver might be close to where wherever it was they were heading.

He didn't have long.

His breath felt hot and sour in the bag, and his breathing quickened, multiplying the heat and the foulness of his own adrenaline-fueled breath. The angle he was cutting at made applying pressure on the blade difficult, but he developed a slow rhythm and felt like he was making progress.

The van turned again, this time the opposite way, sending Shaun rolling onto his front. He outstretched his arms and took the brunt of the landing on his elbows. The blade was perilously close to his neck.

In an instant, his mind flashed with old memories of suicide. Dreams he'd had. The things he'd considered.

Death took a step forward.

Shaun pushed himself to his knees.

But not yet.

He resumed cutting at the tape with added vigour. Soon, he felt the blade break through the final strand of his restraints, and he pulled his wrists apart feeling the cool air on his skin. He set the multi-tool down and immediately tore the remains of tape away then frantically began to pull at the bag on his head.

It was tied at the back of his neck.

His breathing quickened once more, and he was thrown off balance as the van turned, more sharply this time. It began to slow.

He couldn't figure out the knot. He couldn't find the loose end to pull.

The van slowed further and felt like it had turned into a driveway as the tyres found noisy gravel, and the slow crunching of stones began.

Shaun fumbled for the tool. He couldn't lose *that*. He cut a hole by his mouth and sucked in the cool air then cut the bag across his face and pulled it over his head as if removing a hood.

The back of the van was pitch dark, and his eyes adjusted merely to the new shade of black.

The sound of gravel had finished, but the van continued to roll forward over bumpy ground. There was a small incline then the sound of a wheel driving over a stick.

He tried to picture the scene for his escape.

The back of the van had two doors, the side and the rear. He edged closer to the back doors and fumbled for the door release. Perhaps he could run. The van was moving slowly enough; he could easily jump out. He could be gone before the driver knew.

The door was locked.

Which door would the driver open? The side door was on the opposite side of the driver seat. So maybe he'd just walk to the back and open the rear door? But maybe he'd walk around the front of the van and open the side door?

The van stopped.

Shaun stood crouched and ready to pounce.

The engine turned off.

Shaun listened but heard only the sound of his own breathing and the regular beating of his heart.

The driver opened the door and slammed it closed.

Shaun half stood, poised between the two doors, and held the blade ready to slash out at whoever opened the van.

He heard footsteps outside. But which way?

A stream of saliva leaked from his mouth like a salivating animal.

This was survival.

But no door opened.

The footsteps disappeared.

Shaun stood trembling in the darkness for what seemed like an eternity.

Then, out of nowhere, he heard the rush of petrol being ignited.

CHAPTER THIRTY

Harris slowed the car as the camper in front eased to the side of the road. Its brake lights cast hues of red onto the underside of the canopy of trees, formed by the forest that reached across the road as if it were somehow trying to reclaim the space.

"Easy now, George," said Harris quietly. "I'll stay in the car, and you talk to the driver. Get him out of the vehicle."

"But what if-"

"I'll be covering you from here. Nothing's going to happen," said Harris, as he racked a round into the handgun.

"This isn't turning out to be a fun night for me, is it?" said George, as he reached for the door handle.

The interior light flashed on brightly, and Harris squinted through the windscreen to keep an eye on the camper.

George climbed out of the car, closed the door and the interior light slowly dimmed, returning Harris to darkness. He watched as George took a wide path around to the driver's door, then saw him ask the driver to step out.

Suddenly, the rear window sprang open and the muzzle of a high calibre rifle shot out. Within moments, it had fired a round, and Harris felt the car drop as the front left tyre burst. Before Harris could react, the rifle aimed at him.

The camper began to indicate then pulled out onto the road again and drove away casually.

"Shit, shit, shit," said Harris. He thumped his hand on the steering wheel and tossed the handgun into the back of the car.

George had dropped to the ground when he heard the gunshot and now sat up in the middle of the road looking confused. Harris climbed out and surveyed the damage.

"What the hell just happened there?" said George.

"Did you get a good look at the driver?" asked Harris.

"Male, IC1. Small frame, gaunt face, glasses, messy brown hair, I think. He looked almost nerdy. Who took the shot?"

"There was a woman in the back of the camper," replied Harris.

"The one from Rettendon?"

"Can't be sure, George," said Harris. "I was concentrating on the rifle she aimed at me."

"*She aimed at you?* Shall we get uniforms to stop them? They can't get too far."

Harris thought about it. "No, wait," he said. "They're going somewhere local. Get that wheel changed. They won't be going far."

George dropped his arms to his sides and shook his head, then walked to the back of the car to get the tools and the spare wheel. Harris joined, and took the jack from him.

"Do you know where we are, George?" asked Harris.

"Yeah, this is Waltham Abbey," said George.

"No, I mean, do you know *where* we are?"

George looked puzzled. "*Waltham Abbey*, sir," he replied. "Essex?"

Harris had found the car's jacking point and was winding

the jack handle to lift the vehicle. "What's that way?" he asked, nodding west, back towards the direction they had come.

"London, sir," replied George.

"In particular, what part of London?"

"East London I guess, sir."

Harris stopped winding and looked up at George, who was pulling the spare wheel from the boot.

"Okay, I'll spell it out for you, George," said Harris. "We're in Essex. East London is a spit away. But not only are we in Essex, we're literally *inside* Epping Forest." He motioned at the trees around them.

George's eyes widened. "The murders, sir."

"The magnetic board in my office, George," continued Harris. "Think about it. That camper didn't just turn around and go back to the motorway, did it?"

"No, sir."

"They headed that way, and the black van on the motorway, George, it wasn't in the fast lane, was it?"

"No, sir, it was in the slow lane, as if it was going to take the next exit," said George, suddenly seeing where Harris was going.

"We're close, George."

"But where?" asked George. "I mean, it's a big old place, Essex."

"All the murders so far have taken place in the victim's homes, or somewhere quiet like a forest, right?"

"Right. Apart from Rettendon, that one was out in the open," said George.

Harris cracked the last wheel nut with the tyre brace and began to spin the tool in his hands. "But," he said, as he removed the last nut, "it was *still* a quiet place, beside a forest."

"Yeah," said George, "and there's no saying he didn't do the killing *in* the forest and carry the body to where we found him."

"Right," said Harris. "Your man, the driver, was he short?"

"Short, sir?" said George, as he took the damaged wheel off Harris and rolled the new one to him.

"In height, George, was he tall or short?"

"Short, sir," replied George. "Well, not tall anyway."

"And slight, you say. He was small framed?"

"Yes, looked like he'd break if the wind blew too hard, sir."

"Did he look like the man who flattened the grass beside the Rettendon murder?"

George pictured the image in his head for a moment. "No, sir, but-"

"That means there's a few of them in on this," said Harris, as he spun the wheel brace and secured the spare tyre in place. He stood, tossed the brace to the floor and wiped his hands on a cloth that George offered.

"They're covering for each other. They're covering each other's tracks. They're creating alibis. It's not one man doing this, it's a bloody team, George."

"You think the bigger man was in the back van?"

"That's exactly what I think," said Harris, nodding for George to pick up the old tyre and put it in the boot.

"But we don't know where, sir. We still don't know where they're going to be."

"They like seclusion, George. They like to take their time. They're re-enacting the killings, perfecting them, every detail improved."

"Every detail, sir?"

"Every detail," said Harris. "The photos, George. The stakes that he carved to pin his victim to the ground."

"What about them?"

"Think of the photos of the first time. The stakes were hand-made, but they were amateur. The second time around, George, the stakes were perfectly smooth, as if someone had taken the time to-"

"I'm with you," said George. "He wanted to make it better than before."

"He wanted it perfect, George."

"And Noah Finn," continued Harris, "the first time he did it, the body sat there for so long that nobody could even tell what had happened until it was examined."

"But this time he made sure we would find it straight away."

Harris' mind wandered and pictured the image of the boiled man, where Shaun Tyson had been found.

"The boiled man, the last of the old murders," he said.

"What about him?" asked George.

"Where was he found? Where was Tyson found?"

"I think it was in the basement of some big house."

"Can you be more specific?"

George opened the car door and reached for his notes and files. He flicked through until he found the printout.

"Theydon Bois, sir."

"The boiled man, George, that's the next death. And what better place to re-enact the scene than the original location? The place where Shaun Tyson was spared the first time around."

"They're going to boil him," said George.

Harris slammed the boot of the car.

"Not if we can help it, George."

CHAPTER THIRTY-ONE

"Go, go, go, Reg," shouted Melody, as soon as she saw the tyre explode.

She aimed at the driver as a warning not to try to follow them. Once they were far enough away, she collected the spent round that was ejected from the rifle and ducked below the camper's rear window in case return shots were fired.

"How's that right foot of yours, Reg?" she asked.

"Erm, fine," replied Reg, turning to see her making her way up the aisle.

"Well stick it to the floor," she said. "We've got a murder to stop."

"And where exactly is it we're going? We lost Harvey, remember?"

"There's only one place he *can* go," she said thoughtfully. She glanced across at Reg's face and saw his expression turn to dismay.

"Not?"

"The same place he took Shaun before, Reg," said Melody. "It's the only place he'll get the privacy he needs. The place is special to him somehow."

"He needs privacy?" asked Reg.

"And time."

"To prepare?" asked Reg.

Melody gave him a look.

"He's going to boil him, isn't he?" said Reg.

"Not if we can stop him, Reg."

"What happens if they call it in?"

"Who? The boys in blue back there?" asked Melody. "They won't be calling anything in. The force is full of wanna-be heroes like that. They stumble onto something like this and see the potential glory. Greed and a step up the ladder are far too attractive for them to consider sharing the reward with a bunch of uniformed police."

"Ordinarily I'd agree, Melody," said Reg. "But we're not talking about stopping a mugging or a car theft. This is Harvey Stone we're talking about."

"They don't know that, Reg, do they?" she replied. "As far as they're concerned they're onto a madman on a killing spree. What could be better than bringing him in single-handed and nailing him for the recent murders, *and* dragging up the past with all the historical stuff?"

"But Frank wiped his slate clean. They can't nail him for those now, surely?"

"Either way, Reg, it's not going to be a fun time for Harvey. He's already looking at five life sentences back to back, six if we don't get there in time."

Reg was silent for a while, and Melody stared out of the window at the passing trees.

"Thanks, Reg," she said.

"Thanks for what?" he replied.

"For staying and helping. For being a friend. I'm not sure I could do this alone."

Reg forced a smile. "You have a plan yet?"

"I need to talk to him," said Melody. "I need to get to him before he finishes Shaun Tyson. If he kills Shaun, he'll be gone again, and that'll be the last I see of him."

"Maybe that's for the best, Melody," said Reg. "Maybe letting him finish what he started will really be the end of all this."

"I'd love to believe that." Melody held back the tears. "But I got so close to him Reg. He was normal; or rather, I thought he was. Things were great. I just didn't see this coming. Sure, I knew about his past, but we all did, right? We saw the change in him. We saw the good in him. I just can't believe that this evil was suppressed inside him for all this time."

"Are you sure you even *want* to see him again?" asked Reg. "I mean, knowing what you know now."

"I'm one of the few people he won't kill, Reg," said Melody. "I owe it to myself to close this off before he either goes missing or is killed himself."

"You think he'll die for this?"

"He won't go to prison, Reg. I think we both know that much."

"Yeah but he wouldn't-"

"Kill himself?" finished Melody. "No, he'd never do that. But he'd die fighting." She turned away and wiped a small tear that had formed in the corner of her eye. "Of that I'm certain."

CHAPTER THIRTY-TWO

Only the crackle of a nearby fire could be heard outside the van. Shaun remained poised to jump out of whichever door opened first.

His ears were now attuned to the sounds around himself and the van. The darkness had dulled his vision and heightened his audible sensitivity. The crack of a branch or snapping of a stick, the sounds of something heavy being dragged across the rough ground.

A man breathing heavily from exertion.

Shaun tried to remember what the other man had looked like, all those years ago. He remembered the night well, seeing a man boiled alive and knowing that he was next in line had left an indelible mark on Shaun's memory. He remembered the eyes most of all.

The eyes of the beast.

They had been cold eyes, hard and emotionless, and given the chance, Shaun could probably draw them. They were like no other eyes he'd ever seen.

A vision of the beast that had tied him to the wooden beam and forced him and the other man to reveal their dirty secrets ran across Shaun's mind. Death had hung in the air and seemed to take a step closer with every word Shaun had said during his confession. He'd tried to prolong the story, to keep death at bay, but the story had eventually ended.

Shaun had then been forced to listen with horror as the man who lay beside him had recounted a night long ago when he'd raped the beast's sister. It hadn't been just him, there'd been others. But he'd confessed, and he'd paid the price.

Shaun saw the man in his mind's eye, dragging wood to the fire outside, preparing Shaun's death.

Harvey. That had been his name, thought Shaun. He hadn't thought of the name for a long time, and now it came back, clear as day. The boiled man had begged and cried. He'd used the name, and the beast had responded.

Hannah had been his sister.

The memories flooded back, and he began to relive the night. The beast had been cruel and cold, but he'd shown that he had a heart. He'd left Shaun alone. He'd heard Shaun's story. So why now? Why not kill him then when it was all set up? If Harvey *had* murdered Shaun back then, the misery of the past three years would never have happened. Shaun's mum might have recovered from her grief, and he would now just be a memory.

Maybe he'd even be missed.

Another pair of eyes stared at Shaun through his darkened mind, white and lifeless, yet rolling in their sockets, desperately searching for light. The boiling water had cooked them like eggs. The searing heat of the ancient bathtub had melted the skin of the man's arms to the copper. His flesh had peeled away in gloopy chunks as he'd frantically dabbed at his ruined eyes.

Yet the eyes had still roamed.

For a while, anyway.

Shaun wondered what manner of death the beast was planning outside the van. The fire must be large, from the sound of the rush he'd heard, with hot fiery coals. How long had he been there? In the darkness, it was hard to tell. Amongst the fear, it was a lifetime.

A twig broke outside.

The side door was yanked open.

Shaun pounced from his crouched position and slashed at the beast with his small knife, who stood silhouetted by the fire. Shaun caught him off guard. His hands shot up to defend himself, and Shaun felt the blade connect with skin. But he didn't look back. He landed and ran.

He ran past the fire into the trees, away from the light and into the darkness. He ran until he could barely see himself then he ran some more. The jelly-like feeling in his legs took hold like he was running in tar. He was sure he could hear the beast behind him. He needed to hide. The fire was small, maybe three hundred meters away. Shaun ducked behind a tree and searched the darkness for movement.

The thump of his heart and his breathing was loud in the quiet night, and holding his breath only made his heart beat louder.

Was he safe?

Should he wait there until light? Where was the road?

Shaun's breathing eased enough for him to begin to hear the noises in the trees. The scratching of a small mammal on the ground a way off. The rustle of the leaves in the gentle breeze. The occasional pop and crackle of the fire in the distance that sent sparks into the air.

But no other movement.

Shaun stood slowly. His eyes never left the direction from which he'd run. He hoped to see the silhouette of the beast, of Harvey. At least then, he would know which way to run.

He took a step back, keeping the tree between his body and the fire.

His heart started to pound once more, as he began to make his escape.

He was close to the edge of the trees. He could see the long grass beyond the forest that shimmered like water in the pale moonlight.

That was his escape.

"Shaun."

He froze. His mouth was bone dry with fear. He was unable to swallow. The whisper had seemed to come from nowhere, yet everywhere.

He spun.

Darkness.

Had he imagined it?

The long grass beckoned. It was just forty feet away.

His head swivelled back and forth, searching the blackness for a sign, for a shape, for movement. Anything.

"Shaun."

The hushed whisper had come from the grass.

There was nobody there.

"Shaun."

No, it came from the trees.

The beast was all around.

He turned once more, stepping backwards, edging towards the grass, to safety, to anywhere, to nowhere.

Somewhere to run.

"Shaun."

Behind him.

He spun.

Those eyes.

CHAPTER THIRTY-THREE

"Kill the lights," said Melody, as the camper approached the open wrought-iron gates of John Cartwright's estate. "Drive straight past. We'll park further down the lane and walk back."

"We?" said Reg. "I thought I-"

"You've got two options, Reg," said Melody. "You can either stay here in the creepy dark lane all by yourself, knowing there's a serial killer out there." She turned to face him and saw the look of dread on his face. "Or you can come with Boon and me."

"You're taking the dog?"

"Of course I'm taking the dog. His eyes and ears are better than ours."

Reg pulled the camper to the side of the small lane and let out a long breath.

"I don't like this one bit," he said.

"And what about me?" said Melody. She opened her door. Her voice fell to a whisper. "You think I'm in love with this whole idea? A few days ago, I was talking about my wedding with my fiancé." She tucked her SIG into the back of her cargo pants and clicked her fingers for Boon to come. "Now I'm hunting him down."

"That puts things into perspective," said Reg, as he climbed down. He gently pushed the door closed and joined Melody in the lane.

"Just remember, you're his friend, he doesn't want to hurt you," whispered Melody, as they started to walk back up the lane towards the two iron gates.

"What if we're too late?" asked Reg. "What if-"

"We're not too late," interrupted Melody. "If I know Harvey as well as I think I do, he'll take his time with this one."

"Why?" asked Reg. "Why not just get the job done and get out of here? I mean if he's looking for closure-"

"He's looking for suffering," said Melody.

"Suffering?"

"Suffering, Reg." She stopped in the middle of the dark lane and explained in whispered tones. "The people he targets are sex offenders. They've destroyed lives. They're sick and twisted people, and each one of them represents the men who raped and killed his sister. To him, they're just as bad." Melody looked up into Reg's eyes to make sure he was following. "A quick death wouldn't bring the justice he's looking for. It wouldn't offer the retribution, and it wouldn't bring peace to Hannah's memory."

Reg nodded slowly. "I understand."

"So, let's go. Walk quietly."

They turned into the gates and hopped across the gravel to the much quieter grass.

"Didn't there used to be a house there?" asked Reg.

"Harvey burned it down," said Melody.

"Speaking of fire," said Reg, "look over there."

In the distance to their left, the tall flames of a large fire lit the surrounding area and the underside of the trees that stood at the edge of an orchard

"It's the orchard. Of course. That's where his parents are buried."

"In an orchard?"

"Follow me," said Melody, ignoring his questions.

Melody walked slowly, keeping Boon by her side, and listening for him to alert her to anyone approaching in the darkness with his low growl. She'd always hated the place. It was large, old and creepy, and now that it had fallen into disrepair, the wild, overgrown gardens had begun to overcome everything that stood in its way. She took a wide path around the fire. Her eyes scanned the area for movement, for Harvey's shadow. She saw the black van parked nearby the fire, but no movement.

Melody lowered to a crouch, as she grew closer.

"Keep down, Reg," she whispered blindly.

The flames were large next to what looked like a huge pile of wood. But no sign of anyone tending the fire. He'd be near. He'd show himself. It was just a matter of time.

Maybe Tyson was still in the van? Maybe she could get him out.

She stopped beside a lone willow that sat beside a trickling stream and turned back to Reg.

"Stay here," she whispered. "I'll be back for you. If you see anything, whistle."

Reg nodded with wide eyes. Melody could plainly see he was scared out of his mind. She handed him Boon's lead then pulled her SIG from her belt and made her way slowly towards the van.

The long grass made staying quiet difficult, so she lowered herself to the ground, softly and quietly, and for the last hundred yards, she crawled.

One elbow.

One knee.

Push.

Scan for movement.

One elbow.

One knee.

Push.

It was slow going, and the thick grass obscured her view, but gradual progress was her safest option.

Melody drew close to the van. The sound of the fire was loud and clear. She attuned herself to the environment. She tried to understand the noises, the crackle of wood, the gentle swish of grass as the soft breeze rolled across its tips in waves.

The thud of heavy wood hitting the ground.

Melody froze.

Another thud.

She peered beneath the van to the fire behind it.

Something dragged across the earth.

A rush of sparks flew high into the air, and the flames reached up higher than the van, just licking the lowest of the tree's outstretched limbs.

Footsteps.

Melody pulled the grass in around her.

Two black boots stopped and stood in front of the fire. A garden spade slammed into the earth beside them.

She needed to move. She was too open.

One knee.

One elbow.

Push.

Stop.

She listened. The boots hadn't moved. If she could just get beneath the van, she'd be safer. She could watch him prepare. She might even understand him a little more.

Melody crawled forward, her eyes fixed on the boots. The space beneath the van was just large enough for her to squeeze in and lay on her front with her SIG ready to fire. She crawled in slowly and felt him there, a few feet away.

Beyond the boots, in the fire, Melody saw for the first time what the pile of wood had concealed.

Melody shuddered.

In the very core of the fire was the main act, with flames licking its sides greedily, and its cast iron claw feet embedded into the glowing hot coals like some kind of creature from hell.

The old copper bathtub.

CHAPTER THIRTY-FOUR

"Turn here," said George, looking at the map on his smart phone. "The estate is on the left. That's it there. See the big iron gates?"

"Jesus," said Harris. "Would you look at this place?"

Harris pulled the car onto the gravel driveway, stopped, and killed the lights.

"We're on foot from here," he told George.

"Sir, do you think we should tell someone where we are?" asked George.

"What's the matter with you?" replied Harris. "You're not afraid of the dark are you?"

George huffed and climbed out of the car.

They pushed the car doors closed quietly and began to move into the long grass.

"Sir," said George, "look over there. Fire."

Harris held the handgun down by his side. He fingered the safety catch, nodded in reply to George, and then began to move off slowly in a wide circle to the right of the fire.

He strode carefully through the grass, as quietly as he could, and keeping an eye on the fire for any sign of movement. He made it as far as the tree line at the edge of the orchard, and began to hug the shadows as he worked his way along towards the fire.

"George, do you see the van?" said Harris, "Just through the trees there. Bingo, my friend. We're in the right place."

But George didn't reply.

Harris glanced back, but there was no sign of George.

"George?" he hissed.

Harris' eyes scanned back in the direction of the car, but there was no movement.

He carried on alone, and with his gun in front of him, he made straight for the van.

His footsteps were bolder. There was no need to be scared, he told himself. He *was* armed after all.

He raised the weapon, switched the safety off and worked his way along the tree line toward the fire. Stopping thirty metres from the van, he surveyed the darkness. Nothing but darkness.

Around the fire were five tall trees that formed a C shape that half-enclosed the area, creating a little clearing. A thick bough stood out proudly from the largest and most central of the five trees, from which hung what looked to Harris like a heavy chain.

In the centre of the fire beneath the chain was a shape.

What was it?

He focused harder, trying to make out the shape. His night vision was ruined from staring at the bright firelight, but then the shape took form and Harris froze.

It was an old-fashioned bathtub.

His heart began to race.

Clearly, the killers had taken the time to set the scene up perfectly, but the lack of movement and noise added to the anxiety. He wiped his sweaty palms on his trousers and ran his tongue across his lips.

Should he approach? What if the killers were waiting in the trees? Who knew if they were also armed? Where was the camper?

He lowered to a crouch and scanned behind him for George. Harris sucked in a few deep breaths to calm himself, then stood and took two steps forward.

Something wasn't right.

He wasn't alone.

Slowly he turned his head and stared into the darkness of the trees beside him.

There was something in there.

He took a step closer.

Something shined briefly in the moonlight, so faint.

Teeth?

A smile?

Suddenly, a hand reached out of the darkness and clamped onto his throat.

Harris tried to call out, but there was no air.

He pulled at the hands but they were too strong, like iron, and sticky with blood.

Harris kicked, but was dizzy and weak.

He fought for breath.

The hand squeezed tighter.

A brief inhale of chemical.

Harris knew the smell.

But it was too late.

He dropped to the ground.

CHAPTER THIRTY-FIVE

The two black boots took a small step back then swivelled sideways on one heel and one toe, like a soldier might begin a left turn. Then, they began to move as they made their way from the fire towards the orchard and disappeared into the long grass.

Melody shuffled forwards to see which way he'd headed. But in the darkness with just the dancing flames to light her surroundings, finding the shape was futile.

She tapped lightly on the underside of the van with her SIG. Three taps, slow, but enough to let him know he wasn't alone. She hoped Tyson would respond to let her know he'd heard.

He didn't reply. Why would he? He was probably tied up and gagged, sitting in the darkness terrified beyond imagination.

Melody would need to let Shaun out, but she didn't have much time. Who knew when Harvey would return and begin his gruesome plan? She took a couple of long breaths and planted her hands on the ground, ready to slide out backwards.

Suddenly, two hands grabbed her ankles. Two iron-like grips, strong and large. She inhaled sharply and gave a soft murmur. Wrenched backwards from her hiding place, she watched as the SIG slid from her grip and fell to the ground.

A hard knee pressed down and he forced her hands together behind her back.

"Harvey," she hissed, "it's me."

Harvey didn't reply.

Her hands were bound with cable ties that immediately began to dig into her skin.

"Ow, Harvey, what are you doing?"

Harvey didn't reply.

A canvas bag was forced over her head, and she heard the familiar zip of a cable tie fastening it tightly behind her neck.

"Stop it," she said. "I just want to help you."

Dragged to her feet, she tried to kick out at him, but her arms were forced up behind her, nearly dislocating her shoulders.

"You're hurting me, Harvey," she hissed. "Just stop it."

Harvey didn't reply.

A gentle nudge encouraged her to start walking. She felt the heat of the fire to her left and imagined where she was being led. Powerful arms forced her against a tree then she heard the rattle of heavy chains.

"Harvey? What are you doing?" she said gently. "This is too far."

No reply.

"Harvey, just talk to me. Please?"

She was forced to turn around and the heavy chain was thrown around her neck. She knew it was coming, but when the chain pulled tight, she gasped at the feeling of it against her throat.

The click of a padlock added a tense finality to the silence.

She didn't even hear him leave.

Was he behind her still?

Had he moved off?

Then a stark reality hit home and her stomach rolled with disgust, fear and hatred. She'd been too confident of his feelings for her.

He was going to boil *her*.

"Harvey?" she said softly. "It's me. You're not going to hurt me." She tried to command him.

But silence.

"Is anyone there?" she called out, louder this time. "Help."

The heat from the fire a few yards away warmed her skin and her neck prickled. She could feel a bead of sweat run down her chest.

This is fear. Don't be afraid.

But her inner strength was forced to the back of her mind by the muffled whimpers of someone close by. Something was dragged to the tree beside her. A man cried out in the darkness. He begged for mercy, and chains rattled once more.

Was that Reg?

Melody guessed he would be hooded and fixed to a tree just as she had been.

"Harvey, you're out of control," she shouted blindly. "This is it. This is the end. It's over."

Harvey didn't reply.

"Who's there?" said a man's voice, thickened from his tears.

That's not Reg, she thought.

"Don't worry," replied Melody. "This isn't over yet. Just hang in there."

"I can't die," he said. "I have a family. I have children."

"Take it easy," whispered Melody. "Try to control your breathing."

The man took several breaths.

"That's it," said Melody. "Just relax. If he wanted you dead, you'd be dead by now."

"Somehow I find that hard to believe," he replied.

"What's your name?"

"George, Dave George."

"You're police?" asked Melody.

"Yes, how did you-"

"It was me. I shot your tyre," said Melody. Somehow, honesty seemed a way to induce trust with her condemned companion.

"You?" he said. His breathing began to ramp up again. "But you-"

"Easy, calm down," said Melody. "You shouldn't have come here."

George took a few more breaths and then sobbed loudly from inside his canvas hood. "I know, I didn't want to, but-"

"But what?" asked Melody. "Your boss? He's here too?"

George didn't respond.

"Is he armed?" asked Melody, quietly.

George began to reply, but once more, the silence was broken by the sound of something else being dragged across the ground in front of them. The familiar rattle of chains clattered in the night.

The click of a padlock.

Once more, no footsteps of him walking away.

Was he close?

She spoke in hushed whispers, blind to her surroundings.

"Who's that?" whispered Melody.

No reply.

"Harris?" said George. "Is that you?"

"George?" came the muffled and groggy reply.

"Sir, are you okay?"

"Not really, George, no."

"Are you chained to a tree?" asked George.

"And hooded," he confirmed.

"I'm guessing you both are too?" said Harris.

Melody didn't reply.

"How many of us?" asked Harris. "Do we know?"

"Three of us, as far as I can make out," said Melody. "I don't suppose you boys bothered to call uniforms for backup?"

"How do you know we're police?"

"She shot our tyre, sir."

"She what?" said Harris, louder than he meant to. He lowered his voice to a hiss. "It was you? In the camper?"

"You shouldn't have come," replied Melody flatly. "This isn't the place for a small town detective. You're in way over your heads."

"Tell me something I don't know," said Harris.

Melody heard him test the chains and then succumb to the fact that he was stuck.

"Hang on," said George. "The camper? There were two of you. Where's the driver? The small guy?"

Something landed on the ground to their left with a thud.

It began to whimper.

"Reg, you're okay. You're with us."

She was quietened by a hard hit to the side of her face.

The temptation to call out to Harvey was strong, but the two police didn't need to know about their relationship. It would cause distrust, and right now, they needed to stay together.

Reg moaned as he too was bound to the tree with chains.

"Melody?" he called. "Are you there?"

"We're here, Reg," she replied. "Don't worry. We're all here."

"The detectives?" he asked hopefully.

"We're here," they both said at once.

"I don't suppose you-"

"Called backup?" finished Harris. "No, I'm afraid not."

The sound of a spade digging into the ground silenced them all. Melody tried hard to see through the tiny holes in the canvas, but it was no use. He was digging. A rhythm built up somewhere to Melody's left, beside the fire.

A sharp rasp, as the spade sank into the earth. A dirty crunch, as it was forced backwards. Then the scatter of dirt onto a pile.

A hole?

To bury them all?

She fought back tears and a small part of her was thankful for the hood. She didn't need the men to see her cry.

It's not over yet. She told herself.

George began to cry again. Melody heard him quietly. She heard him try to refrain, to hold it in, but he'd broken with a loud sob and the gates had opened.

It was too much for Melody.

"You pig," she spat.

The digging stopped.

"I thought you were better than this," she continued. "But you're not. You're just a cold-blooded killer. You deserve to go to prison. You deserve to rot in hell."

She felt him stand in front of her. His presence darkened the limited light that the canvas allowed. Melody trembled. She no longer knew the man who stood in front of her.

She could hear his breathing.

"Stop," she whispered, so only he could hear. "It's not too late."

She felt a finger on her throat, below the thick chain that held her bound to the tree.

"What are you doing?" she said. A soft unintentional whimper followed. She tried to move away, to slide up and down, anywhere, just away from his touch.

His finger lowered and caught on the neck of her shirt.

"Stop."

He pulled.

"No," she began to beg. "No, no more, just stop."

The shirt began to rip.

Melody cried out.

"Melody, what's happening?" It was Reg.

"Nothing, Reg," said Melody, her voice nearly an octave higher than normal. "Just be cool."

Her shirt fell open, and she felt the warmth of the fire on her skin.

His soft touch ran across her chest.

Tears came silently inside her hood, and she lowered her head.

She was powerless against him. He'd opened her up, he exposed her deepest fears and now flaunted them.

She began to visibly shake.

Her knees buckled, but her throat hung on the chains and forced her to stand straight.

His finger lifted her chin.

"Please, Harvey," she whispered. "No more. It's too much."

He stepped closer.

The shape grew darker.

He kissed her through the thick canvas.

CHAPTER THIRTY-SIX

Harris felt a tug at the back of his hood and heard the clip of cutters on the cable tie, then felt the canvas hood pulled roughly from his head. He breathed in the cool air with an open mouth and groaned.

The hot coals in front were bright on his eyes. He looked down, trying to focus on the ground. There wasn't much to see, just tufts of grass and mud, and a wash of orange that grew and faded with rhythmic intensity.

The man had slipped away, back into the trees as silently as he'd come. Harris was glad. He tried to turn his head to see the tree beside him, but the chains were tight on his throat. All he saw were shapes, four of them.

To his right was open grassland. Beyond the fire, the soft tips of wild grass ebbed and flowed with the breeze, the breeze that he now breathed with pleasure. A man groaned to his left, far away, the furthest tree maybe. But Harris couldn't see. Another groan of pleasure.

Another hood removed?

Who was it? Was it George?

"Tell us what's happening at least," called Harris to their captor.

The killer.

"Tell us *why*."

The killer didn't reply.

The faint sound of the cutters travelling through the air and the sound of another canvass hood being ripped off a head. Another sound of temporary joy and the sharp intake of air.

That's three of us, he thought.

"George, are you there?" called Harris.

"I am, sir," came the reply.

Harris closed his eyes. He'd gotten George into this; it was on him. If George died, Harris would die. He wouldn't be able to face George's family and tell them what had happened and why.

Why was it happening?

It had all snowballed. Harris saw it now, clear as day. He'd made a connection, George had added solidity to his theory, and now, they were both stood tied to a tree before a fire with a hideous ancient copper bathtub that was almost glowing with heat.

The fire had died down.

Red-hot coals shimmered like the fires of hell, and Harris was lost in the movement of light. He imagined the saddened faces of George's children. He imagined Susan's face. The devastation. The shame.

And all the time, why?

"He idolised you," she would say. "He would have followed you anywhere, and you should have known. You should have called for backup."

It's my fault.

Harris craned his neck to see George. But at the furthest

reach of his neck, he saw only blurred and dark shadows stood waiting by trees.

Snip.

The final hood was ripped off, and the girl sucked in the cool air just as he had, as they all had.

"Are you okay?" he asked when the shadow had slipped back into the darkness.

"You talk when I tell you to talk," came a harsh whisper from behind his right ear.

It had been almost silent, like the wind or some drug-fuelled imagining.

But it had been real.

Harris took deep breaths, closed his eyes, and calmed his racing heart. The man was obviously sick. Things were out of control.

Was this really his fault?

He thought of his own wife, Patricia, and wondered if she'd be devastated. Harris knew she'd be upset, as any wife might be. But devastated? Not like Susan. In some ways, his death might be a release for her. A release from the grind of daily life they'd developed. A release from the monotonous routine of courteous manners, asking the right questions at the right time, and not doing certain things to upset the other, or doing other things just to save an argument.

That had been when he'd known his marriage was over, the day he realised that the reason he did certain things for Patricia had turned from enjoying the look of joy on her face to preventing the look of disappointment.

The thick chain that hung from the tree trailed out on the ground beside the fire. It began to pull tight as someone slowly pulled on the loose end.

Harris heard the girl beside him, who was lost to his peripheral vision, begin to question what was happening.

She called him Harvey.

Did she know him?

He failed to see the connection between the camper and the killer. Who were they? What were they doing here? Were they helping him? Were they trying to stop him?

The girl was released from the tree in a clatter of chains and shoved forward onto her knees. Harris saw her face for the first time since she'd looked down the length of the rifle.

The rifle.

It had been military grade. It wasn't an ordinary *dad's got a gun* type of rifle; it had been heavy firepower.

A big black boot sprang from nowhere and kicked her in the side.

She didn't move.

She was tough.

Maybe she was military. Maybe they'd been undercover and George and him had been in the way. Maybe that was why they had shot the tyre, to keep them away. But he'd been greedy. George had protested, and he hadn't listened.

It's your fault.

The man wore a hood to hide his face and stepped from the darkness. He pulled on the chain that hung from the thick bough above and fastened it around her neck. Then he dropped a single white envelope onto the ground beside her, before stepping back into the darkness.

"What is it?" whispered Harris. "What does it say?"

She looked up at him. Her tangled flock of curly brown hair hung limply on her shoulders, and her top was ripped open, revealing a white bra. But she didn't seem to care. She didn't try to cover herself.

Had she lost her own fight?

The girl slid a slender finger into the envelope, ripped the paper then pulled the note out. She let the discarded envelope drift with the breeze into the hot coals, where it shimmered and shuddered before curling and burning.

And then it was consumed.

The girl read the note to herself, and then stared at each of the men who stood by the tree.

"So?" said Harris. "*Read it to us.*"

The girl's eyes hung lazily on his.

"What does it say, Melody?" called the other guy, the driver.

Her head turned slowly to face her friend. But then it dropped and hung low, and she let her hand fall to her side. A deathly silence hung in the air as all three men anxiously waited for the girl to speak, their eyes pleading for news, anything, good news, bad news. But Harris' heart knew it would not be pleasant.

The girl took another single short look at all three men once more, just quickly, no eye contact. Then she returned her stare to the note in her hand.

"It's a game," she said.

CHAPTER THIRTY-SEVEN

Shaun was sitting cross-legged with his arms and legs tied around the tree in front of him with what felt like strips of material. His head rested on the rough bark, which hurt his skin, but he no longer cared. The time for caring about pain was over. The time for escape had passed.

It was his time to die.

At the back of his mind, the idea that his mum would never know this pain he endured eased him. The three years he'd spent crying and wishing he was different had just delayed the suffering process.

The beast had been waiting for him.

It was him. It was the same man. Shaun had seen the eyes. Just like in his dreams. Those cold eyes had shone from the darkness. His strong hands had held him until any morsel of help had been squeezed from his fragile mind.

He wished the end would come soon.

The beast had disappeared into the darkness and left him alone. Somehow, being alone with his thoughts was worse. At least when somebody was near, he wasn't alone.

Shaun heard screams somewhere close by, and a woman shouting, but the tape across his mouth muffled his efforts to join in the cries.

Maybe he wasn't alone in death.

If there was one, maybe there were more. Maybe the beast would offer him a chance of living again, just like before.

Maybe not.

More shouting rang through the trees and fell silently away. No reply came.

No help would come.

"Do you know who I am?" said the beast quietly from behind him in the darkness.

Shaun startled and shook his head. Where did he come from? How is he so quiet?

"But you recognise me?"

Shaun squeezed his eyes shut tight and shook his head.

"I don't want to know," he mumbled through the tape.

"Do you remember, Shaun?" said the beast. "Do you remember that night?"

Shaun was breathing hard through his nose. He nodded softly, reluctantly.

"So you know who I am then?"

Shaun was silent.

"Do you know why I killed that man that night, Shaun?"

The beast was talking softly, not menacingly and not kindly, just softly.

Shaun nodded.

"You heard his story, didn't you?"

Shaun nodded again.

"Who do you fear the most, Shaun?" asked the beast. "Yourself, with your afflictions, or me, with my own afflictions?"

Shaun shrugged his shoulders.

The beast stood from behind him and began to pace around Shaun. He disappeared into the darkness in front and emerged beside him, then behind him.

"Why do you think I let you go, Shaun?"

Shaun looked behind him, but the beast had moved, vanished into the trees.

He shrugged.

"You were supposed to be my last."

Tears flowed from Shaun's eyes. He wished the beast would just finish him. He wished he'd stop the games. The beast spoke like they were old friends, or like they somehow shared a common affliction or weakness.

The beast lowered himself to the ground beside Shaun, crouched on one knee.

"Do you think this is easy for me, Shaun?"

Shaun stared wide-eyed.

"Do you think that taking a life is satisfying?"

Shaun didn't reply.

"Do you think I'm evil?"

Shaun looked away.

The beast seemed somehow disappointed in his response. It was almost as if behind those cold eyes was a heart, or a genuine desire to be liked. He turned to face him again and understood.

"People think you're evil, Shaun. Yet you try so hard not to be. Do the voices inside you battle over good and bad, Shaun?"

Shaun nodded.

"Is it like the goodness inside you tries to keep the evil away?"

Shaun nodded. He was breathing hard and wanted the tape to be removed from his mouth so he could reply.

Somebody understood.

"Do you ever wonder if the good will win the battle?" said the beast. "Or does some part of you realise that no matter how hard you try, no matter what good you do, the evil inside you will strike when you're weak, and destroy everything you've worked for?

Shaun nodded softly, blinked once, and let the tears roll.

"Do you want to beat it?"

CHAPTER THIRTY-EIGHT

Melody knelt on the ground with the hot coals warming her back and the note in her hand. A shadow passed through the trees in front of her, behind the men. He was silent. He was toying with them, and now the end was near.

To her right was a large hole, more like a grave, only half as deep. But deep enough for a body or even four.

"Tell us what it says," said the detective, the one in charge.

His voice stirred Melody from a daze. So much had happened, and there was so much yet to come.

"We're all going to die," said Melody, softly and with a hint of acceptance.

The three men all reacted in their own way.

She looked up at the second detective, who emitted a high-pitched whine that turned into a sob and then full on crying, like how a child might cry. She felt for him. Harvey used to say that fear was stage one in the process.

The detective on her far left became angry. Harvey would be watching from the shadows, and he would call that stage two.

She couldn't look at Reg. But she heard him breathing loudly, controlling his thoughts. Reg wasn't a tough guy, but he'd seen enough of Harvey to know that this was real. Reg was at stage three, acceptance.

"How?" spat the man on the far left. "How is he going to kill us? He can't boil us all."

Melody pulled at the chain around her neck and noted the length.

It was perfect.

She looked around the scene and saw the last tree, empty of prisoners, and she thought of Shaun. Maybe that was where he was supposed to have been standing. Why wasn't he there?

Melody glanced into the angry water that simmered in the bathtub. It was dark, but she could see the water was clear, not bloody. Shaun hadn't been boiled before they'd arrived.

The van.

"Are you going to talk to us?" said the man on the left. "We deserve to know."

Melody snapped back to the game.

"I have to choose one person," she said.

"Choose?" said the man. "What do you mean, choose?"

"One of us will be dropped into the tub, and I have to choose who."

"What if you don't choose?"

"Then it's me that boils," said Melody bluntly.

"And the rest of us?"

Melody took a deep breath and sank lower onto her knees.

"I have to kill two of you," said Melody. "The third person..."

She looked back at the fire and stared transfixed at the claw-foot tub.

She felt Reg's eyes boring into her. She turned to face him. Their eyes met. An understanding passed silently between them.

A single tear ran from Melody's eye.

"So you get to live?" asked the man on the left. "You get to go free after this?"

"Free?" snapped Melody. "Do you realise what I've been told to do? Do you think that by doing this, I'll somehow skip out of here and live happily ever after?"

"You know him," he replied. "You said his name. I heard you. It was you in the camper, you shot at us, and you're part of this, him as well." He gestured at Reg, who had hung his head low but flinched at the attack. "And where's the pervert? Is he in the van? Isn't that for him?" He nodded at the bathtub in the coals.

"You don't get it, do you?" spat Melody. "You don't understand that I have to choose two people to kill. I have to take their lives." Her voice broke. "'Two of you get to die quickly." She paused. "And one of you will die a slow and painful death." She stared at the tub and the grass beyond, which was blurred by heat. "You're making it harder for me not to let that one person be you."

"*I'm* making it harder for *you?*" said the man. "Am I supposed to-"

"Shut up," shouted George. "Just shut the hell up." He fought to crane his neck, but couldn't turn his head far enough to see his boss. "It was *you* who wanted to come here, it was you that wanted the glory, and it was you who said not to call for backup. So just shut the hell up. We're in this together. If anyone needs to boil, it's you."

"Reg?" said Melody. "What do you think?"

Reg kept his head down low. It took a few moments for him to respond, and when he did, he could manage only one mumbled sentence.

"I don't want to die, Melody."

CHAPTER THIRTY-NINE

"How are you going to do it?" asked the man on the left. His voice had dropped to a monotone tenor. The fight inside him seemed to have vanished.

Melody noted the change in his attitude and dismissed the man's temper as nerves, fear and the unknown. She'd taken various courses when she worked on the force. Hostage situations and post-terrorist attacks were prone to elicit various forms of emotions from people. Dealing with them required a certain amount of emotional intelligence. What they hadn't taught her was that when her own life was in danger, she'd have to deal with her own fears, thoughts and demons too, as well as those of others.

"My bare hands, I guess," she replied.

George broke the silence that followed.

"You think you can do that?" he asked.

Melody set the note on the ground.

"It wouldn't be the first time," she said, quietly. "And he *knows* it. He's testing me."

"Testing you?" said George. "Don't you think it's a test for all of us? I mean, after all, we're all chained up here. Maybe he's watching us, analysing us."

Melody shook her head. "No," she said, and pushed herself up to her feet. "He's testing me. He's pushing me."

"You two are close?" asked the man on the left. "You know his name."

"Yeah, we're close. We *were* close, once upon a time."

"So get through to him. Talk to him." He was almost pleading. "Can't you do something?"

The chain around Melody's neck suddenly moved. It was being pulled up.

"I'm running out of time."

"So kill me," said the man. He stopped as soon as he'd said it, and realised the gravity of his words.

"It's not as easy as that."

The chain crept another link over the thick bough.

"What did it say?" asked Reg. "The note. Read it to us."

Melody fumbled with the paper. Her hands shook, and she could barely make out the words with just the light from the coals.

"It's just what I said," said Melody. "Kill two and one will boil. Then below, it says, or I'll be the first to go."

"Holy crap," said Reg. He was beginning to panic. "Melody, I trust you. Do what you need to do." He gave her a long hard look. "I don't think any of us are getting out of here."

"But how do I decide?" asked Melody. "Who am I to say who deserves to die slowly?"

Another link crept over the bough.

Melody held it tightly in her hand and stepped back to gauge the length of her leash.

"I think it reaches all of you, but the longer I wait, the harder it'll be."

Another link.

Melody glanced at the bathtub.

"I choose me," she said. "I can't decide."

"Melody, no," said Reg. "We don't even know how he's going to kill you, or what he's going to do with us when he's done."

"He's right," said the man on the left. "If you can't decide, and he puts you in the water, we might all face the same fate. Who knows?"

"Melody," said Reg, "surely it's better to finish two of us on our terms? Not his."

"How about drawing straws?" said George. "We each pick some grass, and the shortest one-"

"Dies horribly?" finished Melody. "No way. That's not on our own terms."

Another link.

"Oh my God. I can't do this."

"Just get on with it, you fucking bitch," shouted the man on the left.

Melody was taken back by the attack and began to respond, but he continued with his insult.

"You know you want to save your friend, so there's one of the two. Now all you need to do is choose between George and me. Well, I'm making it easy for you. Give George the easy way out. I'll do it. I'll be the one. I'll take the short straw. I deserve it, he doesn't. This was my idea. I talked him into it. So just get on with it and stop pitying yourself."

He turned away from her, panting slightly from the emotional outburst, to let his own words sink in.

"I'll be the one," he repeated quietly. "I won't hear another word on it."

CHAPTER FORTY

Harris let his head drop.

He wished there was some way he could end it all himself. Maybe he could strangle himself with the chain? But he could barely move, and as much as the chain dug into his throat and caused him to gag, that would be the extent of it.

He began to twist and wrench his body away out of frustration. No control. Why should someone else be the one who dictates how he dies?

And the girl? The bitch was making it sound like she had a choice, making it sound like it was some kind of hardship for her. What would happen if she did kill two of them and save one for the tub?

She was in on it.

The more he thought about it, the more it made sense. She was sitting on the ground with the note looking sorry for herself. How did they even know what was written on the paper? She could have said anything.

Another link rolled over the bough, and her leash grew smaller still. Pretty soon, she wouldn't be able to reach them, and who knew what that meant.

"Just hurry the fuck up, will you?" he shouted. "You're making it harder for all of us. If we're going to die, then just bloody do it."

He wished he could see her face, but a part of him was grateful for not being able to see George. He doubted he'd be able to look him in the eye. He couldn't bear the look of hate, of blame.

It's all your fault.

"You want to be the one?" she asked. "Are you sure about that?"

Her voice was authoritative. She was a leader. Her tone was flat, but she was in control, and she knew it.

Another link.

Then a thud.

"What was that?" he asked her. "What just happened?"

"I know how I'm supposed to do it," the girl replied.

"Well, are you going to tell us?"

Instead of replying, she stood. He heard the chains rattling and her shuffling feet, bound at the ankles.

She approached him and stopped directly in front of him.

The chain was nearly at its full length.

Harris admired her. She was strong, very pretty, and with her shirt torn open, he could see how fit she was.

She held up a knife.

"You wanted to see?" she said. "This is how it ends."

A knife. There it was. She could end it all right now.

"Come closer," he whispered. His eyes darted back to the others and then returned to hers.

She stepped forward and leaned in so he could whisper in her ear.

"You're a pretty one," he said, his eyes fixed on her chest. In the dark, the white of her bra seemed to glow. "How about you give me one last request and show me what you have in there?"

The girl's face tightened. She stepped back half a step.

"Or maybe even a kiss," he said.

A look of disgust.

"Or maybe more. Come on, it'll be our last time. You have such pretty lips."

Her arm swung up and over her shoulder.

Harris instinctively flinched, shut his eyes, and waited for the pain. Nothing but the thud of the blade digging into the tree.

"There's nothing more I'd like," she whispered, "than to sink this blade into your head."

Another link reminded them of time.

"So do it," he snapped. "Just bloody end it."

"An easy death for you means a harder death for someone else, and right now, if anyone deserves a slow and painful death, it's you."

She began to step backwards, holding the chain away from her feet with one hand and the knife in the other. That was it. That had been his chance, his only chance at antagonising her into ending it all for him.

Now he would surely boil.

CHAPTER FORTY-ONE

The chain seemed to be shortening faster as if Harvey was growing more impatient as time went by.

Melody needed to make a choice.

For the briefest of moments, the thought of suicide crossed her mind. But she knew that all men would suffer for her cowardice. She couldn't let Reg suffer. She somehow felt responsible for him, for this.

He'd be at home with Jess if it weren't for her.

Melody doubted he would ever see Jess again. But if he was going to die, he was right, they should all die on their own terms.

She also considered running from man to man, a quick slice of the jugular, exactly how Harvey had shown her, and they would die quickly.

But Melody knew that he'd tighten the chain before she reached the last man. He deserved to boil anyway. She knew he was playing her, trying to provoke her into using the knife. But she owed it to Reg and George. She owed them a clean, quick death.

But who to do first?

She stopped between Reg and George, glanced up at them, but turned away.

Could she really do this?

"Me," said Reg. "Start with me."

It was as if he'd read her mind, as she battled to make the first move.

George's face began to screw up, and he sobbed loudly. Shame, pride and dignity had long since vanished. All that remained was a condemned man. He'd been reduced to a snivelling wreck.

Melody pulled her chain and took the few steps toward Reg, whose face was downcast with his eyes closed as if waiting for her to just do what had to be done.

Another link.

Reg was at arm's length now. She could reach his neck. But she wished she could hug him, tell him she'd see him on the other side, thank him for being a friend, and for all the times they'd had together.

She thought of his smiling face. He'd always been happy, always been the one to make jokes, no matter how inappropriate.

He opened his eyes, looked up at her and nodded.

Another link.

She was running out of time.

"Do it," he croaked.

She wanted to reach out and smooth his hair, touch his face, anything. Just feel. Just let him know how she felt. To ease him.

To ease her.

Another link.

She reached out with the knife and set it on his neck. All she needed to do was push and slice. The knife handle was slippery in her sweaty hands and they trembled in the night.

"Do it, Melody," he said with urgency.

Another link.

The point of the blade pressed into his skin, and he lifted his head. He was ready.

"I love you, Reg."

Tears rolled freely from his eyes and he began to pant.

"Just get out of here, Melody," he said. "Do it, save yourself, and get out of here."

"I don't think that's-"

"Just let me have that thought, Melody," he said softly between sharp, heavy breaths. "Just let me think you're going to be okay."

Melody closed her eyes. She felt his neck through the knife. She could see it in her mind's eye.

She pushed harder.

Another link rolled over the bough.

She pushed harder, but her trembling hand fought to hold the knife.

"Do it, Melody," shouted Reg.

She pushed. But she couldn't grip the handle, as if her subconscious was holding her back.

"Melody, do it," said Reg. "Just push."

"I can't," she said, her voice high and broken.

Another link.

"Now, Melody."

"I can't."

"Reg gritted his teeth and forced his neck forward as far as the chains would allow, but the knife slipped through Melody's hand.

It fell to the ground.

He stared at her in disbelief. His jaw hung open as if realising for the first time that it would be his friend who suffered the most. It would be her that they would all watch die horrifically.

Another link rolled over the bough, then another, and another. Faster and faster, the slack chain began to tighten, and then pull on her neck. Melody stumbled backwards, fell to the ground, and gasped for air.

The chain grew tighter still. It began to choke her and pull her towards the fire and the evil bathtub.

Melody fought back, trying to grip the ground with her feet. But the chain was relentless. It seemed to drag her with ease. She felt the heat on her head and tried to roll away. But each time she tried, the chain pulled tighter until eventually, and at the base of its arc, it began to lift her into the air.

The pulling was smooth at first, but as more weight hung from the biting links of steel, the pulling turned to harsh jerks.

Her head was soon above the red-hot coals. The skin on her neck prickled and began to burn. She felt it tighten and smelled her hair as it began to give in to the heat.

Melody was choking. She allowed her body to fall limp but clung desperately to the chain that was cutting into her throat. Air was barely getting through, but she sucked as hard as she could.

She dizzied.

Another pull of the chain and Melody lifted higher, so high she could see into the bathtub now, and the darkness beyond.

The chain grew tighter still. She rose higher.

Brightly coloured dots began to dance across her vision in long kaleidoscopic swirls as if her very soul was preparing to leave.

The long grass ahead appeared inviting somehow, soft, lush, and natural. But there was more. There was movement amongst the grass. Slowly but surely, a shadow grew larger.

The chain pulled tighter.

Shouting, distant and muffled.

A wave of black passed before her eyes.

Voices.

No air now.

Footsteps nearby.

It was close. She felt the warmth of death's embrace.

A man.

Darkness.

CHAPTER FORTY-TWO

Harvey scooped Melody up in his arms and took the weight off the chain. He stood on the hot coals, holding her above the copper bathtub.

"I'm here," he shouted. "I'm here."

He stared into the darkness of the trees, past the open-mouthed men who stood wide-eyed. His vision scanned the shadows for movement.

"It's me you want. Let her down," he called out. "Come and get me."

Harvey loosened the chain from Melody's throat with one hand while supporting her head.

"Let her down," he screamed again.

Suddenly, the chain began to loosen. Harvey stepped away from the hot coals that had begun to melt the soles of his boots and lowered Melody down to the ground.

She lay unconscious, and thin rasps of breath were the only indication she was alive, but barely.

Harvey found the padlock behind Melody's neck.

"Keys."

He left no room for debate.

"If you want *me*, throw me the keys, or you get no-one at all."

A gunshot rang out, and Harvey felt a punch to his shoulder, sharp and hot. He stumbled back to the ground, but scrambled back to Melody, clutching his wounded shoulder.

"*Keys.*"

A pair of keys on a ring landed in the grass beside him.

Harvey fumbled with the padlock, desperate to release the chain from Melody's neck. The keys slipped in his hands, but then the lock snapped open with a click. He frantically pulled it away, tossed it behind him into the fire, then loosened the chain and freed her throat.

Melody was unconscious still, but a faint pulse gave a small glimmer of hope.

Another gunshot, another punch, another run of hot, sticky blood. This time, it was his other shoulder.

Harvey sat back away from Melody and slowly stood like a condemned man with his arms outstretched as much as his new wounds would allow.

"You have me," he called out. "Now show your face and finish me like a real man."

Harvey glanced across at Reg, who seemed to smile at his presence. Harvey gave him a little nod.

"Come on," he shouted, working himself up, preparing himself for death. "I'm ready. Come and get me."

He stood tall, panting from pain, adrenaline and anger. A rage he'd fought so hard to control over the years, a force so powerful it had taken years of training to suppress, now coursed through him. It was as if, in death, it would be the rage that eventually took him down.

"Come on," he shouted again. "Where are you?"

"Put the chain around your neck," said the voice from the trees.

Harvey placed the voice directly in front of him. A London accent, almost familiar, but not quite.

"You can't get me without chains?" shouted Harvey. "After all you've done? You need chains to take me down?"

"I don't need chains, Stone," said the man. "I want the chains."

A cruel laugh rang out, cold and bitter. "I want to see you suffer, Stone. That's all I want. I want to see you suffer, and then I want to watch you die slowly." He paused and dropped the tone of his voice. "I want to put an end to Harvey Stone, once and for all."

"So show yourself," said Harvey. "Let's get this moving."

Melody began to cough and rolled onto her side.

"The chain, Stone," said the voice.

Harvey pulled the chain towards him and wrapped the slack end around his neck.

"There," he called, "it's done. Now show yourself."

The chain was suddenly pulled hard and fast, and snapped tight against Harvey's neck. He gasped for breath. He'd left room to breathe, but the chain had tightened and now closed off much of his airway. He gripped the links that dug into his throat, fighting for air.

Then slowly but surely, the shape of a man stepped from the shadows. He stopped on the edge of darkness like death himself.

"You should have died a long time ago, Stone."

Harvey didn't reply.

"So much death. Think of all the pain and suffering you've caused."

Harvey didn't reply.

"How many, do you think?" asked the shadow. "Fifty? A hundred? More?"

Harvey didn't reply.

"Tell us about them, Stone."

"About what exactly?" replied Harvey.

"Which one was your favourite?"

Harvey didn't reply.

"Stuck for words, eh?" said the man.

"My favourite?" said Harvey, through gritted teeth. He stood on tiptoes, striving to keep his airway open. "It was a scene just like this."

"Do go on," said the man in the trees.

"But it was *you* with a noose around your neck, and not me."

"You must be mistaken," came the reply. "I don't recall ever being in such a position."

"You've had a noose around your neck ever since I saved your sorry ass."

The shadow didn't reply.

He stepped from the trees into the light of the fire.

"Jackson?" said Reg in surprise. "But, you-"

"Quiet, Tenant," said Jackson, without turning. "If you hadn't worked it out already, you're in the wrong job."

He stepped up to Harvey.

"But *you* worked it out just fine, didn't you?" he said.

"It wasn't hard," said Harvey.

"So tell me. Entertain us all with your insight."

"You had the access."

"I did," agreed Jackson.

"You had the means."

Jackson nodded.

"And, out of everyone out there, you wanted me dead more than anybody."

"Very good," said Jackson. "And for what reason?"

Harvey's feet were tiring. He was struggling to keep the chain loose enough to breathe.

"I'm a risk to you," Harvey began. "I saw you kill. If anyone can bring you down, it's me."

"You would have made a good operative, Stone," said Jackson. "You think like a villain."

Harvey didn't reply.

"You are a villain, Stone."

"So it was you all along?" said Reg. "It was you that killed-"

"Like I said, Tenant, if you can't keep up with the conversation, best you keep quiet, eh?"

"You bastard, sir," spat Reg.

Jackson's eyes didn't leave Harvey's face.

"You win some, you lose some, right Stone?" said Jackson. "Isn't that what you told somebody a long time ago?"

"Moments before you tortured him?" said Harvey. "Yeah, it was something like that."

"I'd love to stay and chat, but you know I have a busy morning ahead. It'll be light soon. Besides, we don't want your bath to get cold, do we?"

"Jackson?" rasped Harvey.

Jackson turned back to face Harvey.

"Any last words, Stone?"

"Come closer."

Harvey fought for breath, and stumbled onto the coals, causing a flash of angry sparks to jump from the fire.

Jackson waited for Harvey to stop swinging and steady himself, and then stepped forward.

"Any regrets, Stone?" he asked.

Harvey smiled.

"How did you know where we'd be?" asked Harvey.

"Oh, come on, Stone," he replied. "I've been listening to Tenant's calls now for more than a year." He laughed to himself. "You should hear some of the things your girlfriend has to say about you, Harvey. They're like two old women."

"That was you in Athens too, wasn't it?" asked Harvey. "It was you behind it all."

"You've been a marked man for years, Stone. Don't be offended."

Harvey was struggling with the intense heat. His neck was swelling in the grip of the steel chain.

"I'm not offended," said Harvey. "But I do like to have a good reason when I kill a man. It pleases my moral compass, Jackson."

"What do you mean?" said Jackson, his head cocked and intrigued

"I have to give it to you, Jackson," said Harvey, "this is a fantastic set up you have here, even by my standards."

"What are you talking about, Stone?"

"But for all your planning and eavesdropping, you forgot one important point."

Harvey smiled.

"I told you before that your last word will always be the one that kills you."

Harvey gave a short sharp whistle.

Jackson's eyes widened with fear.

"Boon?"

A sudden look of doubt and fear wiped the smug look from his face, just before Boon leapt from his full speed run, launched himself up and sunk his teeth into Jackson's neck.

CHAPTER FORTY-THREE

Melody woke with the rhythmic beat of her heart loud in her ears, and the stinging of burnt and scratched skin to remind her she was alive. She opened her eyes from the darkness that had welcomed her with its inviting warmth to see the black sky and shadows of the trees overhead.

Men were talking nearby. They weren't shouting. The conversation wasn't heated, but hatred ran thick in the tones of their voices.

A familiar friend rested his head on Melody's chest. His ears pricked up when Melody began to raise her head, and his tail thumped the ground when she smiled at him.

Was it a dream?

She looked around her.

Reg was still chained to the tree. But he smiled at her in the dim light with genuine relief.

Her vision blurred with every movement of her head, but the two other men were still there. George and his boss, the angry man. She tried to wipe her hair from her eyes, but her hands had been bound once more behind her back.

Melody tried hard to remember what had happened. She

was being pulled. Her neck still stung. She'd fought for breath, and she'd felt death beside her.

But now? Was this real?

"It's time, Jackson."

It was Harvey's voice.

"Harvey?" said Melody. "It's time to stop this." She winced at the pain in her temple when she spoke.

Harvey didn't reply.

"Let me down, Stone."

That's Jackson, she thought

"Jackson," said Melody. Though her eyes failed to focus, she stared blindly in the direction of his voice. "Jackson, help us."

"Please, Stone," said Jackson. "You don't understand. Melody, tell him. Tell him to stop."

Slowly the scene began to focus, and Melody rolled to her side to take it all in.

Jackson now hung above the old copper bathtub. A great loop of the chain had been fastened around his chest and under his arms. His head fell forward and his bound feet tried in vain to avoid the heat and steam that grew angrily from below.

"I understand, Jackson," said Harvey. "If *anybody* understands, it's *me*."

Harvey stepped into view.

"Harvey?" said Melody. "Is that you? It's time to stop now. No more. Please."

Harvey bent and smoothed the hair on her forehead then planted a light kiss on her smooth skin.

"*This* is my last," said Harvey. He then smiled weakly and stood.

Melody watched with fear and astonishment as the man she loved began to circle Jackson like a wolf might circle a deer.

"Tell me about the murders, Jackson," said Harvey. "Tell *me* how it made *you* feel."

Jackson didn't reply.

"I don't have time to play games, Jackson. How did it feel to burn the limbs off someone?"

No reply. Instead, Jackson just struggled against the chain.

"How will your wife feel when she finds out who the killer was?"

"No," said Jackson. "*She* can never know."

"Detective Chief Inspector Harris," said Harvey, "would you agree that you've found the man you're looking for?"

There was a short silence, and then a weak voice from the far side of the small C-shaped clearing spoke. "That's fair to say," he said. "But I don't think it matters anymore, does it?"

"Oh it matters, Harris," said Harvey. "Jackson, tell Harris about how you glued Noah Finn to the bathtub."

"No," said Jackson. His voice suddenly broke. "I'll deny it all."

"You probably won't get a chance, Jackson. But if there's one thing I've learned in life, it's that people always feel better after a confession."

Harvey began to pace again in a wide circle. He stopped with his back to the fire and looked out over what was once the grounds where he and his sister had played when they were young.

"I've encouraged many confessions, Jackson. It's what I do best. I enjoy retribution. I can't help it. I'm not sick or twisted, and I'm certainly not the psychopath you say I am."

He turned again to face Jackson.

"I just enjoy seeing people get what they deserve."

He nodded into the darkness among the trees, and the chain links slowly began to pay out. Jackson began to lower.

"No, stop. Harvey, *no*."

"Don't fight it, Jackson. All you have to do is tell us."

"Harvey stop, you sick bastard."

Jackson's toes dipped briefly into the scalding hot water. He fought to keep his tired legs bent and away from the heat.

"Are you ready to talk, Jackson?"

Harvey's face was emotionless.

Jackson's face was a picture of perfect misery.

He began to sob.

"Tears won't help you, Jackson," said Harvey. "You've been a very bad man. The only thing that might help you now is a confession."

"I can't. It was a blur," sobbed Jackson. "I wasn't thinking straight."

"What was a blur? Was it cutting Noah Finn's nuts off and stuffing them in his mouth? Or was it slicing his stomach open and letting his guts fall into his lap in front of his waking eyes?"

Harvey paced once more.

"Which was it? Perhaps it was the pinning somebody down with stakes through their wrists and ankles, and letting them drown in their own blood? Maybe *that* was the blur? What do you think?"

Harvey nodded into the trees again, and slowly, a few more links of chain rolled across the thick branch above.

Jackson's feet sank into the scalding water.

He began to holler and growl, deep, carnal and angry. More of the chain was released and Jackson's feet hit the sides of the red-hot copper tub. His ankles began to blister as they succumbed to the vicious hiss and sting of the boiling water. The growl became a shrill scream.

"Ready to tell us about it, Jackson?" said Harvey. "The longer you take, the harder it'll be. But confess, and I'll make it as quick as possible."

"No Harvey," said Melody. "Stop. He's had enough. Let the law deal with him."

She tried to stand, but could only manage to get to her knees.

"You're innocent, Harvey. Stop and all this will be over."

Harvey offered her a smile.

"Last chance, Jackson," he said.

Jackson continued to sob and mumble apologies aimed at nobody.

"I'm sorry. I'm so sorry. It was the only way."

"Then it's over," said Harvey. "Goodbye, Jackson."

Harvey turned to the trees.

"Shaun?" he called.

Shaun Tyson appeared at the edge of the darkness.

"Are you ready for your new beginning?" asked Harvey.

Shaun nodded.

"Are you ready to leave the weak and perverted mind of the old Shaun Tyson behind?"

Shaun nodded once more.

"Say it, Shaun," said Harvey. "Tell me you're a new man. Show me how strong you are."

"I'm strong," said Shaun, a little weaker than he'd hoped.

"Louder, Shaun."

"I'm strong."

"Louder. I want you to feel it when you say it."

"I'm strong," yelled Shaun. "I'm strong."

"Are you weak?" asked Harvey.

"No," said Shaun.

"I can't hear you, Shaun."

"No," shouted Shaun.

"Are you perverted?"

"*No.*" Shaun's face had reddened from the shouting and his windpipe stuck from his neck.

"Are you a new man, Shaun?"

"Yes."

"Then show me," said Harvey.

Without hesitation, Shaun cast the end of the chain away. It ran freely over the thick branch above, and Jackson landed with a splash into the searing water. His scream seemed to pierce the very darkness around them. His thrashes sent the boiling water onto the hot coals, which sent up clouds of steam that partially hid the horrific death.

The chain fell down on top of Jackson. He thrashed from left to right, unable to stop the pain from biting every nerve in his body. He flung his bound hands out over the edge to pull himself out, but the scorching copper seared his skin, melting it, so he simply slid back inside from the inescapable agony.

His visceral screams were lost to the trees and the dark night.

Melody turned away and held Boon with her bound hands, who grew excited at the commotion.

"Harvey, get him out," she said. "Enough is enough."

Harvey didn't reply.

He stepped over to Melody, and once more, bent down beside her.

"What have you done, Harvey?" she whispered, in disbelief at what she'd seen.

"I finished it," replied Harvey. "Once and for all."

"But you were innocent," she said. "You could have walked."

The thrashing and splashing stopped with abrupt silence. There was just the sound of hissing coals and the searing hot water settling.

"I'm still innocent, Melody. Only not in your eyes. I was always guilty in your eyes, wasn't I?"

"No, Harvey. You changed, you-"

"I've always been me, Melody." He spoke softly. The time for violence and rage had passed, perhaps for good.

"I'm sorry," said Melody. "I'm sorry I doubted you. I'm-"

"Don't apologise, Melody. We had a good time, didn't we?"

He kissed her forehead and smoothed her hair for the last time.

"No, Harvey, don't go. It doesn't have to end like this," she whispered, pleading.

Harvey stood and stepped away.

"Harvey, stop," she shouted.

Harvey didn't reply.

"Harvey, come back."

Harvey didn't reply.

"Harvey, *stop*," Melody shouted, then took a breath. "It doesn't have to end this way," she said softly to the empty night.

She paused.

"Harvey."

Harvey didn't reply.

FINDING a hostel so late at night had been difficult. Shaun had to beg to be let inside, and then had paid double for the little room, which wasn't much to look at, but to Shaun, it was everything he'd dreamed of. Outside his little window, the rain fell hard, bouncing off the surface of the road and the parked cars. Headlights illuminated each drop as if they sparkled.

Shaun thought of his mum.

She'd be sat in her kitchen at the little table they'd eaten so many breakfasts and dinners at before. She'd probably be smoking and cradling a cup of tea in her hands as she often did.

He wondered if she'd be crying. It was a question he'd asked himself when he'd been tied up in the back of the van, and when Harvey Stone had caught him the forest. But this time, his mind was clear. His thoughts ran wild, with the freedom and innocence of a child.

She'd be okay. She'd be happy for him. He made a mental note to call her, just to hear her voice.

A group of people walked by his window, and he moved back away from the glass, but then stopped. He was allowed to look out of the window.

He was free now. Free to as he pleased. Free to live his life.

Thanks to Harvey Stone.

Of all the men in all the world that might offer Shaun a second chance, Harvey Stone had been at the bottom of the list.

But the man had done something to Shaun. He'd awakened something inside him, something that he'd never had before, but had seen in other men.

A confidence.

Shaun emptied his rucksack onto his bed and separated his belongings. He folded his clothes neatly, and placed his wallet, passport and money carefully together. Then, while his freedom ran amok inside his newborn mind, he changed into his smart set of clothes. He ran some water into his hands and smoothed his hair then pulled his coat on. He pocketed his multi-tool, wallet and loose items. Then Shaun walked out into the hallway, locking the door to his room behind him.

The rain was hammering down, but he stepped onto the pavement of Amsterdam anyway, and let the water splash onto his face.

He smiled at how fresh it felt, the rain, the cold air, and freedom.

A man and a woman stood beneath the canopy of a closed restaurant a few doors away. They argued in another language, French maybe or Italian; Shaun didn't know.

He ignored them and focused on his own joy.

How powerful he'd felt when he'd cast the chain away and let that man fall to his death. How in control he felt of his own destiny.

A loud slap caught Shaun's attention. He turned to see the man recoil from the blow the woman had delivered, in time to see him retaliate with a blow of his own.

Shaun stepped back into the doorway and out of sight.

The woman gave a cry, and even the loud rain couldn't hide the dull thuds of punches and kicks. Shaun had heard them on many occasions in prison. It was a noise he'd never forget. It wasn't like the sound of a punch in a movie; the sound of a real punch was unlike any other noise.

"Are you strong?" asked Harvey, a voice inside Shaun's head.

Shaun closed his eyes.

"Are you strong?" he asked again.

"Yes," Shaun whispered.

"Louder, Shaun," said Harvey. "Are you strong?"

"Yes."

"Are you in control?"

"Yes."

Shaun stepped from the doorway.

"Are you a new man?"

"Yes."

"Louder."

"*Yes*," shouted Shaun.

He began to walk towards the couple. The woman was on the wet ground, trying to scramble away from the man. Her dress had pulled up from the struggle, and she was screaming.

"Are you a new man?"

"Yes," shouted Shaun.

The man bent over with his hand on the woman's throat.

"Are you strong?"

"Yes."

A silence seemed to fill Shaun's mind. The man landed a slap across the girls face, but the scene played out in slow motion.

"Are you a new man?" asked Harvey's voice.

"Yes," whispered Shaun. "But..."

Another slap sent the woman's face to one side. Her pleading eyes landed on Shaun's.

"But what, Shaun?"

"Am I ready?" he whispered.

Harvey didn't reply.

The End

STONE RAID

CHAPTER ONE

"We're in position, Fingers," said Dynamite into his hands-free comms. He pulled his scarf back up to cover his face and checked the darkness around them. "Give us a countdown."

"Copy that," replied Fingers, tapping away on the keyboard. "Perimeter security is going down in three, two-"

"Hold on, hold on," said Dynamite. "Give us a bit longer than three bleeding seconds, will you? How long is our window?"

"When I kill the security system, you'll have twelve-seconds to get inside and close the window before the backup power kicks in, and the systems boot up."

"What happens if we don't have the window closed within twelve-seconds, Fingers?" asked Lola. She stood beside dynamite beneath a large window.

"Well," replied Fingers, "for a start, it's going to get awfully loud, and I imagine the place will be lit up like a Christmas tree. Then, of course, the automatic locks will kick in, steel intruder barriers will drop down over the doors and windows, and that lovely manicured lawn that you two just crawled across will likely be a car park for the dozens of police that will no doubt arrive in a matter of seconds. Not to mention, their helicopter will need somewhere to land. You two, of course, will be none the wiser as you'll both be shut inside waiting to be caught like a right old pair of donuts."

"You paint a pretty picture, Fingers," said Dynamite.

"It's a pretty diamond, Dynamite," replied Fingers. "From what *I* hear anyway."

"You heard right."

"Right, let's get our act together, boys," said Lola. "Fingers, give us ten seconds."

"Copy that."

His fingers danced across the keyboard, entering a string of code into the command line interface of the security hub, and then stopped, poised above the enter button.

"You ready?" he asked.

Dynamite lifted the jimmy bar to the window lock and worked the pointed end into the small gap between the window and the frame.

He took a breath and looked at his partner, who nodded in silent reply.

"Go," said Dynamite.

Fingers began his count.

"Ten."

"Lola, get ready to climb up," said Dynamite.

"Seven."

Lola readied her boot on the smooth surface of the wall and reached up to the window, ready to grab onto the frame as soon as it opened.

"Three."

"Our lives will be very different in about fifteen minutes' time," said Dynamite.

"One."

Dynamite heaved back. Wood splintered loudly in the quiet

night as he forced the window open. Lola was up on the ledge before it had opened fully, then she launched herself inside. She immediately turned and helped Dynamite inside, who fell to the floor then bounced back up to force the window back into place.

The tiny copper connections touched.

"Perimeter security is back online," said Fingers. "It's all on you guys now. You've got approximately one hundred and eighty seconds until the infrared fires up, which means that you have one hundred and sixty seconds before I kill the security again."

Lola was already running her hands along the glass cabinet in the centre of the room. Even in the darkness, the golf ball-sized diamond reflected tiny fragments of light.

"Hello, sweetheart," she spoke softly.

Dynamite stepped over to her. "Don't just look at it, Lola," he said. "One-thirty and counting."

Lola fumbled beneath the cabinet, pulling at wires. She flicked on her head torch.

"One-twenty."

Lola closed her eyes and began pulling a tiny wire from its connector.

"Just pull it out, Lola," said Dynamite.

"Hold on," she replied. She reached further into the cabinet. "Aha." Her tongue slithered out between her lips in concentration.

"Don't give me that bleeding *aha* business, Lola," said Dynamite. "One hundred seconds."

"Dynamite, just keep cool."

"Yeah, we'll both be bleeding keeping cool in an eight-by-five cell for about twenty years."

Lola tugged at something and brought out a little black box.

"What's that?" asked Dynamite.

"It's a keep alive," said Lola. "It's attached to the alarm system and the backup power. It sends a tiny voltage to the sensors, so even if the power to the security system goes down, the alarm won't. My guess is that it's attached to an independent network that goes directly to the police."

"Your guess?" said Dynamite. "We don't have time for a guess. He checked his watch. "We have ninety seconds to get the diamond and get out. It was your bleeding job to do a recce."

"Eighty-seven," corrected fingers.

"If I pull this wire, there'll be police all over this place in a matter of minutes. And yes it was my job to do the recce. But you know what, Dynamite? When I came here on a tour, for some reason, the guide wouldn't let me look underneath the cabinet and refused to answer my questions about the alarm wiring."

"Fingers, are you scanning the police frequency?" asked Dynamite.

There was no answer.

"Fingers?" said Lola.

"What happens if we smash the glass?" asked Dynamite.

"Smash the glass? Dynamite, this is *not* a smash and grab. We are a pair of highly-skilled professionals. It's bad enough that you broke the window. Talk about leaving a calling card. No wonder they call you-"

"Okay, okay," said Dynamite, holding his hands up defensively. "So what do you want to do? Leave *without* it?"

Lola looked down at the diamond.

"It's awful pretty, isn't it?" she said.

"Second only to you, babes," said Dynamite.

Lola continued to stare at the diamond, mesmerised by the perfect sparkles.

"We have thirty-five seconds, Lola."

Lola looked up at Dynamite from where she crouched

beside the cabinet. "Get ready to run like you've never run before."

She pulled the wires. There was silence.

"Silent alarm?" asked Dynamite.

Lola lowered the panel beneath the cabinet then stood cradling the velvet cushion with the rock sat on top. Dynamite grabbed the diamond and stuffed it into his pocket.

"Fingers, come back."

No response.

Lola replaced the velvet cushion, and then returned the wires to their connections.

"Fifteen seconds," said Dynamite. "Fingers, we're ready. Shut it down."

No response.

"Bugger this," said Dynamite. He yanked the window open, which immediately sounded the shrill alarm that pierced their night like a banshee. Flashing red lights fixed above the doors and windows began to spin and sent the dark room into a frenzy of beams.

They both dove through the window together and landed in a pile on the gravel pathway that wound around the old building. It acted as a border to the immaculate lawns, which were now fully illuminated by giant spotlights on the rooftop that covered every inch of the grass around the house.

The steel intruder barriers slammed down into place behind them.

"Go," said Dynamite, half-dragging Lola along. "We need to move."

Lola ran alongside him towards the tree line at the far side of the lawn. Her heart thumped with adrenaline. They'd done it; they had the diamond. It had taken a few weeks of planning, and everyone said that it couldn't be done, but they'd finally got it.

Dynamite burst through the trees in front of her into the small clearing where they'd left Fingers in the back of the van.

"Fingers, start the engine," shouted Dynamite as he ran. "Fingers?"

Lola could just make out the shape of the van in the darkness. She saw Dynamite come to a sudden stop. Lola stopped beside him.

"What?" she asked.

Then, as if they'd just run into a football stadium, lights hit them from all around. Five sets of car headlights, all on full, all turned on together and pointed directly at where Lola and Dynamite stood.

"Shit," said Dynamite.

A man in a long, black leather jacket stepped out of the shadows and into the centre of the mock arena, his huge frame silhouetted by the dazzling car headlights. Without a second's hesitation, he pulled a handgun from his jacket, raised it and fired once into Dynamite's face.

Without stopping, he lowered the gun, remorseless, as Dynamite's body folded to the ground in an undignified heap.

Lola stood stiff, too scared to move or even to wipe Dynamite's spattered blood from her face and lips.

The man in the jacket turned to her and spoke with a cold, deep voice that seemed to rumble like thunder.

"Hello, sweetheart."

CHAPTER TWO

For Harvey Stone, being back in London was less than ideal. But the fact of the matter was that he was laying low, and laying low meant finding somewhere unfamiliar, somewhere he'd never been before, and keeping out of sight. He'd spent eighty-nine days staying inside his bedsit. On the occasions that he had to venture out, he tried to blend in. He'd enjoyed a few early morning runs before the sun rose. But he tried to limit them to once or twice a week.

It was a far cry from his preferred lifestyle. Although Harvey typically led a basic life, far from lavish, his main issue now was that he had nothing to occupy his mind. His home in France had taken much of his time. It was a small farmhouse and each day he'd set about completing the minor jobs that needed doing. He'd replaced the roof tiles, sanded and painted the wooden window frames and doors, and cleared the gutters ready for winter. But then his life had been turned upside down. He felt it was wise to stay away for a few months.

It was the thought of returning to his house, walking on the beach and riding his motorcycle along the winding lanes of the southern French coast that kept him going, and staying away for a few months was the sacrifice.

He was beginning to get stir crazy. It would be time to return home soon, just one more day. He could, of course, return any time he wished and deal with whatever came his way. But he'd set the three-month target, he'd made the plan, and breaking the plan for the sake of boredom and one more day didn't sit well with Harvey.

That's how mistakes happen.

Harvey sprinted the final stretch of forest and tore out of the trees into the small back streets of South London. Harvey was an East London man through and through. But laying low in East London was too dangerous. He was too well known by the wrong people. South London had enough migrants and cultural diversity for him to become just another person in the crowd.

He walked the short distance to his bedsit, a small room with an attached bathroom in a terraced house. It offered a view of the houses on the street behind and a dull, grey sky.

The entrance to the old Victorian house was up three stone steps and through a wide front door into a hallway. His room was directly in front of the stairs on the first-floor landing. When he'd agreed on the rates with the landlord, he'd had the choice of the basement room, the first floor or the second floor. Harvey had selected the first floor because the peephole gave him a direct view of the stairs and the length of the hallway. Plus, if the worst happened, he could always get out of the sash window and become quickly lost in the maze of gardens.

The room had a single bed and an old, tired-looking, wooden wardrobe. An ageing lamp with a yellowed, frilly shade stood on top of an even older bedside table. The room was slightly larger than a prison cell with just enough floor space for Harvey to do push-ups and sit-ups. An old TV sat on top of the wardrobe, but Harvey hadn't turned it on in the three months he'd been there.

In some ways, the time had been good for him to reassess his life, make decisions, and to reflect on his past. In other ways, it had been a prison sentence.

Harvey climbed the stairs to his landing quietly and respectfully of the other tenants. He hadn't even reached the top stair when he noticed the shiny new lock on his door. A few steps later, he saw his bag sitting on the floor outside.

There was no point in trying his key in the new lock. He picked up his bag and checked his belongings. A small secret pocket at the back held his few personal possessions. Nothing was missing.

A younger and less mature Harvey might have kicked in his landlord's door and said farewell. But the older and much more tired Harvey took the hint. The landlord had eyed Harvey with suspicion from the off. Harvey had paid in full for three months with fresh banknotes in a bank seal from a small stash of cash he kept for emergencies. The landlord had also asked questions that Harvey had preferred not to answer. Instead, he'd topped up the bundle with more banknotes; one hundred pounds per question, plus an extra two hundred to avoid providing a copy of his ID.

Harvey's total words spoken during the entire process of viewing the room had been only six, while returning the old man's feeble prompts at conversation with cold stares.

He swung his pack onto his shoulder and dropped his key on the floor by the door. It was useless anyway.

The landlord occupied the room beside the front door. As Harvey stepped off the stairs, he sensed rather than heard the man standing behind the door, peering through the peephole, dressed in the same old grey cardigan and slippers that he always wore.

Harvey opened the front door, stepped outside and breathed the fresh air. It was summertime, the air was cool but not cold, and Harvey felt good to be out of the house. The decision had been made for him, and although the following night would be uncertain, he was grateful.

Freedom could be measured in so many different ways, he thought. For some, freedom meant being released from a term under Her Majesty's pleasure. Or it might mean financial freedom. For Harvey, right there and then, stood on the doorstep of the old Victorian house he'd holed up in for nearly three months, freedom meant going home.

But the mantra that Julios had etched into Harvey's mind as a young man seemed to burn at the thought of breaking a plan so unnecessarily. One more night. He could do that. He could find somewhere to get his head down.

One more night. Then the long trip back to France.

CHAPTER THREE

"What do you mean you let her go?" asked Charlie Bond. "You're six foot four and had a dozen blokes with you."

Rupert stood from his desk. His chair scraped across the floor. "Don't talk to me like that, Charlie. I've told you before, I won't stand for it."

"What do you want me to say, Ru? Never mind, come sit down, and have a cup of tea?" He sighed with frustration. "Did you get it, or not?"

Rupert stepped across the floor of their shared office. His brogues sounded solid on the hardwood. He poured himself a whiskey from their crystal decanter and sank it back in one hit.

"You need to give me a little more credit, Charlie," he said, as the liquid fired through his throat.

"So you got it then?" asked Charlie. His voice was serious but a creeping smile betrayed his tone.

"You need to keep the boys low for a while, Charlie," said Rupert. "The old bill turned up within minutes of the bells."

"You said they would," replied Charlie. "Anything I need to be concerned about?"

"Glasgow George had to kill her fella."

"He had to?"

"Yeah," said Rupert. "We've got his body down at Doctor Feelmore's morgue."

"And what was the particular reason he felt it necessary to kill him?" said Charlie. "I mean, other than his passion for blood."

"I told him to. We needed to get her attention."

"Pour me one of those, will you?" asked Charlie.

Rupert poured another glass and refilled his own.

"So you got her attention, and then what?"

"The old bill turned up," said Rupert. "Just like I told you." He set the crystal-cut glass on Charlie's desk, which was the twin of Rupert's own.

"And did you all stop and *wait* for the old bill, Rupert?" said Charlie. "This is like getting blood from a stone."

"Well, if you want to be in the know-"

"I know, I know," said Charlie. "I should have been involved. But some of us had other things to attend to, didn't we? We can't all go gallivanting around in the countryside late at night."

Rupert smiled at his brother and sank his drink once more.

"We're rich," he said. His smile broadened into a grin showing his perfect teeth.

"I know we're rich, bro."

"No mate, you don't understand," said Rupert. "We're even richer."

"So you did get it. I wondered when you were going to drop the bombshell and put me out of my misery."

"You need to see it to believe it," said Rupert. "I've never seen anything like it. It's almost..." Rupert searched for the right word to describe the diamond.

"Almost what?"

The words found Rupert as another scotch burned its way to his stomach. "Otherworldly," he said finally.

"Otherworldly?" said Charlie. "Is it from another planet?"

"It's beautiful."

"You look like you just saw your first naked woman, Ru. Get a grip and don't get attached to it. We're selling it."

"Yeah, but you should see it, Charlie. And feel it."

"I'd love to see it and feel it, Ru. So where is it?"

"Somewhere safe."

"Somewhere safe?" said Charlie. "Where?"

"I had Smokey take care of it. He's trustworthy."

"Smokey the Jew?" said Charlie, leaning forward in his chair. "You've got to be having a laugh with me."

"He's sound, Charlie," said Rupert. "What would *you* have me do? Bring it back here?"

"Rupert, you could have given it to anyone. In fact, I told you to get it straight to Dirty Thanos down at the kebab shop. He owes us a favour or three. He could have kept it hidden in a slab of meat or something. What the bloody hell did you give it to Smokey for?"

"Because, Charlie," replied Rupert, as he made his way back to his desk with a freshly poured scotch. "Dirty Thanos is exactly as his name suggests, a dirty kebab shop owner. He only knows two things, how to make a kebab and how to butcher a carcass." Rupert took a sip of his drink. "Now, if we were getting rid of something, such as a body or something we never wanted to see again, I'd have taken it to either Dirty Thanos, so he could cut it up into tiny pieces and feed it to the Albanians, or Doctor Feelmore down at the funeral parlour, so he could incinerate it. But as it happens, Charlie, this is the one thing we don't want to have cut up into tiny bits and it's definitely not something I would suggest incinerating. It's a priceless diamond the size of bloody golf ball. So I gave it to Smokey the Jew to keep at his house, which I might add, due to his family's light-fingered habits and passion for rare and expensive art, is like a bleeding fortress."

"Who else knows Smokey has it?" asked Charlie.

"The only people that know Smokey has it is me, you and Smokey."

"And what happens if he does a runner? He could leave the bloody country with it. Actually, no sorry, let me rephrase that, he could *buy* a bloody country with it, then go live there while we suck it up here in London in the freezing bloody cold."

"You talk crap sometimes, Charlie," said Rupert, leaning back and putting his feet on the desk. He ran a soft tissue across the front of his shoe. "You know what your problem is?"

"Enlighten me, oh wise one."

"See, Charlie, you've always been the same. You're lucky to have me around, you know?"

"Is that right?"

"Yeah, it is. You just don't have the vision, Charles. You can't see past next week. It's all now, now, now. But what about tomorrow, eh? What about when all this comes crashing down and the clubs are shut? Booze is getting more expensive. I'm sometimes embarrassed how much we charge for a glass of Chablis."

"And what is it that gives you this all-seeing eye then, Rupert?" said Charlie. "What is it that sets you apart from the rest of us mere mortals?"

"I can read, Charlie," said Rupert.

"We can all read."

"Yeah, but I like to read the things that matter. I don't just stare at the pretty pictures of pretty ladies, do I?"

Charlie continued to stare at his twin brother as he sat, looking smug in his fine leather chair. "Go on, then," he said. "What have you read?"

"I thought you'd never ask," replied Rupert. He put his feet down to the floor, straightened his cuffs, and smoothed the back of his head with his hands. "We're going to be double rich, bruv."

"What are you on about?" asked Charlie.

"That diamond, Charlie," said Rupert, leaning forward with his elbows on his knees, identical to his brother. "It's a bit like you."

"Good looking, you mean?"

"It's worth a small fortune."

"Yeah, we established that. That's why we-"

"But," said Rupert, raising his index finger to quieten Charlie, "it's worth a fucking mint when it's with its twin brother."

CHAPTER FOUR

"Morning, Melody," said Reg Tenant as he entered his office.

Melody had already been sat at her desk working on her laptop for an hour. She didn't look up. "Hey, Reg," she replied, barely distracted from her work. "Did you bring coffee?"

"You're empty?" asked Reg. "Do you want to take a walk? We can grab a cup, and I have some news you need to hear. It might be best to discuss it off-premise."

"Sounds ominous," said Melody.

"Ominous? No," said Reg. "Dangerous? Yes."

Melody glanced away from her screen.

Reg smiled back at her.

"You're going to love this one. It's got your name written all over it."

Melody scrambled a few more words onto the keyboard, hit save then shut the lid of her laptop.

"What was that?" asked Reg.

"Just a report I'm finishing off."

"The Jackson case?"

Melody nodded but couldn't meet his eye.

It had been close to three months since their boss, Jackson, had tried to frame Melody's fiancé for murder. Jackson had been killed when his elaborately prepared grand finale backfired, and they had all escaped. Harvey hadn't been seen or heard from since. In the end, the wrong man wasn't found guilty, but Melody's life was still turned upside down. She'd moved from their farmhouse in France back to London, and buried her head in work to get through it.

"Why don't you let me finish that off?" said Reg. "Come on. I'll brief you while we walk."

Melody sighed and stood. She followed Reg out of the office, and they waited by the elevator.

Reg checked around him then began to talk.

"Have you ever heard of the Demonios Gemelos?"

"Demonios Gemelos," repeated Melody. She thought for a few moments. "That's devil twins in Spanish?"

"Well, it means twin demons to be precise, but yeah, it's the same thing."

"No," said Melody. "I can't say I have."

"Well, you'd better learn what you can because your foreseeable future revolves around them."

The doors to the lift opened and Reg, ever the gentleman, ushered Melody inside first. Another man occupied the lift, so the pair remained silent until he got out on the next floor. Melody waited for the doors to close fully before she spoke.

"Are you going to give me a clue?" she asked.

"A clue? Okay," said Reg. "Put it this way, if that engagement ring that Harvey bought you had one of them in it, you'd be dragging your hand across the floor."

"It's a diamond?" asked Melody. She subconsciously glanced down at her engagement ring. She hadn't been able to bring herself to remove it.

The elevator stopped on the ground floor and the pair walked through the security barriers, flashed their badges and stepped out of the Secret Intelligence Services building onto the footpath of London's Southbank.

Melody usually felt an immediate tension release each time she left the building, but she was deep in thought.

"Twins?"

"It's a pair," said Reg. "They aren't the largest diamonds ever found, but together, they're almost up there with the Crown Jewels."

"What's with the name?" asked Melody. "Twin demons. I mean, it's quite a negative name considering what they're worth."

"Rumour has it that whoever holds them both at the same time comes to an unexpected and unfortunate end."

"Folklore?"

"Just a series of unexplained mysterious deaths, I imagine, mixed with a large dose of coincidence. They were dug up by the Dutch in South Africa during the days of the British Empire. Some English guy had a fight with some Dutch guy and won. So, as the legend goes, he stole them. From there, they were exported to England as a gift to Queen Victoria. No doubt a ploy to win her favour."

"But?" asked Melody, sensing the direction of the tale.

"The ship sank."

"Funny that," said Melody.

"The opportunist captain killed the diamond thief when he knew they were going down and jumped ship with them. He made it as far as Europe."

"Then what happened?"

"He made it in a lifeboat to the shores of Portugal, evaded capture and wound up in France with a few of his shipmates.

They, in turn, robbed him of his quarry and turned themselves into the British Army in France seeking safe passage back to England."

"I have a feeling they didn't survive?" said Melody.

"Two of them did actually," said Reg. "There were three of them, but neither could agree on who looked after the diamonds, so one of them stole them one night."

"Don't tell me," said Melody.

"They caught him, and he was killed," continued Reg, "and the remaining two kept one each."

"And because they didn't carry them both together, they both survived?"

"So the legend goes, Melody."

"Coincidence?"

"That's my opinion," said Reg. "I'm a tech guy remember. Things are black and white."

"You sound like Harvey," said Melody quietly.

"I might have stolen a line or two from him." Reg grinned.

They strolled along London's south embankment at a slow pace. Reg left the silence for Melody. He knew she would be devising a list of questions.

"So the diamonds," began Melody, "was that what the robbery in South London was about? The one I read about in the paper?"

"Yes it was," said Reg. "Very sharp." But he offered no further insight.

"And they are considered unlucky when together?"

"Yes, apparently."

"So my guess is that if someone robbed the first diamond," said Melody, "a diamond like that might be worth a small fortune. But both of them together?"

"Who knows?" said Reg. "They haven't been in the same

country since nineteen forty-eight when the second diamond was stolen."

"Nineteen forty-eight?" said Melody. "And they're both in the UK now?"

Reg nodded.

"The current owner, a Dutch gentleman, as a matter of fact, came forward and was putting one up for private auction. He said his family acquired it shortly after the Second World War. It was being kept at a private house out in the country somewhere."

"That's where it was robbed from?"

"Yeah, crazy, isn't it?" said Reg. "The old guy who owns the house is an Earl of something who agreed on the use of his safe room, as the Dutch guy didn't trust the greed of the English."

"It wasn't a very safe room though, was it?"

"The room had steel slam doors and windows, a direct connection to the local police who were notified the second the security system connection went down, and laser motion sensors. All of which were powered by UPS backup power supplies."

"Sounds serious. What else does he have in there?" asked Melody.

"We don't know. But we do know that they didn't take anything else and they only just got out in time. The slam doors and windows were down. Whoever stole it took all the precautions they could to get in, but the secondary circuit beneath the display cabinet had been pulled. It was shoddy work, Melody."

"How would the thieves have known about the security systems?"

"Same way they always do," replied Reg. "Research, visits, and talking to the right people, I guess."

"It's open to the *public*?" said Melody, incredulous. "What were they thinking?"

"It's a National Trust building, Tudor, I think, maybe earlier."

"So how did they get in?" asked Melody. "I mean, I'm guessing they got in without raising the alarm?"

"Yeah. I took a look at the system. It's definitely the work of a team, minimum two, probably three or four."

"Three or four," said Melody thoughtfully. "One to break in, someone light on their toes with knowledge of security and nerves of steel."

"Or just plain greedy," said Reg.

"They'd need someone with tech skills," said Melody. "Someone like you, Reg. What were you doing last night?"

Reg laughed. "I have an alibi. I was having dinner with Jess in the local curry house."

"A likely story," said Melody, toying with her friend. "The other two may have included a driver and some muscle."

"I'd agree," said Reg. "We can't be sure of the exact skill set of the team, but something this big couldn't be done alone."

"So they got in without raising the alarm but triggered it when they took the diamond?"

"The circuitry beneath the cabinet looked as if they just ripped the cables out."

"Not very pro," said Melody.

"Nope."

"You think someone came along and disturbed them?"

"The guards were all doped. Three of them were found face down in the control room."

"So what happens when the circuitry is broken?" asked Melody. "Where does the alert go?"

"The police station gets an instant alarm. It's a special arrangement the owner of the house has with the local unit."

"Would they have known that?" asked Melody. "The thieves, I mean, would they have known about the direct link?"

"They had a false alarm last week," said Reg. "Some guy leaned on the case and set it off."

"My guess is that he was number three or four in the clan."

"Copy that," said Reg. "Some guy with a false name, fake ID, he even had fake prints. Police arrived on the scene in under three minutes. The thieves would have been timing it and drew their own conclusions."

"So I presume the thieves still have the diamond?" asked Melody.

"Yep," said Reg. He held the door of the coffee shop open for Melody.

"And can I presume that you now think they will target its evil twin brother?"

"Demonios Gemelos," said Reg with a smile.

"But it's a diamond robbery case. Why are we dealing with that?" asked Melody, under her breath as she joined the small queue. "It's not exactly secret intelligence, is it?"

"We're not dealing with it," replied Reg with a smile. "*You* are." He continued to watch the barista as she darted around behind the counter, foaming the milk for one drink while hot water ran through the grinds into two other cups.

"*Me?*" said Melody. "On my own?"

"Special orders," said Reg. He eventually turned to face her. "You've been selected, Melody."

"Me? But why me?" she asked.

"You were an excellent operative. Plus, you had success with the jade buddha case. If you remember, most of that operation was accredited to you."

They were called to the counter, and Reg placed the order. A flat white for Melody and a tall hazelnut latte for himself.

"It's a great opportunity," said Reg. "A real chance to get back in the game. You *are* going to take it, aren't you?"

"Of course I'll take it," said Melody. "Do we know where the other demon twin is kept?"

Reg smiled at the cashier as he received his change, and they moved to the collection area of the counter.

"You're going to like this, Melody. It's in the Natural History Museum."

CHAPTER FIVE

"It's not much, Fingers, but at least it's out of the cold," said Lola. She dropped another Daily Express into the fire they had created in the old disused warehouse. She bent down to the bundle of unsold papers and grabbed another one.

"How long did you say we're going to stay here?" asked Fingers. He looked around the room, which seemed to be an old office when the warehouse was habited, and saw nothing but gloomy shadows. Strange noises issued from the larger space outside, the creaks of old beams and groans of walls, and ceilings cooling after a day of rare British sun.

"As long as it takes, Fingers," replied Lola. "I still can't believe-"

"Hey, Lola, don't go there," said Fingers. "Come on, we're still in this, and we won't get through it unless we-"

"Unless we what, Fingers?" snapped Lola. "Forget about him? Is that what you were going to say?"

"No, I-"

"Well, I can't forget about him. He meant too much to me to just forget."

"I'm not talking about forgetting Dynamite, Lola. God, he

was my mate. But you know what? We can still remember him. Remember how he used to be able to make you laugh at just about anything?"

"Yeah, he did," said Lola. Her voice was quiet and thick with suppressed emotion.

"He was always like that, you know?" said Fingers. "He always had this way of making people smile, especially at the most inappropriate times. This one time we were in school and the teacher, Mr Day his name was, kept picking me out to answer his questions. So I'd have to stand and answer him in front of the whole class. Dynamite was sat behind me, and I can't remember what he was saying now, but all I could hear was Dynamite's voice, and all I could do was try not to laugh. Mr Day, as you can imagine, was slowly getting more and more frustrated with me. I couldn't even look at him. I just stared at the floor. My face went bright red, and my body was shaking with laughter until finally he exploded, Mr Day that is. He went into an absolute rage, which was even more hilarious because he was bald with these two tufts of hair above his ears, and when he got mad his entire bald head creased up."

"So," said Lola, "what happened?"

"I couldn't hold it any longer. I burst out laughing and, of course, the rest of the kids all fell about too. Mr Day was apocalyptic. He began screaming at everyone, and you know what?"

"What?"

"The only two people in that room that weren't laughing was Mr Day and Dynamite. I don't know how he did it, but Dynamite just sat there straight-faced, looking at me like I was completely nuts and didn't understand what was happening, which was even worse because I took one look at him and it sparked me off again."

"Always the joker, eh?"

"He was a legend, Lola. An absolute legend."

A moment's peace followed as the pair were each lost in their own thoughts of Dynamite. Lola broke the silence by tossing another newspaper into the small fire.

"Shame we don't have a little bottle of brandy to toast him, eh?" said Fingers.

"We will, Fingers," said Lola. "We will."

"Have you thought about what that bloke said at all?"

"I can't do it," replied Lola. "How could I? He just killed..." Her voice broke off.

"But you know if you don't do it, you'll be hiding like this for a long time? You're going to need a bigger stack of papers, Lola."

"I could disappear," she offered. But immediately, she knew the idea was weak and impossible.

"Disappear, yeah?" said Fingers. "Where would you go? You know it's just a matter of time before they track you down."

"Yeah, but honestly, how powerful do you think these people are?" asked Lola.

"The Bond brothers?" asked Fingers. "Only the most powerful villains this side of London, Lola. They've got their fingers in a lot of little pies, and if there's a cash business this side of the Thames, you can bet your arse they're involved somehow. They own most of the clubs, they run the security for the ones they don't own, and the rest of the firms all fall under their protection. Trust me, I know them well."

Lola gave him a grave stare across the fire. The shadows ran deep beneath his eyes.

"Mark my words, Lola," said Fingers. "Doing the job is the only way out of this."

"It's a betrayal, Fingers," replied Lola. "Imagine what Dynamite would have said? Besides, it was only ever about that one diamond."

"Dynamite isn't here, Lola. I know it's hard to hear. But you know what? You need to survive. You need to live and you need to remember him, whatever it takes. Giving up and having the Bond brothers on your case for the rest of your life isn't going to solve anything, and it isn't going to give you much chance of remembering Dynamite."

"How, Fingers?" said Lola. "I've got two options. One is certain death. The other is almost certainly prison time."

"You don't reckon it's possible at all then?"

"Listen, Fingers, you've seen the place, right? You know the security. If jobs were like dinners, what we did last night was cook sausage and mash potato. Robbing a post office would be like making a sandwich. But robbing the other diamond would be like cooking a lobster thermidor with one hand and knocking up a crème brûlée with the other. Do you know what I'm trying to say?"

"I've never known you to back away from a job before, that's all, Lola," said Fingers.

"I'm not backing away. I'm laying it on the table, Fingers. Whichever way you look at it, my life is over."

Fingers suddenly flinched. His eyes widened and turned slowly to listen at the door. Lola questioned him with a look. Fingers returned the question by mouthing two words.

"Someone's coming."

CHAPTER SIX

The plastic tarp crinkled loudly as Harvey ran his hand along it. It hadn't been moved since he was last there. Old dusty boxes full of meaningless junk, a few battered oil drums that had been used as rubbish bins, and some heavy machinery with a thick coat of grease across their cast iron housings stood against the far end of the warehouse as if they had been forgotten. Perhaps the removal firm had placed them there to be removed last but had never returned to collect them. The machinery looked outdated and useless. The boxes were filled with ancient printouts on dot matrix paper. Whatever was printed on them had long since been relevant to anybody.

On the cold and dirty concrete floor beside the boxes, and stacked neatly in comparison to the other random items, were twenty or thirty large bundles of newspapers. They were probably dumped there by a lazy paperboy with better things to do than walk the streets. There was a pile of old timber, which was likely scrap from when the chainlink fence had been erected around the property. All the doors were boarded up.

The warehouse itself was over a hundred meters long with a wall of offices along one side and huge, arched windows on the other. The ceiling stood high above Harvey's head, maybe thirty or forty meters, and the occasional pigeon made himself known with a shake of feathers and some verbal warnings.

The daylight was fading, but any romantic imaginings of times gone by or sentiment had been lost on the place. It seemed as if life itself inside the old factory had been lost to the shadows for decades, despite the enormous windows.

Harvey stayed close to the wall. A faint glimmer of flickering orange shone briefly from an office at the far end of the warehouse.

A fire?

Maybe a homeless person?

They would be no trouble, thought Harvey, as long as they kept to themselves.

Harvey stepped into the first office space in the long row that ran along the far wall. It was a small space with the same high ceiling as the factory floor and similar large windows. Harvey imagined the office once belonged to the manager of whatever production line used to be immediately outside the room. The same for the rest of the offices. Each manager might have been responsible for a particular production phase.

Harvey had no knowledge of such things. He just imagined.

Long shadows began to reach across the warehouse space outside as the sun dipped low enough to find the floor through the arched glass. The light cut through the dust in the air, forming identical golden beams that grew brighter and weaker as clouds moved across the sky.

Harvey sat in the corner with his rucksack beside him. It wasn't so bad for one night. He'd stayed in worse places for longer. At least he had a roof over his head. During his walk along the canal outside, Harvey had seen the thunderheads moving in from the west, patiently waiting like an ancient army stood at the edge of a city before the command to strike unleashed hell.

As if on cue, a scatter of rain danced across the roof high above, and the golden beams of light faded to shadow, leaving nothing but darkness in their wake.

A scuffle of feet on the concrete floor outside caught Harvey's ear. He listened harder. People. But they were moving away. He glanced around the corner.

It was two men.

Harvey moved towards the doorway but remained inside the small office. He clung to the shadows and followed their movements across the vast open space outside.

A lifetime of finding people, watching them and following them had taught Harvey a great deal about body language. The two men weren't casually taking shelter from the rain; they were creeping towards the room at the end of the warehouse. The room with the fire.

The two men each wore a short bomber jacket, jeans and boots. Harvey noted their appearance; they weren't homeless. Maybe it was a gang meet. They looked like heavies. They walked with the confidence of men who carried weapons, were used to hurting people, and who stayed at arm's length of the law.

Harvey knew the type all too well.

What Harvey found odd was that a deserted warehouse should see so many visitors in one evening.

Harvey didn't believe in coincidence.

In Harvey's mind, either things were, or they weren't. They were black, or they were white. Idealism might be good for businessmen. But in reality, ifs and buts created cracks in plans, doubts in minds and failed missions.

Failed missions often resulted in death.

The angle of Harvey's view became too narrow to track the

men, so he waited a full one minute, which was his standard practice before making any moves. The full minute had been a lesson from his mentor, Julios. If anyone was listening for him or waiting to jump him, most men would grow impatient long before a full minute passed. It also allowed him time to formulate some kind of plan and question his motives.

He could and perhaps should stay sitting in the corner of his empty office on the hard floor and listen to whatever was happening. It was none of his business anyway.

Or he could stick to the shadows and watch from a distance. It was the closest he'd been to anything exciting for three months.

Lightning flashed outside. It lit the windows and left a photographic image of the empty warehouse bathed momentarily in unnatural light on Harvey's retinas.

The lightning passed, and his vision faded back to the darkness. Rain drummed on the roof like the well-timed footsteps of a thousand soldiers marching to war.

The warehouse appeared darker than before as if the thunderclouds had banished the golden sun and cast long, dark fingers across the eyes of the world.

Harvey peered from the office. The men had disappeared.

Finally, a crack of thunder announced the arrival of the storm. It was followed quickly by another flash of sheet lightning that once more lit the open space, while a rumble of thunder rolled across the sky.

Small drops of water had found a leak in the roof and landed on the floor close to where Harvey stood with an increasing rhythm.

Suddenly, a girl screamed somewhere at the far end of the rumble.

Battle had commenced.

The screaming continued. Harvey pictured the girl in a

room much like the one in which he was stood. She would be cornered and frightened with no exit.

One of the men shouted for her to shut up. His rough, baritone voice seemed to carry across the floor and below the girl's screams, which sung through the eaves of the huge ceiling.

Harvey stepped outside.

CHAPTER SEVEN

Rupert put his phone down on the desk and opened an internet browser on his computer.

"Who was that, Ru?" said Charlie, looking up from his own screen.

"Glasgow George," replied Rupert. He ran a search for a satellite map of South London and began zooming in.

"Are you going to tell me what he said?" asked Charlie. "Or are we playing guessing games now?"

"He put a GPS tag on the girl. He's found her and has sent Mad Bob and Cannon Bill to keep an eye on them."

"Oh, so not important news then? Was you actually *going* to tell me?"

"Charlie, when I receive a piece of information as important as this, I like to digest it. I like to think of all the possible outcomes and then articulate a reasoned summary of A, what might happen, B, what I'd like to happen, and C, what the plan might be if indeed circumstances lean towards the non-preferred option A."

"You do talk crap, Rupert," said Charlie. "They found the girl, so there's only one option."

Rupert looked across at his brother who span his chair to gaze out of the floor-to-ceiling windows covering the wall behind their desks.

"And that is?" asked Rupert.

"Grab her, give her a slap, and make sure she does exactly what she's supposed to do."

Rupert shook his head. "And that is why I prefer to absorb the information before it's allowed to be put through your simple mind only to have answers spat out like a wood chipper, Charlie."

"Where is she?"

"In some factory somewhere down by the canal. I'm just looking it up now."

"So she hasn't gone home then?"

"No, obviously she hasn't."

"So why do you think she hasn't gone home then?" said Charlie. "She's planning on doing a runner, and if she does a runner, you can bet your arse she's planning on an anonymous call to the police with a little tip-off about who has got the diamond."

"Charlie, you're a muppet sometimes," said Rupert. "She knows that if she goes home, we'll know where she lives." He turned back to his screen and found the factory that Glasgow had described.

"Care to explain?" asked Charlie, tapping away on his phone and letting the insult wash over him. The two brothers enjoyed the banter, but they only tolerated the insults from each other. Nobody else dared to talk to them in anything less than a respectful manner.

"She's scared, mate. She's just seen her bloke get his face blown off, and then a dozen big blokes, namely Glasgow George and his mob, gave her two choices. Neither are favourable for her future."

"She's scared?"

"Yeah, she's scared. The only way out of this is for her to get the second diamond for us. If we go in there and give her a slap, she's even more likely to do a runner, which means in turn that we'll have to find her, kill her and finish the job ourselves. So that means we'll either be less rich than we had planned or we'll have to risk bringing some other thief in to do the job for us. That's a bit risky, mate. We're not robbing cash vans here. This is serious stuff, Charlie. It needs to be handled delicately."

Charlie was silent. He put his phone in his pocket and carried on looking out of the window at the big black clouds that had begun to roll in. Small specs of rain dotted the outside of the glass and lights across the city started to blink on as the sunlight was quenched.

"Charlie?" said Rupert.

"Yes, brother," replied Charlie, in the mock tones of a well-to-do manservant.

"Do you realise that if we do get this other diamond, that's it for me, I'm out?"

"What do you mean you're out?"

"Charlie, we're talking millions here, mate."

"We already have millions. We'll just be richer," said Charlie. "No, nothing will change. The business needs you. It needs us both."

"No, you don't get it, do you? We won't need the business. We won't need to sit up here and make sure people are doing their jobs. We won't need to make sure none of the men are helping themselves or taking liberties. And we won't need to cock about with backhanders, which, by the way, are getting way out of control now. Do you realise how much we paid last month just to stop the old bill giving us grief?"

Charlie looked across at his brother, but let him continue his rant.

"Fifty grand, Charlie," said Rupert. "Fifty bleeding grand in some copper's skyrocket, just for him to turn a blind eye."

"It's been happening for years, Ru. I wouldn't let it worry you. We make that back in a night."

"Yes, I know we make it back in a night, Charlie. But my point is that we wouldn't have to, would we? No, we wouldn't. We'll be sitting on a beach in the perpetual sunshine, someplace classy with a cocktail in one hand and a tart on each knee fighting over which one of them is going to rub the suncream on my chest."

"Is that right?" said Charlie, smiling at the picture his brother had painted.

"Yes, it is right, and all we have to do, dear brother, is keep our nuts firmly screwed on, keep our beady eyes on the beady little bird, and wait for her to deliver us from evil, as it were."

"Deliver us from evil, Ru?"

"Yes, Charlie. With what little Lola is going to give us, and what we've already taken off her, I intend to live within the remits of the law. I'd like to walk down the street one day, preferably in the sunshine, and not have to look over my shoulder, and not have a carload of Mad Bobs and Glasgow Georges following me. I'm tired of it all, Charlie. We could have a great life. Think about it."

"And all we have to do is...What was it? Keep our heads screwed on and keep our beady little eyes on the beady little bird? I'm pretty sure I can handle that."

"That's it, bro," said Rupert. "Think of the sun, the sand, the semi-naked women." He stopped. "*Charlie?*"

"Yes, bro."

"What have you done?"

"What do you mean what have I done? I haven't done anything."

"You just agreed with me," said Rupert. "You *never* agree

with me that easily. Who did you just text? I saw you on your phone."

"Ah well, you know," said Charlie. "The sun and...What was it? The semi-naked women. I'm game for it. Look at this rain, eh. I'd love a bit of sunshine right now."

"Charlie?"

Charlie fell silent.

"Charlie, *who* did you text a minute ago?"

"No-one special."

"*Charlie?*" Rupert raised his eyebrows. He'd caught the bit between his teeth. "You just text Mad Bob, didn't you?"

Charlie didn't reply.

"You *did*, didn't you? You bloody *idiot*. You told him to give her a slap."

"I might have," said Charlie. A grin began to ease itself across his face. "But in my defence that was *before* you gave me all the talk about beaches, sun and semi-naked women."

"What have you done, you idiot? If he hurts her and messes this up, *I'll* kill him."

Rupert jumped up from his chair, grabbed his phone and hit Mad Bob on speed dial. He listened intently to the dial tone until the call was eventually answered.

CHAPTER EIGHT

"Oh finally," said Melody, sitting back from her laptop. She was sat on the guest side of Reg's large desk. Behind Reg was a view over the River Thames and Vauxhall Bridge. Melody enjoyed watching London from Reg's office. The day had been particularly nice with a rich blue sky that seemed even to brighten the river of endless, murky, brown water.

By evening, however, the blue sky had been pushed to one side to make way for an approaching storm. The soft hues of blue had been replaced with an impenetrable layer of grey. The clouds quenched the distant parts of the horizon with imposing shadow and banished the city into darkness.

"Finally *what?*" asked Reg, engrossed in his work.

"I've finally managed to get hold of the technical drawings and CAD files."

"For what?"

"The museum," said Melody with an accomplished smile. "They don't make it easy, but it's all out there ready for the taking."

"So why do you need the CAD files?" asked Reg. "You know you can walk right in, don't you? You're a member of secret intelligence. I'm sure a few phone calls could arrange it."

"*I* know that and *you* know that. But the thieves don't have our credibility, so they can't just walk right in, and for me to understand how they're going to do it, I need to think like them."

Melody sat back in her chair.

"The thieves will need to go through the same research as I have, with a little help from the tech guys, which means that I can study the same drawings and files to work out how *I* would rob the museum."

She smiled across the desk at her friend, who remained focused on his work.

"What's the matter? I thought you'd be proud of me."

"Well done, Melody," replied Reg. "Sorry, I am proud. But to be honest, I have no doubt whatsoever that you can stop them. I wouldn't have asked you if I thought otherwise."

"Hey, Reg?"

"Yes?" he replied, his eyes still on his computer screen.

"Reg?"

He glanced at her.

"Are you happy?" asked Melody. "With the job, I mean. You miss the tech stuff, don't you? The nitty gritty."

Reg sighed and closed his eyes.

"I guess I do," said Reg. He pushed his keyboard away and leaned on the desktop. "I see Jess and the guys down in the operations room, and I see you getting small wins, and yeah, I totally miss the challenge. All I seem to do is write reports. If I need research done, I have a team to do it for me, and even watching them is frustrating, Melody. Is it wrong to think that..."

"To think what, Reg?" asked Melody.

Reg sighed. "To think that I can still do it better and faster?"

Melody set her laptop down on the desk and crossed her legs. "You want to talk about it?"

"What's to say?" replied Reg. "I just remember the times we used to work for Frank. We pretty much had free reign to do what we wanted, *and* we achieved excellent results."

"You feel constrained here?"

"A little, yeah," said Reg. "I'm ready for a change. I used to love seeing a problem, and in my mind, I'd match a technology to the problem then I'd go away and create something." He met Melody's eyes. "All I create here is reports for someone upstairs to read and then file."

"You're not solving crime," said Melody.

"I'm not solving anything, Melody. I'm barely using my brain, and yes, it's great to see you being given a case and to see you immerse yourself in it, and believe me, all I want to do is jump on that case with you, but I can't. I'm tied to this chair with so much red tape."

"Why don't you help me?" Melody asked.

"How can I? I have to finish this report, then I have to pull up performance stats, after that, I have the hugely unsatisfying task of creating a resource forecast. A *resource forecast,* Melody. A forecast that tells my superiors what resources I will need for the forthcoming year."

Melody held his gaze but pitied him. She could see he was frustrated.

"How the *hell* am I supposed to know how busy we'll be in a year's time?" Reg continued. "*I* don't know how many people I'll need or what technology we'll need. The technology we'll be using in twelve months might be totally different. And to top it off, it should be *me* creating the technology. That's what I'm *good* at. That's what I *enjoy.*"

"So, why are you doing this, Reg?"

He let his head fall into his hands. "Oh, I don't know. It seemed like the right career move, you know? The one that would take me to new levels."

"And has it?" asked Melody.

"New levels of boredom is where it's taken me."

"Boredom?"

"Well," said Reg, with a sheepish grin, "mostly."

"Reg," began Melody, "I've known you a long time, right?"

"Yeah."

"And we're good friends?"

"I think so," Reg confirmed.

"Since you've had this job, you've had a gun put to your head, you've been held hostage on a cliff face, and you've been tied to a tree waiting to be boiled alive."

"Rough, isn't it?" said Reg.

"The reports are just the end of a job, Reg. The truth is, and I say this as a friend, that maybe you're not the type of guy that enjoys the wild rides of an active case. You're always in your element at a computer, close to the action, but not in it. I can't remember how many times you've saved my butt from the comfort of your chair. There's no shame in doing what you're good at, Reg, not when you're as good as you at doing it."

"What are you saying?" asked Reg. "That I'm weak?"

Melody laughed at the comment. "No, Reg. You're one of the strongest men I know." She tapped her temple indicating his mental abilities. "I just think maybe you should dip your toe into the tech research side of things again. When is the next report due?"

Reg shrugged.

"Five days maybe?" he said.

"Okay, come help me work the diamond case. I'd say they'll hit the museum in less than five days anyway," said Melody. "Nobody is going to want to hang onto the dreaded Demonios Gemelos for too long."

Reg let his head hang low, and leaned his elbows on his knees. He looked up at her with a sheepish grin.

"*Come on*," urged Melody. "It'll be like the old days."

"You mean I can sit in a van with a laptop, while you go and risk your life?"

Melody's smile broadened, it was clear that Reg was up for the challenge.

"With you in my ear to keep me company, Reggie," she said, "it'll be an absolute pleasure."

CHAPTER NINE

"Evening all," said Mad Bob, stepping into the room. "Well this is *cosy*, isn't it? All we need is a few steaks and sausages and we've got ourselves a right little barbecue."

Lola backed up against the wall. The arched window above her did little to light the room, but the fire threw flashes of orange light. It was enough for Lola to see that the man's face looked like it had been chewed by a dog. He was large framed and moved with confidence, but his shape was nothing compared to the monster that stepped into the room behind him.

"What do you want?" asked Lola.

"What I want is for you to *shut up* and *listen*, sweetheart." He stared down at her as if to emphasise the point. "When I ask you a question, you can take that as a prompt for you to talk. But if I do not ask you a question, the best thing for you to do is keep that dirty little trap of yours shut." He glared at Fingers who stood close by Lola, keeping the fire between them and the two men.

"Now," he continued, "do you remember me?"

The pair nodded.

"Do you know who I am?" he asked. "I don't think there was time last night to make a proper introduction."

The pair shook their heads.

"You was one of the men that shot our friend," said Lola.

"Okay, we're making progress. But sadly, I didn't pull the trigger. Do you know who I work for?"

"No," said Lola, a little too quickly.

"No?" said the man. "Would you like to hazard a guess?"

A flash of lightning lit the room and his face. He looked like pure evil. His face was more scar tissue than skin. He grinned when he saw Lola's eyes widen in horror.

"Pretty, ain't I?" he said, his voice deep and grumbling.

Lola didn't reply.

"Let's start from the beginning, shall we?" he continued. "My name is Mad Bob. I wasn't christened Mad Bob, but my friends decided to call me that from an early age and it kind of just stuck, you know?"

Lola nodded.

"Do you know why they called me that?"

Lola didn't reply. Fingers stared at the floor.

"No?" he said. Then he raised his voice. "Right, let's get one thing straight, it seems I have to explain the fundamentals of basic human interaction. When I ask you a question, you answer. You speak loud enough for me to hear and clear enough for me to understand. When I don't ask you a question, you keep your mouth shut. But while you are holding them pretty little lips together, Lola LaRoux, you will listen to *every* word I say. You will make it your sole mission during the longevity of our conversation to ensure that every little word issued from my lips, every little detail whether spoken or insinuated, is understood. Carefully place it at the front of your grey matter, ready for you to call upon at any given moment, because, and I cannot stress this point enough, if I ask you to recall a detail, no matter how small, and you fail, then that is likely to upset my friend here and me."

He stopped and glared at Lola and Fingers who were listening intently.

"So, let's make it easy then, shall we? Do you remember playing a game when you were younger called Simon Says?"

Lola nodded.

Mad Bob stared back at her in disbelief.

"I don't believe it," he said. "I have just explained the fundamentals of basic human interaction, less than thirty seconds ago, and yet she still-"

"Yes," said Lola, growing tired of his voice. "Yes, I understand Simon Says."

"Good." Mad Bob turned to Fingers and raised his eyebrows, a gesture that, if it weren't for the firelight, Fingers wouldn't have seen.

"Yeah," said Fingers. "I remember."

"Excellent," continued Mad Bob. "We are making progress, or as my old man used to say, we are cooking with gas. Are we not? Now, are you both ready to play Mad Bob Says? It's similar to Simon Says, but with a slight variation."

"What's the variation?" asked Lola.

"Here we go," said Mad Bob. "I like it. We're interacting. The variation of Mad Bob Says to Simon Says is quite simple, Lola. Just as in the game of Simon Says, when I give an instruction, which is preceded by the words, Mad Bob Says, you are obliged to fulfil the request. But the variation is that, unlike in the game of Simon Says, whereby failing to fulfil your obligation merely results in you being out of the game, in the game of *Mad Bob Says*, failure to fulfil an obligation results in the breaking of bones. Your bones."

Mad Bob let the first variation to the rules of the game sink in before speaking again.

"The second difference between Simon Says and Mad Bob Says is this. In the game of Simon Says, you might get three lives before you are out. I think the rules vary from game to game. But when I was a child, we had three chances, and then we were out. However, this is the important bit. This is one of those bits of information I spoke of, which you need to stick in the front of your grey matter, darling. In the game of Mad Bob says you will only get one life. One attempt at fulfilling your obligation. Failure to do so will result, as I before mentioned, in the breaking of your bones. Every single one of them. One by one. Bone by crunching bone."

Another silence hung in the air.

"Now, shall we begin?" Mad Bob asked.

Lola didn't reply.

"Good girl," said Mad Bob. "She's sharper than she looks this one. *Mad Bob says* shall we begin?"

"Yes," said Lola.

"Yes," said Fingers.

"Good," continued Mad Bob. "Now, *Mad Bob says*, do you know why they call me Mad Bob? There's a nice easy one to start you off."

"Because you're mad?" said Fingers. "Ruthless?"

"Ruthless," said Mad Bob. "I like it. Yes. Although I am quite sane, some people tend to lean towards me being a bit of a psycho. Perhaps it's due to a combination of my lack of empathy, an unwillingness to recognise the needs and feelings of others, and an ability to inflict incredible amounts of pain onto another human being." Mad Bob gave his own statement some thought. "What do you think?" he asked.

Both Lola and Fingers remained silent.

"*Good*," said Mad Bob. "You're learning the rules. Now, *Mad Bob says*, are you having fun?"

Lola and Fingers glanced at each other then back at Mad Bob.

"No," said Lola.

"No," repeated Fingers.

"Good," said Mad Bob. He pointed a huge fat index finger at them both. "Because this is not supposed to be fun. This is supposed to be an exercise in ensuring that you fully understand the consequences of cocking me about and failing to fulfil your obligations."

Mad Bob stood straight again and cleared his throat.

"Now," he continued, "standing behind me in the shadows is my friend Cannon Bill, but you can call him Mr Cannon. He likes that. It appeals to one of the basic needs that Maslow set out as a framework for a human to feel part of society."

Lola looked past Mad Bob into the shadows but saw no-one.

"Why don't you say hello, Mr Cannon?"

Mr Cannon didn't reply.

"He's a man of few words," said Mad Bob. "Lola, why don't you throw some more of those newspapers on the fire? See if we can't light the room up a little."

Lola didn't move.

"Okay," said Mad Bob. "*Mad Bob says*, feed the fire, Lola."

Lola bent and pulled two more newspapers from the pile. She rolled them up and tossed them into the dying flames. The paper landed on the burning embers, shrivelled, then succumbed to the heat in a show of flames. The room flickered a bright orange haze, casting a Mad-Bob-shaped shadow onto the wall behind him.

A man stepped into the room.

Mad Bob sensed the movement.

"Ah, here he is. Mr Cannon. I knew he wouldn't be too far away."

He turned to face his friend, but instead he was met with an uppercut that rocked the big man's jaw and sent him crashing to the floor like a felled tree.

CHAPTER TEN

It took a few moments for Harvey to bind the big man's hands with his own bootlaces and take his weapon, which was a Glock. Harvey removed the magazine, made sure the chamber was empty, and tossed the gun on the fire. He pocketed the magazine and the man's phone.

Two terrified-looking faces stared at him from across the room.

"You've nothing to be frightened of," said Harvey. He stood over the man on the floor, waiting for him to come around.

"Who are you?" asked the girl.

"What's his name?" asked Harvey, ignoring the question.

"That's Mad Bob," said the small-framed man who stood beside the girl, "and that outside is Cannon Bill."

"Mad Bob and Cannon Bill?" repeated Harvey.

"Yeah, that's all we know," said the girl. She gave her friend a sideways glance.

Harvey dragged the man closer to the fire and rolled him onto his front.

"What are you going to do with him?" asked the girl. "Are you going to kill him?"

Harvey ignored her and stepped from the room into the darkness. He found Cannon Bill where he'd left him, dragged the huge man back across the concrete floor into the room, and dumped him down beside Mad Bob.

"Make yourself useful," Harvey said to the pair. "Take them newspapers apart and screw the pages up tight."

"These newspapers?" asked the man, pointing to the only pile of newspapers in the room.

Harvey gave him a look and then continued to arrange Mad Bob and Cannon Bill so they sat upright back to back.

"What's your name, son?" said Harvey to the man.

"I'm, erm, Fingers," he replied.

"Fingers?"

"Yes, that's what they call me, my friends, that is."

"Okay, Fingers," said Harvey. "Give me your belt."

"My belt?" said Fingers. "What do you-?"

The girl suddenly jumped into action. She stripped him of his belt then walked across to Harvey, who had sat Mad Bob and Cannon Bill back to back. She wrapped it around the two men's necks, fastening it tight with a snatch of her wrist.

She stepped back and admired her handy-work.

"What's your name?" asked Harvey.

"Lola," she replied. "Lola LaRoux."

"You've done that before?"

"I've seen movies," she said. "Why else would you want his belt?"

"You two are in trouble?" asked Harvey.

"Yes," said Fingers.

"No," countered Lola. "It's nothing we can't handle."

"I'll leave you two to it then," said Harvey, and made to leave the room.

"No, wait," said Lola, a little over anxious.

Harvey stopped but didn't turn.

"We might be in a *little* trouble."

"That's what I thought," said Harvey. "Good luck with that."

"What?" cried Lola. "You mean you're just going to leave these two here tied up?"

"Do you want me to untie them?"

"Well, no, but-"

"I didn't think so." Harvey left the room.

"But what's your name?" she asked after him.

Harvey didn't reply.

"We can pay you," said Lola, clearly clutching at reasons for Harvey to stay.

Again, Harvey stopped but didn't turn around. "What makes you think I need your money?"

"Why else would you be here?" said Lola. "It's an abandoned warehouse."

"It's raining," replied Harvey. "It's got a roof."

"You don't strike me as the type of man that minds getting wet."

Harvey didn't reply.

"You also don't strike me as the type of man who minds getting his hands dirty."

Harvey heard Lola step closer. She stood half in and half out of the doorway. The left side of her body glowed orange from the firelight, the right side awash in shadow.

"What was the point in helping us if you aren't going to finish the job?"

"I don't like bullies," said Harvey.

"So what was the point of having us screw up the newspapers?"

"Stuff the paper down their shirts, cover them with that fire-lighter and light a match."

"That's barbaric," said Fingers. He squeezed passed Lola and stepped out into the open warehouse.

"Why not just spray their clothes?" asked Lola.

"Paper ignites quicker and burns for longer than fabric. You'll do more damage."

"Who *are* you?" asked Lola again. "You're what, an expert in burning people alive?"

Harvey turned to face them. They stood side by side, like two children asking their older brother for help against a bully.

"I've dealt with men like that all my life," said Harvey. "They all have their weaknesses; you just need to find it. Fire is always a good place to start. We have a primal fear of fire. It'll break even the hardest of men."

"You've burned someone alive?" asked Fingers.

"You ask a lot of questions. Maybe that's why you're both in trouble," said Harvey. "You want my advice? Do what I said, then get out of here. Go find someplace else. Start over."

"That was the plan," said Lola. "But they'll find us. They have more resources than we know about. Besides, do we want to spend the rest of our lives looking over our shoulders?" She glanced at Fingers, who shook his head.

"So what did you do?" asked Harvey. "Men like that don't normally go after someone without good reason. My guess is that those two clowns work for someone else, someone with money and power. The type of man that employs people like your mates in there would need a strong reason to go after a girl and..." Harvey looked at Fingers, searching for the right word to describe him. "You," he finished.

"We haven't done anything wrong," said Lola. "They want us to do a job."

Fingers nudged Lola as if to shut her up. She glared at him and continued to talk.

"They want us to do a robbery," Lola finished.

"What are you robbing?" asked Harvey.

"A diamond."

"A diamond? Singular?"

Lola nodded.

"It's a big diamond then?" asked Harvey.

"Biggest I ever saw," said Lola.

"So you're thieves then," said Harvey. It wasn't a question, it was a statement.

"They work for the Bond Brothers," said Fingers. "They said they'd kill us both if we don't do the job."

"The Bond Brothers?" said Harvey. "Never heard of them. And you definitely can't run?"

Lola shook her head.

"What makes you think they'd actually kill you?" asked Harvey. "I mean, at a guess, I'd say that Mad Bob and Cannon Bill were sent to rough you up, to make sure you do the job. Am I right?"

Lola nodded.

"And where is the job?" asked Harvey.

"So you'll help us?" asked Lola. "You're *interested*?" Her voice perked up at the thought of help.

"Professional interest," he replied. "But I don't do robberies. You're on your own." Harvey turned away again

"*Wait*," said Lola.

Harvey stopped.

"You asked what makes us think they'd actually kill us."

"Yeah I did," replied Harvey.

"They shot our friend," said Lola. "Last night. I was there."

Harvey didn't reply.

"I was stood beside him. They shot him in the face." Lola's voice broke off as she finished the sentence. "Please, we need help. If not for the robbery, at least help us with these guys? Look at what they did."

Lola pulled up her sleeve and showed Harvey a wrist tag.

"Do you know what this is?" she asked.

Harvey nodded. "That's what you get when you're released from prison on parole, so the parole officer can keep tabs on you. It's GPS, right?"

"If I go home wearing this, they'll know where I live and my family..." Her voice trailed off.

"Was it Bill or Bob that shot him?" asked Harvey. "Your friend."

"Neither," Fingers said, taking over the chat from Lola, who was crying into her hands. "Some other guy, but just as big."

"They run this part of town?" asked Harvey. "The Bond Brothers?"

There was a small silence as Fingers clearly recalled the event. "Yeah," he replied.

Harvey digested the information. He'd seen many firms being run by all types of men. Some were hard, some were rich, and once they reached a certain level of power, they rarely got their own hands dirty.

"Fingers, do me a favour, will you?"

"What?" replied Fingers. "What do you need?"

"Stuff all that paper down Cannon's shirt."

Lola looked up from her hands as Fingers tentatively slipped past her and back into the smaller room.

"What?" she asked. "You're going to-"

"I'm going to get these clowns off your back. You can stay if you want. But I'd suggest you get out of London sharp, find some way of getting that thing off your wrist, and forget about your friend."

Harvey took six long steps to the room and entered in time

to see Fingers step away from Cannon Bill, who had begun to stir.

"You're awake," said Harvey. He reached out, took hold of Fingers' belt, and sliced it with his knife to separate the two men. Then he dragged Mad Bob away by his feet and sat him against the wall. Mad Bob stared up at him in silence, but his look said all he needed to say.

Harvey returned his attention to Cannon Bill.

"Where can I find your boss?" asked Harvey.

Cannon Bill remained silent.

Harvey landed the sole of his boot onto Bill's face, sending him back onto the concrete floor. He struggled with his bound hands but eventually managed to sit back up. Blood trickled from his nose and the pages of rolled up newspaper stuck out from his shirt like a cheap scarecrow. The big man remained silent.

Harvey walked behind him. He felt Mad Bob's eyes follow him and saw them widen when Harvey bent to pick up the plastic bottle of fire starter.

"Are you two betting men?" asked Harvey.

Neither of the men replied.

"No?" said Harvey, answering his own question. "Okay, nor am I typically. But sometimes I enjoy a flutter when the stakes are high enough."

He turned the bottle upside down, stuck the nozzle inside Cannon Bill's shirt and squeezed a healthy amount of fuel onto the newspaper. Bill struggled, but Harvey held him still with one hand on the back of his collar.

"I bet," continued Harvey, "that one of you tells me where I can find your boss, or bosses, as the case may be."

Cannon Bill had begun to pant heavily. The smell of lighter fuel was heavy in the air, and he was sat just two feet from the fire.

"What about you, Bob?" said Harvey. "You like games, don't you?"

Bob glared back but remained silent.

"I'll ask the question once more," said Harvey as he began to spray a thin jet of fuel from the bottle onto the floor to form a circle around Cannon Bill. "Where can I find your boss?"

Lola began to get anxious and waved her arms. "Okay, this has gone far enough," she said. "Honestly, we'll deal with it. We can take care of ourselves."

"You asked for my help."

"Yeah, but we didn't know you were going to set light to someone," said Lola. "I can't be a part of that."

"You told me they shot your friend in the face?" Harvey held the bottle above Cannon Bill's head.

"They did," said Lola. "But, no, please don't do that."

"And you told me you can't go home because of the tag on your wrist."

Cannon Bill looked up at Harvey, his eyes wide with fear but masked with anger. Harvey had seen the look a thousand times and returned the stare. He squeezed the bottle. A stream of the flammable fluid ran onto Bill's face and soaked the newspaper stuffed inside his clothes.

"Fingers," said Harvey.

"What?"

"Can you count?" asked Harvey.

"Of course I can count."

"So count down from ten."

"No way. I'm not going to be a part of this."

"You *are* a part of this. Do you want me to let them go? Because I honestly don't mind. It won't be me they come after. You asked me to take care of them. Now I'm taking care of them."

Fingers stood open-mouthed.

"Count," said Harvey.

Fingers looked across at Lola, who turned her face away in horror, then nodded.

Harvey's eyes never left Fingers'. He held his gaze, unblinking even with the fire smoke, until Fingers gave in.

"Ten," he said softly.

"Where?" asked Harvey. He focused on his captive, but received no reply.

With a deft sweep of his wrist, he renewed the circle of flammable liquid around Cannon Bill.

Bill held his mouth closed, making it clear that he wouldn't talk.

"Nine," said Fingers.

Harvey smiled. "The thing you don't know about me is that I don't *want* to know where they are."

"Eight."

"I don't *need* you to tell me."

"Seven."

"I *want* to watch you burn."

"Stop this," said Lola.

"Six."

"I *love* to watch people burn," said Harvey. He doused the big man in fuel once more.

"Five."

"Fuck you," spat Cannon Bill.

"There it is. *There's* the anger," said Harvey.

"Four." Fingers was sounding nervous, but he continued the countdown.

"I won't tell you *anything*. You're going to have to burn me alive."

"Three."

"I cannot wait," said Harvey.

"No more," screamed Lola. "Just put it down. Everyone, just stop."

"Two."

"Last chance, Mr Cannon," said Harvey.

"No," pleaded Lola. "No more."

"One."

Mad Bob's phone began to vibrate inside Harvey's pocket.

CHAPTER ELEVEN

"Bob?" said Rupert. "Where are you?"

Mad Bob didn't reply.

"Bob, it's Rupert. Listen, do me a favour and steer clear of the little tart. I need her in one piece. So whatever you do, don't listen to my brother. Do not scare her off. Do you understand me?"

Silence.

"*Bob?* Can you hear me?"

Suddenly the tiny speaker inside the phone roared into life with the agonised screams of what sounded like a wild animal.

"Bob? What are you doing?"

Rupert held the phone away from his ear and gave his brother a confused look.

"What's wrong?" asked Charlie. "What's that bloody noise? I can hear it from here."

Rupert began to shout into the phone. "Bob? Answer me."

The shrieks grew louder and came in waves, as if whoever was screaming was writhing and rolling on the floor.

Then somebody spoke above the din, calm and controlled. "Which one are you?" asked the voice.

Rupert was appalled at the audacity of whoever the man was. His heart surged into overtime, and his face began to turn bright red.

He was too angry to even think about words.

"You need to stay away, and call your pet dogs off," said the voice.

The screaming began to die down, but panicked breathing and whimpering could still be heard. The noise had an echo, as if they were in a hard-walled room with no carpet or curtains. It was the old factory Mad Bob had mentioned. Rupert was sure of it.

"You're trying to trace where I am," said the voice. "Don't bother. I'll be gone."

"Who are you?" asked Rupert.

There was a pause as if the man was considering his response. "A man who doesn't like bullies."

"Are they dead?" asked Rupert. "My men?"

Charlie placed a crystal cut tumbler of scotch on his brother's desk. The lamplight formed ornate amber-coloured shadows that seemed to rock back and forth on the surface of the wood, before slowing to a stop.

"No," came the reply. "Not yet. Their lives depend on what you say next."

"What I say next, my friend, depends on the question, doesn't it?" replied Rupert.

"There's no question."

"So I'll say nothing."

"Then they die."

Rupert heard the inhale of a sharp breath when the words were spoken, distant, as if someone stood beside the man.

"You're with the girl."

There was no reply.

"Listen, pal," said Rupert. "I don't know who you are, and I don't know how you're involved, but you're muddying some very unsavoury waters. You have no idea who you are dealing with."

"If I wanted to know who you were, I'd have asked, wouldn't I?"

Rupert considered this comment.

The man continued. "And if I was worried about muddying waters, savoury or otherwise, I wouldn't be involved, would I?"

Rupert remained silent.

"And if was scared of who you might be, and what the consequences were, I wouldn't have burned your bloke's face off, would I?"

Rupert closed his eyes. "You burnt his face off?" he asked quietly. "Which one?"

"The one with the big mouth."

Rupert mouthed Mad Bob's name to Charlie, who was busy on his phone. He nodded in reply and continued to round the men up by messaging each of them.

"So what now?" asked Rupert.

"You let the girl go, I let your dogs go, you won't hear from me again, and the girl doesn't hear from you again."

"Oh no," said Rupert. "You see, we have a reputation to uphold. What would the world think if they found out we just let someone like you show up out of the blue, mess with our plans, and then disappear? Imagine what it would do to our credibility."

"So your boys die then."

The call disconnected.

Panicked, Rupert hit redial. His heart pounded. Rage soared through him.

The call was answered, but no greeting came.

Rupert swallowed his drink in one hit and placed the glass back on the table. "Do you think they're the only men we have working for us?"

"Probably not. But you trust them, more so than the rest."

"They're good men," said Rupert. "I've known them a long time."

"Are they worth a diamond?" the voice asked.

"No," replied Rupert. "But I'd gladly give the man that cuts your throat half of what it's worth."

There was no reply. Rupert heard the shuffling of boots on concrete. Mad Bob's whimpers grew louder in the phone and then a sickly gargle of another man choking on his own blood was clear as day in Rupert's ear. It was a sound he'd heard a dozen times before.

"My guess is that you've got every man you can spare on their way here right now," said the man.

Rupert stayed silent.

"You won't find *me*, so you won't bother looking."

"Is that right?" said Rupert. He raised the glass for Charlie to refill then signed with his finger across his neck that Mad Bob was dead.

"It ends now," the man continued. "Life goes on. I'll spare Mr Cannon here. He's having a rough night."

"No, son," said Rupert. "That is where you are wrong. You have, in fact, just entered a whole world of pain, and when I get my hands on you, you're going to find out what pain is." Rupert let his words sink in. "Do *you* understand *me*?"

"I understand you clear enough," replied the voice. There was a noise of movement on the phone, sudden and violent. The girl screamed and howled louder than before, and another man began shouting, but Rupert couldn't make out what he was saying.

The gargling sound faded to a stop.

Rupert didn't speak. He knew that Cannon Bill had just been killed. He pictured the scene. Lola LaRoux still screamed, and she had begun to cry hysterically with loud sobs and the heavy, anxious breathing of a child.

A silence fell between the two men until Rupert could finally bear it no more.

"You just started a war, mate."

CHAPTER TWELVE

The fishbowl was the nickname that one particular team of secret intelligence operatives gave to the small glass meeting space at one end of their operations room. Inside was a small table with four seats. The corners of the ceiling had foam cubes to prevent echo and the glass was half an inch thick and sound-proof. Outside in the operations room, along the length of one wall were three banks of wall-mounted monitors, below which sat a row of tech researchers, including Reg's girlfriend, Jess.

Behind them in the centre of the room were logistics, comms, and team leads, all lost in their own worlds and oblivious to the very secret investigation with which Melody had been tasked.

Melody pulled the blinds down in the fishbowl, while Reg laid out the CAD files of the Natural History Museum.

"Impressive, isn't it?" said Melody, catching Reg admiring the detail that had gone into the drawings. "They were all transferred to digital a few years ago when the museum was extended," she began. "I can only guess that the thieves have the same drawings."

Reg smiled at her.

"Welcome back to crime fighting, Mr Tenant," said Melody. Then she turned her attention to the plans. "Right, well as far as I can tell the diamond is held in this room." She indicated to a small alcove of the museum's main gallery on the drawing. "We'll need to go there to identify the actual placement, but we can see on this MEP drawing that there's network cabling to this point here and this point here, both at high level." Melody indicated the spots on the technical drawing with an immaculate fingernail.

"CCTV probably shares the same cabling," said Reg.

"I think so too," said Melody. "But we need to be sure. I believe the museum also has a state-of-the-art firefighting system that runs off both network cabling and the original copper wiring."

"So that's the room. But what we need to find out are the entry points and the security weaknesses," said Reg. "They may have gotten into the old house to steal the first diamond, but this is the Natural History Museum. It's going to be virtually impossible to get in there and get out with one of the most expensive diamonds in the world."

"So we have the where. Now we need to work out the how and the who," said Melody. "The how is both the logistics and the technical aspect. Are you able to hack into the museum security? Could you give me a breakdown of what you can control and what you can't?"

"Yeah, I did that already," replied Reg. "I've still got a bit more to do, but as far as I can see, there's two or three layers to the security."

"Two layers?"

"Yeah, think of it as two networks," Reg explained. "The first layer is the public layer. It uses a network of fibre and category six cabling around the building. This is where the wireless access points will broadcast free internet access to the public, and where the screens around the museum will be fed the video feeds from media servers."

"Isn't that what the CCTV runs off too?" asked Melody. She had located the network of cabling that Reg was talking about.

"Nearly," he replied. "The next level is the CCTV and alarm systems for the displays. These will utilise the same back-bone infrastructure as the public-facing devices, but they'll be segregated at the switch level."

"Switch level?" asked Melody. "Less technical please."

"Okay, so imagine all the devices, wireless, alarms, CCTV, everything running to a single room on each floor, and they're all connected to one device; this is called a switch. In this instance, it's not just one switch. We're talking about thirty or forty switches."

"Thirty or forty?"

"Well, yeah. There's so many devices out on the museum floor that you'd need thirty or forty switches to connect them."

"Okay," said Melody. "I'm kind of getting that."

"Okay, so each switch or set of switches is controlled by a security interface. This segregates the devices into separate networks based on their function. So you could have all the CCTV cameras in one network, all the wireless access points in another-"

"Okay, I see where you're going," said Melody. "So all the devices essentially use the same cabling, but they are cordoned off at the switch."

"Exactly. That leads me to the second layer in the security design," said Reg. "The private network. We have the public network with all the WIFI and media stuff, then we need a secure network for the CCTV and alarm sensors, which are all fed to the security control room."

"Where is the security control room?" asked Melody.

"At basement level." Reg lifted the ground floor set of drawings and circled the security room on the basement level with a well-bitten fingernail.

"So that's where they control the alarms?" asked Melody.

"Yep," replied Reg, "the alarms, the sensors, the cameras, you name it, if it's security based it'll be controlled from in there."

"So you think our thieves will hit the control room?"

"I don't see that they have any other option. There's not many people that could get through the layers of security from the public network, so it'd be easier for them to take control of the control room, probably quicker too."

"Not many?" asked Melody. "So it *is* possible then?"

"Oh, it's possible. But there's only one man I know that could do that without triggering the alarms."

"One man?" asked Melody.

"Me," said Reg with a smile. "But I'm not going to be the one that robs the Natural History Museum."

CHAPTER THIRTEEN

"How are you feeling?" asked Fingers.

Lola raised her head a little and sighed.

"Like I just saw the love of my life shot in the face, and was then threatened with death or prison."

"What did the Bond Brothers say about Mad Bob and Cannon Bill exactly?"

Lola sensed he was trying to take her mind off the Dynamite incident.

"Do you want the long version or the short version?"

"Short first," said Fingers.

"I told them we don't know who the bloke was-"

"Which we don't."

"Right, he just came out of nowhere. I told them he must have been homeless or something," said Lola.

"Okay and they believed you?"

"I don't know, but it's true. We don't who he was."

"And what about the other diamond?"

"They still want it. They said that they'd decide what happens to us once they have it, and see how well the job goes."

"And what about the bloke?" asked Fingers. "Are they going after him?"

"They won't stop until they find him, Fingers."

"Do you think he'll come?"

"I told him where to find us, but I doubt it. I mean, would you?"

"How much did you offer him?" asked Fingers.

"We didn't talk about money. Somehow, I think he's not the type to be motivated by cash. I think he has other issues."

"You think? Lola, he set fire to Mad Bob's face. How else would you explain that?"

"Anyway," said Lola, "I doubt he'll come. I'm glad he was there, and that he stepped in, but-"

Her thoughts trailed off to Dynamite.

Fingers was silent for a while, choosing to take the dirty plates and cups to the tiny kitchenette at one end of the little houseboat. He returned to the small living area and hovered over Lola.

"Where did you get all this lot from?" he asked, as he ran his hands across the rolls of paper stood upended against the wall of the houseboat.

Lola glanced back from the window above her then saw Fingers was referring to the rolls of technical drawings. "I borrowed them," she said distractedly. She returned her attention to the huge sheet of paper spread across the small dining table. She held a magnifying glass over the paper and traced the tiny lines that represented the security network.

"Have you come up with a plan yet?" asked Fingers. "Time is running out you know."

"So why don't you help?" said Lola. "I'm here tracing networks and security, and you're sat there waiting for a diamond to fall out of the sky."

"'Tracing networks?" said Fingers. "Don't be silly. I've done all that. It's easy, even easier than that soppy old bloke's house."

"Easier?" said Lola. "This is going to be bloody dangerous. I do not want you thinking it's easy and relaxing; I want you to be worried. In fact, I want you to think one hundred percent of the time about how bloody hard this is going to be."

"Alright, alright," said Fingers. "Get me close, connect a laptop to the internal network and I'm away. From there, I'll need about ten minutes."

"'Ten minutes?"

"Yep, I told you, it's easier than you think. Just because there's a bloody great diamond inside, doesn't mean to say that it's any more secure than anywhere else," said Fingers. "In fact, it's not the digital security I'd be worried about. I'd have said the physical security is a bit trickier."

Lola nodded.

"I agree. There's five guards there at any one time, and another God knows how many close by."

"Apparently there are a few paintings on the walls that are worth an absolute mint," said Fingers.

"Not to mention the antique vases and statuettes," said Lola.

"Are we going to be taking anything else? You know make the trip worthwhile?" asked Fingers.

"No," said Lola. "Absolutely not. We get the diamond and we get out."

"Not even a nice little something to hang over the fireplace?"

Lola gave him a severe look. "I'm not doing this for money, Fingers," she said. "I'm doing this for Dynamite."

"And your freedom," Fingers reminded her.

Lola subconsciously rubbed the tag on her wrist. It weighed on her as if it were made of lead and hanging around her neck. "If we're caught doing this, Fingers-"

"I know, I know. We'll be fed to the wolves."

"We have a chance though, right?" she asked.

"Of pulling this off?" replied Fingers. "Yeah. Look, if you can get me access to the internal network, I'll need a few minutes to crack the security, and then I'll open the whole thing up. Once I've done that, I'll have access to the security console. The only question is how big the window is for you to get in and out."

"Don't worry. I have an idea about that."

"Sounds ominous."

"What's the minimum window you can give me?" asked Lola.

"Honestly?" said Fingers. "How's zero?"

"I won't know until I'm in."

Footsteps on the boardwalk above caught their attention. They saw the boots of their mystery saviour walking slowly along the length of the boat through the narrow portholes. The door opened with a slight creak, and two thuds of heavy boots resonated through the boat's wooden floor.

"I'm in," said the man. "Where and when?"

Lola felt a wash of relief run through her, but kept her eyes on her work. "I'd greet you, but you haven't told us your name yet," she said, without looking up.

Fingers edged away from the man and tucked himself into the corner of the sofa and against the wall behind him.

"Is this your boat?" asked the man.

"Does it matter?" Lola replied.

"Depends, doesn't it?" he said, as he stepped into the dining area. He seemed to loom over the room. His presence almost cast a shadow, though the grey sky outside cast little in the form of daylight.

Lola's eyes followed his until they felt like they would roll around in her head. She leaned back in her seat to get a better view of him and folded her arms.

"Depends on what?" she asked.

"Well, if you're planning to rob the Natural History Museum using a house boat that doesn't belong to you, the plan poses an element of risk that we don't need."

"It's mine," said Fingers. "It's where I live."

The man nodded, and eyed the kitchen mess.

"We?" Lola asked the man. "So you're now including yourself in this, are you?"

"You asked for my help," he said. "I came."

Lola remained silent. She studied his gestures and expressions, a skill Dynamite had taught her, to learn what really goes on inside someone's mind. The man had no tell signs.

"Harvey," he said suddenly.

"Harvey?" Lola repeated.

"Harvey Stone."

Lola repeated the name over and over in her mind. She was sure she hadn't heard it before, but it was strong name, a reliable name.

"It is Fingers' boat," said Lola. "We're safe here."

"Are you being watched?" asked Harvey.

"By who?"

"The brothers," said Harvey. "I'm pretty sure they'll have eyes on you, and will be waiting for me to arrive."

"So?" said Lola.

"So, I won't stay long," said Harvey. He turned to leave. "I just came to tell you I'm in. Tell me where and when." He paused. "You do still want my help?"

Lola's lips clamped the tip of her tongue in thought.

She nodded.

"Tomorrow afternoon. Five o'clock. Meet us at the junction of Denmark Hill and Daneville Road."

He nodded in reply, pushed the door open, and took a step outside.

"Harvey," said Lola, just as he ducked his head. He turned to face her. "Thanks."

He gave her a thoughtful look, nodded once, then left.

Fingers watched Harvey's boots walk back past the houseboat. He waited until Harvey was out of sight before speaking. "You really think he'll help us?"

"Gut feeling?" asked Lola. "Yes, I do."

"Why?" asked Fingers. "Why would someone get involved in something like this? And how can we trust him?"

"I don't know Fingers, but if we can deliver the diamond *and* him, I think we might just get out of this alive."

CHAPTER FOURTEEN

A narrow footpath ran alongside the canal so Harvey took it, preferring the peace and tranquillity of the waterway to the honking of horns and perpetual rumble of engines and traffic on the main roads. Two women pushed babies in prams. A cyclist rode by, and a jogger ran lightly past him. How normal people's lives were, thought Harvey. Most people had complications, of course. He knew that; he wasn't naive. But the complications of everyday people were usually along the lines of earning rent money, paying bills, fighting over custody of a child, or maybe, going to a workplace they hate every day and spending the smallest amount of time at home with loved ones before going to bed, only to do it all again the next day.

Harvey knew he was lucky not to be bogged down by such complications. But normality still appealed to him somehow. In the factory, he could have just stayed out of the girl's troubles. He could have just ignored the two men as they crept across the factory floor. He hadn't even needed to kill them. But it was who he was. Something had taken over him.

Killing was what he was good at.

Harvey took a seat on a bench while thoughts rolled around

his mind. The bench looked like the type of place that the local authorities had installed so that families could sit and feed the ducks. Instead, it had turned out to be a place where local kids could sit and get high without the prying eyes of parents.

The two women with prams walked past, deep in conversation. They took slow steps as if they had all the time in the world or too much to say and not enough distance to say it. They looked happy. Harvey watched them and couldn't help but think of Melody. They were supposed to have their wedding soon. Harvey knew that she'd wanted to have children as soon as they were married.

He pictured Melody in the place of one of the mums.

She would have been a good mother. Hopefully, she still will be one day, thought Harvey. But he doubted his own suitability to be a dad. A kid shouldn't have to grow up with a father who had spent most of his life as a hitman for a crime firm, and the rest of it on the good side of the law. But still killing. He was cold-blooded.

How could he possibly raise a child?

During the three months Harvey had been lying low, he'd had a lot of time to think, and to contemplate his future.

His decision to leave the crime world behind and live alone on his farm in France with a simple routine had been the outcome of many dark nights walking the rain or staring at the ceiling of his bedsit. But there had always been something gnawing at the thought. He knew what it was. It was a phrase he'd said to Melody once to describe how killing had made him feel.

"I enjoy it," he said aloud to himself. His voice sounded loud in contrast to his thoughts.

"*Excuse me?*" said one of the women as they strolled past.

The woman's voice shook Harvey from his daydream. His reaction was to offer a weak smile and wave the comment away as nothing. They walked on with furtive glances over their shoulders at the man sat talking to himself on the bench where kids get high.

"I enjoy it, and it's what I'm good at," Harvey said again. He repeated the words as if saying them aloud was somehow more convincing than losing them in the jumble of thoughts in his head.

"You've got talent," said a memory, somewhere distant in a dark corner. But this time it wasn't his own. "You're unique, Son. Don't waste it."

It was the voice of his foster father, words he'd spoken many times.

Harvey had been training with Julios in the gym at the back of their grand house in the Essex countryside. He had loved that gym. It had everything he needed to train with floor-to-ceiling glazing around the entire room. Even on the dullest of days, when the grey sky felt just a few inches out of reach, the gym had been full of light with no shadows.

Nowhere to hide.

John Cartwright made a habit of watching Julios train Harvey, while sat on the sun beds around the pool and holding a brandy between his fat fingers. When Harvey had developed into a strong sixteen-year-old, with two kills under his belt, John had watched and praised the boy's progress. When they'd finished training, all Harvey had wanted to do was to sit and eat with Julios and listen to a story of when his mentor was young. It was Harvey's favourite time of the day.

One time, they stepped from the gym, both boy and mentor glazed in sweat, and John had put his arm around his foster son and stolen the moment from Julios and Harvey. The mentor was made to stay behind and clean up. Instead of tales of Portuguese back streets and fishing on the Mediterranean,

Harvey had to sit with his foster father and listen to his dreams of what Harvey might be.

Harvey didn't need to hear the praise, he didn't need the push, and he didn't need any more direction. His path had been set in stone. He thought like a beast, with cunning and foresight, and he trained like a beast, with relentless vigour. Harvey had been building a pool of stamina to call upon when Julios pushed him to the edge. He knew he'd already become a beast.

"You're going to be a dangerous man when you get bigger, Harvey," John had said, as they'd sat in the kitchen eating.

In his mind, Harvey had recalled how he'd reached out from the darkness and slit his second victim's Achilles tendon before standing over the much older man.

"I can see it, you know?" continued John, as he shovelled carrots into his mouth. "I can see it in your eyes. And if you follow my advice, do what I say, you'll be feared throughout London. Maybe even further, who knows?"

Harvey chewed his vegetables. He avoided eye contact with his foster father, but let his mind continue to cast images in horrific flashes. First, there had been the boy from school, the sex pest who Harvey had hunted, found, and then slaughtered. Then came Jack, one of John's men. Julios had accompanied Harvey that time. He'd stood in the shadows and watched Harvey bring his own flavour of retribution to the sick man who'd raped Harvey's sister.

"You see," John explained, ignoring the fact that Harvey hadn't replied once. "Some people in this world are born to sit in an office. Some are born to help others, like nurses and doctors. But some, Harvey Stone, are born to even the odds. These people aren't bad people. But if the world didn't have them, and the rest of the men were left to their own devices, well, it wouldn't be safe to walk the streets. They bring balance to the world."

Harvey pictured himself walking the dark alleyways as he often did at the weekends, seeking lowlife to practice what Julios had taught him. He made himself a potential victim of a crime and waited to be attacked so he could unleash his skills.

"You're one of those people, Harvey," said John. "You're special. Some might even say unique."

Harvey imagined what the Bond Brothers might look like. He knew their type; he'd been around people like that all his life. Too much money, inflated egos, and somehow they'd earned respect. He knew they fed off fear, all bullies did. Harvey also knew that they wouldn't stop looking for him. They might find him today, tomorrow or a year from now, but one day the episode would catch up with him. Unless he stopped them.

Harvey felt John's eyes burning into him.

"Don't waste it," said Harvey aloud.

Further along the towpath at the exact location he'd been given, Harvey climbed down the few steps to a small wooden boardwalk. The canal cut through the neighbourhood. It acted as a dividing line between the old run-down factories on one side and the new-build apartment blocks on the other. The entrance to the dock was over a small footbridge spanning the gap adjacent to an old lock. Manicured lawns and trimmed bushes bordered the quiet private roads and parking bays that stood between the residential buildings.

He pushed open the door to one houseboat and ducked inside to find Lola and Fingers poring over building blueprints. The boat smelled of damp wood and greasy food, likely from the used pans and plates in the kitchenette.

Fingers averted his eyes when Harvey looked his way, and Lola kept her head down, engrossed in the plans.

"I'm in," said Harvey. "Where and when?"

CHAPTER FIFTEEN

"We seem to have a dilemma," said Charlie to his brother. They were sat in the back seat of their Bentley. Both wore dark blue suits with white shirts. The only differentiator was the colour of their accessories. Rupert wore a yellow pocket-handkerchief and tie, while Charlie had opted for a light blue.

"There's no dilemma, Charlie," said Rupert. "Merely plans to be made."

"We need to act, bro. We can't be seen sitting on our laurels while some nutter out there gets away with killing Mad Bob and Cannon Bill. It won't take long for word to get about."

Rupert stared out of the window as the streets rolled by. It always pleased him to see the dozens of small businesses that fell under his and his brother's protection. They had control over what was potentially a rough neighbourhood, and while petty crimes still existed as they would anywhere, most of the serious crime was dealt with swiftly and sharply.

"This is our manor, Charlie," said Rupert. "Look at it. Look how peaceful it is. When was the last time we ever had to step in and take care of anything here?"

"I don't know," replied Charlie. "Months ago, I guess. That bloke that tried to rob the betting shop, wasn't it?"

"Yeah, it was. I remember. But look how safe it is now. Look at that woman there on her own with her kids and all that shopping. A few years ago, she would have been ripe for a mugging. Nobody would have dared to walk down the high street with designer shopping bags. Even the teenagers on the corner of the street don't yell abuse at anyone who walks past. Can you remember what it was like, Charlie?" said Rupert. "Can you remember how diabolically crap this place was before we took over?"

"I remember, Rupert. But what are you saying?"

"I'm saying it's a bloody miracle, Charlie. That's what I'm saying." Rupert straightened his tie for the twentieth time and pulled his cuffs from his sleeves. "I'm saying that when all this is over, how long will it be before this place goes back to how it used to be? When women couldn't walk the streets without fear of being mugged or worse, and shopkeepers had to worry about being robbed every week just so some junkie could get his fix."

"Why are you dead set on leaving then?" asked Charlie.

"When I go, I want to leave a legacy. I want to leave this place better than how we found it. You know what I mean?"

Charlie gazed out of his own window with contempt as a scruffy old woman in slippers and a cheap coat with a cigarette hanging from her mouth stepped out of Better Odds betting shop.

"I couldn't care less what happens to these people, Rupert," he said. "What I care about, bruv, and something I think you've lost sight of is that somebody set light to Mad Bob's face and slit Cannon Bill's throat. And that certain somebody is out there somewhere thinking he can have one over on the Bond Brothers."

Rupert stared from his window in silence.

"What is it, Rupert?" asked Charlie. "Have you lost your bottle, or what?"

Rupert tore himself from the view of his world and turned to face his brother. "What do you reckon we should do then, Charlie, eh?" he said. "Why don't you tell me your master plan? You seem to be full of thought-provoking suggestions this morning."

"I don't care about thought-provoking suggestions, Rupert. Not when I know that scumbag is out there. I don't even need a plan. We get the boys to put the word out to find him and set light to him. See how he bloody likes it."

"Good plan, Charlie," said Rupert. "But it is those brash decisions that you are so fond of that wind up getting us into bother."

"Right and I suppose you have a master plan, do you? I suppose you plan to find him and give him a cuddle and a pocket full of cash and ask him politely to leave?"

"So what happens if we do find him?" asked Rupert. "We have the boys kick the crap out of him, maybe drag him round to Mad Bob's house so his family can have their say, and then to Cannon Bill's?"

Rupert paused and let the image run through his brother's mind.

"Then what?" continued Rupert. "You just scare the hell out of the girl, and she does a runner. Maybe worse, she calls the old bill."

"So what?" said Charlie. "Who cares about the girl?"

"So then here's what happens. The girl calls the old bill and the heat gets put on us, maybe they put the heat on someone a little more fragile than us, such as Smokey or Doctor Feelmore, and maybe the old bill finds the diamond."

"They can't prove it was us. We never stole it. None of our prints are on it," said Charlie.

"Even so, maybe the old bill turns the heat up anyway. Then maybe it starts getting harder to do business here. Maybe the police even start letting some other firm in, offering them more favourable deals. And then what? People begin to take the piss, Charlie, that's what."

Charlie shook his head and turned away as Rupert carried on.

"And even if none of that happens, even if the old bill don't come, and they don't find the diamond, and it's business as usual, by hitting the nutter that killed Mad Bob, you are going to scare the life out of the girl. And guess what?"

"What?" said Charlie, uninterested.

"She won't nick the other diamond for us, will she?"

"We'll sort her out too then. We'll hit them both together," offered Charlie.

"Don't be a moron, Charlie. If you hit her, she won't be nicking nothing. If you hit him, she won't be nicking nothing. If you hit either of them, we don't get the other diamond."

"The diamond?" said Charlie. He faced his brother. "The bloke just killed two of our best men, and all you can think about is the diamond."

"Charlie, the bloke just killed two of our men, yes. But, if we play this right, not only can we get our hands on the other diamond and leave this wonderful place behind, but we can also take care of the bloke, take care of the girl, and live happily ever fucking after. But mark my words Charlie; he will die a very slow and very painful death."

"You live in the clouds, Rupert. You know that?"

"I live in a world that I created, Charlie. A world where those who plan, live longest."

The car pulled to a stop in a bus lane in West London.

"And what is it we're doing here?" asked Charlie. "Another part of the master plan, is it?"

"I sometimes wonder how we actually have the same parents, let alone come from a single egg," said Rupert. "This building here is the Natural History Museum."

"What are we doing here?"

Rupert opened the car door and placed one polished brogue on the ground.

"We are learning, Charlie. That is what we're doing. Learning and planning."

CHAPTER SIXTEEN

"So that's it, is it?" asked Melody. "I thought it'd be bigger."

She sidestepped to allow a man and his two children to exit the small alcove where the diamond was displayed.

"Its reputation is bigger than this museum, Melody," said Reg. "Besides, it's not how big it is, it's what you do with it that counts."

"And what exactly would you do with that?"

The small alcove somehow shielded much of the ambient noise from the main gallery where the herds of schoolchildren and gaggles of tourists roamed free, so they were able to speak quietly.

"Retire," said Reg. "Tomorrow."

"You'd be even more bored than you are now," replied Melody. "I remember when you were signed off for two weeks after the Athens job, and you were on the phone every five minutes."

"I have an active mind, Melody. It needs stimulation. But I tell you what; I reckon I could stimulate my mind on a beach in the Maldives pretty well."

Melody gave a little laugh. "The Maldives, yeah?"

"Something like that. Somewhere warm with diet coke on tap and soft sand to rest my weary bones."

"Well before you get carried away with dreams of resting those weary bones of yours, Reg, how about you help me figure out this display cabinet?"

"That's easy," replied Reg.

He rested his hands on top of the glass. The lone Demonios Gemelos diamond sat encased in a small, round glass display unit resembling an upside down fish tank. It sat on an ornate pedestal as if it were a bust of Julios Caesar.

"See these?" said Reg, pointing at three small clips on the inside of the display. They looked as if they fixed the soft velvet cushion to the inside of the glass.

"Yeah, the clips?" said Melody.

"Not clips, Melody. These are sensors." He bent his knees to get a closer look. See in here, look, you can just see the ends of the two wires. Each of those three clips has a pair of wires that feed to the middle of the display beneath the cushion. They then run down the middle of the pedestal and into the floor void, where I imagine there are three separate alarm circuits."

"Three?" asked Melody. "Wouldn't they just run into one circuit?"

Reg stood from his crouch.

"No, that's the idea of having a round display," he explained. "There's no way on earth to lift one side of the display without triggering at least one other sensor."

"So if someone were to disable one sensor, surely they could disable the others?"

"They could, but the sensors won't be together and they aren't marked on the drawing as part of a display. Plus, displays move, right?"

"Right," said Melody. "So where are the sensors' alarm systems?"

"They'll be small black boxes," said Reg. "Each one of them will be connected to the private data circuit which is-"

"Security layer two," said Melody.

"And they'll also be connected to two power supplies running active passive."

"Active passive?" asked Melody.

"If the active power supply cuts out, the passive supply takes over. The sensor is down for less than two or three seconds."

"But doesn't that trigger the alarm? Surely the sensors are in contact with the security system?" asked Melody.

"Yes, but there's typically a tolerance to take into consideration the cut over between power supplies."

"So effectively, a thief would need to cut both power supplies on all three sensors to give themselves a two-second window to open the cabinet and steal the diamond?"

"Yes. But the diamond is also likely resting on a sensor of its own, which is held in place by its weight."

"Another sensor?" asked Melody.

"Any variation in weight within a given tolerance triggers a separate alarm." Reg smiled at the sheer genius of it. "And that's if they even manage to get into the building. This place has more security than Buckingham Palace."

Melody stepped around the display, her eyes never leaving the thousands of sparkles produced by the innocent-looking diamond.

"How would you do it?" she asked eventually.

"Me?" said Reg. "I wouldn't."

Melody gave him a glare. "If you had to?"

Reg began to play the scene out in his head. He looked up at the camera behind him then stared down at the floor and around the room at the other artefacts on display.

An ancient skull belonging to an African Masai warrior stared at him from behind the glass of a much taller display.

Various forms of early axes and stone tools had been carefully placed nearby. But the skull was the centrepiece. In another cabinet were carved items including tiny stones, hewn to a particular shape to suit a specific purpose. There were also small bird bones that had been used as awls centuries ago.

"Three tech guys," said Reg at last. "Three tech guys, two hard men to deal with physical security, and one man with balls of steel."

"So you're saying the thieves have six men?" asked Melody.

"No, but you asked how I would do it. Three tech guys, one for the power, one for the security, and one for the CCTV. I wouldn't even bother trying to disarm the alarms from here. They're all under the floor."

"You'd override the security and the power?"

"Easiest way. Once I get access to the remote security site, it's a doddle," said Reg. "The problem is that you still need to get inside the building and into the security control room, and you'd need to take care of the secondary security."

"Can't somebody guide the intruder using the CCTV?"

"For a while. But they'd need to shut the CCTV down. There's no way of knowing who else would be monitoring it."

Melody stood still, deep in thought.

"There used to be a diamond exhibition here at the museum, you know?" said Reg.

"There did?" said Melody. "I don't remember that."

"It was only open for a few months. Apparently the museum had some backlash from protesters about African tribes being forced out of their homes to make way for diamond mining."

"So they shut the exhibition down?"

"Well, shortly after that, the Metropolitan Police advised them to shut it due to increased risk of criminal activity," explained Reg.

"Increased risk-"

"Of criminal activity," finished Reg. "That's when they upgraded the security here. Makes me wonder if it's the same mob?"

"So what we're dealing with here is a group of highly-skilled criminals," said Melody. "That narrows the suspects down."

"Potentially, yes. However, most known villains that are even remotely capable of pulling this off are either dead or already in prison," said Reg. "I can't see it being done."

"Oh, it'll be done alright," said Melody. She was transfixed by the diamond. "If they have one of these already, there's no way they'll leave the other behind."

CHAPTER SEVENTEEN

"Here, Charlie," said Rupert. "Get Glasgow George on the phone, will you?"

"Glasgow?" replied Charlie. "It's eleven o'clock in the morning; he'll be in the pub by now having a liquid breakfast."

"Just do it, and trust me, will you?"

Charlie carried on walking, pulled his phone from his pocket, found Glasgow George's number and hit dial. "Do you want to talk to him, or should I?" asked Charlie. But Rupert wasn't beside him.

He'd stopped beside a display of some early hunting knives from around the globe, and feigned interest in a long curved blade of Damascus steel with a heavy wooden sheath.

Charlie stopped and took the few steps back to his brother with the phone in his outstretched hand.

"You talk to him," said Rupert. "I can never understand what he's bloody saying."

Charlie shook his head and put the phone to his ear. "What am I asking him?" he asked.

Rupert's eyes were focused on a man and woman stood either side of a large diamond in an ornate glass cabinet inside a small alcove off the main gallery. Above the arched entrance to the room was a model of an African tribesman and a sign with two words printed on it.

Demonios Gemelos.

Charlie followed Rupert's gaze and put the pieces together for himself. Rupert was transfixed.

"George?" said Charlie, breaking the tense silence that had built up in a few short seconds. "It's Charlie."

Rupert could hear the Scotsman's angry and slurred tone even from a few feet away.

"Yeah, yeah," said Charlie. "Listen, you remember the girl from the other night?"

Rupert watched as the man crouched beside the cabinet and seemed to gesture to beneath the floor.

"Yes, George, the diamond girl," said Charlie. "Do you want to say it any louder? There's a small tribe in a yet undiscovered part of the Amazon rainforest that didn't quite hear you."

Rupert listened to the one-sided conversation, but his eyes were fixed on the girl. She was looking up at the ceiling, perhaps checking the security cameras.

"What did she look like?" asked Charlie.

Rupert's eyes bore into the pair stood beside the diamond, picking up every little detail of their faces.

"Small," said Charlie, out loud for Rupert's benefit. "With long dark hair, and a face you'd want to take home to your mum."

It was her.

"And the bloke?" asked Charlie.

Rupert stared at the girl. She had a confidence in her manner and moved with the fluidity of a dancer.

"No, not the one you shot in the face. The other one."

Rupert turned his attention to the male.

"Short," said Charlie. "And skinny with glasses. Apparently, he looks like he needs a good meal."

"That's them," said Rupert.

Charlie disconnected the call and pocketed his phone.

"Shall we take a look?" asked Rupert with a raised eyebrow.

The two men strode into the small room, which somehow seemed to block all the ambient noise from the gallery outside. Charlie stood looking at the head of an ancient axe, while Rupert made his way to the cabinet that displayed smaller tools made from bone and rock.

He edged closer to hear the hushed discussion the pair were having, but could make out nothing. Charlie, who also feigned interest in the small rocks and bones, soon joined him.

"Three thousand years old," said Rupert.

"How do they know that?" asked Charlie. "They could have found that last week. The caretaker probably hit a bird with his car and put it in here as an exhibit."

Rupert didn't respond to his brother's retort.

He was watching the girl in the reflection of the display. It seemed to him that the dynamics of the conversation switched between the girl leading and the man taking control as if they were equals. Rupert moved closer still and studied the diamond in the glass cabinet from a few meters away.

"Shall we go and take a look around?" said the girl. "I haven't been here for years."

They slipped out of the small room and into the main gallery.

Rupert stepped out after them.

The ambient noise returned as if a switch had just been flicked, and a combination of smells hit him. The place smelled like a dusty attic with a hint of fried food.

He watched the pair walk away. They didn't look back. They didn't hold hands or link arms. All the time, the girl seemed to be glancing up at the huge expanse of ceiling forty meters above, as if checking for security cameras.

"Are you sure that's them?" asked Charlie, who had silently joined his brother at his side.

"Positive," said Rupert.

"I thought you wanted them left alone?"

"I do," replied Rupert. "But it's nice to know what they actually look like."

"You know," began Charlie, in a rare moment of reflection, "in the olden days, we'd of hacked their heads off and put them up on spikes so everyone would know not to mess with us."

Rupert gave a little smile. He enjoyed the fact that the only piece of interesting knowledge his brother could offer was on the subject of violence.

"Maybe when we've got the diamonds, that's what we'll do," offered Rupert.

Charlie's eyes narrowed into evil slits. "You think they were checking the place out? Maybe making a plan?" he asked.

"I'm certain of it," said Rupert. "In fact, that's what they're doing now. Watch them. She's checking the security, and he's on his phone."

"He's the tech guy, right?" said Charlie. "He hacked into the old geezer's place to get the first one, didn't he?"

"Yeah. I imagine what he's doing right now is finding a way into the security, so he can take it all down later."

The two brothers stared after the man and woman as they made their way along the first-floor mezzanine towards the two great staircases.

"I can't believe that one man and one woman could pull off a job this big," said Charlie. "Surely they'll need some help."

"If he's as good as Glasgow says he is," said Rupert, "and if she's as light-fingered as I hope, then I reckon they just might pull it off." He turned to face his brother. "But the truth is,

Charlie boy, I don't actually care if there's two of them or two bloody thousand of them. Because in less than twenty-four hours, that little tart over there will be handing me the other diamond, and we'll be richer than the bloody queen."

"I'm not really fussed about the money, Rupert," said Charlie. His voice had dropped to a growl, and he stared unblinkingly at the pair. "I'm going to nail her head to a stake."

CHAPTER EIGHTEEN

Harvey stood like a rock in a fast moving river as swathes of schoolchildren, families and tourists carved their way around him in waves of excitement and intrigue. Dozens of cameras hung from the necks of museum visitors, who posed for selfies and family pictures before the giant bones of a dinosaur.

It took Harvey a few seconds to scan his surroundings inside the huge gallery called the Earth Hall. According to the floor plan, pinned to a wall behind scratched Perspex, the diamond was displayed on the first mezzanine floor.

Harvey had no intention of visiting the diamond. Such a move would be like signing a confession, should the robbery go south. But nothing was stopping him from looking at the emergency exits and checking out the security.

With practiced and cautious movements, Harvey was able to identify the security cameras without being blatant about his research. Cameras seemed to cover every single area. The fire exits beside the washrooms were alarmed, the main entrance resembled a fortress, and security was patrolling every floor. The tiny room holding the diamond, an offshoot of the main gallery, had two cameras on the entrance and likely more inside the room, in addition to the sensors.

Harvey was keen to see Lola's plan. He saw two possible options for stealing the diamond. Although admittedly he was not a professional thief, he had experienced robberies and criminals for most of his adult life, and virtually all of his childhood.

Option one was to walk through the main door in the middle of the day, hole up someplace and wait for dark, have someone on the outside cut the alarms and divert the CCTV, then take the diamond and get out whatever way you could.

Option two was to storm the museum with ten to fifteen trustworthy men and take the diamond by force. The museum would automatically shut down if the alarms were triggered, making escape virtually impossible.

Both options were flawed. The museum sat in the middle of Kensington, London. The whole area was monitored day and night by Metropolitan Police CCTV control rooms based in Bishopsgate. A car wouldn't make it five hundred yards before the entire police force swooped in.

Harvey stepped back to the edge of the walkway and leaned against an ornate column. He felt eyes boring into the back of his head. A presence.

He turned slowly. His fingers found the moulded grip of his knife. The sheath had been sewn into the lining of his leather biker jacket. His trained reaction sent lightning-fast, multi-dimensional scenarios playing through his mind of escape routes and nearby weapons. He found himself standing face to face with a wax model of a Neanderthal man, who stood, ignorant of the reaction he had caused, behind the glass of a large, eight-foot-high display cabinet.

Amused by the idea of the waxwork model triggering his senses, Harvey smiled to himself.

He studied the man, with his furrowed brow, long wild hair

and strong jaw. The designers had placed him in a slightly crouched posture with one arm up, pointing at the far end of the hall as if some great danger lurked there, such as a predator making its way through the trees.

Harvey followed the Neanderthal's gaze. He saw no man-eating predator, no sharp teeth, no claws designed to tear the flesh off early man. Instead, he saw two identical tall men dressed in matching dark blue suits. They stood beneath the archway entrance of the small room where the diamond was being displayed.

The men stood motionless as a predator might. They stood at the edge of the alcove and were wildly out of place. It was the suits, the movements, and the way they interacted; they just didn't fit into their surroundings.

Harvey followed their gaze and scanned the herds.

A group of schoolchildren grazed on snacks from packed lunches, huddled in groups of three, while under the watchful eyes of two teachers, who seemed more interested in each other than the kids. Tourists formed small, closer herds and seemed to move as one along the edge of the mezzanine, flowing from display to display.

But two of the herd moved quicker than the rest, making their way towards the grand staircase at the far end of the gallery. They disappeared behind a thick column and reappeared briefly again on the other side.

The girl seemed alert, checking the ceiling space and voids. The man was occupied by his phone.

"Is that...?" Harvey whispered to himself.

He pushed off the wall. His senses pricked.

Harvey glanced back at the two men, who hadn't budged an inch but continued to sight their prey. He took a step back and fell in behind the column to watch from the shadows as Melody and Reg strolled down the huge staircase.

CHAPTER NINETEEN

"So how are we going to do this?" asked Reg, as he stepped from the last stone step of the museum's entrance to the pavement. "What's going on in that mind of yours? Now that we've seen the place, how are we going to catch them?"

Melody tried to refrain from beaming, but she allowed a hint of joy through pursed lips and showed a glimpse of her perfect white teeth.

"Why don't you tell me your plan first, and then I'll tell you mine?" said Melody.

"My plan? I think you'll find I asked first."

"Okay, but it seems to me that you're keener to hear my plan than I am yours." She skipped a small puddle of rainwater and put her hands in her pockets to make sure Reg knew she wouldn't give up her own ideas until he spoke first.

"Alright, alright," he said. "I gave it a lot of thought in there. To manage the security, the power and the data networks would need three men minimum. There's only one man I know who could handle all that himself, and he's standing right here talking to you. So we'll need to assume they'll have at least three tech guys."

304 J. D. WESTON

"Copy," said Melody. "Physical security?"

"I said two inside before, but thinking about it, three minimum. One in the control room and two taking care of the guards. If they could have someone pose as a guard, even better. But I'm not sure how long they've been planning this, so let's assume not."

Melody nodded.

"Copy. What about the thief?"

"Like I said inside, Melody," replied Reg. "Balls of steel."

"How would they enter?"

"Loading bay. The only weakness I could find. The tech guys can deal with opening it, and from there the thieves could access the walkways that run behind the walls. They'd come right out beside the display."

"I saw that on the drawing. Do we know if security patrol the rear walkways?" asked Melody.

"We have to assume so. They'd have to force a few doors, but the tech guy could take care of the alarms, which would make the job much easier. If they took over the control room before the alarms were raised, they'd have free rein of the place."

"What if their hacker is good enough to control the security from outside?"

Reg's eyebrows raised as if the statement was a tall order.

"Then they'd have free rein all the way to the diamond, save for the guards."

"Okay," Melody replied. "Transport."

She knew the curve ball would trip Reg. He would have thought about the technicalities of the actual robbery, but not the logistics of the escape.

"This is West London, Melody. There's more armed police here than anywhere else in the UK."

"Yep," agreed Melody.

"Get away would be tough."

"Copy."

"In fact, it would be almost impossible."

"Mm-hmm."

"By car would be out of the question. You'd be shut down before you reached the main road."

"Agreed."

"By air might be good...But no, they'd have the police helicopters all over them in seconds."

"They'd be shot down," said Melody.

"Which only leaves the river," said Reg, as if in revelation.

"It does," said Melody.

"But where would they go from there? Surely the river police would be all over them?"

"It's harder to respond in a boat than by air or road," said Melody. "Besides, there are a hundred places they could dock and get out, only to disappear into the unknown."

"But how would they get there?" asked Reg. "To the river I mean. It's got to be nearly a kilometre from here."

"It's your plan, Reg," said Melody. "Why don't you tell me?"

"I don't know," replied Reg.

"Think about Harvey," she said.

"*Harvey?* What's he got to do with it?"

Melody didn't reply.

"Harvey?" said Reg again. Melody saw his brain engage. He always looked to the side through the gap in his glasses when he was in thought.

Then he fell in with what Melody was getting at.

"Motorbikes?"

"From here, straight onto Queen's Gate." Melody pointed at the junction a few hundred yards away. "From there, it's a straight road all the way to the river. On a motorbike, it's under a minute away."

"Motorbikes," Reg said again. "That means helmets too, so they'd avoid the cameras."

"If they have the right team, I'd say you just came up with a solid plan right there."

"It's all speculation, Melody," said Reg, deferring the praise. "We can't know how they'd do it exactly. All we can do is be ready for it when it happens."

"You think we can be ready for something like this?" asked Melody. "What are we going to do? Escalate the job and make sure the river police, the eyes in the sky and the response units are all lined up ready for the next two to three weeks? We don't know who they are, how they'll do it, or even when they'll try. All we can ascertain is that, given our experience and your knowledge of digital security systems, they stand a better chance of success if they go through the loading bay and into the service corridors. We also know that they're going to need three technical experts to control the cameras, the alarms and the power at the same time."

"There's one other problem," said Reg.

Melody gave him a sideways glance but didn't respond.

"I can't actually be involved. I mean, I can't escalate this. The job came from above and sits with you. If it needs to be escalated, and as you say, requires the river police, air support and armed response units to be primed, you're going to have to provide evidence for that kind of mobilisation. The chief isn't going to risk a massive waste of time and resources on a hunch based on experience."

"That's what I thought," said Melody.

"So what was *your* plan?" Reg asked. "Do you have something better than what I came up with?"

Melody gave a little laugh. "No. Actually, your plan works well, but we're missing something to make it work."

"Missing something?" said Reg. "You mean confirmed suspects and reliable data?"

"No," said Melody. "Much simpler than that."

She watched as Reg's eyes peered to the side of his glasses again.

"What?" he asked.

"A motorbike," replied Melody.

"A what?" said Reg. "Why?"

"Easy." Melody couldn't contain her smile any longer. "We're going to break into the museum."

CHAPTER TWENTY

The junction of Denmark Hill and Daneville Road was busy with early evening traffic heading out of London. A steady stream of commuters made their way from Denmark Hill Train Station or emerged from the continuous flow of buses that ferried people from the city or nearby underground stations.

Harvey thought it was a great place for a meet. Cars frequently stopped to pick up passengers or for passengers to duck into the nearby shops for a takeaway dinner. He leaned on the shutters of a closed shop while he waited for Lola and Fingers to arrive. The fact that he was about to rob the National History Museum didn't raise his pulse. He'd done worse things in his life. But the thought of getting his hands on the Bond Brothers tickled his excitement.

Lola hadn't mentioned what they would be driving. They'd find him. As much as he blended into the melee of commuters who stood waiting for buses or rides, he was easily identifiable to those that were looking. Those that weren't looking for him would pass as if he wasn't there. Just another face in the crowd.

A construction worker dressed in a t-shirt, dirty jeans and heavy boots with a green tool bag and spirit level stood adjacent to Harvey. He leaned on the shelter of the bus stop eating a bag of chips. Harvey smelled the salt and vinegar, and it reminded him of Fridays, the day when Harvey's foster father, John Cartwright, used to always demand fish and chips. He said it was a tradition. Friday was fish day.

An office worker dressed in a smart suit carrying a laptop bag stood behind the construction worker. He checked his watch then peered along the road for the bus before loosening his tie and opening a well-read newspaper.

Normal lives, thought Harvey. He wondered if they were going home to families or going home to be alone. He wondered if they might stop at a pub for a pint on the way, as many men used to do in John's pubs. Harvey had always wondered what it might be like to work in an office, to walk in at the same time every day and see the same faces. Maybe they'd ask how your evening was or what you have planned for the weekend. That all sounded very normal to Harvey.

But the chain that held them in that same room until five o'clock every night seemed restrictive. At the end of the day, what did they really achieve? What good did they do? It all seemed like a waste of time. Harvey had heard people talk of hitting sales targets, but it didn't make them wealthy enough to leave their jobs. They'd still have to go back and clamp the chains on the next day. They didn't help people, they didn't save lives, or-

Harvey's trail of thoughts jolted.

-make people suffer for their actions.

How many people had Harvey made suffer for their actions? How many grown men had he seen cry as he'd burned their limbs off in front of their own eyes? Sometimes, he did not even need to touch them before they shattered. Often, Harvey's words had broken men. He'd never threatened anybody; it wasn't his style. Threatening to hurt a big man would only antagonise him, but pulling out a confession, making them say the words out loud and admit the terrible things they'd done, that would destroy him. Verbalising the actions somehow made them all the more real. That was how to break most men.

Harvey wondered how he might break the two brothers. They would be different. Men of that stature usually were. They didn't typically perform the terrible actions. They only gave instructions and communicated their desired results. How the subordinate achieved the results was of no concern to men like the Bond Brothers.

John Cartwright had been the same. He would never have told Harvey to open a man up and pull his intestines out. He would merely state that he wanted a piece of information, and Harvey would extract it using the tools at hand, often using just his voice.

Mad Bob and Cannon Bill had been prime examples of subordinates. They were loyal and viscous, capable of almost anything, and guilty of worse than the construction worker with the fish and chips or the man with the newspaper could ever imagine.

Harvey had a clear picture in his mind. The two brothers had somehow learned of Lola and her team's plans to steal the diamond. Men of power, fuelled by greed, could easily intercept their escape. That was exactly what they had done, then stolen the diamond. It wouldn't have taken a genius to learn that the diamond was one of two, so they'd forced Lola to steal the second, which was a far riskier task than the first.

He could understand why Lola wanted Harvey to be part of the job. Her motive for that was clear; she wanted Harvey to protect her. She'd already seen what the brothers were capable of when they shot her friend.

But then what?

And where did Melody and Reg fit into the plans? Were

they investigating the first robbery, or preventing the second? Did they know about the second robbery, or was it a hunch? They were walking away from the Bond Brothers. Had they met? Were Melody and Reg somehow in cohorts with the villains?

Harvey wondered what Melody might do if she found Harvey at the robbery. Would she try to arrest him? How would he react? He could never hurt her.

Then two pieces of Harvey's puzzle seemed to come together to offer an alternative scenario. Harvey's chest tightened at the thought.

What would the Bond Brothers do if Melody cornered them?

A horn honked on the far side of the road. Harvey snapped back to reality. A four-door BMW was half pulling out of the side road. He could just make out Lola driving and Fingers sat beside her. Lola caught Harvey's attention with a discreet single wave of her hand.

Harvey shoved off the wall he was leaning on and made to cross the road, just as a large Ford van screeched to a halt in front of the BMW. The side door was thrown open, and two men in masks jumped out.

Harvey stepped into the road, watching the scene play out, deciding who to hit first. He focused on the driver of the van, who also wore a mask.

Another horn sounded, louder and closer. Harvey jumped back just in time as a large, red, double-decker bus came to a halt at the bus stop. Harvey was suddenly engulfed in people as they tried to board the bus. He shoved them away. All the time, his eyes watched the van on the other side of the road through the bus windows.

"Easy, mate," said the construction worker as Harvey began to jostle his way out of the crowd, knocking the man's dinner to the ground. Harvey ignored the comment, pushed free from the crowd, and stepped in front of the bus in time to see Lola being dragged into the van.

The side door slammed, the driver gunned the engine, and the van roared off in a squeal of tyre smoke. Harvey gave chase for a few seconds. He ran between the moving cars and dodged a man on a bicycle, but the effort was futile. The van turned into another side road and was gone.

Another loud car horn honked behind Harvey, followed by a stream of abuse. Harvey turned to find an impatient man behind the wheel of a Mercedes, gesturing that Harvey was mad by tapping his finger against his own temple and urging Harvey to get out of the road with wild waves of his other hand.

Harvey's head cocked to one side. He stared at the man through the windscreen and watched as the impatient anger turned slowly but surely to confusion, then fear. The driver slowly brought his hands down and stilled them. He locked the doors. As soon as Harvey stepped to one side, the man accelerated away with cautious looks in his rear-view mirror.

The world had just witnessed a kidnapping, but as soon as the van disappeared, life had returned to normal.

The BMW was also gone. But lying on the ground where the struggle had taken place was Lola's wrist tag.

"So, what's the plan?" asked Charlie. "Do you actually trust her to bring us the diamond?"

The two brothers sat in the back of their Bentley and passed over the River Thames on Battersea Bridge. Their driver kept the speed to a cool thirty-five miles per hour, giving his bosses a smooth ride in the style of which they'd grown accustomed.

"She has no choice but to bring us the diamond," replied Rupert. "She knows what will happen to her if she doesn't."

"And what about after?" said Charlie. "We can't just let them go free, not after what they did to Mad Bob and Cannon Bill."

"You're right," said Rupert. "And that's why we're not going to let them go free. She's going to meet us at Doctor Feelmore's funeral home, where she thinks she'll be handing over the second diamond and walking away with a fresh start."

"However?" said Charlie.

"However, we'll be waiting there to receive her, and when we get that second diamond in our own grubby mitts, she'll be taking a turn for the worse. We'll be handing all of them over to the good doctor along with all our troubles and sins."

"What about this other fella?" asked Charlie. "The new guy."

"Glasgow is putting the feelers out. If he's got any sense he'll stay low. But if he decides to come for us we'll be ready. Lola knows I want him. She'll stay well clear of him if she's got any sense."

"No, Ru," said Charlie. "It's too easy."

"Too easy?" said Rupert. "You want me to make it harder?"

"Alright, listen," began Charlie. "Picture this. You did a robbery with a mate and got away with a priceless diamond. I mean, I haven't seen it yet, but I'm guessing it's the last robbery you'll ever need to do, right?"

"Right," said Rupert.

"But on the way out, some better-equipped men with guns take the diamond off you, shoot your mate, and tell you to go get the second diamond. Oh and by the way, it's in the Natural History Museum."

"Right," said Rupert. "I'm following."

"So you do the second robbery, and somehow by some godforsaken miracle, you manage to get out alive and with the diamond. So for the second time in a week, you're holding the keys to a life of luxury. How did you put it? Sun, sand and semi-naked women?"

Rupert didn't respond.

"Do you honestly think for one second that you're going to waltz down to the local morgue to meet the blokes with the guns and hand it over to them?"

"If she's got any sense, yes. She'll want her freedom."

"She wants the diamond more, I bet," said Charlie. "She'd have to have a screw loose to give up a life of luxury. In one hand, she'd be Lady Lola LaRoux of some sun-kissed island in the Maldives, and in the other hand, she'd be Unlucky Lola of Peckham, the bird with a council flat who could of had it all, but didn't."

"You reckon she'd do a runner?" asked Rupert, doubting his own judgement.

"I reckon she might. But you know what, bruv?" said Charlie.

"Go on."

"I know for sure that if we're sitting on our arses waiting for someone to deliver us the second diamond, while they're skipping their way to Heathrow Airport, we'll be laughed out of London."

"Shit," said Rupert.

"You ain't the only one with brains, bro," said Charlie, sitting back in the fine leather seats with a smug look on his face.

"I hate it when you're right, Charlie," said Rupert.

"Don't beat yourself up," replied Charlie. "That's why there's two of us."

"You know London will be locked down if she does actually get out, right?" said Rupert.

"Yeah, we'll be quiet for a while," said Charlie. "We'll get the obligatory questioning from the plod, but they won't have nothing on us. No prints, full alibis and the rest. We'll let it blow over then we can talk about this sun, sand and semi-naked women thing."

"What's to talk about?" asked Rupert. "There'll be sun, there'll be sand, and guess what?"

"There'll be semi-naked women?"

"You'll be drowning in them, Charlie," said Rupert. "You mark my words."

The two brothers stared out of their own windows, both deep in thought. The day was drawing to a close, but the long summer sky still held hints of blue.

"I love London at this time of year," said Charlie.

"I like the blue sky," replied Rupert, but his mind was elsewhere.

Charlie gave a little snort of laughter. "The blue sky?" he said. "You carry on admiring the blue sky, bro. I'll carry on admiring the short skirts."

"Glasgow," said Rupert.

The driver caught Rupert's eye in the rear-view mirror.

"Yes, boss?" he replied.

"Do me a favour, drop me here," replied Rupert.

"What are you doing?" said Charlie. "We're miles away."

Glasgow George pulled the car to a stop in the bus lane, to the annoyance of a black taxi driver who was trying to pull out into the traffic.

"Is here alright, boss?" asked Glasgow.

"Perfect."

"Rupert, what the bloody hell are you doing?" asked Charlie, as Rupert pushed the door open and climbed out. Charlie leaned across and peered up at him.

"Charlie," said Rupert, feeling energised by his new plan. He enjoyed the flourish of confidence a new idea gave him. "Meet me at Doctor Feelmore's later and bring our passports."

"What about you?" asked Charlie.

Another taxi beeped its horn, and the driver gestured rudely at Rupert for stopping in a bus lane. Rupert gave the man a stare he wouldn't forget. The taxi pulled out around the Bentley.

"Me?" said Rupert, when the taxi had passed. "I'm going to make sure old Lola LaRoux delivers us from evil, bruv."

CHAPTER TWENTY-TWO

Car horns shook Harvey from his thoughts. He casually stepped to the side of the road, hearing but ignoring the angry comments that passing drivers made through open windows. The noise was just a background blur.

Were they too late? Had the Bond Brothers grown tired of waiting? Where did Fingers go? Was he scared? Was he in on it?

Harvey began to walk away from the junction. A girl had just been dragged from her car and thrown into a van; someone would have called the police, and Harvey couldn't afford to be questioned.

He ducked off the main road into an alley and pocketed the wrist tag. The alley led into a series of back streets that Harvey knew would eventually lead to the canal. He kept walking, using the time to think.

Walking away and leaving London as originally planned was an option. That was one thing Harvey loved about his life; he had options. First and foremost was the option to go home, put his feet up and forget about it all.

But forgetting was easier said than done.

He'd spent a lifetime dealing with bullies, hard men that preyed on the weak and gained from it either financially or in status. Harvey couldn't abide bullies.

Standing tall, a few hundred yards along the back street and adjacent to the main road, was a library. Harvey approached the building in thought. He pushed open the door and in a few sweeping glances had the place mapped out. The washrooms were in the far left corner with the fire exit beside them. In the centre of the large room, a middle-aged lady with glasses on her nose sat behind the curved reception desk. She didn't look up at Harvey. To Harvey's right was a bank of six desks with computer screens. Teenagers with books occupied two; the other four were empty.

Harvey took a seat at the furthest desk, facing the window and giving himself a view of the outside, with easy access to the fire exit. It was an old habit, but one that had proved useful on more than one occasion.

He clicked on the mouse button, which seemed to wake the computer up, and presented a box on the screen stating that the user agrees to the terms and conditions of the library's free internet usage policy. The terms and conditions looked long. There was no time for that. Even if he did break an internet law, it wouldn't be the worst thing he'd done.

Harvey opened the internet browser to begin his search. He started with the words, *Natural History Museum Diamond*, and hit enter.

The page filled with results. Some were about a diamond exhibition that closed just a few months ago due to police warnings about potential organised criminals robbing the place. Other results gave a brief description of single diamonds, and enticed the reader to click on the link to read more.

One of the results, close to the bottom of the web page,

briefly discussed a pair of diamonds, Demonios Gemelos, or Demon Twins.

Something twitched in Harvey's mind. There was a connection there that he couldn't quite grasp.

He clicked the link. Another web page opened up. At the top was an image of the two diamonds, the demon twins. Below the image was a single paragraph of small italic text.

Demonios Gemelos, or Demon Twins. A pair of 200-carat diamonds found in South Africa during the mid 1800s. The diamonds are believed to be cursed, bringing a quick death to any man that holds the two together. The diamonds have been separated since nineteen forty. One was donated to the National History Museum. The other was retained by the Abrams family, but was subsequently stolen in nineteen forty-eight.

Harvey ran an internet search for *Demonios Gemelos*.

Once again, the page filled with results for various websites all encouraging the internet user to click. But one result stood out from the rest. It stated that the missing Demonios twin might have been recently found. Harvey clicked on the link.

A new web page opened showing a stock image of diamond mining in Africa in the nineteenth century. The page went on to describe a pair of very precious diamonds discovered by a man called Roland Steinbach, who owned several diamond claims in Kimberly. Servants found Steinbach dead at his desk. Both of his hands had been removed, and the diamonds that he'd kept so proudly in a small safe were also missing.

Harvey went on to read that people believe the diamonds somehow ended up in the hands of a Dutchman who brawled with an Englishman and lost. The Englishman then took the diamonds as a gift for Queen Victoria, but he was drowned at sea. The captain of the ship stole the diamond and escaped with a few of the crew on a lifeboat.

However, the crew soon learned of the diamond and killed the captain before they washed up in Portugal. The three men found the British Army and requested safe passage to England. But before they left France, one of the men tried to steal the diamonds. He was caught and killed by the remaining two men. The two men agreed to carry one diamond each. They went their separate ways at the busy port of Calais, and never saw each other again.

One of the men, Jack Penn, sold his diamond to Hans Sloane, who eventually created the Natural History Museum and donated his huge collection of natural artefacts. The remaining diamond remained in the Abrams family up until nineteen forty-eight when it was stolen. Despite the Abrams' large offers of reward, it was never returned.

More recently, the diamond was spotted by a collector who wished to remain anonymous and is due to be sold at a private auction in the UK.

Harvey checked the top of the article. It was dated three days previous.

He opened a new web page and searched for *Stolen Diamond*. A fresh page of results appeared, and at the very top of the page, the headline read, *Missing Cursed Diamond Stolen*.

Movement outside caught Harvey's attention. Two armed policemen ran past the window of the library towards the door. Harvey closed the internet browser, ran the sleeve of his jacket over the mouse and keyboard, more out of habit than necessity, and then casually made his way toward the washrooms. He took a quick look around him then bolted for the fire exit.

The alarms sang out immediately.

The alleyway behind the library was clear, but neither left nor right was a great option. Harvey took a few steps forward then leapt up and grabbed onto the wall in front of him. He pulled himself over and dropped down to the garden on the other side. Dogs barked nearby, and he heard the heavy engine of the police arriving behind the wall. Car doors opened and radios sang as the police closed in.

Harvey tore up the garden. He ducked down the side of the house, burst through a garden gate, and found himself in a back-street. He glanced left and right, then bolted into an alleyway in front.

The thump of an approaching helicopter stopped him dead in his tracks. He dove for cover beneath a large bin and waited for it to pass, knowing that the police would be using infrared to find his heat signals.

Sirens sounded in all directions. Harvey knew they would close the area down, and he had to get out fast.

The whomp of the helicopter's rotor blades was suddenly deafening in the air above. His subconscious readied himself to fight. The familiar iron taste ran around his gums, and the tingle of adrenaline surged through his veins.

The helicopter hovered for a while. At the far end of the alleyway, a police car stopped. It as if the driver was daring him to move.

Harvey lay dead still, his senses alive, interpreting, planning and preparing.

But as fast as it had arrived, the helicopter banked and continued its search elsewhere. The police car slipped away, leaving an empty run of alleyways in front of Harvey, all the way to the canal.

Seeing his chance, Harvey slid from beneath the bin, checked around him then sprinted through the network of alley-ways. Slowly, the noises of the sirens and helicopters began to fade away, and eventually he burst onto the quiet canal-side footpath.

But Harvey didn't stop running. He ran with everything he had until less than a kilometre later he reached the factory where he'd first met Lola and Fingers, Mad Bob and Cannon Bill.

After finding the gap in the fence, Harvey kicked the door open and stepped through onto the factory floor. It was empty, as he knew it would be, save for the pigeons that scattered on his arrival. He wondered if Mad Bob and Cannon Bill had been found and their bodies removed. But he didn't stop to check.

Instead, he walked up to the pile of boxes and old pieces of machinery that were stacked to one side of the vast room. He pulled back the dusty tarp and breathed a small sigh of relief.

In the midst of the boxes of papers, greasy machinery and random factory objects, exactly where he'd left it three months before, was his beloved motorcycle.

CHAPTER TWENTY-THREE

"I can't believe you talked me into this, Melody." Reg's voice came across loudly over Melody's ear-piece. "This has got to be one of the stupidest ideas you've ever had."

Melody was crouched in the shadow of a tree one hundred yards from the huge rolling shutter doors that were the loading bay entrance to the Natural History Museum.

"You said it yourself, Reg," she began. "We're missing credible evidence and confirmed suspects. What better way to get both of those than to catch the thieves red-handed?"

"What makes you think they'll do it tonight?"

"They have one diamond already. Greed will have set in by now. The longer they leave the second hit, the harder it will be. All eyes will be on the museum's diamond and security will tighten. Anyway, we don't have facts, but we do have years of experience on our side."

"Melody, if you're caught, you'll be locked up," said Reg. "And I won't be able to get you out of it. You'll have years of experience in something altogether different."

"So let's not get caught, Reggie, eh?"

Melody heard Reg's sigh loud and clear across the comms.

"Let's just stay focused, Reg," said Melody. "Run through the plan once more."

"Okay," said Reg. Melody had worked with Reg long enough to recognise when his reluctance was tinged with a hint of excitement at the challenge. "I'm connected to the public network and I've accessed the remote security facility. From here, I can see all wireless access points and media channels. In a few minutes, I'll be onto the secure layer, which is the CCTV and alarms. Once that's done, I'll pop the single rear door to the side of the loading bay. That'll be your cue to go in."

"Copy," said Melody. "Any other locks?"

"No. The internal doors are all secure key card access that run off electromagnetic locks. I can isolate the power circuit that runs those doors and release them for you so you should have a clear run."

"Easy," said Melody. "What are you worried about?"

"What am I worried about?" said Reg. "Ah, let me see. Well, first off, there's not seeing Jess for the next ten years. Then there's showering with an entire wing of men much bigger than me who haven't seen a woman for God knows how long. Then, of course, there's the little thing of being locked in a tiny cell with one of them every night and becoming their sex slave."

"Anything else?" asked Melody, as she pulled her hood up over her head.

"I hear the food isn't great either," replied Reg.

"Are you finished?" said Melody.

"Finished listing the things that I'm dreading or finished opening the doors?"

"The doors," said Melody. "Your insecurities merely amuse me."

Melody could hear Reg's fingers tapping away at his keyboard. She had every confidence in his abilities.

"I'm glad I get to amuse you one last time," said Reg. "The

rear door is open, and the cargo area is free of guards for one full minute. You are good to go."

Melody darted the twenty yards to the building and edged along the wall to the small door. It sat inset into the brickwork to one side of the giant rolling shutters. She glanced up at the keypad; no LEDs were blinking. A small set of eight concrete stairs led up to the door, which opened easily and silently. Within a few seconds, she was inside, standing on a raised concrete walkway the exact height as the rear of the four trucks that were parked up below. Presumably, so the workers could easily push trolleys of fragile goods out of the truck cargo areas and wheel them inside the museum.

A goods lift stood open, full of dark shadows with a set of double doors to one side. A narrow pane of reinforced glass set into both doors showed Melody the empty corridor beyond.

"I'm inside. Is the corridor free?" she asked.

"For the next thirty seconds, you need to be in that corridor. Then move into the first turning on the right in under forty-five seconds," said Reg. "I've been watching the guards' movements. They seem to have a pattern. But from here on in I need to kill the CCTV until you're in position. Otherwise, you're going to have a dozen guards rush you from all angles."

"That's fine, Reg," replied Melody. "Once I'm in the service corridors, I should be okay. I'll hear them coming."

She pushed through the double doors and let them close behind her, just in time to hear another door open in the loading bay. A few cautious moments passed as she listened for any signs of movement. Then, once she was happy the coast was clear, she sprinted to the first junction in the corridor.

There was a smell of disinfectant. The long walls that trailed off in various directions were painted cream up top and green on the lower half. The concrete floor had been painted dark grey. Melody thought that the place was immaculate like a hospital but with a distinctly industrial feel.

The smaller corridor led to another set of double doors, beyond which was a staircase.

"Up the stairs?" asked Melody.

"You got it," said Reg. "Up to the first floor. The corridor up there leads left and right. You'll need to head right."

"Copy," said Melody, and pushed the doors open. Immediately, she heard footsteps coming down the stairs. She darted into the dark space beneath the stairwell and edged into the shadows.

A deep voice echoed from the stairwell walls, and the footsteps stopped.

"Yeah, I'm here. What's up?"

His radio crackled into life.

"Just had a call from control two, Stevey. They're saying the cameras are down. Be advised, mate."

"Again?" said the man apparently called Stevey. "They went down last week too."

"Just be on your toes, mate. That's all."

"Yep, will do."

The footsteps continued. Stevey's loud breathing disappeared when the double doors closed behind him. Melody made her move up the stairs.

"Sounds like they're onto the cameras being down, Reg."

"Get yourself in position and I'll turn them back on. They'll think it was just a glitch."

"I'm in the first-floor corridor. I turned right."

"Great. You should see that the corridor turns to the left about a hundred yards in front of you. The room with the diamond is the last door on the left-hand side before the bend. Get to the door but don't open it," said Reg. "I need to kill the alarm system first."

"Okay, sit tight." Melody ran the hundred yards as quietly as she could. "I'm outside the door," she whispered.

"I'm working on it," replied Reg. "Give me twenty seconds."

Voices approached from around the bend in the corridor. It was two guards discussing how antiquated the security was in the museum. Their voices grew louder.

"You need to hurry," whispered Melody.

"I'm trying Melody," replied Reg. "But I just found a bypass. The alarm sensors are well-protected."

"I have about ten seconds until I'm discovered and I have nowhere to hide," said Melody.

The two men's voices were so close now that Melody could hear their breathing. Their footsteps were slow and casual, not the footsteps of two guards who were on the lookout for trouble.

"Reg," said Melody, "come on."

"Okay, how about this?" said Reg. The lights in the corridor flicked off, leaving the long chamber in pitch darkness.

"What the bloody hell now?" said the first guard as he rounded the corner. "I can't see a bloody thing."

Melody pinned herself to the wall, making herself as thin as she could to let the two guards pass.

"Here, hold on," said the second guard, who sounded a lot younger than the first. A flashlight flicked on, illuminating the corridor in front of them as they moved past.

Melody stood motionless as the beam of light danced across the floor in front of the two men. It wasn't until they disappeared into the stairwell that Melody dared to breathe out.

"Nick of time, Reg," she said, as her heart began to calm down.

"Nothing to it," replied Reg. "You want some light in there?"

"It'd be nice," said Melody, just as the corridor lights burst on again. The hum of electricity she hadn't heard before became very apparent in the otherwise silent space.

"Try the door," said Reg.

"Are we good to go?"

"Only one way to find out."

Melody pushed the lever on the door handle and stepped into the live side of London's Natural History Museum.

CHAPTER TWENTY-FOUR

Standing in the shadows, silent and still, Harvey watched his ex-fiancé edge along the outside museum wall. Had he not known it was Melody beforehand, he'd have recognised her now from the grace and style with which she moved.

From where he stood, he couldn't hear her talk, but from her actions, she was waiting for something. Somebody would be accessing the museum security for her, clearing a path and guiding her through. There was only one man she knew who could do that.

Reg, thought Harvey.

Melody took the concrete stairs in a few silent steps and opened the small door to the left of the loading bay entrance.

Harvey gave his surroundings a final check then followed. He caught the door before it closed, and watched Melody through the tiny reinforced glass. She disappeared into a corridor.

Keeping his noise to a minimum, Harvey followed on her heels. He was in the corridor in seconds and waited at an intersection. He heard Melody talking on her comms to Reg. Her short, sharp comments over the stealth comms units were familiar to Harvey. It felt good to be so close to her. If it wasn't for the strong scent of disinfectant, he thought he'd be able to smell her familiar fragrance.

Her whisper faded away as she crept through the double doors into the next corridor. But a man's voice, loud and clear, echoed off the flat, hard walls. A few seconds passed as he stopped to talk on his two-way radio, and a loud crackle of a distorted voice announced that the guard had opened the doors and was heading Harvey's way.

The guard's footsteps stopped. Harvey chanced a glance around the corner and saw a heavyset man peering back through the doors.

He was pulling a telescopic cosh from his utility belt.

Harvey saw Melody dart from behind the stairs, and the guard began to re-enter the stairwell after her.

In three long, silent steps, Harvey had a hand over the guard's mouth and his arm bent behind his back. A sharp knee to the man's leg sent him to the floor.

The door closed silently behind Harvey, leaving the two men staring at each other.

"You have a family?" whispered Harvey, as he unclipped the man's radio, turned the volume down and pocketed it.

The guard nodded.

"Are you going to be quiet?" asked Harvey. He took the cosh, closed it and tucked it into his own belt.

The guard nodded once more.

In less than a minute, Harvey had the man's wrists zip-tied behind his back and his ankles bound with the laces of the man's boots. A sock was stuffed into his mouth and secured with a long length of duct tape wrapped around his head.

Harvey dragged him to the dark storage space beneath the stair well.

"If you be good, I'll tell someone you're here when I'm done," said Harvey. "If you make a noise, I won't be so nice."

He slipped away and bounded up the stairs after Melody, just as the lights flicked off, leaving the stairwell dimly lit by the hazy green glow of the emergency exit signs.

The first-floor corridor was pitch dark. Harvey stood in the doorway holding the door open and listened. Two men were talking to his right. Then a flashlight switched on and began to wave a fat beam of light around the corridor. Harvey closed the door and stepped back into the stairwell.

He stood to one side and waited.

The bouncing torch light announced the arrival of the two men and the double doors shoved open revealing one man in his twenties of medium build and an older, more portly man who Harvey placed in his fifties.

Harvey waited for the doors to close then struck the younger of the men hard to the side of his head with the cosh. He went down without a noise, and the torch fell to the floor with a crash.

The older of the men began to voice panicked questions. The white of his eyes shone bright green in the emergency lights.

"Who's that?" he said, clearly unready for an attack. "Jimmy?"

But before he could say anything else, Harvey had whipped the cosh back and slammed it into the man's temple.

Tying the men together using the last of his zip ties took a few minutes. He took their radios, removed the batteries, and dropped their mobile phones over the edge of the stairwell to smash on the concrete floor below.

Two more lengths of duct tape secured their mouths. The two men were still out cold by the time Harvey had finished. He tied them back to back with their wrists joined and a strip of tape wound around their foreheads.

Harvey admired his work for a second, and then pushed through the doors and stepped out into the corridor. The lights in the long empty space had been turned back on.

The corridor to the left was long and empty. To the right a few doors led off, and the corridor bent to the left. Presumably, the walkway ran around the perimeter of the mezzanine feeding the little alcoves Harvey had seen. He turned right and pictured the place where he'd stood earlier that day on the first floor of the gallery. If his judgement was right, the diamond display would be the last door on the left-hand side of the corridor.

With an ear to the door, Harvey listened. He knew he wouldn't hear anything; the doors were thick, and Melody would not be making a noise.

He pushed the door open slowly.

CHAPTER TWENTY-FIVE

Melody gazed at the perfect sparkles that reflected from the diamond's surface even in the low light.

"Pretty, isn't it?" said a voice behind Melody.

It wasn't just any voice. From the first syllable he spoke, she knew it was Harvey. Her mind recognised his tones and powered into overdrive. Her heart skipped and her chest tightened, then her knees felt weak as if they might give under the weight of his presence.

She froze and felt her gun being lifted from her belt.

"What are-"

"No questions," said Harvey. "You wouldn't like the answers."

"Then you're here to steal the diamond?"

Harvey didn't reply.

"I can't let you take it," said Melody. "You'll be shot dead before you step foot outside."

"I doubt that Melody," said Harvey. "Besides, *I* won't be carrying the diamond."

"You expect *me* to walk out of here with it?"

"That's an option."

"*No*, Harvey. It is not an option," hissed Melody. She turned to face him before he could stop her.

Their eyes met.

He looked gaunt and unshaven.

A silence grew between them that felt harder to break as each silent second ticked by.

"How have you been?" he asked. His voice had softened.

Melody swallowed what felt like the diamond itself.

"Don't do this," she whispered. "It's not you."

"It's a means to an end."

"An end?"

Harvey remained impassive for a few seconds then spoke quietly.

"Not my end."

Melody stared at the shine of his eyes in the soft light. The room was unlit, but enough light spilt from the main gallery for them to see each other and to bring the diamond's glittering surfaces to life beneath the glass.

"I can't let you take it," said Melody.

"It's not me that's taking it," replied Harvey.

"I miss you, Harvey. Don't do this."

"Take the diamond, Melody."

"You can't make me."

"What if I told you that I know who has the other one? The second diamond."

"It's not you then?" asked Melody, fishing for clues as to his motive.

"I'm not a diamond type of guy, Melody," replied Harvey. "You know that."

"So why then?" she said. "Why do this?"

"What if I told you a girl will die if I don't?"

"Who?" said Melody. "Tell me. We can help."

"You can help by lifting that lid and taking the diamond."

"I could scream. There'll be twenty guards here in a matter of seconds, and the police will be right behind them."

Harvey didn't reply.

"It might take some explaining, but I'd likely be okay. I can't say the same for you though."

"Am I still wanted?" asked Harvey. "Are the police looking for me?"

Melody shook her head and felt her eyes water.

"No, Harvey, no. You were *never* wanted. You're a free man. But do this, and there's no more I can do to help."

Harvey reached for his belt and pulled a telescopic cosh. He swung a short stabbing swing by his side and it extended with a series of sharp clicks.

"Move aside, Melody."

"Please, don't do this, Harvey. I can't watch you go this way."

"So move aside and get out. Run."

Melody stood her ground.

Harvey reached back with the cosh. Their eyes locked. He tensed and swung the cosh down.

"Okay, okay."

Harvey stopped mid-swing.

"I'll get the diamond," said Melody. "But you need to tell me exactly what's going on."

"I told you," said Harvey. "A girl will die. Help me save the girl, and you can have them both. You'll be a hero."

Melody let her head fall forward. She gave a sigh then looked up at Harvey. His eyes hadn't changed. His cheekbones were a little more pronounced, his hair unkempt and his beard was rough and scraggly.

Footsteps sounded not far away. It was the slow, bored pace

of a security guard following the same route he took a hundred times a night.

Harvey stepped away from the display case and dragged Melody with him. The pair stood chest to chest in the shadows to one side of the arch. Melody could smell his scent, familiar, warm. She closed her eyes and breathed him in, then rested her head on his chest.

Two boots stopped at the archway, as if they were afraid to step further.

Melody could feel Harvey's heart against her cheek. She felt his muscles tense as he made himself ready to pounce.

The guard stood a few seconds, then spoke to his radio. "All clear on mezzanine one. No sign of Stevey or the other two."

A short silence was broken by the scratch and crackle of the radio.

"Ah, no problem, Del," the controller replied. "They're probably skiving as usual."

The heavy boots turned away and returned to their slow, bored plod. The pair listened to the guard move off, and then both breathed out slowly.

Melody placed her hands on Harvey's chest. "Just like old times." She smiled.

Harvey matched her gaze. He bent forward, bringing his lips close to hers. Melody closed her eyes and waited for the soft familiar touch of his mouth. She felt his warm breath, and the way he rubbed her forehead with his own. Their noses touched just briefly.

"Get the diamond, Melody," whispered Harvey. "Then we'll talk."

He pulled away, leaving her hanging with pursed lips.

Melody watched as Harvey approached the arched entrance, being mindful not to step too close to the boundary that the guard had clearly avoided. He gave her a wave as if to tell her the coast was clear.

Melody took a deep breath and let it out slowly, then hit the little button on her ear-piece to talk to Reg.

"Reg, I need a little help here," she said.

CHAPTER TWENTY-SIX

A small tinny speaker crackled into life in the rear of the van.

"Reg, I need a little help here," said a female voice. "Are you there? Talk to me."

Rupert stepped up into the cargo area and glared down at the thin man sat in front of a small bench whose face was lit by a pair of computer screens. He slid the sliding door closed behind him.

"This is not the time to go quiet on me," said the girl, her voice a little more urgent than before.

The man sat motionless, his eyes wide.

"Can I answer her?" he asked.

Rupert nodded and placed a finger over his lips. His other hand held the gun to the man's head.

"I'm here." Then the man released the push to talk button, never removing his eyes from Rupert's.

"Where is she?" asked Rupert.

"The diamond display," replied the man. His voice quavered just a little.

Rupert lowered the gun, leaned on the back of the van's front seats, and nodded at him to continue.

"Reg, I need a little help," said the girl.

"Can I answer her?" asked the man again.

Rupert nodded again. "Do whatever it takes, but *do not* do anything stupid."

The man at the computer cleared his throat. He hit the push to talk and spoke quietly into the microphone.

"What do you need?"

A long silence followed then the girl replied with an equal tremor in her voice.

"The alarm is on the display," she said. "You still think you can get me a window?"

Rupert's eyes were locked onto the man's.

"How long do you need?"

"Max ten seconds," said the girl.

"It'll take some doing, but I think so." The man shifted in his seat and began to tap on his keyboard. "Have you run into difficulties?" he said into the mic.

"You could say that," replied the girl. Her voice was tinny over the comms and blocked in part by the museum's thick walls.

He released the button and turned to face Rupert.

"I need to get busy," said the man. "It might take a few minutes."

"Go ahead," said Rupert. "I'll be watching. No funny business."

From where he stood, Rupert could see the screens. The man was typing into a black interface. White text flowed in streams of what looked like code. Although Rupert couldn't understand the commands, it was clear that the words were computer talk.

Another interface opened, which looked like an internet browser. A username was entered followed by two failed password entries in quick succession. A message displayed informing them that a third failed attempt would lock the user out.

"You know the password?" asked Rupert.

The man tilted his head back as if in thought, then gave a huff, a spit of keystrokes, and slammed the enter button down.

The screen went blank then re-opened into a graphical representation of what looked like symbols for electronic switches.

"What's that?" asked Rupert.

"These are the sensors placed around the various displays in the museum."

"All of them?" asked Rupert, slightly impressed.

"As far as I can tell."

"So which ones do we need?" asked Rupert.

A few clicks of the mouse and the screen showed a 3D model view of the museum as if it had transparent walls.

The man zoomed in, rotated the view, and then zoomed in some more, until a vague resemblance of the alcove with the diamond display was on the screen.

There were nine sensors in the room. Two were beneath the floor of the entrance under the archway. The man waved the cursor over them.

"Pressure sensors," he said, as if to confirm the obvious to Rupert.

He then moved the cursor to the sensors on the walls.

"Artwork, cabinet, and then the other cabinet and one more piece of artwork."

Rupert remembered the pictures on the walls beside the cabinet containing the stone tools. They'd been photos of ancient cave paintings found somewhere in Africa.

"That leaves three," said the man. He brought the cursor to the three sensors that seemed to float in the air to form a triangle.

"How long?" said the girl. "It's not a good time for me here."

The man reached forward and hit the push to talk button.

"I'm close," he said. "One minute, and for the record, I'm not exactly having a ball."

He released the button. Then he stared at the screen.

"So you can disable the sensors?" asked Rupert.

"I can disable them okay, but they have a backup sensor which will need to be disabled first."

"Where's the backup?" asked Rupert.

"It's hidden beneath the cushion."

"How do you know?"

Rupert's comment seemed to aggravate the man.

"Because I looked, and I'm not stupid."

"You've done this before?" asked Rupert with a smile. "But how do I know you're not trying to bluff me?"

"Listen, I don't know who you are, but my friend is in there, and I'm going to get her out without this place lighting up like a Christmas tree and half of London's police carting us all away."

The two men stared at each other in the dim light.

"Now," the man continued, "are you going to carry on asking questions, or can I just do this?"

"I'm running out of time here," said the girl over the comms.

"Don't pull any tricks," said Rupert.

"Can you at least lower the gun?" said the man. "This is tense enough without having that thing in my face."

"I'll lower the gun when the diamond is in my hand," replied Rupert.

The man exhaled audibly then returned his attention to the computer. Another black screen appeared, and the familiar white text began to run across the screen.

"What are you doing?" asked Rupert.

"I thought you were done with the questions?" replied the man. His attitude had stiffened.

"I'll ask all the questions I like," said Rupert. He leaned forward to place the muzzle of the gun against the back of the man's head. "Now, tell me what you're doing."

"The hidden sensor is on a sub-system of the sensor network. If the first three sensors are disabled, the sub-system kicks in. I'm finding the IP address of the sub-system so I can then hack into it and disable it. If I don't do that, the alarms will go off as soon as the diamond is lifted from the cushion. It's a pressure sensor."

Rupert watched the commands he was entering and saw nothing untoward. Another browser opened, and the man entered the IP address of the sub-system. This time he entered the right password first time around.

A similar graphical representation of the building appeared, and the man flipped the building, zoomed and found the diamond display.

A single sensor floated in the air where the previous screen had shown three.

"That's it?" Rupert asked.

The man didn't reply. Instead, he hit the push to talk button on the mic.

"Secondary sensor is going down in three, two, one."

He clicked a button on the screen to disable the sensor; the icon turned red.

A few strokes of the keyboard and he switched back to the first screen then located the three sensors beneath the glass display.

"Primary sensors going down in ten seconds, but I can't keep them off for long before it's noticed. You've got about five seconds to lift the lid, grab what you need, and close the lid again."

"I'm ready," said the girl in response.

"Okay. Three, two, one."

CHAPTER TWENTY-SEVEN

Centuries of history stood silent and still before Harvey. He waited at the edge of the small alcove with the diamond and Melody behind him. Their own history was thick in the air, and the tension between them was electric.

"Harvey, I need your help here," said Melody.

He turned as she pushed the button on her ear-piece.

"I'm ready," she said to Reg. "Harvey, I need you to lift the edge of the glass when Reg gives the signal. I'll take the diamond."

Harvey stepped over to her, looked at the glass, then back at Melody. He pulled on a pair of thin cotton gloves and placed his hands either side of the display.

"Now."

Harvey raised the glass just enough for Melody to reach in and grab the diamond, which seemed to sparkle and glitter in response.

Harvey lowered the glass lid.

"It's down. We're good," said Melody to Reg, as she pocketed the diamond. "Now get us the hell out of here."

She listened to Reg's commands then gave Harvey a nod.

"Okay, we're leaving," said Melody, heading for the door to the service corridor. "How long do we have before the cameras come back on?"

She pulled open the door and stepped through into the walkway with Harvey right behind her. Immediately, two hands reached out and forced her to the floor. A guard stood over her, holding her arm behind her back. She'd hit her head in the fall; her body fell limp and her eyes closed. A small track of blood was smeared along the corridor wall.

Harvey sprang into action.

He swung the cosh, hard, fast and with violence. It connected with the back of the guard's head. His knees buckled, and he crumpled to the floor on top of Melody. Harvey pulled the guard off her and stole the man's radio. The channel was alive with crackled and frantic messages.

"They're on to us," said Harvey. "Come on, Melody. You need to wake up."

He rolled Melody onto her back and straightened her twisted arm. Without hesitation, Harvey reached down, removed her ear-piece and put it on his own ear before flicking the small switch that permanently opened the comms channel, eliminating the need for the wearer to push the button to communicate. He scooped Melody up in his arms and made towards the door.

"Reg, come back," said Harvey. He made his way along the corridor. "Reg?"

A familiar but timid voice came back in his ear. "Harvey? Is that you? What have you done with her?"

"No time, Reg," said Harvey. "She's down. I need an exit and fast."

"I'm just clearing the cameras."

"No time. We're blown. Get me out of here," said Harvey. "Fastest exit possible."

He shoved through the double doors just as two more guards reached the top of the stairs. Harvey kicked one directly in the chest sending him back down the hard steps. The other swung his cosh, but Harvey was faster. He twisted Melody out of the way and landed his forehead directly onto the man's nose.

The guard held his face with both hands. Harvey stamped down on his knee, bending his leg the wrong way, then stepped aside to allow the man to fall down howling like a baby with shrill screams that echoed through the stairwell.

"Fastest exit is the loading bay," said Reg.

"I had a feeling you were going to say that," said Harvey. "Can you meet me around the back?"

"Copy that," said Reg.

Three more guards heaved through the double doors as Harvey reached the bottom of the stairwell. One held a Taser pointed at Harvey, but all three hollered panicked commands at him to stop and get down on the floor.

"Easy, boys," Harvey replied. "Do you mind if I put her down first?"

Two of the men looked at the man in the middle, a middle-aged officer who stood tall and confident of his team's success.

"Do it slowly," he said. "Then lay on the floor beside her with your arms stretched out in front of you."

Harvey nodded as if submitting to his request. He bent and placed Melody on the cold, hard floor. Then, in an instant, he pulled Melody's Sig from his belt.

"Taser down now," said Harvey.

The three men all raised their hands in the air.

The Taser clattered to the floor at their feet.

"Kick it away," said Harvey.

The man closest to the weapon did as he was told.

"You, fat man," said Harvey, nodding at the large man who was closest to Harvey and holding out a bunch of zip ties. "Grab his wrist." Harvey gestured at the boss. "Tie it to the boy's wrist." Harvey gestured at the younger man on the end who had dropped the Taser.

The large man did as he was told.

"Now tie your own wrists to them both," said Harvey. He bent and collected Melody, keeping a firm hold on the handgun.

"Tight," he reminded them.

He heard the short, sharp zips of the ties being pulled tight.

"Good," said Harvey. "Nobody needed to get hurt, did they? Now sit down."

The three men sat down in unison as Harvey collected Melody from the floor and slipped through the double doors with her in his arms. She began to stir but was incoherent.

As Harvey entered the loading bay through the last set of doors, one more guard came at him. He was young and over-enthusiastic. Harvey heard his wild run up even before he saw him.

Harvey stopped.

Almost in disbelief, Harvey stared at the young man who was running full pelt at them both, readying to launch himself and take them to the floor. Their eyes met.

The guard carried on running.

Harvey didn't move.

Still running, the guard drew closer.

Harvey didn't look away.

The young guard suddenly lost momentum. His death cry waned to a murmur and then petered out to nothing.

Harvey glared at him.

The boy stood motionless in front of Harvey with his head hung low as if ashamed.

"Sit," said Harvey.

The boy dropped to a cross-legged position on the floor in front of Harvey.

Harvey kicked the single door open to the side of the loading bay, dropped down the small flight of concrete stairs, and walked calmly to Reg's waiting van.

Approaching sirens blared from all directions.

The van's side door slid open as he approached.

CHAPTER TWENTY-EIGHT

"Stop here," Rupert shouted.

The man had transferred from his place by the computers to the driver's seat to move the van.

"You won't get away with this," he replied with fresh confidence. "You don't know who's in there."

Rupert laughed. "My friend, I believe Harvey and I have spoken already. Interesting chap. Talented too, I hear."

"If you knew him, you wouldn't be waiting out here for him," said the man.

Rupert gave a soft laugh in the tense darkness of the van.

"He has quite the reputation, doesn't he?" he said. "Well, let's see how he deals with me."

"You'll need more than a gun to stop him."

"We'll see about that," said Rupert. He popped the magazine from the handgun, checked it and reloaded.

"What do you plan on doing with *us?*" the man asked.

Rupert watched for the single door of the loading bay to open through the tinted side window. Police sirens began to grow close and seemed to multiply the nearer they came.

"It's Reg, isn't it?" asked Rupert. "I heard him call you Reg."

"Yeah, it is," Reg replied.

"Well, Reg," said Rupert. "I have some ideas, and it all depends on how you and your friends react. Play nicely, and you might not get hurt, but mess me about, and you'll find that I have a sharp side. I can be quite playful." Rupert smiled as if to confirm his statement.

"He's coming," said Reg.

Rupert glanced out the window and saw a man carrying the girl in his arms. Rupert slid the side door open and stepped back with the gun raised. Harvey laid her down on the van's wooden floor and took a step up.

"Go, Reg," he said. "Don't hang about." He began to pull himself into the van.

"Not so fast, hero," said Rupert from the shadows.

Harvey froze.

"Come on guys. I can see the police," said Reg from the front of the van. "We're running out of time."

"Step down, Harvey," said Rupert.

"You're going to leave me here?" Harvey replied.

"Oh no, Harvey. This is the end for you, for what you did to Bob and Bill. But I wanted to look you in the eye before I killed you." Rupert offered his warmest smile again.

"Guys, can we discuss this on the way?" said Reg. His voice was racked with nerves, which were at their breaking point.

"Shut it," screamed Rupert. "Just shut your mouth and do as you're told."

He turned to back Harvey.

"You," he gestured at Harvey with the gun, waving it at his foot. "Off. Now."

Harvey slowly removed his foot from the van, his eyes never leaving Rupert's.

Rupert re-aimed the gun at Harvey's face. The two men shared a tense moment. The man didn't seem frightened at all.

If the girl he clearly cared about hadn't been lying at Rupert's feet, he would probably have jumped on him, a fact that Rupert made careful note of.

"Where's the diamond?" asked Rupert.

It was a few tense seconds before Harvey finally spoke.

"In my pocket. Why don't you come and take it off me?"

"Is that right?" said Rupert. He bent and ran his hands along Melody's pockets.

Rupert's grin grew into a laugh. He shook his head at his own luck as his hand closed around a golf ball-sized lump.

"Bad luck, Harvey," said Rupert. He stood, preparing to squeeze the trigger.

"Reg, *now*," said Harvey, and span out of sight.

Reg gunned the engine. The van lurched forward and Rupert lost his balance. He pulled a single shot, but it went wide into the air. Rupert clung to the side of the van, dragged himself upright, and then slammed the side door in anger.

"I didn't tell you to go," he screamed at the driver. "Turn back."

Reg cowered at the wheel.

"Turn around?" he asked. "We can't turn-"

Rupert kicked out at the chairs with fury. "Just drive, and don't do anything I don't tell you to do."

"Where am I going?" asked Reg, visibly scared. "There's police everywhere."

"To the river," said Rupert, as he fumbled through the girl's pockets. "Turn onto Queen's Gate and don't stop for lights."

Rupert searched through the girl's black hooded sweatshirt. His hand fell on something familiar. He reached in and pulled out the GPS tag that Glasgow George had fixed to her wrist. He tossed it aside then felt through the pockets of her black cargo pants where he'd felt the lump a few minutes earlier.

He slid two fingers into her pants pocket then slowly pulled out a perfect diamond the size of a golf ball and identical to the one he had stashed at Smokey's house.

It glittered in the soft light. The weight felt reassuring in his hand. He was mesmerised.

Reg swung the van hard to the left as he turned onto Queen's Gate. Two police cars screamed past in the opposite direction. Rupert held on tight with one hand, and holding the diamond up in the air, he closed his fist, kissed his newfound fortune, and pocketed it, tapping his pocket as if to confirm to himself that it was safe.

He felt his anger dissipate and a calm relief washed over him. "It's turned out to be a successful night, Mr Reg," said Rupert. "You get me to the boat, and you just might live after all."

CHAPTER TWENTY-NINE

The van pulled away and left Harvey standing outside the rear of the museum in the dead of night. Police sirens were growing louder. Flashing blue lights approached in front and to both sides of his peripheral vision. He remained still for a few more seconds, pinned to the ground as he watched the van turn onto Queen's Gate then disappear. Then Harvey jumped into action as if shaken from a dream.

He ran directly away from the museum along Museum Lane. His head pounded with anger, and his chest thumped at the loss of Melody. A police car pulled into the lane in front of him at high speed, blocking his exit.

The driver accelerated towards him.

Harvey didn't slow down, nor did he move to the side of the narrow road, which was blocked on either side by huge buildings. He could see the passenger's face prepare for a collision as the car grew nearer. Harvey ran faster, giving everything he had.

Then, at the last possible moment, the driver pulled the wheel to the left and pulled the handbrake up. The length of the car almost filled the width of the lane. Harvey jumped across the front of the car as the doors opened. He landed on his backside, slid off the car's polished surface onto the road, and was away.

"Stop. Armed police," yelled the passenger, who was closest to Harvey. The policeman gave chase and tried to grab onto Harvey's jacket but missed. Harvey pumped his arms as he ran. He sprinted towards the edge of the building, waiting for the shots to begin. He dived around the side of the Science Museum, which occupied the other side of Museum Lane, and stopped. Jumping back against the wall under a small copse of trees, he stopped and listened as the policeman's boots approached. At the first sign of the man appearing around the corner, Harvey whipped out the telescopic cosh, reached out from the shadows and swung it hard against the policeman's knees.

He fell to the grass in a silent whimper and rolled to a stop.

Harvey wasted no time. He heard the car turning behind him in the lane, and cut through the trees beside the Science Museum, then sprinted through an alleyway another hundred yards along the road. There, he found his motorbike parked beside two expensive-looking saloon cars, exactly where he'd left it.

Squealing tyres and brakes told Harvey that more police had arrived at the museum. The area was lit with flashing blue lights. Bouncing headlights in the alleyway behind Harvey showed that the other cop was hunting for him behind the Science Museum.

He pulled his helmet on quickly, started the bike, and rode casually away from the scene. Winding his way out of the back streets, he passed the Natural History Museum less than two minutes after Melody had been taken. At least twenty police cars had since blocked Museum Lane and they had begun to block the main road to the front of the building. He took a quick look at the scene before turning towards the river, where the van had disappeared at the junction of Queen's Gate.

Harvey waited until he was out of sight of the police then dropped into second gear with his sights firmly set on the river less than a mile directly ahead of him.

There was no need to brake or change gear on the bike once he hit one hundred and ten miles per hour. The roads were quiet, and he passed the few cars in a flash before they even knew he was approaching.

As the black strip of the river came into view, Harvey eased off the accelerator. At the entrance to the small dock, sitting with its doors wide open, was the van. Harvey approached carefully, but the van was empty.

The buildings on the far side of the river reflected lights of red, blue and yellow off the water's surface. By the time Harvey reached the water and had slowed to a stop beside the little dock, the lights were shimmering in the wake of a distant boat. Its waning portside light grew smaller and disappeared into the night.

Harvey stared after the boat heading south on the river. He was too late. A rage began to boil inside him.

He revved the bike's engine once. Then his anger got the better of him, popping in his mind like a pressure valve. With a hard twist of the throttle, the engine roared, screaming in revolt, but he held it, venting his anger and frustration through the engine. Then he slipped into first gear, popped the clutch and locked the front brake hard down. The rear wheel span on the cobbled road, sending the back of the bike in a slow circle. A cloud of tyre smoke filled the night around him. Once the bike had turned to face the way he'd came, he released the brake and roared up the street, his mind firmly set on South London.

CHAPTER THIRTY

A heavy stale smell of charred meat intertwined with an acrid, acidic odour clung to the back of Melody's throat. She gagged then dry-heaved but couldn't lean forward to spit. Instead, fiery saliva dribbled from her lips onto her lap.

A hood had been pulled over her head, which shut out any direct light and view of the room. But she felt strong heat and just faintly saw a glow of orange in front of her through the loose fabric of the hood. Everything else was dark.

Somewhere far off, in another room perhaps, Melody could hear the soprano section of an orchestra, though she couldn't make out the exact piece.

A desperate fight for life kicked in.

Melody was immediately aware that she was sitting down with her hands bound behind her and her ankles tied to the chair legs. She fought her restraints, pulling her arms and legs in all directions, but to no avail.

"Harvey?" she called, with a breathless, weak, dry rasp. "Is that you?"

No reply came for a few seconds until a slow, crying hinge

turned, like some wild animal's dying breath. It pierced the space around her, and the heat of the room intensified.

"Reg?" she called. The force of her voice on her dry throat scratched and sent her into a coughing fit. She spat blindly to rid her throat of the burning saliva.

"Melody?"

It was Reg's voice.

"Reg?" she wheezed. "Where are you?"

Reg didn't reply.

"Reg, talk to me," said Melody.

"I can't, Melody," said Reg, his voice high with emotion.

"Reg? Tell me what's wrong."

She could tell he was somewhere in front of her, but the hot glow was all she could vaguely see.

Reg sniffed once and sighed.

"Are you crying?" asked Melody. "Talk to me. We can get out of this, Reg."

"You'll be going nowhere fast, young lady," said a voice, cold and hard, with a twang of a Welsh accent.

Blind to her surroundings, the voice conjured an image in Melody's mind of a man in his fifties with a flock of silver hair above each ear and small spectacles resting gently on the bridge of a large nose.

"Who are you?" she asked. "Where am I?"

"You're in purgatory, dear," the voice replied. "Relax while your path is decided. You're on the cusp of heaven and hell. There's a tug of war happening between the devil and the big man himself."

His face suddenly blocked the glow of the fire. He almost whispered.

"And you're the prize."

"Who are you?" asked Melody.

The shape of the man's face moved away, and the orange

glow returned to the centre of Melody's view. With it came the dry heat that prickled every tiny hair on Melody's skin.

"That's an easy one," he replied. "I am the shepherd. *I* am the shining light which will guide your way, and I am your soulless chaperone from this world to the next."

"Reg, are you hearing this?"

"Silence," the voice spat. "The time for questions is over. Your friend is about to begin his own journey."

"Melody?" mumbled Reg.

"Reg?" cried Melody. "*Reg.*"

A strong smell hit Melody's nose of chemicals, but not familiar.

"Reg?" Melody screamed.

The flat palm of a hand struck Melody hard across her face.

Then the hand returned to her cheek, but this time the touch was soft. His thumb reached into the hood and gently caressed her skin. She tried to move away, but her restraints held her there.

"Don't fight it," the man said.

His hand slid slowly to her neck. His body passed in front of her, once more revealing the orange glow like a beacon in the dark.

She felt him standing behind her. His hand was working its way along her collarbone, soft hands, but cold to the touch.

A small moan of relief issued from his throat as he inhaled the smell of Melody's hair. She pictured him standing behind her with his head tilted back, his face half lit by the glowing orange fire in front of where she sat.

His hand dropped further. His fingers found the top of her tight black t-shirt.

Melody's heart raced. Her breathing quickened. His hand slid across her clammy skin and found what he was looking for.

"Get your dirty hands away from me," Melody spat.

The man responded with a small groan and pushed himself into Melody's back. As much as she struggled, Melody couldn't get away from the push of his groin and the squeeze of his hand.

"Don't fight me, dear," he said. "I can make your journey easy." He gave a hard squeeze. "Or I can make it painful. The path you take is not my decision, but how I lead you there, well, you decide."

He slipped his hand out of her shirt and walked away. Melody felt his presence move around her like a shadow in the darkness. He began to hum to the soft music that played somewhere far off. She heard the metallic clangs and clatters of what sounded like tools being placed on a surgical trolley. It was followed by the gulp and gargle of a liquid container being turned upside down, like a water dispenser. Finally, Melody heard a small squeak of a tap or a valve and the roar of open flames growing louder.

A door opened behind Melody, allowing a cool breeze to enter the room. It sent a chill from Melody's ankles to her face, forming goosebumps that shuddered through to her very core.

"Doctor Feelmore," said a new authoritative voice from behind Melody. "Are we ready?"

CHAPTER THIRTY-ONE

With a tug of the thin material, the hood pulled away from the girl's head. Rupert tossed it into the glowing furnace behind him, which sat like a hungry beast at feeding time.

He watched as the girl blinked her eyes and squinted. Then, as her vision adjusted, she focused on his feet. Her head rose as she took him in, slowly letting her eyes fall onto Rupert's for the first time.

Rupert gave her time to look around the room as far as the restraints allowed. She gave a distasteful glare at Doctor Feelmore, who smiled like the creep that he was in return. Then her eyes fell on her friend who lay on the gurney.

The girl's face fell in dismay at the sight of him. A drip of embalming fluid was inserted into his arm, just waiting to be turned on, and a draining tray lay beneath his thigh.

It would be a painful death. The worst imaginable.

"How long does it take for a man to die like this, doctor?" asked Rupert. He fixed his gaze upon the girl.

"It will be interesting to find out, Mr Bond," replied the doctor. "I've never embalmed a *live* person before. But I would say seven or eight minutes. The acid will very quickly eat away at his veins and arteries, which will be excruciating. I would suggest then heart would give out before the loss of blood takes effect, through the pain, you understand. But we'll see."

Rupert glanced at the doctor, nodded his thanks for his professional opinion, and returned his stare to the girl.

"How's your head?" he asked.

She returned his stare with equal distaste.

"Fine," she said.

Rupert nodded at her friend on the gurney. "You love this man?"

"Like a brother," the girl replied.

Rupert allowed silence to ensue before speaking. He enjoyed seeing how people reacted under pressure.

"You understand what we're doing here, right?" he asked. "You can see the lengths we're going to in order to make you suffer."

"I can see," she replied. "But for the life of me, I can't understand why."

"Do you know who I am, Lola?" he asked.

She looked confused.

"No," she said. "No, I don't know who you are. I've never seen you before and my name is not-"

"Well, let me enlighten you," said Rupert, cutting her off before the conversation deviated from where he intended. "My name is Rupert Bond. You may have heard of me?"

"No. I can't say I have."

"Your friend Harvey has, Lola, and if I may jog your memory a little, you helped him burn the face off my good friend Mad Bob and cut the throat of Cannon Bill. I knew them both for many years, and they were very loyal men."

"I have absolutely no idea-"

"Don't interrupt me, Lola," said Rupert. Anger began to rise in his voice. "You and your friend Reg here, or should I call him

Fingers? Not only did you both help our friend Harvey kill my two good friends, but you have potentially damaged our reputation. I can't have the good people of South London running away with the idea that it's okay to knock off the Bond Brothers without a sniff of retribution or retaliation. Or punishment," Rupert finished.

"You've got the wrong-"

"You don't talk until I tell you to talk, Lola," snapped Rupert.

The girl let her head drop.

"So, I needed a way to make you suffer, and luckily for me, my good friend Doctor Feelmore here not only has the skills to prolong that suffering but as you can see, being a doctor of mortuary science, he also has the necessary tools to dispose of your bodies."

"You have the diamond. Let us go," said the girl.

"No," replied Rupert, cold and hard.

"Can I speak?" she asked.

Rupert nodded. "You can talk, but the only thing I want to hear from you is the word, sorry," said Rupert. "And *sir*," he added with finality.

"He'll find you."

"I doubt that," replied Rupert with a laugh.

"The harder you make this on me, the longer it'll take for you to die."

"Not very convincing."

"You've got to believe me. He won't give up. He'll find you and-"

And?" said Rupert. He held the back of her hair and pulled her head back in a swift, sharp movement. "That's just it, you see. I want him to find me. I want him to show his face because I'm going to tear it off."

She blinked away the pain.

"You don't know him," she said. "You don't know what he's capable of."

"Oh, no, no," said Rupert. "It is he who doesn't know what *I* am capable of."

The girl's expression dropped to a submissive tone of pity.

"Then do what you will," she said. "But believe me, you'll be sorry."

Rupert shoved her head away and put his face close to hers.

"I'll look forward to it, sweetheart."

Rupert's pocket began to vibrate.

"Think about your next words, Lola," he said as he straightened. "They'll be the last ones Reggie over there ever hears."

Rupert pulled his phone from his pocket, recognised the number and hit the connect button.

"Smokey," he said. "I wondered when I'd hear from you."

CHAPTER THIRTY-TWO

The thin wooden door of the little houseboat was no match for Harvey's heavy boot. It swung back and smashed against the tiny kitchenette, breaking free from its top hinge. It rocked back and forth for a moment, then crashed to the floor.

Harvey ducked inside the cabin and stood tall over Fingers, who had frozen at the sound of the crashing front door. Fingers stood poised with the bundle of rolled up drawings in his arms and a small holdall on the floor beside him.

"Going somewhere, Fingers?" asked Harvey.

"Oh, thank God it's you," said Fingers. "I thought they'd come for me."

"Who?" said Harvey. "Who would have come for you?"

"The Bond Brothers," whispered Fingers. His eyes darted to the narrow view of the canal's towpath through the side window.

"There's no-one out there," said Harvey.

"Are you sure? I heard the police helicopter go over a while ago."

"You're the geek, right?" asked Harvey.

Fingers responded with a confused look.

"The geek, the computer guy," said Harvey. "You're the one that gets Lola inside so she can do her job. Am I right?"

Fingers nodded.

Harvey took a step forward.

"Find me Lola," said Harvey.

Fingers took a step backwards.

"I don't know where she is," said Fingers. "You saw yourself; she was thrown into the back of that van."

"Find me the tag she was wearing."

Harvey held his gaze.

"She dropped it," said Fingers. "I saw it fall."

"I picked it up," said Harvey, "after you drove off and left me there."

Fingers lowered his eyes to the floor. "I was scared," he said. "I didn't know what to do."

"Sit down," said Harvey.

Fingers remained standing, open mouthed and staring at the floor.

With a single sweep of his arm, Harvey cleared the small dining table that stood between the two men.

"I said sit down," he shouted.

Fingers dropped back onto the small U-shaped couch, still clutching the rolls of building plans to his chest.

Harvey collected the holdall from where it sat on the floor, unzipped the zipper, and tipped the bag upside down. The contents scattered across the old rug that covered the boat's polished wooden floor. Some paperwork, a passport, a few items of clothing and a laptop lay in a heap. Harvey bent and picked up the laptop. He tossed it at Fingers, who dropped the rolls of paper and caught it as if it were the most precious thing he owned.

"Find the tag."

"What tag?" asked Fingers, stalling. "I don't know how to find it."

Harvey didn't reply.

With an air of reluctance, Fingers set the laptop down on the table, opened it and began to type.

Harvey moved around the tiny room to see the screen.

Fingers edged away.

"You're afraid of me?" Harvey asked.

"With all due respect, sir, I watched you set fire to a man's face and cut another man's throat," said Fingers. "It's fair to say I'm a little wary of you."

Fingers' fingers danced across the keys in short spurts. Harvey noticed how they moved in fits then hovered as his eyes scanned a line of text, and then burst into life again. The movements reminded Harvey of Reg; he used to do exactly the same thing.

"That's why they call you Fingers then, is it?" said Harvey.

Fingers kept his eyes on the laptop screen and issued a quiet, "Mm-hmm." It was exactly how Reg used to sound when he was focused on something.

"Okay," said Fingers. "I'm into the GeoTech Tracking Platform. There's about six hundred live tags in the London area. I have no way of knowing which is Lola's."

"Seven, four, five, six," began Harvey. "Six, eight, two, five, nine, three, four."

"You memorised the serial number?" said Fingers, clearly impressed. He tapped the number that Harvey recalled into the search function.

"Have you found it?" asked Harvey.

Fingers sucked in a lungful of air through his teeth and let it out with a long hiss.

"The Crematorium of Greater South London," said Fingers, spinning the laptop around for Harvey to see a little icon on a map. It hovered over a patch of green in the middle of what was clearly residential streets.

Harvey zoomed the map out, fixed the location in his mind then shut the laptop. He reached up to the window, opened it a little, and tossed the laptop out. It landed with a splash in the canal below.

"You just..." began Fingers. "That was my..."

Harvey glared at him.

"So you're *leaving* now?" asked Fingers, with hope in his voice.

Harvey sighed then leaned on the couch opposite Fingers.

"What's your real name, Fingers?"

"Jeremy, sir."

"Jeremy what?"

"Jeremy Hawes," replied Fingers. His voice quavered, and his eyes were wide open as if they'd been glued.

"Mind if I call you Fingers?" asked Harvey.

Fingers shook his head.

"Good. So is there something you want to tell me?" asked Harvey. "And before you feed me a pack of lies, you should know that I'm extremely good at knowing when somebody is telling the truth." Harvey pulled his knife from the sheath sewn into the inside of his jacket. "And I know when they're playing me for a fool," he finished.

He turned the knife in his hands, feeling the familiar texture of the wood. It was the same knife his mentor had given him when he was a teenager, and the same knife Harvey had used to extract the truth from many men of all shapes and sizes.

"I'm waiting," said Harvey.

"It was her idea," said Fingers. "I just helped." He gestured at the empty space where the laptop had been.

Harvey didn't reply. He raised an eyebrow.

"The diamond was all she thought about," said Fingers. His

head dropped in defeat. "She said it belonged to her. It was rightfully hers."

"Lola LaRoux," said Harvey.

"Exactly. You know the story? It belonged to her family or something. I don't know. But they've been after it for years and when-"

"Yeah, yeah," said Harvey. "When the diamond was spotted, she convinced you and the other fella-"

"Dynamite," interjected Fingers.

"She convinced you and Dynamite to rob it?"

"That's right. It was all her idea. I just-"

"Helped?" asked Harvey.

"Yeah, I just helped. We knew each other from way back. I went to school with Dynamite, we did a few jobs years ago."

"Something doesn't add up," said Harvey. "I'm a simple man, Fingers. To me, everything is either black or it's white. It either is or it isn't. I don't believe in God. But I would never disrespect someone who does, you understand? That's their choice. Do you see a picture of who I really am?"

"A simple man," said Fingers. "Black or white. Yeah, I understand."

"Good," continued Harvey. "Can you tell me the story about when the brothers put the tag on Lola?"

"The wrist tag?" said Fingers. His eyes somehow grew larger as if he could sense where Harvey was taking the conversation. "We did a job."

"Tell it like it is, Fingers," interrupted Harvey. "You stole the missing diamond."

Fingers nodded.

"Yeah, we did. We stole the missing diamond. But when Lola and Dynamite went in, the Bond Brothers found me in the van hidden in the trees. So when Lola and Dynamite came running from the job, they shot Dynamite and put the tag on Lola. That's when they told her to rob the second diamond."

"And if she didn't rob the second diamond, they'd kill you both?"

Fingers nodded. "And our families."

Harvey began to pace the few short steps from the small dining table to the broken front door, and back.

"So, who took Lola then?" asked Harvey. "Who threw her in the van the other day?"

"I don't know," said Fingers. "It all happened so quick."

"Yeah, I saw it. One minute you were both there, the next she was in the back of the van, and it was tearing off down the road. I saw it all, you know, Fingers?"

Fingers held his gaze. His eyes had begun to shine with the inevitable tears that would come soon.

"Did you see me?" asked Harvey. "Did you see me there, Fingers?"

Fingers nodded. It was almost indiscernible, but it was a nod.

"You saw me, and you just drove off. And don't tell me you were scared."

Fingers stayed silent.

"You see, that's another thing I can't understand. Why would someone drive off in the opposite direction so quickly after their friend had just been kidnapped?"

Fingers looked at the floor.

"And why, if they took Lola, would they not take you as well?" asked Harvey. "You're a witness, right?"

Silence.

"And this is the big one, Fingers. Why, if they found you at the first robbery, did they not either shoot you or put a tag on you?"

"I guess they didn't need-"

"Didn't need to?"

Fingers began to cry. Silent tears fell from his cheeks to the old rug that lay beneath the table.

"It's not me they want, is it? They want Lola. She's got the skills they need. She's the one who can break into places, not me."

"So you set Lola up? *You* had her kidnapped?" said Harvey. "You also set me up. You *knew* that I'd go and get the diamond, didn't you?"

Fingers nodded.

"And now, two of my good friends are in trouble, Fingers, and the Bond Brothers still have the diamond."

A loud sob announced the arrival of a full confession. The waters broke. Fingers crumpled into a folded mess on the couch. He drew his knees to his chest and buried his head between his legs.

Harvey stepped out through the broken door and reached for a fuel can he'd seen resting on the prow of the boat. He stepped back inside, unscrewed the lid and tossed it to one side.

Fingers' eyes lit up with horror.

"I did it to save her," whined Fingers. "You have to understand. Her father knows some men. I told him she was in trouble and we made a plan. He helped me."

Harvey waited for the rest of the story. He'd seen it a hundred times. The confessor usually felt glad to finally tell someone their secret. Once they started, the whole story came out.

He began to douse the furniture in petrol while he waited for Fingers to open up.

"If Lola got the diamond, I knew they'd still kill her and probably me as well."

"I'm listening."

"And if we didn't get the diamond, then they'd still kill us both. But if we gave them you-"

"Right," said Harvey. "So are you saying you had Lola kidnapped because you knew that I'd go in and rob the diamond anyway?"

"I'm sorry. You were the only one capable of getting away. If I let Lola do the robbery, she'd have got the diamond for sure. But they'd of killed her anyway, just like they did Dynamite. It was the only way to save her," said Fingers.

"But what about if I killed you?"

Fingers shrugged and stared at the floor.

"I'm dead anyway, let's face it. I didn't know what else to do," said Fingers.

He looked up. His eyes glowed red and snot ran from his nose in a stringy gloop. He looked wretched and simply stared at the floor.

Harvey placed the empty fuel can on the table with a loud thud like a drum. He kicked the passport on the floor over to Fingers' feet.

Fingers saw the movement. He reached down and picked it up, but looked at Harvey with confusion on his face.

"You're letting me go?" he asked.

Harvey didn't reply. Instead, he stuffed a wad of unopened letters into the toaster, which sat surrounded by breadcrumbs on the surface of the kitchenette. He pulled down the lever and set the timer to max, then turned the gas hob onto full.

Fingers jumped to his feet, scrambled over the drawings and his belongings to the door, and disappeared onto the footpath. Harvey gave the boat a cursory glance. Once he was happy that all the evidence would be burned, he stepped out to find Fingers, who was cowering behind a tree on the towpath fifty yards away.

"What have you done?" called Fingers, as Harvey causally approached him. "That's my boat."

A loud click cut through the night as the toaster popped up, followed by the rush of gases expanding, igniting, and seeking pockets of oxygen to burn, which combined in a whooshing ball of flame that mushroomed in the night sky.

The wooden hull of the boat exploded, sending shards of wood high into the air, which landed in the trees and grass behind Harvey.

"*Was* your boat," said Harvey, without turning back. "You just died in a very nasty explosion, Fingers. I suggest you get on the next plane out of here."

CHAPTER-THIRTY-THREE

"Charlie," called Rupert from the door. "Where are you?"

"Here," said another voice from somewhere further down the corridor.

"Well, get your arse in here," said Rupert, stepping back into the room.

He snatched the bag off Melody's head, but there was no painful stab of light in her eyes. The room was dark with just the dull glow of the furnace flames. The heat from the fire prickled her skin.

She stared up at Rupert, who stared back with the smug grin of someone who'd won, as his identical brother stepped into the room.

"Charlie, get Glasgow ready. We're going to the factory," said Rupert. "What were you doing out there anyway?"

"Not a lot."

Melody looked around once more and noticed they were in a chapel behind a large curtain. The cool breeze on her ankles came from the curtain. It was a crematorium.

"What were you doing, Charlie?"

"Looking at the bodies," he replied. "They're quite fascinating."

A broad grin ran across Doctor Feelmore's unashamed face.

"They're what? They're dead bodies," said Rupert. "You aren't supposed to be fascinated by them."

"What factory?" asked Charlie, ignoring his brother's distaste. "And what for?"

Rupert shook his head. "I just got a call. Smokey the Jew wants to meet us there for the handover."

"In a factory?"

"Yes," said Rupert.

"You mean the one where-"

"Mad Bob and Cannon Bill were killed? The very one," said Rupert.

"Can't we meet at a bar or something? Somewhere a bit nicer. I just had my shoes cleaned."

"When we're done, Charlie, you'll be able to buy a new pair every time you get one pair dirty. Now, I'm going to finish up here, you go get Glasgow George ready with the van."

"The van?" said Charlie. "It gets bloody worse. Why don't we go in the Bentley?"

"Are you going to question my every decision tonight, Charlie? Or can we crack on with this?"

"Alright, alright," said Charlie. "So who's that then?"

"Who's what?"

"Her?" said Charlie, nodding at Melody.

"That's Lola, you idiot. Who do you think it is?"

"Aren't we going to stay and watch the fun?"

"Charlie, you've got problems, you have," said Rupert. "We're about thirty minutes away from being richer than you can imagine, and you want to stay and watch this lot get burned alive?"

Charlie smiled at the comment.

"For Mad Bob," he replied. "And Bill."

"Charlie, we're leaving in five minutes. Get Glasgow ready."

Charlie huffed and left the room, muttering to himself. Rupert turned to Melody. He lowered himself down in front of her and spoke slowly and clearly.

"You, sweetheart, are a very stupid girl. You could have had it all."

Melody stayed silent.

"Doctor, do we, or do we not, pay extremely well?"

"Oh yes," said the doctor. "Very handsomely, I'd say."

"And how long have you worked for me, doctor?"

Melody began to hate the smug confidence with which the man spoke. His tailored suit, Italian shoes and well-groomed face were results of everything she opposed.

"Oh, about ten years, I'd say," replied the doctor. "Give or take."

"And, in that time, have either myself or my brother spoken to you with anything other than the highest respect?"

"Oh no, sir," the doctor replied. "Always a pleasure, it is."

"Did you hear that, Lola?" asked Rupert. "*Sir.*"

He eyed her up and down. His lip curled and he spat in her face.

"You don't come to South London and mug off the Bond Brothers, sweetheart. When the good doctor here is done with you, your ashes will go in the toilet, and you should count yourself lucky. Mad Bob and Cannon Bill worked with us for a very long time, and you know, every single man that works for us would have quite gladly paid you a visit here to make your last few hours that little more..."

He flicked at Melody's chin to lift her head.

"Unbearable," he finished.

"So why don't they?" she asked.

"We, as it happens, Lola, we have a more pressing night ahead of us, and thanks to you, we'll be moving on to bigger and better things. So, you know, plans to make, people to see. But not to worry, of all the men that work for me, I'm certain the good doctor here is capable of making sure that my friends Bob and Bill are remembered."

He leaned forward and whispered into her ear.

"He's a sick man, and having a girl with a pulse will be a real treat for him, especially one as pretty as you."

Melody closed her eyes to block out the thoughts.

"Isn't that right, doctor?" said Rupert aloud.

"A pulse, why yes, sir," the doctor replied. "That'll make a nice change."

Rupert stared down at Melody. "See what I mean?" He stood to leave. From the doorway, he turned and spoke once more. "I'll leave you in the capable hands of our friend Doctor Feelmore, Lola."

Melody didn't reply.

"Doctor?" said Rupert.

"Sir?" the Doctor replied from his place in the corner.

The tiniest of moments hung between the sentences, but it was enough time for Melody to hear the music and picture Harvey and her on the beach near their farmhouse.

"Do your worst," said Rupert. "And make sure she suffers."

CHAPTER THIRTY-FOUR

Rain pelted the van as the three men journeyed the short distance through the South London suburb. Glasgow George drove the van. Charlie sat in the middle. Rupert was in the passenger seat.

"We're close, Rupert," said Charlie. "So bloody close. I can almost taste the sangria now. Why do you think he wants to meet here?"

"I don't know, Charlie, probably because he doesn't want the likes of us at his nice house."

"Well, what did Smokey actually say?"

"He said to meet him at Mad Bob's factory," said Rupert. "The instructions are quite clear, Charlie."

"Yeah but how did Smokey *know* that Mad Bob was killed there?" asked Charlie.

"Because it was his men that came and cleaned up the mess," said Rupert. "You don't think I'd have sent one of our own guys to clean up their mates' bod-"

Rupert stopped, aware that Glasgow was listening.

"That's what mates do, Charlie. When they lose a friend, they help out. Smokey's family and the Bonds go way back.

They've been wasting their money on art and big houses, while you and I, brother, have built a bloody empire."

"You put too much trust in that man, Rupert," said Charlie.

Rupert ignored his brother's lack of foresight and spoke directly to Glasgow. He was a stocky man, short, but fierce looking.

"Are you carrying, Glasgow?" asked Rupert.

Glasgow tapped the breast of his jacket where his handgun sat in its holster.

"Always, boss," he replied.

"You're a man of few words, Glasgow," said Rupert. "But tell me something. If this all works out how it should, Charlie and I will be shutting up shop here in London. We'll have enough money to retire. I think we've earned the chance to see out our mature years in the warmth and comfort of warmer climates-"

"And the warmth and comfort of several semi-naked women," said Charlie.

"So, Glasgow, tell us what you're going to do if we fold all this up?" continued Rupert, once more ignoring his brother.

Glasgow George's eyes didn't leave the road in front. His brow didn't furrow. His face remained impassive.

"What are my options?" he replied.

"Your options?" said Rupert. "That's a very level-headed question, Glasgow. So I'll give it to you straight. But remember this before you make up your mind. There is one more job you need to do for us in order to earn whatever you decide."

Glasgow nodded.

"The first option, Glasgow, is for you to take over here."

"Run the firm?" asked Glasgow.

"You've worked for us a very long time, and I've given the options an appropriate amount of consideration. If anyone was to take over, you're the only man I can see pulling it off. It'll be all yours, Glasgow. Naturally, you'd buy the assets from us at mates rates, and we can work out some kind of payment plan. But other than that, it'll be yours to run as you see fit."

Glasgow nodded once more.

"Option two. You carry on working for us. You come with us to wherever we decide to go and resume your role as head of security."

Glasgow, as ever, showed no preference to either.

"You'll be well paid, Glasgow," said Rupert, as a sweetener.

"What's the job?" asked Glasgow. "You said there was one last job."

Rupert considered how best to sell the idea to a man as ruthless, yet simple, as Glasgow.

"As I recall," he began, "Mad Bob and Cannon Bill were mates of yours, were they not?"

Glasgow's mouth turned into a grimace. Rupert watched at the effect the two men's names had on the man.

"They meant a lot to us too, Glasgow. They worked for us for a very long time and helped us build the empire we now enjoy. I wondered what it might feel like for those of us who knew Bob and Bill so well to get our hands on the man that killed them."

Glasgow nodded.

"Is he coming?" asked George.

"He is, Glasgow. He's coming right for us."

Glasgow's face seemed to bunch up in the dim light. It was difficult to tell if the expression was of hate, pain, or perhaps a smile.

"One last act to close off this whole episode, George, and to allow them the rest they deserve. What do you say to that?"

"You want me to kill him?" asked George.

"Oh no, Glasgow," said Rupert with a grin. "I want you to *catch* him. I want him caught, so that we can all take turns in killing him. We're going to kill the fucker so many times he's going to wish he'd never set foot in London. He's going to wish he'd never been born, Glasgow."

Glasgow nodded once more. The silhouette of his huge face rocked twice against the driver side window.

"You don't have to make a decision now, George, about if you'd prefer option one or option two. But I have a feeling that the chance to complete your little mission might come tonight, and if it does, I want you to be ready."

"So you reckon he'll definitely come, Rupert?" asked Charlie. "This Harvey bloke?"

"He'll be here alright," said Rupert, "and we'll close this little episode off once and for all."

Glasgow George stopped the van in the little lane outside the old factory. A chain-link fence secured the perimeter, and trees grew wild in the scrubland that bordered the lane and the building. The scene was empty of cars, people and movement, except the howling wind that tore at the treetops and sent the rain down diagonally.

"How do we get in, George?" asked Rupert.

"There's a hole in the fence over there," replied Glasgow, gesturing with a nod of his head.

"Good. Charlie, you come with me. Glasgow?" Glasgow George looked across at Rupert, his face as serious as it could be. "Go find our man Harvey."

"We're going to get soaked," said Charlie.

"No bruv," replied Rupert. "Tonight, we're going to get even, and we're going to get very bloody rich."

CHAPTER THIRTY-FIVE

The touch of Doctor Feelmore's hand against Melody's shoulder made her skin crawl. He'd closed the door behind the Bond Brothers and stood directly behind her.

The flames continued to burn inside the cremator but on a low setting as if they were only to warm the room and keep the furnace alight.

Reg had passed out on the conveyor belt.

"Just you and me then," said Feelmore. "I told you we'd have plenty of time to enjoy ourselves."

"Is this how you get your kicks?" said Melody. "You're a seriously disturbed man."

Feelmore reached down to Melody's chest, took a deep breath and groaned.

"So warm," he said. "My guests are usually much colder, you know?"

Melody struggled against the restraints. She was sure she could overpower him. She was held tight, but if an opportunity presented itself, she'd need to be ready to take it.

Feelmore laughed. "And they don't usually struggle so much. In fact, they rarely complain at all."

He slipped his hand from Melody's shirt and rested it on top of her head.

"I must say, you're a real treat," said Feelmore. "In addition to the warmth of your skin and the youth of your face, it's an absolute delight that you're so..." He searched for the words. "Alive with spirit," he finished. "I rarely get to sample one of your kind."

"My kind?" said Melody. "Do you have many guests?"

"Not so young, and hardly ever as pretty. But more importantly, you have a debt to pay," said Feelmore. "And for once I get to have you all to myself. I was once lucky enough to have the company of a female magistrate, who by chance or good fortune had recently brought the hammer down on some of the brothers' men. It was armed robbery or something, in the early days before they bought the clubs and bars."

Feelmore walked away from the chair. Melody couldn't see where he went but could hear his breathing close behind her.

A rustle of clothing.

He was undressing.

"Of course," continued Feelmore, "the boys all took delight in seeing her dead on my gurney one night. A few stayed for the after party. Not the brothers, no, they wouldn't get involved in that type of thing. But some of their boys would. And did."

A rattle of a belt broke the silence between Feelmore's rambling. Melody closed her eyes and thought of Harvey.

She thought of all the times she'd been in danger. It wasn't the first time she'd been caught, tied up and threatened. But for the first time, she could truly see no way out.

"The brothers turn a blind eye. They know what happens here. It doesn't make someone a bad person, you know? One bloke, in particular, Bill his name was, that's right, Cannon Bill, he came here often and paid well to get his kicks."

As much as Melody tried to picture Harvey, their farmhouse in France, and the life they had shared however briefly, she couldn't shake the image of Doctor Feelmore standing naked behind her with his face upturned as he recalled times of old.

"He was a quiet one, old Bill. Nice guy, don't get me wrong. Just quiet. You couldn't read him. Do you know what I mean, Lola? He was as hard as nails, built like a bleeding house with hands like shovels."

He rested his hands on Melody's shoulders from behind.

"Then he deserved what he got," spat Melody.

"I don't care what he did, but Bill didn't deserve to die like that. He didn't even need to be brought here. Apparently, they just scooped the bodies up with a shovel."

He moved away again. But this time, he stepped to the side of Melody and moved around in front of her, proud and smiling with the confidence of a child.

"It's strange, isn't it?" he said.

Melody let his words hang in the air a while, then fixed his gaze.

"What's strange, doctor?" she asked, her voice almost a whisper.

Feelmore looked down at Melody with curiosity and answered in a whisper equal to her own, but riddled in spite.

"How a man can be almost forgotten, a distant memory tucked somewhere in the far corners of your mind, until one day, the memory is recalled for some reason far removed from its purpose. Then the person is once again alive in your mind. But, as if to solidify the thought, that same person arrives in your life by virtue of an altogether separate interaction with somebody in another circle of life. Synchronicity, I believe they call it."

Melody opened her mouth to reply, but before the words found her voice, a distant sound, familiar and warm, brought hope to her heart.

A descending arpeggio of piano notes indicated the initial

bars of Beethoven's Moonlight Sonata. It was her father's favourite piece of music.

The music rose in volume from the speakers mounted high in the ceiling and beyond the curtains to Melody's side.

Feelmore looked around and up at the speakers.

The lights went out.

"I'd call it retribution," replied Melody.

Shadows danced on the walls of the chapel.

"Who's there?" called Feelmore.

But there was no reply, just a reassuring cool breeze that seemed to flow beneath the curtains and shake the furnace flames.

"I said who's there?" called Feelmore once again. "Announce yourself."

The curtain twitched to one side. Feelmore's head snatched at the movement. He grabbed a scalpel on the tray of surgical tools and stepped away behind Melody.

Melody closed her eyes and waited.

"I'm armed," called Feelmore. His bare feet scuffed the worn carpet as he edged away and his breathing quickened. "Show yourself or-"

His sentence was cut off with a gurgle. Then a loud sob left his lips. It was the type of involuntary cry that comes from the mind.

Melody heard Feelmore drop to the floor. He began to drag himself along the carpet, each movement accompanied by a soft pain-filled whimper. He turned himself and wrapped his arms around Melody's legs as if she would save him.

Feelmore was suddenly ripped away. He gave a cry like that of a child, which merged into long, painful sobs.

Melody strived to turn in her seat to see what was happening, but her restraints held her fast.

A few short moments of silence followed. Then Feelmore's

body slammed down onto the conveyor belt with a bang that sounded around the large room beyond the curtains.

A dark shape moved in front of the orange glow.

Melody hesitated then spoke softly. "Harvey?"

A long silence filled the room, but Melody felt his presence. She felt his security.

"Where are they?" asked Harvey.

"Who?" replied Melody. "The brothers?"

Harvey didn't reply.

"Some factory, I heard one of them say. But, Harvey, leave them. Forget it. We can move on."

Doctor Feelmore sniffed. He was crying like a child, Melody thought. How apt.

Harvey moved away from the whimpering man and stepped into the shadows. "The canal?" he said.

"I don't know. Something about Mad Bob's factory."

"It's the canal," said Harvey.

The dark shape of Doctor Feelmore was black against the glow of the furnace. From where Melody sat, she could see the knife that still stuck in the top of his spine, tall and erect.

Proud.

It was a wound Harvey had used before to disable the enemy, but prolong their life long enough for them to suffer.

"Is Reg okay?" asked Harvey.

"He's fine, just drugged I think."

"Are you okay? Did he hurt you?"

Harvey's hand rested on her shoulder as Feelmore's had, but it was warmer and stronger.

"Harvey, don't-"

"Did he hurt you, Melody?"

She took a deep breath and let it out slowly.

"No," said Melody. "You came in time."

"And if I hadn't?"

Melody couldn't bring herself to say the words.

Suddenly, the conveyor clunked into life. Its tiny gears worked themselves up to speed and the black shape of the doctor began its slow journey into hell.

"No," said Feelmore. "Stop, I tell you. I can explain."

He tried to roll away, but even from where Melody sat, she could see his limp body edge closer to the fire. His useless arms flailed, searching for something to hold onto, but they found nothing.

Melody felt a tug on her wrist ties.

"I'm going to cut your arms free," said Harvey. "You'll have time to untie your ankles and save him. Or you can watch him burn."

Feelmore's feet were inside the furnace. He gave a wild scream as the flames found his bare feet. His skin began to blister and smoulder.

"Harvey, no. Stop it. Stop the belt."

Harvey didn't reply.

"Harvey?" called Melody. "Harvey?"

A breath of cool air licked at Melody's ankles but it was quickly quashed by the heat from the fiery furnace.

Melody reached down and pulled at the loose ends of the rope that bound her ankles. She glanced up at Feelmore who was inside up to his knees and crying with the pitch of a soprano. His voice was hoarse from screaming, and sheer terror was carved on his face. His neck twisted to one side to see Melody.

"Help me," he croaked.

Melody stood from the chair and leapt to the big red button.

Her hand hovered over it.

She stared at the man on the belt as his waist began to disappear. Only his arms and head moved. His head rolled from one side to the other, and his hands beat down on the conveyor as if they were trying to beat it to a stop.

But the belt rolled on.

And the fire began to scorch his chest.

Feelmore had stopped moving by the time the furnace had fully consumed him. Maybe his heart had given up. Maybe his organs had failed. Or maybe his blood had boiled.

Melody wasn't sure of the exact cause of death, but she'd been enthralled by the spectacle, unable to remove her eyes from Feelmore's journey to hell.

Melody hit the stop button then turned the valve on the side of the furnace until the gas shut off. The orange glow fell to reveal a darkness and a silence. Just the ticking of the cooling metal and the popping and crackling of Feelmore's baked body could be heard.

A voice broke the silence, innocent like that of a child, but with the depth and wisdom of a man.

"Melody?" said Reg. "Are you there?"

Melody composed herself, took a few breaths, and then spoke.

"Reg, you're okay?"

"A little groggy. What happened?"

"It's over," she replied. "We're getting out of here."

Reg groaned and lay his head back down.

"Where are we going?"

Melody considered the various options. But there was only really one.

"We're going to get the devil twins, Reg."

CHAPTER THIRTY-SIX

Four large oil drums had been pulled into the centre of the huge, empty factory floor, twenty meters apart to form a square. The drums themselves had been filled with wood and petrol. The fires cast an orange light across the vast expanse of space.

A thick odour of petrol hung in the air from the oil drums. It mixed with the age-old grease and damp of the night.

Somewhere far off, a thunderstorm rolled by. Wind-swept rain hammered on the roof and the skylights of the old Victorian building like waves on a beach. They pelted the huge arched windows with millions of tiny *tap taps* as if a swarm of insects were fighting to get inside and escape the rain.

In the centre of the square of oil drums, standing with his hands tucked into the pockets of his long overcoat and facing the only open door, was Smokey the Jew. He stood alone and seemingly unafraid of the Bond Brothers. In front of him was one more oil drum, empty and upturned.

Lola LaRoux stood in the shadows of the first small office space, close to the pile of random boxes and machine parts that had been left behind by the last tenant. From where she stood, she had a clear view of the factory floor and the single doorway.

388   J. D. WESTON

The two brothers eventually stepped into the room. The first stopped, shook his jacket, and then looked around before his eyes finally landed on Smokey. The second walked in close behind the first, ran his hands through his short hair and immediately saw Smokey.

They approached him side by side and entered the square, stopping a few meters before him with the upturned drum between them.

"My boys," said Smokey. "It's a nice night for it."

"Smokey," said Rupert in greeting. "How have you been?"

"I can't complain, Rupert," Smokey replied. "In fact, if the sun was shining out there and I was sitting by a pool drinking cocktails, life would be perfect."

"But it isn't perfect, is it Smokey?"

"No, Rupert. But we do our best, don't we? We make of it what we will."

"We do," said Rupert. "And lately we seem to have made quite a lot of it."

"You've certainly done well, boys. That you have."

"So where's the diamond?" said Charlie. "Did you bring it?"

"Ah, Charlie," said Smokey. "You always were the hasty one, weren't you?"

Rupert held his hand up to Charlie to quieten his brother.

"It's a fair question, Smokey," he said. "Did you bring it?"

Smokey lifted his hat and ran his fingers through his long hair.

"I did, Rupert," said Smokey. "But before I simply hand you your fortune, and as long-standing friends, I was wondering if you could tell me something."

"What?" said Charlie. "Why don't you just hand it over?" He turned to Rupert. "I told you we can't trust him."

"Rupert, I suggest you keep your dog on a leash, and might I remind you that you both put me in a very serious position when you asked me to look after the diamond. But I asked no questions, did I?"

"No, Smokey," said Rupert.

"I told no lies?"

"No, Smokey."

"So perhaps you could afford me a little respect and credibility before you attempt to tarnish my impeccable reputation with your slander, young Charlie."

Charlie didn't reply, but Smokey continued anyway.

"Before I begin, and to appease young Charlie here, let's see them both in all their glory."

The brothers looked at each other, then back at Smokey, who had pulled from his pocket two silk handkerchiefs, black, with the initials SA embroidered in gold thread in one corner.

He stepped forward and, keeping one hand in the pocket of his three quarter length overcoat, laid the two silk handkerchiefs down side by side on top of the upturned oil drum.

CHAPTER THIRTY-SEVEN

The he turned a watchful eye on the brothers as his hand felt inside his coat. With no more grace than if he was reaching for an apple, he pulled out the diamond and placed it on one of the handkerchiefs.

Smokey the Jew stepped away from the diamond, returned his hand to his pocket, and glanced from brother to brother.

"Your turn," he said.

Rupert dug into the pocket of his suit.

"What are you doing?" asked Charlie. He put his hand on Rupert's arm. "Just take the diamond and let's go."

Smokey observed the dynamics of the pair with keen eyes.

Rupert stepped forward and placed the second diamond on the second handkerchief beside its twin.

The three men stared in awe at the two rocks between them. Thunder grumbled its way closer, and the rain fell heavily onto the roof.

"Are you both aware of the story of the diamonds? Or to be more accurate, Demonios Gemolus?" said Smokey, breaking the silence.

"There's two of them," said Rupert. "They were split up years ago and have never been together since."

A deafening crash of thunder split the sky outside.

Charlie flinched at the noise. Rupert held Smokey's gaze.

"Do you know why they haven't been together since, Rupert?"

Rupert shook his head.

"No," he replied. "No, I don't."

"Would you like me to tell you?" asked Smokey. "I think you should know."

"Oh, this is bullshit," said Charlie. "Just hand-"

"Charlie, shut up," snapped Rupert. "I want to hear the story."

Charlie stuffed his hands in his pockets and looked away from them both.

"If you were twice as smart, Charlie, you'd be an idiot, you know that?" said Smokey.

"What's that supposed to mean? Charlie replied.

Smokey offered him a pitiful grin.

"It's just a saying we have," he replied. "Just a saying."

Smokey returned his attention to Rupert.

"The story goes, Rupert," he began, "that the diamonds were found in the years of Queen Victoria, somewhere in the arse end of what is now South Africa. They were found by a Dutchman, whose name I do not know, but is quite insignificant."

Smokey began to pace with small steps, but he kept to his side of the upturned drum.

"I won't bore you with every detail. I'm sure you're both quite capable of finding the story on the wonderful world wide web for yourselves. But legend has it that the diamonds were stolen by an Englishman who wanted to present them to Queen Victoria as a gift. But during his passage back, his ship sank and he drowned. As luck would have it for our sparkling little friends there, the captain of the ship took them and climbed aboard a lifeboat with two other men. They floated around at the whim and mercy of the ocean for weeks. Then they eventually washed up in Portugal. From there, they made their way to France and found the British Army, with whom they planned to travel back to England."

"Not much of a story, Smokey," said Rupert.

"But there's more, my boy," said Smokey. "You see, they couldn't decide on who carried the diamonds, seeing as none of them trusted each another, so they took turns in carrying one each. Eventually, one night, when all around them was silent and stars filled the black sky, one of them stole the pair."

"He stole off his mates?"

"That he did, Rupert, that he did, and God did strike him down, you see. The other two woke just as he was leaving and found the diamonds missing. They were both overcome by some kind of godly power. No longer in control of their own senses, they tore the third man to shreds with their bare hands."

"So then there was two," said Rupert.

"That there was, Rupert, that there was," replied Smokey. "From that point on, and to this very day, the diamonds have never been in the same pair of hands. When the two regained their composure and realised what they'd done, they were shamed and went their separate ways. The first diamond stayed with the man's family for years, hidden and deemed too dark to reveal to the public, as if it were possessed by some kind of demon."

"And the second?" asked Rupert.

"The second, my boy, was given to Doctor Hans Sloane, who in case you didn't know, was the man that founded the Natural History Museum from his very own collection of natural wonders from around the world. It was a collection worth a small fortune in its own right."

The brothers took in the story in silence.

"And that," continued Smokey, "if I'm not very much mistaken, is the very diamond that sits before us, reunited with its demon twin brother for the first time in nearly two hundred years."

Smokey stopped pacing and faced the twins.

"Fascinating, isn't it?" he said with a jovial tone.

"Yeah, fascinating," said Charlie. "So can we take them now?"

Just as he spoke the words, a crash of thunder ripped through the night and seemed to shake the old building. The skylight high above them smashed, sending hundred-year-old shattered glass raining down on the men, along with the body of Glasgow George, which landed with a sickening crunch of breaking bones beside the upturned oil drum.

Standing in the rain outside the factory, on the canal towpath and in the shadow of a willow tree, Harvey took in the scene.

On the far side of the canal, the south side, residential apartments stood new and clean. Lit windows with open curtains showed families or bachelors closing their days off with TV or dinner. Two women ran from a building to a waiting taxi, laughing, and drove away to somewhere more glamorous.

On the north side of the canal where Harvey stood, the scene was far bleaker. Old factories stood in a line. Once, they might have loaded canal barges with their produce, or taken deliveries of coal that may have floated down from further north.

The buildings were all derelict, and it was only a matter of time before a wealthy investor tore them down to mirror the south side. The buildings were all dark save for one, in which the tall arched windows glowed liked fiery orange eyes cast from the fires inside.

A van was parked outside on the narrow lane, and an old chain link fence ran the perimeter of the factory. It was the only security for the property.

Harvey stood and watched.

He'd seen two men enter the building through the single door he himself had used before. The two men had been identical and were the exact two men he was looking for. But the absence of other people tugged at Harvey's mind. Men like the brothers rarely came to a meeting alone.

An iron bench had been placed on the towpath for walkers to rest. Beside it was a waste bin. Harvey checked inside and found what he was looking for, an empty glass brandy bottle. Someone who had sheltered in a nearby factory probably left it. Harvey fetched it out and returned to the tree.

He waited a full minute before he moved again.

Nothing stirred except the trees and the perpetual rain.

A huge crack of thunder and immediate lightning carved a hole in the sky and lit the factory in three successive flashes.

Outlined against the old brickwork, Harvey saw the shape of a man beside the door. He was stood with his hands in his jacket pockets, a sign that he was either over-confident or ill-trained.

The full minute finished. Harvey stepped forward and launched the bottle high in the air. It came down and smashed on the ground twenty yards to the man's right.

As planned, the goon heard the shattering glass and went to investigate. He was a wide man, stocky but short. The way he walked gave Harvey the impression that he was mostly muscle and trained heavily.

Harvey stepped out from the trees and walked slowly across to the factory. He fell into the shadows just as the man looked around, confused as to who had thrown the bottle.

Harvey worked his way behind the man, taking small, slow

steps. The rain covered the sound of his boots, but Harvey could still hear the man's heavy breathing like grunts from some docile beast.

The man stopped. He seemed to sniff the air.

Harvey slowly pulled his knife from the sheath inside his leather biker jacket.

"I hoped you'd come," said the man without turning.

Harvey froze.

The man turned to face him.

"They said you would, and you did," he continued. Then his eyes caught the shiny blade in Harvey's hand. The man gave a laugh then stopped. "It is *you*, isn't it?"

He'd been waiting for Harvey.

"That depends on who it is you think *I* am," replied Harvey. Raindrops were now dripping from his brow.

"You're the one that killed my mates," said the man. "You're Harvey."

Harvey didn't reply.

"Let's settle this like real men. Put that away, son." He gestured at Harvey's knife.

"You first."

The man grinned and reached inside his jacket. He pulled out a handgun, black and slick with the rain.

He threw it to one side.

Harvey let the knife fall from his grip. The weighted blade found the soft mud and stuck in, leaving just the carved handle sticking out of the ground.

"They were two of the toughest men I ever met," said the man. "You must be pretty tasty."

Harvey didn't reply.

In an instant, the man charged at him. Harvey braced his feet and swung an uppercut to the oncoming man's face. It connected but had no effect. Instead, the full weight of the charging man collided with Harvey, taking him off his feet and onto the ground.

Before Harvey could react, punches rained down on his face. His arms were pinned by the man's knees, and they rocked from side to side with the hammer of each blow.

The man reached back to get his full weight behind one last final blow, but Harvey twisted, raised his leg, and hooked the punching arm. Using the momentum, Harvey pulled the man off with his leg and reversed positions before landing his forehead into the man's nose.

Harvey landed three bone-crunching head butts before he was thrown off. Both men rolled away from each other, each wiping rain and their own blood from their eyes. With three confident paces, the man came again at Harvey. His left hand was cocked to defend his face, while he held his right ready to deliver a jab.

Harvey raised his own hands, but the jab smashed through his block and into his throat. Harvey gasped for air as his crushed windpipe recovered. But more punches came through. A shot landed on Harvey's left side, and immediately, a right hook connected with his face.

Harvey went down.

"Come on, boy," said the man. "I thought you were tough."

Harvey dragged himself away, putting distance between them.

"Get up," the man shouted.

Harvey pulled himself to his feet and stood just as the man collided with him again. Harvey landed on his face only to receive a succession of rapid punches to his kidneys. He tried to suck in air, but only managed to cough up blood, thick warm and metallic.

Suddenly, Harvey was hoisted into the air like a rag doll. The man held him high above his head, took three steps, and tossed him into the factory wall beneath one of the arched windows.

"This is easy," he said. "There's no way you killed Mad Bob."

Harvey rolled onto his back and saw the man walking away. He was working himself up, breathing heavily.

Then Harvey saw his chance. A maintenance ladder fixed to the side of the factory wall was a few feet away. Harvey pulled himself to his feet, using the wall to balance, and slid along the old bricks to the first iron rung. He clung to it as if his life depended on it. Then he took a glance behind.

The man had seen him.

"Where do you think you're going, boy?" he said, and charged at Harvey once more.

Harvey dug deep. He jumped up and grabbed the highest rung he could reach. The iron was slippery with rain and sharp with years of rust. His kidneys screamed in protest, but he pulled his body clear of the man, who slammed into the wall beneath.

Harvey's feet found the rungs and he began to climb. Each pull of his arms to the next rung tore into his beaten body. His head swam from the blows, and more than once, he swung to one side as his mind tried to regulate his balance.

Harvey cleared his throat and spat blood down at the man, who was slowly catching up. Just when he thought the ladder might go on indefinitely, Harvey fell forward onto the huge, shiny and slippery pitched roof.

Dragging himself clear, Harvey rolled onto his back and clambered backwards to the apex. The big man lumbered over the crest of the ladder a few seconds later, grinning.

"Is this it, is it?" he asked. "You want to be thrown from the roof?"

Thunder rumbled closer and the rain felt heavier.

Harvey pushed himself to his feet once more and stood. He

was taller than the man who followed him. But the height advantage was nothing compared to the lightning-fast jabs that came at him. Harvey dodged, bending right and left, his eyes planted on the man's.

But the punches kept coming. There was no room for Harvey to return a blow. Then suddenly, the man stopped.

He was catching his breath.

Harvey had been waiting for the moment. He lunged out with a straight kick to the man's chest. It connected and sent him stumbling backwards, but not down.

Instead, he returned with a vengeance, swinging wild punches at Harvey's head, chest and stomach. Most missed, but a few destroyed Harvey's attempts at blocking and connected.

The last blow stopped Harvey dead.

The man stepped in close, reached up and put his fat fingers around Harvey's throat.

He squeezed.

In an instant, tiny lights swam in Harvey's eyes. His breathing grew thin, like sucking air through a tiny straw.

The man grinned up at him.

Harvey reached up, groping for the man's face, until he found his eyes and jammed his thumbs into the sockets.

His throat was released, and Harvey fell to the wet, tiled rooftop. He slid down and dug his boots in, just managing to stop himself from sliding to the edge.

He looked up at the man who was now several meters away and bent double clutching his face. For the first time in the fight, Harvey charged. Just as a rumble of thunder built somewhere far above, Harvey gathered his strength, took a deep breath and ran with everything he had up the pitch of the roof.

His full weight slammed into the man's legs. Jamming his shoulder into the man's mass, Harvey lifted him, barely off the roof tiles. But it was enough. Harvey carried on pushing with his legs. He roared as he called upon all his strength. As the man toppled forward and Harvey's momentum began to falter, the two men fell together.

Harvey slammed into the rooftop with his arms wrapped around the man's legs. The sky split with an enormous crash of thunder and a flash of lightning that seemed to light the entire world.

Suddenly, the man's full weight dragged Harvey fully up the roof and he glanced up, expressing a split second's realisation that it was over. Just moments before Harvey too fell through the hole, he let go.

There was no scream, no thud of a body hitting the floor. From where Harvey lay, there was only an empty expanse of wet and shiny rooftop with a smashed skylight, pouring rain and a grumbling sky.

CHAPTER THIRTY-EIGHT

The two brothers jumped back in surprise, but Rupert noted the lack of reaction from Smokey. He pulled his handgun from the inside of his suit jacket.

"What the hell was that, Smokey?"

Smokey peered at Glasgow's twisted and smashed body.

"He's one of yours I think," replied Smokey.

Charlie pulled his gun. Both brothers held their weapons aimed at Smokey, who seemed unperturbed.

"That's fucking Glasgow George, Smokey," said Rupert.

"Ah, George," said Smokey. He returned his gaze to Rupert. "Shame. But you really should be careful where you point those things. They can be lethal, you know?"

"Smokey, we're going to take the diamonds and we're going to leave," said Rupert. "Who do you have up there?"

"I have friends in many places, Rupert. But on the roof of this here factory?" He shook his head. "None that I am aware of."

Rupert stepped forward and reached out for the diamonds, but Smokey pulled back one side of his coat and lifted the gleaming double barrels of a shotgun.

"Do yourself a favour, my boy," he said. "Step away from the diamonds."

"Smokey," said Rupert, "what are you doing? There's two of us and one of you."

"There is indeed two of you," said Smokey. "But I have two barrels, each with a nice red cartridge in, and you know what, boys?"

"What, Smokey? This is not going to end well for you, mate."

"Before I loaded my shotgun, I took a marker pen, a black one. On one cartridge, I wrote the letter R. Tell me, Charlie, what letter do you think I wrote on the other one?"

Charlie fixed Smokey's questioning gaze with his own hateful stare. "C?" he replied.

"C," said Smokey. "That's right. Well done. But the only problem is I cannot for the life of me remember who is on the right..." He returned his stare to Rupert. "And who is on the left."

An awkward silence hung as the brothers tried to fathom Smokey's smug grin.

"I hope you don't mind sharing?" asked Smokey.

"There's no need for this, Smokey," said Rupert.

"On the contrary. You see, those diamonds are a legacy. There's history in them than runs deeper than you can imagine, and well, I just couldn't live with myself if I let you two clowns walk off with them."

"What do you care about history?" said Rupert. "I told you we'd give you a cut."

"Oh you did, you did, my boy. But tell me Rupert, do I look like I need a cut? My house is so big there's rooms I don't even know about. When I make a cash withdrawal, Rupert, the fucking bank manager comes to my house in an armed security van. It is true that I admire and respect what you two pair of degenerate ponces have done for yourselves with your bars, clubs and with the help of Neanderthals such as our late friend Mr Glasgow George here. But you are not ready to wield the responsibility that comes with protecting the beauty and grace of rare and expensive gems such as the Demonios Gemelos."

"I'm not going to bear the responsibility of anything, Smokey," said Rupert. "I'm going to sell them and sit on a beach-"

"With semi-naked women," said Charlie.

"Oh, is that right?" said Smokey. "Oh, well in that case, I'm afraid the answer is irrefutably no. I can't allow these to be sold. Who knows what hands they might fall into? They'd be gone forever, boys."

Rupert gave a little laugh. "*You* don't get to allow the *Bond* Brothers to do *anything*, Smokey. We're *taking* the diamonds, and we can either do that with you standing there, or we can do it with you laying down there, with George, and with a bloody great hole through you."

Rupert took another step towards the diamonds.

"And if we're giving speeches, I suggest you listen hard. Our families go way back. We've always been allies and on account of that, I'd sooner not have to kill you. But if it means the difference between walking away with those two diamonds or not, I *will* kill you, Smokey."

Rupert aimed the gun at Smokey's head.

"So, Smokey," Rupert continued. "The ball is in your court, I believe. What's it going to be?"

Smokey remained completely still with his shotgun aimed from his hip at Rupert. "I told you I have two barrels on this shotgun, didn't I?"

"You did, Smokey. But my patience is running out I'm afraid."

In a flash, Rupert lowered his weapon and pulled the trigger, sending a round through Smokey's knee. Smokey went down. He hit the hard concrete floor with a slap. His shotgun discharged harmlessly into the roof above. Rupert stood over him and watched him writhe on the floor, growling through gritted teeth.

"Dad," a voice yelled from the shadows behind Smokey. A female voice.

Rupert swung his weapon into the shadows.

"Who's there?" he called out.

Smokey continued to laugh.

"I said who's there?"

"Have you met my daughter?" asked Smokey.

"Your what?" said Rupert.

"My daughter, Rupert. I don't believe you've had the pleasure. Lola, would you care to join us by the fire?" he called. Smokey winced at the pain that was shooting through his leg.

"Lola?" said Rupert. "You must be mistaken, Smokey. Lola's enjoying a nice slow death as we speak." He grinned at the man on the floor.

But his grin turned to confusion as Lola LaRoux stepped from the shadows.

Rupert's head suddenly dizzied.

"You can't be..."

Smokey laughed. "You lose, Rupert. You got the wrong girl."

"Regardless," said Rupert, "you're down there and I'm up here. The diamonds are mine."

"No, Rupert, wrong again. The diamond *belongs* to me. It always has. The man that carried it from France-"

"Your ancestor?" said Rupert, as the pieces fell into place.

"It was stolen many years ago from my father, and we've been searching for it ever since. So when you and your greedy brother stole it from us, you woke a very old and angry beast, Rupert."

Smokey laughed hard, then grimaced at the pain in his leg.

"And then you gave it back to me to look after, you schmuck. But I'll give you credit for the plan. It would have been good had you done your research."

"You played me?" said Rupert.

"You always *were* the smarter of the two. But I suggest you use those brains and stop pointing that gun at my dear Lola. I'm quite the protective father, Rupert."

"Charlie," said Rupert, seeing the upper hand shift, "take the diamonds."

But Charlie gave no response.

"Charlie?" said Rupert. "I said take the diamonds."

Rupert glanced around to find an empty space where Charlie had been standing.

"Charlie?" he called.

No answer came.

Smokey laughed through his pain.

"Where is he, you bastard?" said Rupert.

Smokey continued to laugh.

"I said where is he, Smokey? You could have lived. Don't make me do this."

Smokey stared up at him, smiling.

"Put the gun down, Rupert," said Lola. She stepped into the fire light pointing her own handgun at Rupert.

Rupert aimed back at her, but the move gave Smokey a chance to shift his heavy shotgun from his position on the floor. He aimed it directly at Rupert.

"Now, Rupert," he said. "I believe that *we* have two guns, and *you* only have one."

"Rupert," called Charlie from the shadows behind.

"Charlie? Where are you?"

No response came at first. Then a weak and frightened voice replied to Rupert. "I'm here, by the wall."

"What are you doing? Come here," said Rupert.

"Rupert, help."

Rupert looked down at Smokey, who just smiled back.

"We find ourselves in a very tricky position, don't we?" said Smokey.

"Rupert, help," called Charlie.

"I'm coming, bro," said Rupert. "What's wrong?"

Rupert backed away, switching his weapon from Smokey to Lola and back again. He passed the diamonds, collecting them both with one hand, and stuffed them into his jacket pocket.

"I wouldn't do that if I were you, Rupert," said Smokey.

"Rupert, help."

"I'm coming," called Rupert. "Why not?" he said to Smokey. "You don't honestly believe in a curse?" Rupert continued walking backwards. "Charlie, where are you?" he called.

"I'm here," replied Charlie. His voice was weak and raised an octave.

Rupert turned to find a dark wall in front of him, swathed in shadows.

"Charlie?" he whispered, suddenly aware of a presence around him.

As if on cue, thunder boomed, followed a few seconds later by two flashes of lightning. It was then that Rupert's eyes fell on the sight of his beloved twin brother hanging from the wall with two meat hooks protruding from his chest.

"Charlie?" whispered Rupert, and ran to his brother across the soaked concrete floor.

Grabbing him by his waist, Rupert tried to lift Charlie off the hooks, but he was too heavy and Rupert's handmade leather soled brogues slipped on the wet floor.

"Who did this?" he yelled at his brother, as if it was his fault.

Charlie just stared back at him as if he'd accepted death. Pity filled his eyes and his wordless mouth hung open.

"Charlie?" said Rupert.

"Drop the gun, Rupert," said a voice, new, but familiar, with a tone of exhaustion.

Rupert span to find Smokey being supported on one side by Lola, and on the other, a man who held a burning length of wood picked from one of the oils drums.

"I told you I had two barrels, Rupert, didn't I?" said Smokey.

"Get him down," Rupert shouted, his voice thick with tears.

"The diamonds, Rupert," Harvey replied.

"The diamonds?" said Rupert. "Why don't you come and get them."

Rupert stuffed his free hand into his pocket and pulled out the two diamonds. They glittered in the fierce fire light, alive with the power of the flames.

"Take them off me," Rupert spat.

The man simply smiled back at Rupert as if it was the answer he'd been expecting. Then he let his hand fall forward and tossed the burning lumber into the pool of liquid in which Rupert stood.

Immediately, the pool took light. A rush of excited blue flames tore across the room, sucking in the cool air with a hiss.

Rupert cried out in shock as the flames engulfed him. Instinct told him to run, but brotherly love held him on the spot. He reached for Charlie, throwing both arms around him. He pulled and pushed, trying to lift his brother high off the hooks, but the flames licked at Rupert's hands and soon engulfed them both. Charlie's suit and skin simply fell away at his touch. As the flames reached his face, Rupert screamed as every inch of his body was seared and the sickly odour of burning flesh filled his mouth and nose.

Charlie's face seemed to look down at him, retorted in silent agony as the flames too licked at his face. Rupert clung desperately to his brother's waist. But as the fire took hold and the pain overcame any strength Rupert still had, he slid down to Charlie's knees and lay in the pool of burning petrol with his arms wrapped tightly around his brother's legs.

Through the heat haze and his burning eyes, Rupert faintly caught movement. Smokey had lifted the shotgun from beneath his coat. He seemed to watch Rupert's suffering for a few seconds longer until finally, he pulled the trigger.

CHAPTER THIRTY-NINE

By the time she and Reg ran through the single doorway of the factory, Melody knew they were too late. Three figures stood beside the wall to her left, standing over the remains of a smoking and smouldering fire.

A thick, sickly odour filled the huge space.

The man in the centre turned his head to face them as they approached and the girl readied her weapon.

"It's okay," said Harvey.

Melody stepped up to the trio.

Harvey held his hand out to relax the man he and the woman were supporting. "They're after me," he said.

"I get the feeling we're late to the party," said Melody.

"Smokey, Lola," said Harvey, "meet Melody Mills and Reg Tenant."

"Ah, I've read about you, Miss Mills," said Smokey. "It's a pleasure. I'd love to stay and chat, but as you can see..." He gestured at his ruined leg.

"You look like you're in need of medical attention, sir," said Melody.

"Medical attention and a stiff drink, miss," replied Smokey. "It's been a long night."

"And these two?" said Melody. She nodded at the charred remains of the Bond Brothers.

"They won't be much trouble any longer, Miss Mills," said Smokey.

"And you must be Lola?" said Melody. "The brothers had quite the plan for you and your friend Fingers."

"You're police?" asked Smokey.

"Sir, can I ask you to drop the gun?" said Melody.

"Oh, indeed, Miss Mills." Smokey span the shotgun around and he offered it to Melody butt first. "Would you mind taking it? But please be careful. It's a Purdy, very old and extremely expensive."

Melody took the weapon from him.

"One of a pair you know," he added. "Quite apt really, given the circumstances."

"Harvey?" said Melody, as she broke the shotgun, checked it was empty, and hung it from her arm. "What are we going to do here? Someone has to pay for this and the diamonds."

"Is that right?" replied Harvey. He passed Smokey's weight onto Lola and made sure she was steady. Then he stepped forward, bent down to Rupert's blackened and still smoking bones, and snapped back his charred fingers to reveal a pair of perfectly unscathed, flawless, 200-carat diamonds. They were identical in appearance and weight.

Harvey removed them from Rupert's hand, which crumbled to ash as Harvey stood up.

The diamonds, lying cupped in Harvey's hand, sparkled even in the dim light of the factory. Holding them high, Harvey peered through them to catch the dim light from the arched windows.

"Incredible," he muttered.

"They're absolutely beautiful," said Lola.

All five of them were silenced by the almost magical glistening, until Harvey lowered his hand and closed his fist on the two rocks.

He turned to face Melody and the others.

"As I see it, Melody," said Harvey, "the brothers had themselves an accident."

He stepped past the bewildered Lola and Smokey and held out an upturned hand.

Melody held her own hand out, palm facing up, and felt the weight of a single half of the Demonios Gemelos as Harvey released it.

For the smallest fraction of time, he held Melody's gaze. The slightest of smiles appeared on his face then faded to Harvey's standard non-emotional gaze.

As Melody began to speak, Harvey turned away.

"But what about the other-" she started.

"I believe this belongs to you," interrupted Harvey, addressing Smokey. He dropped the twin diamond in the palm of the old Jewish man.

Smokey's hand closed around the diamond without even a cursory glance then disappeared into his pocket.

"Toda," he said.

Harvey raised an eyebrow.

"It means thank you in Hebrew."

Harvey nodded.

"But wait, what about *Fingers*?" said Lola, suddenly panicked. "Did the brothers get him?"

"No," said Harvey. "I got him."

His remark was met with an intake of breath from the group.

"It's okay. I let him go. I told him to get on the first flight he could," said Harvey.

"It's a shame I didn't listen then, wasn't it?" said a voice from behind Melody. "I could be somewhere much warmer by now."

"Fingers," cried Lola. She held onto her father but held an arm out for Fingers to join her.

He gave Lola a hug and shook her father's hand. Then he ran his eyes over Melody and Reg before letting them fall on Harvey.

He gave a small nod of thanks.

Harvey returned it.

"Well," said Smokey, "I'd love to stay and chat. But I'm afraid I'm slowly bleeding to death here. So if you'll excuse me."

Fingers left Lola's side and picked up the side that Harvey had previously supported. The three slowly made their way past Melody and Reg, but before they reached the door, Smokey stopped. He turned and with a voice of authority, wisdom and gratitude, addressed them all.

"Before I forget my manners," he began. "I can't begin to tell you how grateful I am. And the rest of my family too."

Harvey, Melody and Reg all nodded at him.

"I'm sure my father and the generations of Abrams before him are all up there somewhere smiling down that our diamond is back home."

He let the comment hang in the stale air, and smiled.

"You'll be hearing from me," he said. Then with the help of his daughter and her friend, he left the factory.

CHAPTER FORTY

Just two days had passed since the incident at the factory. There was a lot for Harvey to take in but not much for him to do.

He took one final look at the single Demonios Gemelos diamond, sitting prettily on its cushion in the Natural History Museum. A flock of tourists had gathered around to see the now-famous diamond after its recent theft and return.

The tourists closed in and Harvey stepped away, taking the fastest route out of the building and ignoring the strange looks from passers-by who stared at his bruised and swollen face.

He shouldered his backpack, pulled the visor down on his helmet, and rode out of London for good.

His senses felt numbed to the people, places, and cars he passed. But it felt good to be back on his bike and heading back to his little farmhouse in France.

He just had one more stop to make before pointing his bike at Dover and opening up the throttle.

Harvey regretted leaving before he had a chance to talk to Melody, and to Reg. He missed his old friend a little. Melody had tried to talk to him in the factory, but it hadn't been the time or the place. He'd walked away, leaving Melody standing there for the second time in his life.

Part of him regretted walking away. He knew she was good for him. But the beast inside him was volatile, and he knew it. He couldn't bring her down with him.

Thirty minutes later, and around thirty miles west of Guildford, he clicked the left-hand indicator on, slowed the bike into second gear, and rode between two huge wrought iron gates, which he estimated at about thirty feet tall.

Before him was a long gravel driveway, which swooped around past an enormous lake. A series of smaller fountains sprayed water at the foot of a central fountain. The lake was awash with frothing white water.

Past the lakes and the fountains stood a huge grand house, at least three stories tall, with balconied windows and an entrance that even the Royal Family would be happy to walk up.

He parked the bike at the foot of the eight long curved steps, removed his helmet and peered up at the two huge double doors.

A man in a tuxedo and white gloves stood waiting between the balustrades for Harvey to climb the steps.

"Mr Stone?" he asked, as Harvey approached.

Harvey nodded.

"This way, sir," the man replied, and walked briskly to the house.

The huge front doors closed behind Harvey.

"Follow me, if you will, sir," said the man.

Harvey followed once more and allowed himself to be led through a pair of ornate doors of dark wood, past huge oil paintings in frames that looked as expensive as the paintings themselves, and along a corridor so long, Harvey couldn't even count the doors that led from it.

At the far end of the corridor was one final set of double doors, of matching dark wood and intricate mouldings.

Harvey stepped through and was surprised at the sudden change in surroundings. The doors opened out into a huge glass conservatory with brilliant white window frames. The natural light in the room was overwhelming in contrast to the grandeur of the house Harvey had just walked through.

Ahead of Harvey stood two doors that opened out into an immaculate garden filled with manicured hedges and flowers that exploded in colour, contrasting the thick greenery they bordered.

To Harvey's right was a table surrounded by chairs and holding raised plates offering fruits, nuts, and small pastries. A silver tray with coffee completed the scene, containing a small display of china cups, saucers and silver spoons.

But the biggest surprise was to Harvey's left. A large, white-framed bed stood encased in a flowing net curtain.

In the bed, sitting up and beaming at Harvey with grateful admiration was Smokey the Jew. He was dressed in white pyjamas, with his braided payot swinging freely beside his face and a dark skullcap perched atop his head.

"Mr Stone," said Smokey, "I'm so pleased you made it. Won't you join me?"

"How's the knee?" said Harvey as he stepped up to the foot of the bed, noticing for the first time that Smokey's half of the Demonios Gemelos sat in a rich purple cushion on his side table.

"I won't be walking unaided again," replied Smokey. "They removed my leg below the knee. But I'm breathing, and my heart is strong." He followed Harvey's gaze and smiled gratefully.

Harvey nodded.

"Good," he said. "I'm glad to hear that you're feeling okay."

"You look like you've been in the wars yourself, Harvey," said Reg.

"I'll heal," replied Harvey. "I always seem to."

"Well," began Smokey, "without further ado, I'd like to offer you my sincere appreciation for helping my family regain its long lost property."

"It's okay, Smokey," said Harvey. "I don't need your money."

"My money?" said Smokey with distaste. "I'm not offering you money, my friend."

He swept a smile across the room, as if checking they were alone, and then rested his eyes on Harvey's.

"I have a proposition for you."

Harvey didn't reply.

The End.

STONE DEEP

CHAPTER ONE

The Defeat of the Floating Batteries at Gibraltar commanded the opulent gallery; even Cordero Diaz thought so, whose knowledge of the fine arts could be written long-hand on the rear of a cigarette packet.

The painting was more than just a scene painted on a canvas. The brush strokes, visible in the texture of the oils, had purpose. They were not the simple result of applying colour to creation using a brush as a medium. Instead, the strokes conveyed tones, shadows and direction, and complemented neighbouring colours, tones and shadows. The depth of the foreground, with its hues of green and deep shadow, was not there to fill a gap between the background and the content. The foreground had lines that drew the viewer's eye to the life of the art, its heart and soul. Soldiers on horseback were described in so much detail that a modern photograph could not portray the scene with more clarity. A washed blend of pastel colours, used to invoke a terrifying scene of battle, anguish and carnage, invoked the smell of gunpowder to the viewer, along with fire, smoke, and death.

The painting was a masterpiece.

At close to seven metres by five metres, removing the frame from its position of glory five metres high on the wall of the gallery would require planning. But it was not impossible. If it was possible for one man to create such a masterpiece, it would be possible for a team of men to steal it.

Falling in with a guide and a host of tourists, Cordero played the part of an inquisitive visitor well; this wasn't his first rodeo. He knew the rules of engagement. Invisibility was key.

The remainder of the tour, although interesting, was spent examining security, adding more research to what the team had already discovered through their planted security guard. Lasers did not protect the Guildhall Gallery in the City of London. A web of infra-red beams was not switched on when the doors were locked, ready to sound the alarms should an inexperienced intruder fall foul of their purpose. But behind the walls and beneath the raised floors was a mesh of sensors. They all connected to the control room in the basement, where a team of guards monitored them around the clock.

Cordero noted the camera positions, and with a series of timely nods from one of the planted guards standing nearby, he managed to photograph the security challenges they might face under the guise of artistic interest.

"Erm, excuse me," said the guide, as Cordero leaned over the barrier to photograph a Monet in the corner of the room beneath a security camera. "There is no photography allowed. Did you see the signs?"

Cordero stepped back from the painting.

"No entiendo. Lo siento," he replied.

"No está permitido," said the guide.

"Ah," said Cordero, feigning a sudden understanding. "Sí, lo siento."

He finished with an embarrassed smile as the eyes of the tourists all returned to the guide, who continued to explain how German bombers destroyed the gallery during the blitz of World War Two. He described how many of the paintings that were displayed had been temporarily removed and sent for safe keeping just three weeks before a lucky hit from a Nazi pilot destroyed the gallery. Cordero ignored the speech, aware of the gallery's history. Instead, he memorised the brand of the security camera. It was a detail that his photo would have captured, and would allow his tech guys to plan the security breach.

The tour took another forty minutes to complete, during which Cordero noted several paintings that would be far easier to remove and steal, and were likely worth a great deal more, black market or not. But Dante had specified The Defeat of the Floating Batteries at Gibraltar, claiming it to be a lifetime ambition to own the masterpiece, and because of his ambitious nature, the logistics of the operation were minor details. If Cordero knew Dante as well as he thought he did, it would not be long before the painting would be installed in Dante's house, although he couldn't think where it would go. A painting of such magnitude would require a room with walls far greater and grander than Dante possessed.

As the guide completed the tour and answered the final question from an Asian tourist, Cordero loitered for the opportunity to thank the guide in his best broken English, and to apologise for his lack of thought, stating that he became overwhelmed with admiration for the painting.

"It happens every day," said the smiling guide. "I hope you enjoyed the tour?"

"Ah, sí," said Cordero, in an attempt to sound enthused. "Perfecto."

The guide opened the door to the staff-only room, and offered Cordero a "Ciao," as he stepped away.

Cordero took a final glance up the sweeping staircase into

the gallery, catching a final glimpse of the target, then turned to leave.

The walk from the gallery to Liverpool Street Station took just five minutes, and the train to the leafy London suburb of Brentwood was waiting at platform eight. Cordero chose an empty carriage. But three schoolgirls, who appeared to be skipping school, joined him and took a booth a few seats away, laughing at nothing while playing music through the loudspeaker on one of their phones. The girls disembarked at Stratford Station where a man entered and selected a seat at the far end of the carriage.

Cordero searched through the images he'd taken before the guide had caught him snapping photos. He sent them to Diego as instructed. Diego would ensure the team received the images. By the time Cordero arrived back at the garage, plans would already be in motion.

As the train approached Brentwood, Cordero waited by the doors. The man at the far end of the carriage, who was of slight build and engrossed in his phone, ignored him. A lady at the other end of the carriage, who Cordero had not noticed, collected her bag and was standing beside the doors closest to her seat. She checked her watch and peered out of the window. Perhaps she was checking for her husband who would collect her. Or maybe it was a lover? Cordero could smell her perfume; it was rich, not floral, but light with a hint of sandalwood and fruit. She unfastened the top button of her blouse. Cordero smiled to himself and pictured her steamy clandestine meeting with her infatuate. Perhaps she would allow her hands to wander as he drove them to his house. Perhaps she would offer a glimpse of whatever lay beneath the small skirt she wore; a tease before the delights of their taboo relationship unfolded.

Cordero followed the woman from the train, down the concrete steps and through the barriers, which had been left open during the day until rush hour, in a move to reduce the manpower needed to manage the station. He slowed his walk and admired the view of her behind, hoping to glimpse whatever the lucky man would be enjoying over the next few hours with her.

The station was empty. The street outside appeared quiet. The woman turned left.

Cordero followed.

She walked thirty metres from the station entrance then, with a practised casual manner, she glanced back once and slipped into the passenger side of a waiting SUV. Cordero slowed then stopped and made to cross the road. He turned his head to check for traffic as the first blow connected with his throat, crushing his windpipe. With wide panicked eyes, he turned to face the attacker but found nobody.

Cordero gasped for air. He leaned on a post to support himself. Then, from nowhere, his chest felt like it had been hit with a hammer and the static sound of a taser sang like a warning bell as fifty thousand volts raced through his body, stunning his senses. The taser stopped. Cordero reeled from the blast of energy as someone pulled a thick bag over his head. He fought to remove it and lashed out at the attacker, but a hard blow to his gut sucked the wind from him. A second blow, which slammed into his temple, rocked his vision and turned his world from a dizzied array of spinning lights to the peaceful, pitch dark of unconsciousness.

CHAPTER TWO

"Do you remember I asked for your help, Lola dear?" asked Smokey.

"I do," Lola replied, "and can I presume that you have some kind of masterplan and the garage has something to do with it?"

"You'll see," her father replied, and squeezed her hand.

Samuel, Smokey's driver, pulled the sleek Mercedes minivan up to the doors of Smokey's brand new garage, which had been built in a thicket of trees on the far side of the lake at the south end of his vast property. Lola slid the side door open, stepped out, and waited for Samuel to slide the two stainless steel ramps into place, so she could then wheel her father down into his workshop.

"I could walk if you'd help me, Lola," said Smokey from inside the van.

"You heard what Doctor Fenn said, Dad," she replied. "You need to keep the leg elevated and rested to heal."

"Yes, well, he that can't endure the bad won't live to see the good, Lola."

Samuel gave her the nod, and helped her guide the wheelchair to the ramp. She stepped up, tilted it back, and lowered her father to the ground.

"I hate all this," her father complained in his thick London accent.

Lola pushed the chair past Samuel, leaving him to remove the ramps and park the minivan. She pushed the chair into the garage, which was a brick-built rectangle with a forty-foot-high ceiling and electric rolling shutter doors. The garage was a new addition to the property and contained Smokey's collection of beloved vintage cars.

"Well," said Lola, "are you going to tell me what this is about?"

"Lola, sweetheart, before we go inside, I have to tell you something."

Lola recognised her father's tone.

"What have you done?"

"Not me. Well not directly."

"Just tell me," she said.

"I had to get some outside help."

"So? What type of help?"

"I needed..." He hesitated. "There's no easy way to say it, so I shall just say it. I needed somebody kidnapped."

"Kidnapped?" said Lola, then checked her voice. "What on earth?" She craned her neck to see through the door.

"He is exactly who we have been looking for," her father replied. "Now we have him, we will extract the information. It's important, dear. Please, you must understand."

Once inside the garage and on the smooth, painted screed floor, her father wheeled himself, preferring to maintain his independence as much as possible. Lola walked beside the chair as they approached the far end of the large room.

A man lay on his back on the floor. Tied to each of his limbs were thick lengths of manila rope. Each hung in long, sweeping curves over four separate roof beams and collated near a pulley in the ceiling space, which ran through a series of other pulleys. A single length of manila rope hung on the far side of the room, and the manner in which the man was tied meant that a tug on the single rope would lift him from the floor and stretch him apart.

Lola's father stopped his chair at a safe distance from the man, but close enough to see his panicked face. Lola took her place beside him.

"So, you're awake now. You must be Cordero?" said Smokey.

Cordero remained silent but continued to search around him, as if some beast lurked out of sight.

"Do you know who I am, Cordero?"

The man let his head fall back, overcome by his struggles.

"Do I look like I care who you are?" he replied. His Spanish accent was thick.

"Now, now, pleasantries will get you everywhere, my boy. We'll have no more of that."

"What is it you want?" Cordero asked. "I know nothing. I don't know where I am. I don't know who you are. And I don't know what you want. You want to kill me? Just kill me. You want to let me go? Just let me go. But do not sit there and ask me these idiot questions."

"My name, my ill-mannered friend, is Smokey the Jew. But you can call me Smokey. Perhaps you've heard of me?"

"Smokey the what?"

"Smokey the Jew. It's quite simple."

"No, I have never heard the name. I don't care who you are, just tell me what you want. All these stupid games..." His voice trailed off into a rant of heavy Spanish.

"You're in an unfortunate position, and for that, you have your boss to thank. Sadly I don't think you'll get the chance."

Cordero pulled on his restraints, more out of frustration than a genuine effort to escape.

"Dad, are you sure-"

Her father turned to her, his brow furrowed. Lola stopped mid-sentence.

"Lola, can you leave us please?" he asked.

"But, Dad-"

"No buts, ifs or maybes, Lola. Leave the room. Prepare for a small operation. Just as soon as Cordero talks."

"How will you get-"

"I'll call Samuel. I'll be okay. Now leave."

Lola stepped away from her father and took a slow walk back to the door where she stopped, turned, and watched as Smokey wheeled himself closer to Cordero. He spoke softly with genuine compassion.

"I feel I should take the opportunity to warn you, Cordero," he began, "of the lengths I will go to stop your boss' plans."

"You think he will care that you have me?" replied Cordero. "You think that somehow you have now the upper hand?" His laughter seemed to hang in the open space, then died as abruptly as it was spat.

"No, I don't. In fact, I don't think there is one person alive that will miss you. Am I right, Cordero?"

Cordero remained silent.

"I presume by your silence that I am right?" said Smokey.

Lola slunk down out of sight of her father, but with a clear view of Cordero.

Cordero responded once more with silence.

"But you will suffer. Brutality is not in my nature, you know? Oh no. It never has been, and I didn't get where I am by dishing out penance to others. I'm not a violent man, but sometimes, Cordero, sometimes the greed and evil that overcomes others just needs to be stopped. And do you know what I think to myself, Cordero?"

"I don't care what you think. You are insane."

"I think, what is all this wealth? What are all these possessions? And what is this power if I can't use it to bring a little good back into the world? Because, and this is something I truly believe, the world is a good place, Cordero, full of good people. But sometimes they're led astray, as was Judas Iscariot. He wasn't a bad man. He simply fell foul to human nature. So with all this power and wealth, Cordero, I'm able to steer a select few of the misguided onto the right path. The path of righteousness, as it's so often called."

Cordero groaned as his own weight took its toll on his arms and legs.

"What is it you want?" asked Cordero.

"Your boss has veered from the path of righteousness, Cordero. He has taken a path lined with gold and wealth, but sadly, that path leads to nowhere but hell." Lola's father spoke slowly and articulately. "And with your help, I intend to steer him back onto the path of righteousness."

Smokey looked up to the end of the room. His eyes conveyed a silent command.

Lola glimpsed movement from the shadows of a small room at the far end of the garage.

An upright beam blocked her view, but she was sitting on her haunches, waiting for whoever it was to step into sight. A black jacket, dark jeans and heavy black boots were all Lola could see.

"This is your last chance, Cordero," said Smokey. "Your last chance at dying a quick and easy death."

Once more, Cordero's snappy bark of a laugh reverberated around the room.

"Then I'm afraid you have chosen a path that even I can no

longer help," replied Smokey. "You will now suffer. How much, I do not know. But my friend here is highly skilled. He will keep you alive when you hang on the brink of death, and he will reel you back for more. You will tell me what Dante is planning, Cordero, one way or another. How much pain you endure before you do so, well, that's your choice."

Smokey turned to the figure in black, and even from the distance that Lola was spying on them, she caught the slight nod of her father's head.

Lola gasped when the figure stepped from the shadows. Framed in the light of the rear window with an almost childish look of intrigue etched on his face may as well have been death himself.

"Harvey Stone," she whispered.

Harvey stepped up to Cordero, took a deep breath, and then began.

Her father no longer acknowledged Harvey, as if by doing so, he removed himself from the imminent atrocities. Harvey required no acknowledgement. His presence filled the room. Lola kneeled, transfixed, at the door and watched as the man who had saved her life only a few months before, so brutal and yet so righteous, took hold of the rope and worked the pulley system. Cordero hung from his limbs rising six inches at a time, powerless to defend himself. He protested; loud, harsh Spanish insults flew from his mouth in rapid bursts until he hung six feet in the air. Then he silenced.

Lola's father also waited in silence until Harvey had stopped, tied the rope off and reached for five heavy sandbags that hung on the walls from large S-shaped butcher hooks. He carried three in one hand and two in the other, stepped over to Cordero and dropped the three at his feet. He then switched the sandbags to his other hand, positioned himself between Cordero's legs, and lifted the two hooks above Cordero's knees.

Cordero was shaking. He raised his head and peered down the length of his body at the two razor-sharp hooks and heavy sandbags. Then he uttered a reel of Spanish as the reality of what was about to happen hit him.

"Tell me the plan, Cordero," said Harvey, and he let the sharp points of the hooks rest on Cordero's knees.

CHAPTER THREE

"So how do you feel?" Melody asked. "Are you glad to be out of the job?"

Reg sighed and took a sip of his coffee.

"Part of me is. I feel like someone has lifted a weight off my shoulders. I should have left a long time ago."

Melody smiled at him. "It's MI6, Reg. You did have the weight of the world on your shoulders, or the country at least."

"I don't know about that, Melody. I don't think any of my operations were of any significance. The place was so secretive, I never knew what else was happening. I signed so many non-disclosure agreements, I don't even remember what I'm supposed to know and not supposed to know."

"And how did Jess take it?"

"Oh, she's okay. She'll carry on working there. She has a good career in front of her. Sometimes I think if I had just stayed where I was, doing what I was doing, I could have made something of it."

"But you didn't, Reg. You've seen more action than most of those tech research guys will ever see between them in a life-time in the service."

"I didn't want the action, Melody."

"But now you do," she replied. "Now you've had a taste, you wouldn't be happy unless the stakes were high. You were bored out of your mind in there."

Reg turned his cup on the wooden surface of the table, then stared out the window of the coffee shop.

"I just want to do some good, Melody," said Reg. "I know I'm good at what I do. I just want to make a positive impact on the world, and that doesn't mean being shot at or being killed. There's plenty of things I can do. I could go into medical research. I saw a position available online. They're always looking for tech-minded creative individuals apparently, and they're hiring now."

"And what about the other part?"

"Of what?" asked Reg.

"You said a part of you is glad you're out. What about the other part?"

"Oh," said Reg, "yeah, well. The other part is a little more adventurous than the part with the brains."

"You will miss the action then?"

Reg held his finger and thumb in the air and closed the gap until they were an inch apart.

"Maybe this much," he replied with a smile.

"Are you going to take Smokey's offer?"

"Ah, now I see where this is leading," Reg replied. He was sitting back in his chair and let his arms drop to his sides. "You first."

"Me?" said Melody. "Fine. It sounds interesting, and I'm not doing much else right now."

"Don't you think his plan steps over the line of right and wrong?"

"Right and wrong?" said Melody. "No. It lands somewhere in

the grey blur between legal and illegal maybe, but I think he's morally sound. He's got his ear close to the ground, and his finger on the pulse of the black market well enough to assume his intel is legitimate. Besides, he's the chairman of the Society for the Protection of Sacred Arts. He will never do anything to compromise the artwork. All he's doing is saving it for the rest of society to enjoy."

"So you're in then?"

"If you are," Melody replied. "How does that sound? It'd be like old times."

"Don't say that. The last time you said that, I ended up on a gurney seconds away from being embalmed."

Melody laughed, and the woman on a nearby table gave her a disapproving yet questioning look.

The pair laughed again and leaned in close over their coffees.

"So?" Melody asked.

"So what?"

"How about it? Come on. We're a good team. You know we are."

"It does sound like fun," said Reg.

"And his budget is big. You saw the size of the guy's house, right?"

"He said I could have whatever I needed."

"So let's do it," urged Melody. "Come on."

"He already has a tech guy. Fingers."

"Oh, come on. We both know you could wipe the floor with him, and besides, if he's any good, you can have him do all the stuff you don't like doing. Smokey said you'd run the tech operations."

"I have to admit," said Reg, "it's a tempting offer. But what's after this? The time I spend messing around saving these paintings or whatever, I could spend finding a new job."

"Do you think the medical research world will fall to pieces if you don't show up for an interview?"

Reg gave a little laugh.

"You're not <u>that</u> good, Reg," continued Melody. "Besides, this might be the last chance to get your hands dirty and see some real action."

"Oh, behave, Melody," said Reg. "He's asked us to help stop a painting being stolen. How dirty are my hands going to get doing that?"

Reg tipped the remainder of his latte into his mouth and placed the cup back on the table. He swallowed hard and shoved the cup away.

"I bet it'll be over in a few days, and I'll be sitting pretty in an interview in some tech science lab somewhere out in the sticks."

CHAPTER FOUR

"Cordero's a no-show, Dante," said Rosa. She held her mobile phone to her ear with her shoulder while she filed the edge of her nail with an emery board. "He was due in over an hour ago, and his phone is going through to voicemail."

She tossed the board into her handbag, on an old, wooden desk in her tiny office at the back of a mechanic's garage. Outside in the workshop, the loud rattle of the heavy shutters on the back of the truck clanged around the empty space while someone else hammered nails into wooden crates.

"When did you talk to him last?" asked Dante Dumas. His voice was calm as if the news was of no surprise. No doubt, plans were already forming in his mind. Dante's cunning and meticulous plans were his trademark.

"A few hours ago. He was heading into the gallery for a tour." She kicked the door shut to close out the noise from the workshop.

"We planted a guard there," said Dante. His English was better than Rosa's. It was better than the whole team's. Only a twang of Spanish crept through.

"I know. Diego Del Pino. He's a cousin of mine. He's a safe pair of hands."

"So have you spoken to him?" asked Dante.

"His shift finishes at three. He can't take calls at work. He's not even allowed to have his phone on duty. It stays in his locker. But I've messaged him to call me."

"Good. How close are we to finishing the plan?"

"Luckily, Cordero sent through the images of the frame and the placement before he went missing, so we'll be completing it today."

"Camera placement?"

"Cordero didn't get the shots, and Diego can't take his phone on duty."

Rosa heard Dante take a deep breath and let it out slowly. She pictured his nostrils flaring as they did. It was a warning sign.

"So tell me the plan," he said.

"Diego has a kilo of plastic explosives in his locker. Antonio will hack the security system from outside somewhere, disable the cameras and run a dummy loop right about the time that Diego blows the control room door and takes control of the guards."

"What about the guards out on the floor?" asked Dante.

"It's a small gallery. There's only one or two guards on patrol. Antonio will guide the boys and me to where they are and we can take them out."

"The boys?" said Dante.

"Luca and Marco."

"No. Luca and Marco will not be on the job with you."

"They won't?"

"They're too hot, Rosa. They're straight out of prison and I don't want this job compromised. I'll be with them a few blocks away creating a decoy for you to get away."

"Dante, they're our best guys."

"I said no, Rosa. It's too risky. We'll create a diversion. It's the best we can do."

Rosa paused, carefully choosing her words. She knew Dante's volatility.

"I want you on the job, Rosa. I want you inside. Take Cordero if he surfaces. If not, it'll just be you and Diego."

"Just Cordero?"

"And Diego."

"Dante, can I say something?"

"Do I want to hear it?"

"Dante, this is our last job. This is the big one."

"That's right, Rosa. That's why I want you on it."

"And do we get paid when we're finished? We're all getting a little anxious, Dante. You told us three jobs, and this is the third."

"Rosa, have I ever let you down?"

"No, Dante."

"Do you trust me?"

"Of course, I-"

"Well then, do as I ask. Take Cordero and Diego. What do you need?"

"Get me some tear gas and three gas masks."

"Done," said Dante. "Tell me what happens next, once you've gassed the guards, Antonio has hacked the security, and Diego has control of the guardroom."

"Diego will join Cordero and I. Antonio will cut the sensors and the alarms and then give us the all clear to remove the frame from the wall."

"It will be heavy."

"There's a bolt in the ceiling. We'll use ladders and hang a chain hoist from the bolt to lower the painting to the floor."

"Okay, that's ten minutes."

"Fifteen in total, including taking the guards out," said Rosa.

"Then what?"

"We extract it from the frame."

"Another ten minutes."

"Five," said Rosa. "I'm fast."

"What's the exit plan?" replied Dante, neither agreeing nor disagreeing.

"We'll leave by the front door, get in the van and drive away."

"Door security?"

"Diego has access to the keys, and Antonio will cut the alarms."

"You make it sound easy, Rosa."

"It'd be easier with Luca and Marco."

"You'll be fine. Trust me. With the distraction we have planned, you'll have an open road out of the city."

"One more thing, Dante."

"Go on," he replied.

"I want double."

"You want what?"

"Double," said Rosa. "This whole thing has been planned for the four of us. Now all I have is Cordero, who is still missing, and Diego, who is green behind the ears. It'll be his first job."

"Double is a lot of money."

"The risk is double, the effort is double, the reward is double. It's easy mathematics, Dante."

"I'm leaving you in charge of my lifetime ambition, Rosa. It's the biggest job you'll ever do. Get it right, and I'll see that you never need to work again. Call me when you hear from Cordero. I want to know where he is, and I want you on the road by eight o'clock tonight."

"Of course," said Rosa, but Dante had already disconnected the call.

She tossed her phone onto the desk, reached across and banged on the thin partition wall.

"Antonio?" she called.

"Sí?" came his response from the small office next door to hers.

"We are go for tonight. Make sure you have that security under control."

"Ah, sí, sí," he replied.

But Rosa's mind was already in Spain, sitting outside her house in the sunshine with her feet up and a glass of sangria in her hand.

CHAPTER FIVE

"I'm a patient man, Cordero," said Harvey. "I can wait all day if I have to."

"Wait then," replied Cordero. "I will tell you nothing."

Harvey smiled.

"So you do know *something*, in which case all I need to do is extract the information from you. I might add that extracting information from people is my specialty."

"I know *nothing*," spat Cordero.

"How are your arms?" asked Harvey. "Tired yet?"

"I'm fine. You think you can break me?"

Harvey let the weight of the two sandbags and gravity pull the sharp point of the hooks into Cordero's skin. Cordero grunted with the additional weight. His legs shook, and he sucked short, sharp breaths through his tight, pursed lips, fighting to control the pain.

"How much do you know now?" asked Harvey. "In time, those hooks will tear through your cartilage, bone and muscle. The longer you hold out, the more painful it will be."

"Fuck you," replied Cordero, in between breaths.

Harvey nodded in admiration at the man's tenaciousness then turned to Smokey.

"Ten minutes, maximum."

"You've done this before?" asked Smokey. His face was calm, but his eyes betrayed his anticipation of what Harvey might do next.

Harvey didn't reply.

Cordero was grunting. He muttered a long string of illegible Spanish.

"What if he doesn't talk?" asked Smokey.

"How bad do you want the information?"

Smokey stared at Cordero hanging from the four lengths of rope and Harvey felt his contempt.

"Do you like art, Harvey?"

"As much as the next guy," Harvey offered, with a slight shrug of his shoulders.

"Well, this man alone is responsible for the loss of millions of dollars' worth of paintings. Some of them will never be seen again, Harvey. But the monetary value isn't the point. It's the art." Smokey seemed to lose himself in his imagination as he spoke. "Think about the time it takes a man to create mind-blowing scenes. Some of them were five hundred years old, four hundred years, three hundred years. And he robbed the world of things that can never ever be returned. Timeless images, Harvey. Timeless."

Harvey didn't reply.

"I want the information, Harvey. Dumas needs to be stopped."

The seriousness is Smokey's eyes spoke volumes.

Harvey lifted two more sandbags with two more butcher hooks.

"Cordero," he said, catching the man's attention, "we know Dumas is planning another robbery. And we know that you know what, where and when. All you have to do is tell us and all of this stops."

Cordero bit his lower lip, fighting the urge to talk, to shout it out.

"It's there, isn't it?" said Harvey. "It's on the tip of your tongue. All you have to do is say the words and I'll let you down."

The statement was met with more rhythmic grunting. Tears had streamed from Cordero's eyes as his shaking body worked the two sharp hooks deeper into his knees.

Harvey collected two more sandbags by the hooks and held them above Cordero's wrists.

Cordero looked up in clear distress, his eyes wide with fear, and the deep carnal grunts, borne from the pit of his stomach, rose in pitch to a fear-fuelled squeal from the back of his throat.

Harvey ran the sharp points along Cordero's skin, creating two faint scratches that drew a thin line of blood on each arm. He stopped with the point of the hooks above Cordero's elbows then watched with intrigue as Cordero fought a battle in his mind. Harvey had seen the battle before. The result all depended on if the battle was with Cordero's own honour and fear, his loyalty to Dumas, or his fear of what Dumas might do to Cordero should he talk.

The battle played out as if it was on a screen. Cordero's face performed the role of the front line with its desire to deceive Harvey. But his eyes were the stars of the show. He squeezed them closed as Harvey touched the points of the hooks to his skin. If he was holding out for honour, then anger would soon show itself. If he was holding out for loyalty, he would welcome the pain and embrace it. But if he was resisting out of fear of Dumas, his eyes would light up and he would talk.

Harvey lowered the sandbags, letting the weight slip from his hand. The point of the hook sank into Cordero's skin. In just a few seconds, they slipped through his arms to the shank of each hook. Two deep red pools of blood formed on the floor below. But as Cordero screamed and struggled, the hooks in his knees found the sweet spot between the cartilage and the bone. One by one, they too sank deeper into his legs.

The more Cordero struggled and screamed, the deeper the hooks sank, until they could sink no further and hung from his legs, swinging from side to side with his efforts.

Stepping towards the exit, Harvey glimpsed Lola as she ducked out of the garage. He turned to Smokey.

"Maybe we should leave him to think about it for a while," he said.

Smokey's eyebrows raised in admiration of Harvey's control.

Harvey walked towards the door, but he hadn't taken three steps when Cordero broke.

"Okay, okay," he shouted, breathless and hoarse from screaming. "I'll tell you, but let me down."

Harvey returned to his side with two long steps.

"Talk first," he said.

Cordero's face was bright red and shiny with sweat. Four pools of blood had formed on the painted, grey screed floor beneath him.

"No," he begged. "Please, just let me down. I'll talk."

Harvey reached for the last sandbag and picked it up using the last hook.

"I've got one more hook, Cordero," he said, his voice strong and commanding to cut through the man's wailing. "Where should it hang?"

"No, no," Cordero cried. "Please. I'll talk."

"When is the robbery?"

"Let me down, please. I'll tell you anything you want, just-"

Harvey offered the hook up to the man's groin.

"How about here?"

"No. No." Cordero's eyes widened further. "It's tonight."

"Where?"

"Just stop. I can't take-"

"Where?" Harvey repeated.

He let the point of the hook rest on Cordero's groin then moved away as Cordero's bladder gave way, and a stream of clear urine soaked his jeans and dripped to the floor. Cordero let the tears roll. At first, a few sorry sobs emerged from his lips, but then the flood gates opened and he cried like a child.

Harvey lifted the hook once more.

"Tell me where, Cordero."

Between a burst of whimpering and a long sniff, Cordero raised his head far enough to look down at Harvey and the point of the hook.

"Last chance," said Harvey.

Cordero spat his phlegm then laughed as Harvey wiped his forearm across his face.

Harvey waited for Smokey's confirmation with raised eyebrows. Smokey returned the silent question with a nod of his head.

Harvey let go of the hook.

CHAPTER SIX

Two gleaming brogues matched Lola's pace. She knew the
shoes, knew the walk, and knew the reason he was there. She
swam freestyle and increased her speed, yet on each fourth
stroke as she raised her head to breathe, the immaculate shoe
would be right alongside her.

She coasted the final two metres, grabbed the curved coping
stone and leaned on the end of the pool in the shallow end, then
tipped her hair back into the water and pulled it over her shoulder. The shoes were standing in front of her. A fresh white
towel hung above them and above that was Samuel's face,
solemn and expressionless.

"He wants to see me?" Lola asked, as she climbed from the
pool and took the towel that Samuel offered.

"Ma'am," replied Samuel.

"I'll be thirty minutes."

"Very good, ma'am," said Samuel. "Will you be accompanying your father for dinner?"

Lola finished towelling herself off, wrapped the towel across
her chest, and tucked in the loose end.

"Not today, Samuel. I'll eat alone."

Samuel remained impassive.

"Ma'am, if I might say, your father had asked me-"

"Samuel, I'll eat alone. If we're sending messages via the butler now, you may inform your employer that I shall only talk to him so I can express my disgust, and he should be damn grateful I'm even bothering to do that."

"Indeed, ma'am."

"Thank you, Samuel. That'll be all."

"Very good, ma'am."

Samuel turned on his heels with a practiced flourish, and with arms locked behind his back, he strode alongside the pool to the doors that led into the greenhouse, which connected the indoor pool house and the gym to the west wing of the main house.

Lola pulled a fresh small towel from a pile on a nearby table and dried her hair. She couldn't shake the image of what she had seen earlier that day from her mind. Throwing the towel in the basket, she dropped down onto the edge of a wicker lounger and dropped her face into her hands.

The water had calmed by the time she lifted her head and changed from her bathing suit. She stripped naked by the poolside, strode over to the drying rack and dressed in her favourite soft, baggy, multi-coloured striped pants and a vest top. Then she pulled her damp hair back, shook it to give it some life and stepped into her flip flops before following in the footsteps of Samuel through the greenhouse.

The conservatory, where she knew her father would be, was situated at the end of the east wing. Lola found him, exactly as she'd expected, sitting at the head of the large, twelve-seater dining table. One more place had been set for dinner at the far end of the table. Samuel was standing behind the free chair, ready to seat her.

"Ma'am," he said.

"I told you-"

"Lola, please join me for dinner," her father interjected, without looking up from his dinner. He was sitting with his knife and fork in his hands, but waited courteously for Lola. She shook her head, took her place at the table, and allowed Samuel to push in her chair.

Lola stared down the table at her father while Samuel lifted the cloche from a silver serving dish in the centre of the table. He spooned a healthy amount of roast carrots and broccoli onto a plate, and then selected a few of the leaner, finer cuts of lamb from the dish the cook had prepared.

He placed the plate in front of Lola, poured her water, then stepped back and resumed his position with his hands behind his back.

"Thank you, Samuel," said her father. "That'll be all for the night."

"Ma'am?" said Samuel, offering her a chance for a last request before he retired.

Lola shook her head.

"Very good, sir," said Samuel. He turned on his heels, strode towards the exit into the main house, and pulled the double doors closed behind him.

As soon as the doors clicked shut, Lola fired into action.

"How dare you?" she spat.

"You forget yourself, Lola," her father replied.

"I saw what you did to that man. You had no right."

"I told you to leave."

"I didn't know you hired Harvey Stone," said Lola, almost hushing Harvey's name as if they were being overheard.

"I paid him to do a job, and he'll stay until he's done."

"He's a monster, Dad. I don't want him here."

"He gets the job done," replied her father. "And from what I've seen so far, he's better than most."

"Better?" said Lola. "Better than who?"

"Anyone else I've ever seen."

"So now you're an expert on torture, are you? You're suddenly-"

"You have no idea of the things I've done, Lola. And might I remind you who you're talking to?"

"You've changed. Since you lost your leg, you're different."

"I've always been the same, Lola. But now the stakes are higher."

"It's art, Dad," said Lola quietly, edging on pleading. "For centuries, it's been torn from one hand into the next, stolen, buried, and burned. And it won't stop just because some old Jew in the arse end of England takes it upon himself to call in the big guns and stop one guy from stealing a few paintings. I bet out there right now there's some other thief in some other country nicking some other painting that you've never even clapped eyes on. And what's more, and excuse me for pointing out the elephant in the room, but I've been nicking art in one form or another for years. Bit hypocritical, isn't it?"

Lola's father placed his fork to the side of his plate while he chewed his lamb. Lola waited for him to swallow. He wiped the corners of his mouth with a white napkin.

"If some other thief is, as you say, in some other country, stealing some other art that I am yet to clap eyes on, Lola, there's nothing I can do about that right now. And if I crossed a few lines in my younger years, what can I do now but pay my penance?" He raised his finger, resting his elbow on the table. "But what I can do, right now, right here, in the arse end of England, is stop one man from taking some of the finest artwork this country has to offer. As a result, my girl, millions of others may enjoy the art for perhaps centuries to come."

"If you're so sure it's Dumas, why don't you call the police?"

Her father laughed at the comment and picked up his fork.

"And say what, Lola?" He cut a polite mouthful-sized piece of carrot. "Excuse me, officer, but I happen to know who it was that, just a few weeks ago, stole The Sortie Made by the Garrison of Gibraltar, and The Mother and Child. I don't suppose you could send a squad car round to pick them up, could you?"

"You know what he stole already?"

"Of course I know what he stole, my girl. They were two of my favourite paintings."

"And you're going to send Harvey Stone in to stop him?" asked Lola. "You think he can handle Dumas' men?"

"No, dear. Mr Stone is merely extracting the information. He refused to get involved. I have another team who will handle Dumas when the time is right."

"So you paid him to torture Cordero?"

Her father shrugged.

"We came to an arrangement. I asked him to help with Cordero but he drew the line at Dumas. He said he's tired of it all and wants to go back to his house in France."

"Well, I'm out," said Lola. She wiped her hands on her napkin, and dropped it beside her plate. "I can't work with him. And I can't work with you. Not now."

"You knew he was a violent man. He saved your life, remember?"

"'That was different. We were in a situation."

"I need you in this, Lola. Harvey's good, but I need your-"

"My what, Dad?"

"Skills, Lola."

"My skills? Who else have you hired to stop Dumas? I'm guessing they're equally sick?"

"No, they're very different. Together, the four of you make a well-rounded team. Dumas doesn't stand a chance."

"It sounds like Fingers and I are excess. Why would you need four of us?"

Her father shook his head slowly and kept his eyes focused on Lola's.

"Melody Mills and Reg Tenant have skills and links that we do not have. How about it?"

Lola felt her father's manipulation closing in like a ring of guards, each stepping forwards a pace with every word he spoke.

"Of course they have skills. They're ex-police. So you're protecting yourself? But I can't see what help they'd be to stop Dumas."

Her father seemed pleased with the team he was building. The corners of his mouth curled with unconcealed delight.

"They were MI6, my girl."

"They were what? MI6? What the hell do they want with stolen paintings?"

"Nothing. That's the point. Like I said, they have skills and contacts. They'll be helpful."

"You have got to be joking," said Lola. "I knew they were police, but...do you realise what would happen if they recognise most of the paintings in this house?"

"They were MI6, Lola. Unless you can snort it or blow it up, they wouldn't have a clue what it is. In fact, I doubt they'll know a Monet from a Michelangelo."

"I can't do it, Dad. It's got fail written all over it."

"One last time, Lola. It's all I ask."

Lola let the thought of helping her father one last time roll around her head for just a fraction of a moment before reality hit home. She held her hands up in despair.

"Can't you see it? It's crazy, Dad."

"It's what I want. It's what I've always wanted."

"What is?"

For the first time, her father had no reply.

"What's what you always wanted, Dad?"

Silence.

"Dad?"

Her father didn't reply.

"It's it, isn't it? Dumas, he's going to rob the Defeat of the Floating Batteries at Gibraltar, isn't he?"

Her father averted his eyes.

"That's what all this is about," said Lola. "It's not about the art. It's not about you doing good. It's about Dumas stealing the painting that you've always wanted. And you can't have it because now you're the chairman of some art society."

"He needs to be stopped, Lola."

She pushed her chair out, stood up, and began to walk away from the table but stopped, and without turning to face him, she addressed her father for the last time.

"I can't be a part of this."

CHAPTER SEVEN

"Are you okay, Smokey?" asked Melody. "You seem a little off."

Smokey slid himself to one side of his bed in the grand conservatory, lowered his good leg, and then pushed off. He gave a practiced twist, found the arms of the wheelchair and lowered himself into it.

"Smokey?" said Melody.

"I want to show you something," he replied. "Have you finished your tea?"

Melody nodded and looked across at Reg, who sank the rest of his and placed the cup on the small coffee table.

"Let's go into the garden," said Smokey. "I just came inside for a nap and to think. I feel like I've been shut up inside when the weather is this nice. Reg, my boy, would you mind doing the honours and pushing this old chair of mine?"

"Sure," said Reg. "I can think of worse places to be shut up though, Smokey. I've never seen a conservatory so big. It has everything you need."

"Everything except a leg, Reg," replied Smokey. "Let's go out that way." Smokey pointed at the white PVC doors that led onto a wide, flagstone terrace.

Once outside, Melody closed the doors behind them and took in the breath-taking view of Smokey's property. A blue sky with picture-perfect white fluffy clouds framed the expanse of manicured lawns and small clumps of trees. Trimmed hedges and vibrant flower beds lined interweaving pathways that led off in all directions. A small brook cut a shallow gorge through the centre of the landscape and fed into the lake at the front of the house.

"Let's go," said Smokey.

Melody smiled at his ability to control a situation despite his recent disability. She walked beside him.

"It's a beautiful property, Smokey. Have you owned it for long?" said Melody.

"Too long, I think, Melody. I keep meaning to get rid of it. I have a more modest house in North London. But with a leg gone, I'm not sure I could manage the stairs anymore."

"How could you even consider selling this place?" asked Reg, as he steered the chair onto a small, stone footbridge that spanned the brook. "It's incredible."

"My grandfather bought it, you know? That was before I was born. He had all the money. That damn old miser never let a penny go astray. When my father inherited it, the greed got its hold on him too. We never came here, never visited. The place was left to rot. I took over when my father passed, but it wasn't out of duty or desire, you understand? Oh, no. I took a step through those two front doors for the first time, and my eyes fell onto an oil painting so big and so well-crafted that I was standing on that spot, enthralled by it's magnificence and fell in love. Transfixed, I was. That painting was all I could think about for the longest of times."

"Sounds romantic," Melody said, encouraging Smokey to continue with the story.

"I walked around the house, dumbfounded and bewildered

at all the artwork, but I kept going back to the one painting. Like it drew me in."

"So you inherited them? The paintings, I mean. The walls seem to be lined with them."

"I inherited many of them, my dear, and acquired a great deal myself over the years. That's the thing, you see, when you come from nothing and suddenly find yourself surrounded by fine things, you find yourself holding a burning desire. You see something and desire takes over. It grabs you, you understand? And it doesn't let you go until you succumb. Mine is one of the biggest private collections in London now, and as a result, I keep getting voted chairman for the Society for the Protection of Sacred Arts."

"That's quite an achievement, Smokey."

"It's quite a responsibility, Reg. The paintings are considered more valuable than human life sometimes."

"I guess it depends on the human, doesn't it?" Reg joked.

"It often does, Reg," replied Smokey. Then he muttered to himself, "It often does indeed."

Reg caught Melody's attention, and tapped his temple with one finger, indicating that maybe Smokey had a screw loose.

"I can assure you I have all my faculties, Reg," said Smokey. "I might be crippled, but I'm not stupid or blind."

From the corner of her eye, Melody saw both Reg's shocked expression and Smokey's wry grin, and turned to admire the gardens to hide her amusement.

The path rounded a corner at the end of a long, tall hedge, which had been allowed to grow out. Before them, sitting in a bed of gravel, was a brick-built garage with two huge sliding doors at one end, presumably for vehicles to enter, and a smaller door for foot traffic in the centre.

"I wasn't expecting that," said Reg.

"It's my garage where I keep my classic cars."

"Well, your garage is bigger than all the flats I've ever lived in all rolled into one," said Reg.

Melody held the single door open for Reg to push the wheelchair through, then followed them inside as Reg gave a start and called out.

"Holy mother of-"

"Easy now," said Smokey. "This is what I wanted to show you."

Melody turned from the doors. Her eyes skipped past the classic E-type Jaguar, the sixty-seven Corvette, and the nine-teen-thirties Rolls Royce, and landed on a body that hung from thick ropes that reached up into the ceiling void.

Sandbags hung from butcher hooks on the man's limbs. The two that hung from the arms were placed harmlessly over the limbs, but the two hooks at the man's knees had sunk through the cartilage and reappeared at the rear of the leg. One of the man's arms had pulled free of its socket, leaving a grotesque, dislocated deformation that had turned black and blue with a haze of yellow, which had spread across his chest.

A final sandbag hung from a final hook that had been embedded into the man's groin.

A toxic smell of faeces and urine hung like a layer of fog in the air. The man's head hung like the sandbags, an expression of pain and failure etched into his pale face.

"I wasn't expecting that," said Melody.

CHAPTER EIGHT

"Are you guys nearly done here?" Rosa asked. She placed a foot on a stack of two-by-four timbers and leaned on her thigh.

Luca eyed her foot then traced her leg along her knee-length leather boots onto her black skin-tight leggings and up to her chest, which, thankfully, was covered in a loose-fitting checked shirt, tied off in the middle with the sleeves rolled up.

"See anything you like?" she asked him. "How long?"

Luca returned to his work and laughed to himself.

"It's nearly ready," he said, taking a handful of three-inch screws from a box on the back of the van. He stuffed three into his mouth for safekeeping and screwed the fourth into the two-by-four that he was fixing to the bed of the van.

"Nearly ready doesn't answer my question," said Rosa. "Do you ever give a straight answer?"

"Yeah, well, if I wanted to be asked questions, I'd work in a call centre."

Rosa stood up straight and stepped out of the way as Marco carried another length of timber past her and dropped it next to the one Luca was fixing to the van.

"What's this for?" she asked.

Luca finished screwing in the last screw from his mouth and stood up in the rear of the van.

"It's for the decoy," said Luca.

"I see," said Rosa. "You need a van this big for the decoy?"

"Yes, Rosa, we need a van this big."

Rosa nodded. She was intrigued.

"Are you going to tell me what Dante has planned?"

"No, Rosa. Please excuse us. We are very busy."

Rosa decided to try a different approach.

"It's a shame you guys aren't coming on the last job," said Rosa. "I could do with two safe pairs of hands."

She caught Luca's glance at Marco, and they both lowered their heads without answering.

"Why don't you tell me?" she asked.

Neither replied.

"Is it a secret? I thought we were a team. The first two jobs went well. Why pull you off now? Especially as payday is so close."

"You know this third job is the most important to him?" said Luca.

"Of course. This is the one we've been waiting for. It's the grand prize, which makes it all the more strange that he wouldn't have his two best men on the job."

"The robbery is easy, Rosa. My grandmother could do it."

"But the risk is high," Rosa replied. "The painting is the biggest, the oldest and the most expensive of all of them."

"So you'll need all the help you can get."

"What's that supposed to mean?" asked Rosa.

Luca sighed, stopped working and turned his head to face her.

"We're a decoy, Rosa," Luca whispered. He poked his head

from the van and checked around to make sure nobody was nearby. "That's all we know. While you're in the gallery, we'll be somewhere else creating havoc. The attention of the police will be on us, and you will have an easier time of getting away."

"Well why not send the others to do the decoy, and let us three do the job? You know we'll be in and out in less than ten minutes. Who knows how long it will take with the others?"

Luca put his fingers to his lips, gesturing for her to keep the noise down.

"Because, Rosa, Marco and I have been out of prison for exactly three months, and in that time, two very old and expensive paintings have already disappeared like farts in the wind. If we are being watched, which Dante suspects we are, would you like for us to be standing beside you when you take the grand prize? Don't you think that of all the jobs, The Defeat of the Floating Batteries at Gibraltar would be the one that Marco and I would prefer to be on? It would be the highlight of our careers, the encore to our opera of life." He spoke the last words with a flourish, opening his hands and spreading his arms wide.

Rosa considered the statement.

"Alas, we are too hot," Luca continued. "Dante does not want us to compromise the job. But..." He paused, embracing his typical romantic enthusiasm. "We are still helping. We will draw the police in droves, leaving you nothing but empty roads for your escape, and when you are free and clear, you will thank us and we will drink wine."

Luca gave a theatrical bow and the pair laughed at their own humour.

"We are at your service, Rosa," Marco finished.

"You see, Rosa, it is you that will steal our glory," said Luca. "And it will be us that clears the path for you."

"But we will all share the fortune." Marco grinned.

Luca jumped to the ground beside Rosa, dropped to one knee and collected her left hand before Rosa could resist. He kissed it once, holding her gaze with his large brown eyes.

"Is that a straight enough answer for you, my lady?"

CHAPTER NINE

"Who is that?" asked Melody, her voice loud in the huge garage.

"Do you remember I told you about a job I needed help with?" asked Smokey.

"That's the job?"

Smokey laughed.

"No, this is Cordero. He works for a man named Dante Dumas."

"You mean, used to work for Dumas?" said Reg.

From inside the darkened side room, Harvey heard the familiar voices of his old friend, Reg, and Melody, his ex-fiancé. He stood up from his chair, keeping to the shadows, and peered through the small window in the door.

Melody was dressed in her usual black cargo pants, boots, and a tight white t-shirt. She looked good. Unaware of Harvey's voyeurism, Melody began to walk a wide circle around Cordero until she stopped by his feet.

Smokey seemed suitably impressed at Melody's stomach control. Cordero wasn't a pretty sight, but she'd seen worse. She reached out and touched the back of her hand to Cordero's foot.

"He's alive?" she asked.

With a sudden suck of air, Cordero's head raised up, fast and without so much as a warning stir. Melody recoiled. She removed her hand on instinct, then calmed as Cordero held her gaze, pleading with her. Then slowly, he let his head fall to its hanging position.

The sandbags rocked gently back and forth with his movement.

"Cordero has given us information on when and where. All he needs to do is let us know how they plan to steal it, and then we'll let him down."

"It's a painting, right?" asked Reg.

"Not just any painting, Reg," said Smokey. "The Defeat of the Floating Batteries at Gibraltar is considered one of the finest pieces of art of the period."

"What period is it?" asked Reg.

"Ah, you're an aesthete?"

"No," said Reg. "I just wondered how old it is."

Smokey looked up at Melody's gaunt-looking friend, who was standing with his arms hanging by his sides and was dressed in the same old duffel coat he always wore, no matter the weather.

"It was painted by an American called John Singleton Copley in seventeen ninety-one and depicts a failed attempt by the Spanish and French to capture Gibraltar from the British."

"Do you think that's why Dumas wants it? He's Spanish, I presume?" said Reg.

"He would have you think so. He would have you think that it's his heritage, but-"

"But you think otherwise?" said Melody.

"I do," said Smokey. "He is perhaps the most cunning thief of them all. In recent months, since you and I spoke last, Dumas and his crew have stolen two other pieces on two separate occasions. Collectively they are worth a small fortune. But this is his prize. The Defeat of the Floating Batteries at Gibraltar will be the jewel in his collection unless we stop him."

"And that's where we come in?" said Reg.

Smokey nodded.

"That's where I need your help."

"You mentioned his crew. How many are there?" asked Melody.

Smokey rolled himself to a position where he could see both Melody and Reg together. Harvey watched in admiration of Melody as she gathered the facts, exactly as she had always done, and noticed the way she folded her arms, the way she rested her arm on her right hip and rubbed her lips with her left hand when she was thinking.

"Rule number one. Dante Dumas trusts nobody, and nobody trusts Dante Dumas. He has one person who works on nearly every job. The rest are contracted in. He leaves no trail, and he pays well enough that nobody talks."

"He's a pro then?" said Melody.

"He's been in the game long enough that this won't be a walk in the park. Dumas will be one step ahead the entire time."

"Antonio Rodriguez is his technical genius. He's able to hack into security networks and open up the way for the rest of the team. He's good, and if we can take him down, we may be able to stop Dumas without even leaving the house."

"Sounds like you have an opponent, Reg," said Melody with a smile.

"You're able to hack a security system?" asked Smokey.

Reg's eyes widened as he searched for a modest answer, but Melody interjected.

"He's the best, Smokey," she said. "I've worked with dozens of tech researchers and hackers, and Reg is the best the service could ever offer me."

Smokey nodded with approval.

"That's good to hear. We'll have to see about getting you set up in here."

"What? Near him?" asked Reg, pointing a long bony finger at Cordero.

"Are you squeamish?" asked Smokey in reply.

Melody pushed Reg's hand down and replied on his behalf.

"He'll be fine, Smokey. Tell us about the rest of Dumas' crew."

"Luca and Marco Lopez. Veteran thieves, not just of art. These two could steal the shoes you're walking in. They were released from prison three months ago, coincidently just before the first of the paintings was stolen."

"So they're the men on the ground?" asked Melody.

"Yes. They're strong, smart, and not afraid to use force if need be," replied Smokey.

"Anyone else?"

"Rosa Rivas," said Smokey. "Long-time partner of Luca and Marco. Jewel thief originally, but her path crossed with Dumas during Luca and Marco's trial, and she has been leeching work off him ever since."

"So Rosa Rivas and the brothers are a team?" asked Melody.

Smokey nodded.

"As far as I can make out from our friend over there, they were all brought in to do three jobs. Three paintings. All incredibly expensive. And all high risk."

"They've got two already," said Reg.

"The Defeat of the Floating Batteries at Gibraltar is the jewel in the crown."

"Why is it so difficult?" asked Melody. "I mean, they've got the skills and the headcount. What's all the fuss about?"

"The painting is approximately five metres tall by seven metres wide and is set in a solid bronze frame hanging fifteen feet up on a wall in the Guildhall Gallery in the City of

London. It may only be a painting to you, but to some of us, it is the very essence of eighteenth century artwork."

"Where does Cordero fit into this?' asked Melody.

"He's a contractor too. Probably playing the long game, hoping to get something a little more permanent with Dumas."

"Is he going to talk?"

"We're just letting him hang there, giving him time to consider his options."

Melody's head snatched at Smokey's words.

"We?" she said, her face a picture of realisation. "You said we."

"You think I could do this with one leg?" asked Smokey.

There was a long pause as the pieces came together in Melody's mind. She looked at Cordero. The sandbags, the way he'd been tied, even the knots that had been used were familiar.

She spun back to Smokey, her face a blend of terror and joy.

"Where is he?" she asked.

Smokey smiled and raised an eyebrow in innocence.

Harvey pushed open the door.

CHAPTER TEN

"Harvey," said Melody.

She was slightly dizzied at the sight of her ex-fiancé.

"Harvey has been helping me get the information," said Smokey. "He has quite a way about him."

Melody nodded. "I'm familiar with Harvey's ways."

Her statement added to the already electric atmosphere in the garage.

"I'm sensing a history here," said Smokey. His inquisitive gaze switched between Melody and Harvey. "Anything I should know about?"

"No," replied Melody. "We're good."

"Good. Harvey has extracted most of the information. It will be your job to stop Dumas." He turned to Harvey. "Are you sure I cannot tempt you into helping us stop Señor Dumas, Mr Stone?"

Harvey shook his head.

"No. I'm done. The contract was for the information only."

Smokey turned back to Melody and Reg.

"So you see, I need you both."

466   J. D. WESTON

"Are you going to tell us the plan? I presume that's why we're here today?" said Melody, moving the conversation on.

"Let me explain," said Smokey. He linked his fingers, placed his elbows on the armrests of his wheelchair, and then rested his chin on his fingers. "I've known Dumas for many years, and I also know him to be one of the best art thieves that ever lived. He's cunning, devious, and one of the smartest men you'll ever come across."

"When's the robbery?" asked Reg.

"Tonight."

Reg's confused gaze bounced from Smokey to Melody but avoided Harvey.

"This painting took the artist seven years to complete," Smokey continued. "He was commissioned by the City of London. It is worth a small fortune. Eight figures."

"So our job is to stop him stealing the painting?" asked Melody.

"No. Your job is to catch them stealing it and have them locked up, Miss Mills. Your job, Mr Tenant, is to get Mills into the gallery so she can stop the thieves, and to tie Dumas to the robbery. I need solid evidence. He can't get away."

"With all due respect, Smokey, neither Reg nor I are able to arrest anyone anymore. We quit the service."

"But you know people who can."

"Smokey, are Reg and I here purely because of our links to the police?" asked Melody.

"No, you are both here because of your extraordinary talent at getting into places and because you quite recently were police. Therefore, perhaps we might retain a certain element of ethical practice. I see no reason for us to break the law too much to do what we need to do."

Melody caught a rare grin creeping onto Harvey's face.

"Perhaps we're not the best people for that, Smokey," said Melody. "Our reputation-"

"Your reputation is impeccable."

"You had us checked out?"

"Young lady, you'll find me to be a resourceful man. Although I'm a little limited in my own movements since the leg incident, I still have ways and means. That I do."

"You want me inside the gallery? On my own?" said Melody. "So you do want us to break the law then?"

"Bend it, my girl. Bend it. It shouldn't be too difficult. No, the difficulties will come when you try to stop them. So you'll be armed."

"We're not thieves, Smokey. And we're not police."

"You stole a priceless diamond from the Museum of Natural History, did you or did you not?"

"That was different, Smokey. That was to stop it being stolen."

"So what's different here?" said Smokey. "Instead of a diamond, it's a painting."

"Why don't you just call the law? Make an anonymous call if you're worried it'll come back and bite you," offered Reg.

"The law?" Smokey laughed. "Let's just say that my relationship with the law is fractured, to say the least."

"So why do you need to get in there? Why don't you just wait outside and grab them on the way out?" asked Harvey.

"And risk the painting being damaged? Oh no, my boy, we're going to stop them before it leaves the room."

"What about your daughter and the other guy? Fingers? I thought they'd be in on this," said Reg.

"No, I'm afraid not. The less we say about that, the better. So it's just us. Tell me what you need."

"Plans and security details," said Reg.

"I have them ready up at the house. What about hardware?"

"I have everything I need to hack into the system," said Reg. He patted his satchel.

"Good. So listen carefully. This is how things will go down. Reg here will hack the security, which I might add is extremely sophisticated, so much so that if Dumas' man cannot hack it himself, the whole plan will fail."

"That's a good thing, surely?" said Melody.

"No, my dear, that is a bad thing. It means they won't be able to rob the gallery, which means they won't be locked up, which means they will be free to rob something else. The information I have received is by pure chance. We can't afford to let them get away."

"So you want me to open the doors for them?" asked Reg.

"No, Reg, but loosen them up a bit. Make sure that Dumas' man thinks he's done a good job. Make it easy. Do you know what I mean?"

Reg nodded, slowly falling in with the plan.

"Once they're in, Melody will follow. The painting is big, very big. All we need is for them to lower it to the ground and we have them."

"If they resist?" asked Melody.

"Then do what you need to do," said Smokey, without hesitation. "Disable them, tie them up, leave them for the police, and get out of there. Once you're out, Reg will trigger the alarms and the slam doors will come down, trapping them inside."

"We'll need transport," said Reg. "I'll need to be close by."

"We have a van. What else do you need?" Smokey turned to Melody.

"Details of Dumas' men. How many and who," she replied.

Smokey nodded and turned to Harvey.

"Harvey, my boy, it's time to get to work."

CHAPTER ELEVEN

"It's hard not to be impressed, isn't it?" said Lola, as she stared up at the huge painting. "You know, when the gallery was rebuilt, they actually designed the place around this painting, knowing that it would need a wall this big to hang on."

"It is impressive, Lola," replied Fingers, "which is more than I can say for the security."

"Yeah, I thought the same," said Lola. She then whispered, "Does it make you wonder what's downstairs in the control room?"

"How do you know it's downstairs?" asked Fingers.

Lola grinned.

"Professional interest," she said.

"What did you do, Lola?"

"Nothing major. I just took a look at the plans and a security report."

"Where did you get them from?" asked Fingers, apparently hurt that she didn't go through him to obtain the information.

"Dad had them. He is the chairman of the society, you know. I tell you what though, on the outside this place looks like a walk in the park, but behind those walls is so much security you couldn't pass wind in here without half of London's police jumping on you."

"Tell me more," said Fingers. He leaned on the handrail of the mezzanine floor and looked down to make sure nobody was around.

"Okay," said Lola, and leaned forwards to join him. "The control room is at basement level. Eight guards man the desks at all times, twenty-four seven, three hundred and sixty-five days a year. They're monitoring seventy-two high-definition security cameras that cover every square inch of the gallery three times and across three different networks. So if at any time one CCTV system is down, two more are there to cover the space."

"Smart," said Fingers. "And expensive."

"The control room also monitors an array of sensors fixed to the back of every single painting."

"How many paintings?" asked Fingers.

"Over four thousand."

"Four thousand sensors?"

"Not including the pressure sensors in the floor."

"All manned by those eight guards?"

"Yep."

"So surely the way in would be to take over the control room?" said Fingers. "If the tech guy knew his stuff, you'd have free rein over the place."

"Easier said than done," said Lola. "The guards sit inside a self-contained unit. Fireproof, bullet proof, bomb proof, you name it. There's no way in until shift change, when they are escorted by private security, a bunch of ex-special forces guys probably. The doors are locked and sealed until twelve hours later."

"What about the guards on the floor?"

"Basic security. They are literally just a walking pulse ready to hit the alarms."

"And when they do?"

"The slam doors and windows are activated, closing all exits. A direct link to the police obviously sets them in motion while the thieves sit in here and contemplate their bleak futures."

"Well, looking at the lovely paintings at least," said Fingers.

"There's more," said Lola. "If explosives are used, the security system even shuts down the underground and the ring of steel around the City."

"The what?"

"The ring of steel. The barriers all raise. No cars in or out on the roads and the trains come to a grinding halt. The entire square mile of the City is protected by it. The policy started off with the Bank of England but it was extended to other buildings. The City essentially goes into lockdown as soon as an explosion occurs. If you had a painting, this is where you'd want to keep it."

"How many men does this Dumas have?" asked Fingers. "And why is your dad even bothering to try to stop him? The chances of success are minute."

"I don't actually know how big his team is, but the way my dad talks about him, if anyone is capable of pulling this off, it's Dumas. His team is good. They're pros. He would have been planning this for months."

The pair returned their gazes to the painting.

"It's not even my favourite," said Fingers. "It's impressive yes, but-"

"I know what you mean," said Lola. "It's my dad's favourite. And it's Dumas' favourite. Dad has always wanted it, but even he doesn't have that kind of money, and it'll likely never be up for sale anyway."

"Makes you wonder what Dumas wants with it, doesn't it?" said Fingers.

Lola gave a soft, half-hearted laugh. Then she thought back to the last conversation she'd had with her father.

"Dumas wants it for two reasons. The first, because he can, and only he can."

"And the second?"

"Because my dad wants it."

"They know each other?"

"They've been enemies for years, Fingers," replied Lola. "This is the culmination of about three decades of hate, contest, and spite."

"But what's Dumas going to do with it? I mean, it's a bit big to have on the average bedroom wall."

"He'll sell it, and it'll stay on the black market, at least for the rest of my dad's lifetime."

"Why are they enemies? Three decades, man. Get over it and move on, right?"

"You'd think. The way I understand it is that Dumas and my father both worked for some guy when they were younger. They were both thieves, you know?"

"Your dad was an art thief?"

"One of the best, Fingers, as was my grandfather, at least until he could afford to buy his own art. My father is not proud of what he did, but you can't change the past. I think that's why he took the chairman job, to put something back into the art community."

"Yeah, but did he give the stolen paintings back?" Fingers smirked.

"Every one of them. In fact, you're looking at one of them," said Lola. "Now he's dead set on protecting the world's artwork. It's almost like a mission in life."

"Your father stole this?"

"My grandfather stole it. My father returned it. Now Dumas wants to steal it and my father has dug his heels in."

"I don't think we need to worry too much about this being stolen again," said Fingers, nodding at the huge painting before them. "I'll see if I can get into the security and take a look around. I could probably set up a sniffer to alert us when Dumas' men hack in."

"You can do that if you want," said Lola. "But I told my dad last night, I'm out. I don't want anything to do with it."

"What? Why not?" said Fingers. "You just told me it's your dad's favourite painting. I thought we were going to help him stop Dumas?"

Lola contemplated her next words carefully.

"He's my father, Fingers, and I love him. But sometimes..." She paused and looked away to brush a tear from her eye.

"Sometimes?" said Fingers.

"He's gone too far, Fingers. He needs to be shown that money can't buy you everything. Maybe if he loses something close to his heart, he'll re-evaluate his priorities."

The pair took the wide staircase down to the ground floor, turning away from the huge painting and walking out through the main doors onto Basinghall Street. They turned left and crossed the road, where a man stopped them for directions. He spoke in Spanish and seemed agitated.

"No hablo español," said Lola.

But the man's face just broadened into a smile. His eyes darted behind Lola just as a loud screech of tyres filled the street. Lola spun to find an unmarked white van on the road two feet behind her. The side door slid open to reveal two wooden crates. Just as Lola turned to run, she felt a dull thump on the back of her head.

Somewhere, as darkness began to envelop her sight, she saw Fingers fall to the ground beside her. Her own knees buckled. Two hands grabbed beneath her arms as she fell. Unconsciousness took her before she could offer any further resistance.

CHAPTER TWELVE

"Go easy on him, Harvey," said Smokey. "He's no use to us dead."

Harvey didn't reply. Instead, he wandered outside through the single door to a small wood pile. The pile had clearly been made by the gardener or groundsman. It consisted of felled fern trees cut into foot-long logs and a larger pile of dried branches, brown and ready to burn.

He collected an armful of logs and two large, bushy branches then stepped back inside the building.

Cordero hung motionless. His bruised limbs had begun to turn a very unhealthy yellow. His head hung back as if he was peering backwards, but in reality, he no longer had the strength to raise it.

Harvey dropped the woodpile on the floor.

"Harvey, what are you doing?" asked Melody.

Harvey didn't reply.

"He's getting answers, my dear," said Smokey. "It's quite fascinating to watch."

"I've seen Harvey get answers before," replied Melody. Then she turned back to Harvey. "You don't need to do this."

Harvey didn't reply.

Instead, he began to lay the logs side by side in a line beneath Cordero.

"Harvey, no. I can't allow this," said Melody, her voice growing in urgency.

"You can leave if you wish," said Smokey.

Harvey snapped the branches into smaller pieces to form a tinder and lay them over the logs. Eventually, the scene was set.

"Please don't do this, Harvey," said Melody.

Harvey raised his head for the first time. His eyes met Melody's and he winked.

Melody remained silent.

Harvey reached for the single length of rope that ran through the system of pulleys and untied the figure of eight that held Cordero suspended. He lowered Cordero closer to the wood.

The movement seemed to rouse the Spaniard. His groggy eyes fell on Harvey but saw through him as if he was unable to focus.

Soon, the sandbags that hung from his limbs touched the ground, removing the weight from his knees and elbows. But Cordero's elation was short lived as the sharp end of the chopped wood pricked his skin.

"When?" said Harvey.

Cordero exhaled, long and deep. Relief washed over his agonised face.

"I can make the pain go away," said Harvey. "I can make all this stop."

Cordero ran his feeble tongue across his parched and cracked lips.

"Melody, I need some water," said Harvey, without removing his eyes from Cordero. In the corner of his eye, he saw Smokey gesture to the rear wall where a six-pack of large water bottles were standing beside a kettle on an immaculate black work surface.

"Here," she said, offering him the bottle with an outstretched arm.

Harvey took the bottle, removed the cap and poured water from a standing height onto Cordero's face, being careful not to get the wood wet. Cordero came alive. He kicked out, wrenched his arms against their restraints, turned his head from side to side and coughed up a mix of clear bile and water that ran across his face and hung in a long gloopy string.

"When?" Harvey repeated.

Panting for breath, Cordero raised his head to stare at Harvey who loomed over him, expressionless.

"Fuck you," Cordero croaked. "Untie me and I'll talk."

Harvey tipped the bottle up once more, letting the water run across Cordero's mouth and nose until he gasped for air. His body convulsed and once more, clear bile ran from his mouth.

The bottle was empty. Harvey tossed it to one side. It clattered across the hard concrete floor and settled in the corner of the garage.

"So we'll do it the hard way," said Harvey. His voice betrayed neither disappointment nor pleasure.

He pulled once more on the rope, raising Cordero back into the air. The sandbags swung, tearing at his skin, and Melody turned away as Cordero's contorted face let out an agonised scream of renewed pain.

Harvey tied the rope off once Cordero was above his head. Bile, water and urine dripped from Cordero's broken body. Producing a box of matches from his pocket, Harvey removed one and slid the cardboard packet shut.

"How many men?" asked Harvey.

The only sounds that came from Cordero were whimpers, grunts, and some kind of screeching that formed in the man's gut. The grunts grew loud, forming a rhythm. As they pulsed, Harvey imagined the pain that shot through Cordero's body with every loathsome beat of his weakened heart.

Harvey struck the match, letting the smell of burned sulphur drift into Cordero's face.

More urine leaked from Cordero's pants.

"How many?" Harvey repeated once more.

"Let me down," came the reply, feeble but full of anger.

The match burned out. Dead wood smoke carried to Cordero's nose and his nostrils flared with the realisation of what was about to happen.

Harvey retrieved another match from the box. But as he struck the match, Smokey's hand raised to silence the room. Harvey let the match burn and averted his gaze to the man in the wheelchair who was sitting listening to a call.

Smokey's face dropped. The lines etched into his forehead and surrounding his tired eyes all fell with gravity. His mouth sagged open, his eyes closed shut, and he dropped the phone onto his lap.

Harvey remained by Cordero's side.

"Smokey?" said Reg. "Who was that?"

"Are you okay?" asked Melody. "You look like you've seen a ghost."

With a visible effort to control the emotion in his voice, Smokey removed his glasses, pinched the bridge of his nose, then wiped his eye and looked up at Harvey, as if he was the only person in the room.

He took a swallow, then spoke softly, but loud enough for Harvey to hear.

"They've got Lola."

CHAPTER THIRTEEN

The garage suddenly filled with Cordero's cackle, a laugh that seemed to jab sharp spikes of hate into Smokey's sullen demeanour.

Melody tore herself away from Cordero and pulled a blank-faced Reg from where he'd been standing, not daring to move for the past fifteen minutes as he had watched Harvey work.

"Reg, let's go. Now," she said.

Reg was shaken from his daze.

"Laptop. Find her."

He immediately fell in with Melody's idea. Within a few moments, Reg's laptop was out of his satchel and opened up on the wing of a bright red, nineteen sixty-two, E-type Jaguar. He pulled a mobile Wi-Fi hotspot from his bag, clicked the switch on and watched the row of lights flash as they sought an internet connection. After a few seconds, they stayed solid to indicate a signal had been found; three of the five lights stayed on.

"Sixty percent signal. Should be fine," said Reg.

"Find her mobile phone," said Melody to Reg, then she turned to Smokey. "Smokey, listen, we're going to need to know everything that happened, where she might have gone, and who she might have been with."

Smokey stared at the floor then raised his head, seeming to peer through Melody.

"Smokey," said Melody again, "you need to be strong now. We can find her but we need your help."

She had to raise her voice to be heard over Cordero's impassioned and uncontrollable laughter. The Spaniard rocked from side to side in his crazed state as he hung from his bindings, causing the sandbags to find a motion of their own. For a split second, Melody held Harvey's gaze, but then he turned to Smokey, who simply nodded his request.

"Smokey, help us find her," Melody shouted.

Harvey lit a match.

Cordero, seemingly oblivious or hardened to the pain of the hooks through his knees, gave a maniacal screech that filled the room.

"Smokey?"

Harvey dropped the match to the hungry dry ferns.

"Now you'll see," cried Cordero, between fits of raving lunacy. "Now you'll see who's smarter, you old cripple."

"I have her signal," called Reg from the cars behind Melody. "She's moving fast."

"Where?" Melody replied, leaving Smokey to his dreamlike state.

Smoke started to rise up, engulfing Cordero in thick, grey plumes as the ferns began to take flame.

"London. She's in the City," said Reg.

Suddenly, without warning, Cordero's maniacal laughter rose an octave. The crackle of burning wood filled the spaces between as he inhaled a lungful of smoke, coughed, and wheezed for air. His body contorted in wild thrusts as the heat began to sear his skin.

"All of them," yelled Cordero. "It's tonight. They'll all be there. Five of them."

"And Dumas?" said Harvey.

But Cordero burst into frantic, frustrated fits as he tried to escape the heat that was growing beneath him.

"Yes. Yes. He'll be there. Now get me down, please," cried Cordero.

"What time?" asked Harvey. "Tell me and I'll put a stop to it all."

"Fingers," said Smokey, suddenly and without warning.

Melody and Reg's heads spun to find the old Jew, fully composed and staring back at them.

"She's with Fingers," he repeated.

With a few deft swipes of his laptop's track-pad and several clicks of the mouse, Reg had Fingers' contact file open. He copied the mobile number into his tracking software and hit enter.

"Eleven o'clock," screamed Cordero. "It's eleven tonight."

"Why take Lola?" asked Harvey, his voice the calmest in the room.

"Let me down, please," begged Cordero. "I told you what you need to know."

A particularly bushy branch of fern began to catch light. The flames spread across its length, devouring the dead bristles and growing higher.

"Why take Lola?" Harvey asked again.

"Dumas has taken Lola because he knows I'll concentrate my efforts on finding her," said Smokey. He rolled towards where Cordero hung then gestured to Harvey at a wide broom that leaned against the wall.

"They'll kill her," said Cordero, "if you don't let me go."

"That's enough, Harvey," Smokey said.

Harvey didn't reply.

"Harvey, I said that's enough. Move the fire."

Melody and Reg both looked up from the laptop at the tension that was now evident.

The thick, acrid smell of burning flesh had begun to overwhelm the rich aromatic taste of burning evergreen. Cordero had ceased to scream or squeal and had resorted to exhausted whimpers.

Melody made herself ready as Harvey and Smokey were locked in a stare.

"Harvey, please move the fire," said Smokey.

Harvey waited a moment, then nodded, and fetched two bottles of water to extinguish the flames. Cordero hung lifeless in the midst of thick smoke.

With a questioning look on his face, Harvey stared over Cordero's broken form at Melody.

"What is it, Harvey?"

Smokey and Reg turned to face Harvey, who stared back at Melody.

"Harvey, talk to me," said Melody. She knew that look. She knew what his gaze meant.

"I'm in," he said.

Melody nodded in reply.

As if satisfied with the response, Harvey's gaze fell on Smokey.

A silence ensued. All eyes fell on Smokey. All Harvey needed was the go-ahead to make his move. Melody would be by his side. Reg could guide them in.

"What do you think, Smokey?" said Melody. "I can't get her back alone."

After some deliberation, and with steepled fingers held beneath his chin, Smokey finally turned to Reg and spoke.

"Are you able to get into the gallery's security system?"

Slightly taken back to have a question directed at him, Reg stammered but replied with caution.

"Sure," he said.

"Melody and Harvey will need passes."

"Passes?" said Melody. "Smokey, Dumas has Lola-"

"And if we don't stop him, he'll have the painting too."

"What's more important to you, the damn painting or your daughter?" said Melody, disgusted at his nonchalance.

"Lola is my whole world, my dear," said Smokey. "But if we go after her, we'll be playing right into Dumas' hands. No. No, we stop him. We stop the robbery. It's the last thing he'll be expecting."

"And Lola?" asked Melody.

"Lola's a tough girl. Something tells me there's more to this than we know."

"You're risking your daughter's life for a painting, Smokey. If she survives, she'll never forgive you. If she doesn't, you'll never forgive yourself."

"My dear, if we go chasing after her, Dumas will have us running around London, at least until they have the painting. Then we'll be nowhere but a laughingstock. No, that's not how it happens. We stop the robbery." He turned from Melody, bringing the conversation to a halt. "Reg, can you do it?"

"I'm into the back end of the security system now," replied Reg. "I'm adding Melody and Harvey to the security records. Plus I managed to hack into the supervisor's email account to notify the control room, letting them know that there will be two new guards tonight. It looks like the floor is guarded by a different firm to the control room. It's a split security strategy that minimises the risk of internal corruption. But it also means that the guards in the control room are used to seeing strangers from the other firm covering the gallery duty."

"What time does the shift start?" asked Melody.

"Ten," said Reg.

"It's seven thirty now," said Melody. She turned to Harvey who was leaning against the wall. "We've got two and a half hours to get there, find uniforms and get onto the floor."

Harvey didn't reply. He nodded, shoved off the wall, and gave Smokey a look as if offering him a silent chance to voice any last changes.

Smokey returned the stare, then offered a single indiscernible nod.

Harvey began to move towards the door.

"Reg, keep an eye on Lola and Fingers," said Melody as she hurried after Harvey.

"Wait," said Smokey.

The pair stopped.

Smokey wheeled himself to a bright red tool chest that was standing by a bench in front of his impressive line of cars. He opened the bottom drawer and pulled out two black cases that Melody recognised immediately.

"You might need these," he said.

Both Harvey and Melody took a larger case each. Inside each was a single SIG Sauer P226 with two magazines. Smokey pulled two small boxes of ammunition from another drawer and handed them across to Harvey and Melody. Harvey loaded his weapon and stuffed the spare magazine into the pocket of his cargo pants.

Reg then passed them a smaller case, from which, Melody produced two GPS earpieces.

"Wear these. I can track you from here," said Reg.

"Are we ready?" asked Harvey.

"Reg, are we good to go?" Melody asked.

"I'm set," he replied, pulling his headphones from his bag. "But what do we do about Cordero? He's still alive." He gestured at the broken Spaniard who still hung from the ropes. His skin was charred and bruised and his breathing was shallow, but it was deep enough that they could see the faint rise and fall of his stomach.

Melody glanced at Smokey, who in turn looked at Harvey.

Reading the signal exactly as it was intended, Harvey approached Cordero, raised his weapon and fired two shots, one in his chest, and one in his head.

He turned back to Melody.

"Are we ready now?" he said.

CHAPTER FOURTEEN

It wasn't the first time Lola had been trapped in the back of a van.

She came to as the van took a right-hand bend, which rolled her onto her side and sent a hot wave of nausea through her gut. Stomach acid clawed at her throat and trickled into her mouth. She spat into the darkness, blind as to the direction.

"You're awake," said a man's voice. "That was fast." His dialect had a lick of romance, which Lola guessed to be Spanish, well disguised but recognisable.

"You're wondering where you are," he said.

Lola felt the wooden floor beneath her. She sat back and leaned against two large wooden crates.

"I'm in a van," she replied. "Open the door and I'll tell you where exactly."

"You have your father's humour, Lola. It's a good trait to have, but it is useless with nothing to support its enthusiasm."

Lola judged him to be sitting on the wheel arch a few feet away. She felt for the bump on her head, then winced when her fumbling fingers found it.

"What is it you want, Dante?" She held her head steady in her hands, trying to control the dizzying sensation.

"Your mind, Lola."

"Is this about Cordero?"

"Cordero? Oh, so your father does have him? And I'm guessing he now thinks he has control? But you will see who is in control, Lola."

"I'd be surprised if Cordero is even still alive," said Lola. "Last I saw of him, he was having a pretty awful time of it."

"And the last I saw of him, he was planning to betray me," Dante countered.

"You think he'd betray you?"

"I know he'd betray me. In fact, I'm counting on him betraying me."

Lola tried to piece together what Dante was saying, but her head pounded, and she fought to hold back the nausea.

"Don't try to understand it, Lola," said Dante. "It'll all become apparent in a short while."

"My father will stop you. He'll throw everything he has at bringing you down, and he'd die rather than see the painting in your hands."

"The painting?" said Dante. "Oh, you mean The Defeat of the Floating Batteries at Gibraltar? Yes, he would. You see, we've both always had a kind of affinity for the piece. It is, after all, a masterpiece."

"You won't get it, Dante," said Lola. "Why don't you stop now? You know he'll kill Cordero if it means stopping you."

The van slowed, the driver cut the engine, and the vehicle shuddered to a stop.

"You're right, Lola. I won't get it. And if he kills Cordero, well, he'll be saving me a job."

The side door of the van slid open, but Lola wasn't blinded

by a dazzling light; they were parked in a side street with tall buildings that cast the cobbled road in shadow.

Two men were standing in front of the door, blocking Lola's escape. The man on the right tossed her a pair of coveralls.

"Put these on," he said. His Spanish accent was thicker than Dante's. The tail end of the sentence was drawn out, and his esses were more pronounced.

Lola stood up, half crouched, and tried to duck out of the van.

"Are you going to move out of the way?" she asked.

"Marco, let her out. She won't run," said Dante, as he too made to exit the van. For the first time, Lola noticed that Dante was also wearing coveralls. In fact, they all were.

She buttoned up the over-sized coveralls, rolled the sleeves back and put her hands on her hips.

"So I've got the uniform. Now what?"

The other man threw her a hard hat, the likes of which she'd seen construction workers wear. Then the men set to unloading large canvas bags from the van, which clanged when they hit the ground with the unmistakable sound of heavy tools.

"Now, we wait," said Dante, checking his watch. "Antonio, are you joining us?"

A fourth man, slighter than the others, slid from the front seat of the van. He clutched a laptop bag and pushed his glasses onto the bridge of his nose with a habitual touch.

"What are we waiting for?" asked Lola.

"Dante, do we really need her?" said the man who'd thrown her the hat. "She asks too many questions."

"We need her, Luca," replied Dante. "Just wait and you will see."

Dante checked his watch again. Lola instinctively checked hers. It was ten forty-five.

"Okay, it is time," said Dante. "Luca, Marco, get the bags.

Antonio, be ready for Rosa's call. And Lola, please do not try to run. I can assure you that Marco and Luca here will catch you."

Lola's heart began to pump. It was the same feeling she got before a job. Adrenaline began to line the walls of her veins and her hands became clammy. Dumas held out his hand.

"Your phone," he said. "I imagine your friends will be looking for you."

Seeing no gain from arguing, Lola pulled her phone from her pocket and handed it over. But instead of throwing it into the van, Dumas placed it on the wooden crate that had been pushed against the bulkhead.

"That'll lead them to a dead end," he said with a smile.

The van doors were slammed shut. Dante led the way with Luca and Marco taking up the behind. Antonio walked beside Lola but said nothing. As soon as they left the small side street, evening sunlight warmed her face. Lola recognised the area as Cannon Street.

"Are you tunnelling into the gallery?" she asked. "It's a long way."

No reply followed. None of the men reacted at all.

A short walk later, the five entered Cannon Street Station. Antonio handed Lola an Oyster card to swipe through the barriers, and soon, they were descending the escalators along with city workers who'd either had a few drinks after work or worked late. Most people seemed to be alone. But there were a few groups who were louder than necessary, their smart office ties pulled loose.

At the foot of the escalators, the London Underground platforms were left and right, and signs for the overhead main lines pointed back up to ground level.

"This way," said Dante, and the group followed without stopping. Dante's stride was confident as he approached a single door in the wall. He unlocked it, pulled it open and stepped aside to allow his team and Lola to enter before closing it behind him and locking it again.

The door opened into a well-lit, tiled corridor that bore the signs of many years of use by the engineers that maintained the station and the railway lines. Lola guessed it was some kind of service tunnel to the various service areas of the station. It would lead to the power station, the switch room and the escalators, and likely to the actual underground tunnels themselves.

"Antonio, it's time for phase one," said Dante.

The smaller man pulled his laptop from his bag, then opened a panel that was housed in the wall. Inside were various switches and connection ports. He connected a network cable from the laptop to the interface on the panel, waited a few seconds, and then announced that he was online. He then connected his phone to the laptop and set it down to one side.

"We're ready," he said.

"Good," said Dante. "Now it is time for a little mayhem."

CHAPTER FIFTEEN

London's night time lights shone bright and true. Black cabs dominated the roads, city workers dominated the walkways, and in the back streets of the city, only the occasional stumbling drunk or homeless wanderer were to be seen.

It had been an hour since Luca had stopped the van for Rosa to get out, and then he, Dante, Marco and Antonio had driven on to the decoy.

Rosa dialled a number from memory on the burner she'd been given, placed the hands-free earpiece in her ear, and waited for Antonio to answer.

"Three minutes, Antonio. Is Diego in position?"

"Sí, Rosa. He is ready and waiting."

"Okay, at precisely eleven, he is to blow the door to the control room, and you are to disable the alarms on the basement entrance for me."

"Sí, Rosa. Everything is ready."

A couple, neither drunk nor homeless, turned into the street and walked towards her. The man's silhouette showed a confident, unhurried walk. The woman linked her arm with his and leaned into him.

Rosa stepped back into the doorway of an office block opposite the gallery.

She watched as the couple crossed the small street and passed her without looking up. Rosa waited for them to pass and for their voices to fade.

"Okay, we're ready. I'm going to the basement level now."

The gallery's arched doorway was standing in front of her. Thirty feet to her right was a small iron staircase that led to the basement. Rosa checked left and right, darted across the road then took the iron stairs down to a dark entrance.

"Rosa."

"Yes, Antonio," she whispered.

"You are at the door?"

"Yes."

A loud buzzer came from inside, and a small click indicated that the electromagnet had been released. Rosa pushed the door, stepped inside and closed it behind her. A cloud of thick, acrid smoke and the smell of explosives hung in the air. Beyond a glass wall to her right was her cousin Diego. He was standing at the controls with a crazed look on his face. The adrenaline pumping through him made his eyes large and black. Eight guards lay slumped over their desks around him.

He signed that everything was running to plan. Rosa nodded in reply.

"Control room is down. Antonio, kill the alarms and sensors. We're going into the gallery now." She turned back to the control room. "Diego, stay with me," she called, then waited for Diego to emerge from the smoke-filled glass room.

"Antonio, I need eyes on the gallery. Where are the guards?"

"Okay, Rosa. There is one guard at the top of the central staircase. The other is on the ground floor by the main entrance. If you climb the staircase beside the control room, you will enter the gallery on the ground floor beside the second guard. I would suggest one of you takes the staircase to the first floor so you can each take one guard."

"Good call, Antonio," said Rosa. She dropped her heavy backpack, pulled out two gas masks and two canisters of tear gas, and then handed one of each to Diego.

"First floor. There's a guard on the left as you enter the gallery. Put this over your face, pull this pin from here, and toss the canister towards him."

Diego was fired up, breathing heavily, and snatched the items from Rosa's hands.

"Hey," she said, stopping him from running up the stairs. "Are you wearing a watch?"

"Sí," he replied.

"Okay, thirty seconds from..." She held out for the minute hand on her watch to hit twelve. "Now."

Diego took the stairs two at a time and disappeared from sight. Rosa walked calmly behind him. She stopped at the ground floor and checked her watch again.

Ten seconds.

She readied herself and pulled the mask over her face.

Five seconds.

She put her hand on the handle and peered through the glass.

One.

CHAPTER SIXTEEN

All it took was a nod of Harvey's head to the guards behind the glass screen, and a smile from Melody, for the process to begin like a routine. A clipboard was passed through a stainless steel security drawer. The pair filled in the spaces and passed it back with their fresh identification cards, which Reg had printed just two hours previously.

"You pulled graveyard duty, did you?" asked the guard at the screen.

"Looks that way, doesn't it?" said Harvey, with an accompanying glare. One of the other guards looked up from his desk. He pulled the ID cards from the drawer and began to run their details through the security system.

"Well, it could be worse, mate," said the first guard, as the second began typing their names.

"Is that right?" said Harvey. "And how exactly could it be worse?"

He felt a soft kick from Melody beneath the counter. The guard's humour stopped. He began to study Harvey and Melody's faces, then glanced at his colleague who had found the dummy profiles that Reg had planted on the security interface.

A mugshot of both Harvey and Melody filled one screen with a line of text below each photo, too far away to read.

"Don't mind him," said Melody. "He's just grouchy because he won't get his pie and mash tonight. I'm Melody, by the way."

"Pie and mash?" asked the guard, his face twisted with misunderstanding.

"Yeah, we usually work at the Science Museum. They have a cafeteria we can use during our breaks. Harvey here is fond of the pie and mash."

"And you've been pulled off your pie and mash gig to come and spend the night here?"

Harvey didn't reply.

"Well," continued the guard, "you can use the vending machine by the main entrance if you want a pissy cup of lukewarm coffee. There's two more guards from your firm up there already. I'll let them do a handover. They'll show you where everything is."

The second guard tossed the passes back into the security drawer, and the first guard dropped in two walkie-talkies along with two thick plastic key cards. He slammed the drawer shut, allowing Harvey and Melody access to the passes and allocated equipment from their side of the glass screen.

"But it doesn't do pie and mash, I'm afraid," he finished, with a half-smile aimed at Harvey who held his smug gaze.

"Thanks. What do I call you?" asked Melody.

The guard switched his attention to Melody.

"You don't," he replied. "Shift changes in eight hours. One of you upstairs, one of you downstairs. No chatting. We'll be watching." He gestured over his left shoulder at the row of guards behind him, all with their backs to the front desk. Each of them had two screens that showed a variety of camera views and digital readouts from the sensors placed around the gallery.

"Looks high tech," said Melody.

"You fart and we'll know," replied the guard with a wink.

Melody clipped her walkie-talkie onto her belt.

"I'll bear that in mind" she replied with a roll of her eyes. "Come on, Harv."

"Through those doors and up the stairs. We do a comms check every hour on the hour. Don't miss it, eh?" said the guard, as the door to the stairwell closed behind Harvey.

They took the stairs slowly, aware of the flashing LEDs of the cameras fixed to the corners of the ceiling. Making a show of scratching his ear, but hitting the tiny button on his earpiece, Harvey opened the communications channel between Melody and himself.

"You take the ground floor. I'll take the top," said Harvey.

"Copy that," said Melody, who already had her channel open.

Harvey climbed the stairs to the first floor and listened for the beep and click of the ground floor door's magnetic lock as Melody entered downstairs. Then he swiped the card he'd been given and stepped through into the gallery.

The space was open-plan and rectangular. To his right was a long wall lined with paintings, dimly lit, but enough to see by, with soft, patterned carpet underfoot. To his left, thirty feet away, was a sweeping staircase leading down to the ground floor. A guard was standing at the opposite end of the room, leaning over the balcony and looking down. A faint murmuring of voices could be heard.

The door closed behind him with a click.

"Hola," said the guard, turning his head to face Harvey, but retaining his casual position. He looked tall, not particularly well-built, but confident. The Spanish greeting caught Harvey's attention.

"Is this it?" asked Harvey.

"Sí, this is it, my friend," the guard replied. "Nothing but a big empty room to keep you company."

The guard turned back to look over the edge.

"So I'm here now," said Harvey. "Which means you can go."

"Sí," replied the Spaniard, but he didn't move.

Taking a step forwards, Harvey glanced over the edge as the guard Melody had replaced pushed the stairwell door open, leaving her to work the next shift.

Seeing his colleague leave, the first-floor guard pushed off the balcony, rolled his neck and breathed in. In the air-conditioned room, his warm and stale coffee breath reached Harvey from a few feet away.

"You're supposed to give me a handover or something," said Harvey.

"A handover?" replied the guard. He looked Harvey up and down as if sizing him up. "What do you need to know? The washroom is downstairs, the coffee is terrible, and there are no chairs to sit on. Have a nice evening." Then he made his way past Harvey towards the door to the service stairwell. He swiped his card, shoved the door open, and looked back at Harvey once more before letting the door close behind him.

"Are you alone now?" asked Melody over the comms.

"Yeah," he replied softly, being careful to look normal. He began a casual stroll to the centre of the large room. "You think your guard is in on it?" he asked.

A few seconds passed before Melody replied. She would be doing what Harvey was doing, playing the role of a security guard's first night at the gallery and pretending to look at the paintings.

"No," she replied. "Too weak, too eager, and too much of a pussy. How about yours?"

"One hundred percent," Harvey replied. "Small time villain

caught up with the big boys. Even if he gets away with this, he'll be behind bars in under six months."

"You get his name?"

"No, I caught his breath," said Harvey, stopping to look at a portrait of someone of some significance in a time long passed. "He's Spanish, lazy and arrogant."

"You think he'll be alone?" asked Melody. "Have you seen the painting? It's huge. Far too big for one man to steal."

"The one by the balcony?"

"Yeah, you can't miss it."

Harvey turned back and continued his casual stroll to the balcony where he'd spoken to the guard.

"Are you there?" asked Melody.

"I'm looking at the painting."

"Big, isn't it?" said Melody. "How would you go about stealing that?"

Harvey ran his eyes along the huge, ornately decorated brass frame. A series of small electrical wires ran around the edge of the frame and then joined to run up to the ceiling where, presumably, a series of eyebolts had been drilled in to hold it on the wall. When the painting underwent maintenance, Harvey thought, it had to be removed and lowered to the floor.

"I'm no art thief, Melody," said Harvey, taking in the sheer size of the painting, "but I'd say that stealing this is almost impossible. Get hold of Reg and ask him how much it weighs."

"I've been here all along," said Reg's voice, distant and broken. "Your earpieces are connected via satellite."

"So what does it weigh?"

"Well," began Reg, clearly loving the research, "given the frame's size and thickness, plus it's made from brass, so..." He began to mumble to himself as he ran the calculations in his head.

"Reg?" said Harvey, interrupting the genius calculations. "Just give us a rough idea. We don't need the exact weight."

"Oh, well," he replied, a little discouraged by using rough estimates as opposed to fact, "about half a ton."

"Half a ton?" said Melody. "It's a painting."

"It's solid brass and mounted on a hardwood backboard. And it's the size of my flat in Clapham," said Reg, defending his estimation.

"Harvey, I've got a bad feeling about this," said Melody.

"Agreed."

"I think this is a setup," she continued.

Harvey didn't reply. The sound of heavy boots running up the stairs behind the service door caught his attention. He glanced down and saw Melody. He pointed with one hand to the door she'd used and with the other, he cupped his ear.

Catching on immediately, Melody tucked herself flat against the wall and edged closer to the door.

Three long steps took Harvey to the first-floor service exit. He positioned himself in front of the door, feet planted, and waited.

The seconds passed slowly.

"Hear anything?" he whispered.

"There's someone in the stairwell," replied Melody. "They're counting down for something."

Click. The magnetic lock released.

CHAPTER SEVENTEEN

"Rosa and Diego are in position," announced Antonio. He cupped his hand over the hands-free earpiece connected to his phone and squinted, listening for what Lola presumed to be Rosa giving him an update. "The control room is down, and I have access to the security interface."

Lola watched with admiration as the slight man navigated through the various security prompts. He ran a small program Lola had seen Fingers use before to break the passwords of firewalls. Within moments, Antonio had three windows open on his laptop: the alarms, the cameras and the sensors.

"I'm ready, Dante," he said with practiced calm. "Say the word and I'll kill the alarms."

"Disable the sensors first," said Dante. "In the floor and behind the paintings."

A few deft keystrokes from Antonio and Lola saw the green sensor icons blink to red. A flashing warning began at the top of the screen.

"Good," said Dante. "Leave the cameras on. I want to see this."

He turned to Lola.

"You should watch too, my dear. You might learn a thing or two."

Lola glanced past Dante into the tunnel ahead.

"I wouldn't even think about running," said Dante, catching the movements in her eyes. He nodded to Marco who was standing beside Lola, and she felt his grip on her arm tighten.

"Who are the guards I see?" asked Dante to Antonio.

"Just guards. They'll need to take them out first with the tear gas," replied Antonio.

Dante checked his watch once more. Lola noted the diamond-studded bezel and leather strap.

"Okay, give her the green light. Let's do this," said Dante.

"Rosa, you are go on my count of three," Antonio announced over the comms.

The five of them looked on as if they were watching a football game on the screen. But something was wrong. Lola saw the guard on the ground floor jump to the wall beside the door, and the guard on the first floor moved to stand in front of the first-floor exit.

Dante smiled and gave Lola a sideways glance.

"You recognise them?"

She shook her head.

"They're your father's people. Look how prepared they are. Look how confident they seem. Ready to foil my plans."

It was only when Dante had said the words that Lola became very aware of the guards. It was Harvey and Melody.

Dante gave a laugh.

"Always one step behind. Poor old Smokey. He never learns."

Antonio reached the end of his count. The doors to the ground floor and first-floor service stairwells burst open and chaos played out in black and white across two screens. Lola struggled to focus, switching between the action on the first floor and the ground floor.

A woman, who Lola assumed to be Rosa, burst through the ground floor exit and tossed a can of tear gas in front of her. She pulled a gas mask down over her face just as the canister gave off a small explosion, bright white on the small black-and-white screen. But Rosa was caught off guard by Melody, who reached out from beside the door, twisted her arm and performed what looked like some kind of judo roll to bring Rosa down. Rosa fought back, and the two women rolled off towards the main entrance as great plumes of thick smoke began to emanate from the canister.

The fighting women rolled to a stop. Lola was surprised to feel pleased that Melody had Rosa pinned to the ground with her knees on her shoulders. But the pleasure in seeing Rosa taken down was replaced with dread as the cloud of smoke washed over them both, shielding them from the cameras.

Upstairs, the camera was aimed at the top of the stairwell and the service exit Diego had burst through. Smoke billowed out from somewhere to the right, off screen. But neither of the two men could be seen. Lola, Dumas, Marco, Luca and Antonio watched the laptop, transfixed and waiting for some kind of movement.

"Get us another view," Dante snapped at Antonio.

He flicked through the cameras, but each of them showed a different angle of a large, empty, rectangular-shaped room with a stairwell at one end and walls lined with paintings. The canister expired, the smoke dwindled to nothing and the view of the empty room began to clear.

Antonio continued to switch cameras, seeking the men. He then flinched; the screen was filled with the face of a man staring into the camera through the protective gas mask. The smoke was clearing fast. When the view had become clear, Lola saw the man was wearing a guard's uniform.

He moved his face close to the camera, peering up and cocking his head as if intrigued. Then he raised a hand and pulled at the mask. Breaking the rubber seal from his skin, he lifted it clear to reveal wild, primal eyes staring into the camera.

"Who is this?" said Dante.

But nobody replied. They were all captivated by Harvey as he bent out of sight and began to drag Diego into view until the screen was filled with just Diego's face.

"You know him?" asked Dante.

But Lola remained silent. She watched as Harvey's two hands held Diego's head from behind. Diego's eyes were wide with fear and red from the gas. Tears streamed down his face, and even on the poor quality camera, they could see the red veins across the whites of his eyes from the gas attack.

His head began to turn to one side, then further. Harvey's firm hands gripped Diego's head. He forced the head to the right as far as he could, against the will of the muscle and sinew that stuck out from Diego's neck and until he was looking back over his right shoulder. Then with a movement so sudden and sharp that Lola gasped in surprise, Harvey ripped Diego's head the opposite way, snapping his neck in one easy, effortless movement.

Diego's head hung, limp and lifeless, for a moment. He fell from the screen, discarded by Harvey who then stepped back into view. He peered into the lens with eyes as cold as stone.

"I said who is that?" shouted Dante, then backhanded Lola.

"You won't stop him. He's a monster," Lola spat, as she dabbed her lip for signs of blood. "And he'll come for you next. You wait."

Dante took a step towards Lola.

"You think I care about some piece of crap like Diego?

Honestly?" he said, his voice quiet and controlled. "Are you really as stupid as your father? Do you think that I would steal the Defeat of the Floating Batteries at Gibraltar?"

"So why send them? Why plan all this?" asked Lola. Her voice, louder than before, echoed through the tiled tunnel.

"You know the trouble with your father, Lola?"

Lola remained silent.

"He has no foresight. He has such visions of grandeur that he can't see past logic. The Defeat of the Floating Batteries is seven metres long and five metres high, Lola. What would even I do with a painting of such a size?"

He turned away and began to pace along the services corridor.

"Rosa is nothing but trouble. She was destined to fail. Her cousin, Diego, was an ignorant pig who deserved to die. And your father's little pets are now trapped."

Lola stared back at him.

"Trapped?"

"Antonio," said Dante, "sound the alarms. It is time for us to go."

CHAPTER EIGHTEEN

The pounding of her heart was intense. Rosa had never felt it beat so hard. She fought to suck air through the restrictive mask, but the claustrophobic feeling was overwhelming. The woman's knees had Rosa pinned to the floor, but her grip on Rosa's neck was waning as the burn began to take effect and the woman's eyes reddened and began to stream.

Soon, her hands released completely. Unable to hold on any longer, she pulled her shirt up to her face and covered her mouth. But it was too late. The effects of the CS gas had already taken hold.

Just then, a piercing whistle rang through the gallery. Spinning orange lights danced off the ceiling and walls. The noise was deafening, and amidst the smoke, the lights were chaotic.

A series of metallic thuds boomed around the room as the slam doors came crashing into place, blocking the exits and windows.

With a sharp twist of her hips, Rosa flicked the woman off and scrambled to her feet, but whatever her misgivings, the woman still had some fight left. Her hand reached out as Rosa stood up, grabbed her belt, and pulled her back down so they were face to face. The effort was futile. Even as she held her there, her burning eyes prevented any follow-up attack. A hard jab from Rosa's elbow to the woman's face easily released the grip. She stepped over the woman, who had curled into a ball covering her face.

Rosa delivered a hard kick to her face.

But the move was blocked, and once more, a hand caught hold of her ankle, twisted and pulled. Rosa toppled. She tried to kick out again, but she went down, only for the woman to clamber on top of her back. The mask was wrenched from her face, pulling Rosa's head back at an unnatural angle. Rosa retaliated by reaching up for the woman's hair and pulling it down hard, until the two women lay side by side. The assailant tried desperately to pull the mask from Rosa, who with one hand held the mask on and with the other landed two hard punches to the woman's face.

Regaining her breath through the restrictive mask took a few seconds, but as Rosa began to stand to move away from the woman, she felt a hand on her belt. Another grabbed her collar. But before she could react, she was hoisted from the floor high into the air.

She screamed at whoever it was to put her down, kicking out with her legs. But he was moving and gaining speed. Then he launched her.

There was a moment of nothing, brief and filled with anxiety, as the tiny parts of her ear deciphered which way was up and which was down.

But the feeling was short-lived.

Rosa slammed into the inner glass doors. The sound of breaking glass and splintering wood was lost against the piercing wail of the alarm. Rosa rolled to a stop on the granite entrance floor. There was no time to assess the damage to her body. Even through the mask, her peripheral caught the movement of the man as he stepped up beside her.

Rosa jumped to her knees, scrambling for a weapon amongst the broken glass. Her hand found a piece, nine-inches long with a sharp point on one end.

She slashed out at his legs as he drew close, and at his hands as he attacked. But he was fast, and trained, judging by the way he moved. Calculated blows from his legs and fists were met with deft swipes of Rosa's weapon. Warm sticky blood dripped from her hand, forcing her to hold the slippery shard of glass tighter. It was her only hope.

But then, as if a whistle had called an end to the bout, he stood up straight then stepped back out of view, leaving Rosa breathless and leaning against the outer glass doors, behind which, the steely slam doors blocked the exit.

"Antonio," she said, "the slam doors are down. Get them up. I'm trapped here."

But Antonio offered no reply.

The man stepped back into view, emerging from the smoke like some kind of apparition.

"Antonio, raise the slam doors, god damn it," she shouted with her finger on her comms.

But it was too late. The man was standing over her, a bright red fire extinguisher held high above his head.

"No," she screamed.

But her scream was cut off as the heavy canister smashed into her body. A rib broke, of that she was sure, and maybe her arm as well. She let go of the glass shard, letting it drop to the floor as the fire extinguisher rolled away.

"Reg," he said, "it's a trap. Get us out of here."

Rosa backed into the corner. The movement crippled her with pain. He was talking to someone. He had outside help.

The slam doors began to rise, slow, mechanical and reluctant. The screaming alarm ceased and the spinning orange lights flicked off.

Outside in the distance, sirens blared, growing closer with each wail.

With an almost animal strength, be reached down and grabbed Rosa's belt. She tried to fight him off. But each blow she delivered stabbed at her ribs, rendering her attack futile.

He lifted her high in the air once more, turned, and, as the last of the slam door disappeared out of sight, he launched her through the outer doors. Once more, shattering glass slashed at her body. It tore the mask from her head and she hit the cold pavement outside, sliding on her face far enough to feel the pavement tearing at her skin.

Rosa lay there, unable to move. She heard the crunching of glass beneath his boots and braced herself for the follow-up attack.

But it didn't come.

She rolled onto her back, opened her eyes and looked up into his cold stare. He was carrying the girl, and he studied Rosa's face as if committing it to memory. Then as the sirens closed in just a few streets away, he slipped from view.

CHAPTER NINETEEN

Nausea came in waves, washing over Melody and leaving a cold sweat on her skin. Her eyes had stopped streaming and she could focus, but they were sore as if sand lined the inside of her eyelids. She rocked from side to side as Harvey took long fast strides with her in the crook of his arms. Resting her head on his chest, she pulled her arms around him, listening to the calm beat of Harvey's heart. It was as if he was walking in the park on a Sunday afternoon, despite her weight, despite the adrenaline and despite the pace of their escape.

Somewhere in the distance, a swirling mass of sirens silenced.

"I can walk if you want," she offered.

"Can you see?"

"Enough, if you help me."

Melody had always admired how gentle Harvey could be. He was a man known for his violence and brutality, yet with her, he had the softest touch. He lowered her to the ground where Melody felt the cool, soft grass beneath her.

"Where are we?" she whispered, as he leaned across to move her hair and wipe the tears from her eyes.

In the black and blurry night, Harvey was just a shape, dark against an already dark sky.

"In a park. We're safe here," he replied. "Open your eyes and tilt your head."

Cool fresh water ran across her left eye.

"Blink," said Harvey. "Let the water wash the chemicals out."

"What do you think happened?" asked Melody. She tilted her head to the right for Harvey to wash her other eye.

"We were set up."

"What for? Dumas doesn't have the painting. He failed."

"Hold still," said Harvey, as he poured the remains of the bottle into her eye. "There were only two of them. Not five."

"So?" said Melody.

"So if Dumas wanted the painting as much as Smokey does, he'd have been there himself. And he'd be armed with more than just tear gas," said Harvey.

Shifting her position, Melody rested her head on Harvey's knee.

"So now we've lost Dumas, and we don't have Lola," said Melody. "Sounds like we all lost tonight."

"No," said Harvey, "the game is still on. Dumas is still out there, and my guess is that he's got Lola with him. Whoever they were back there in the gallery were also set up."

"What makes you say that?" asked Melody.

"They had back up. What was the name of Dumas' tech guy?"

"Antonio or something."

"That's him. The girl back there told him to raise the slam doors, but she got no response. It was like she was meant to be trapped there with us."

"But I still don't understand," said Melody. "If Dumas doesn't want the painting, what does he want?"

"The painting was bait. He knew Smokey would protect it.

And by doing so, Dumas knew that Smokey would commit his resources, leaving him free to hit somewhere else."

"Something bigger?"

"Bigger than a seven-metre painting?" said Harvey.

"More valuable, at least," replied Melody. "So how do we find him?"

"We need to find Lola," said Harvey. He hit the button on his earpiece.

"Reg, come back."

"I was wondering how you two were getting on. I've got eyes on the gallery. It's swarmed with police. They've got the girl, and they found a body."

"No sign of Dumas then?" said Melody, who opened the channel on her own earpiece.

"No sign of Dumas. Just a control room full of dead guards, one dead criminal and a half-dead girl laying on the pavement outside. How are your eyes?"

"Better. Still sore, but it could have been worse."

"Reg, it's Harvey. We need to find Lola. Where was her last known location?"

They heard Reg's fingers scrambling across his keyboard and his under-the-breath mutterings as he spoke to himself while he worked.

In the reprise, Melody managed to catch Harvey's eye. It wasn't much, but it was enough for her to see that inside him, somewhere buried deep down, there was a chance that he felt the same as she did.

"Righto," said Reg. "I've found her phone. It looks like it's in a side street near Cannon Street Station."

"We can walk that from here," said Harvey.

"I'm sending you the location now," said Reg. "Do you guys need anything else?"

"Yes," said Melody. "We don't think Dumas wanted the painting after all."

"So why go to all the effort?"

"It was a trap, a trap Dumas knew Smokey would fall for. From now on, we call the shots."

"Copy that," said Reg.

"The painting was a decoy. Even Cordero thought Dumas would be there. See if you can find something else that Dumas might want to steal."

"Something else?" said Reg. "You mean you want me to find expensive pieces of art in London? I imagine fifty percent of privately-owned art is in this city."

"Not London as a whole, Reg. The City. It needs to be in the City. You say Lola was last seen near Cannon Street? Start there. It's a twenty-minute walk from here, so have some answers ready."

"Gotcha," said Reg, sounding enthused by the call for research.

Harvey clicked off his comms. Melody followed suit.

"We're on our own now," she said, pulling his hand to her face and holding it against her skin.

"Melody," said Harvey.

"Don't," she replied, savouring the feel of him. "I've missed this."

"Melody," he said again. But Melody ignored him and rolled closer.

A dog barked somewhere close by and the trample of heavy boots on concrete were loud in the quiet night.

Without warning, Harvey scrambled to his feet and pulled Melody up by her arms.

"We have to go," he said. "Now."

CHAPTER TWENTY

Harvey pulled Melody to her feet and dragged her across the grass to the wrought-iron gate on the edge of the little park in London Moorgate.

Melody seemed confused at first, but when she heard the clicking of the German Shepherd's paws on the footpath, she caught on and ran alongside Harvey. A taxi rolled by. It slowed as if the driver was hoping for a fare then drove on when Harvey turned his back on the driver to face the oncoming dog.

"Stop," said Harvey, planting his feet and pulling Melody behind him. The dog's speed increased as it drew closer.

"Harvey, what are you doing?" asked Melody, sliding behind him. "Let's get out of here."

But Harvey kept his ground in the centre of the small, empty road that ran around the park.

"We'll never outrun it," he replied quietly. "Trust me."

He made eye contact with the dog at twenty metres, which at first seemed to aggravate the animal. But as the distance closed and Harvey held his ground, the dog slowed. Its tail dropped low and the hackles on its back flattened.

The large, eighty-pound German Shepherd came to an abrupt stop at Harvey's feet. He sniffed at his legs once then sat and held Harvey's stare, its ears flat against its head. Melody took a step back from Harvey and the dog growled once. But one look back at Harvey and the dog quietened.

"Harvey, I hope you know what you're doing."

The boots Harvey had heard in the park emerged from the iron gates as a six-foot-something policeman with a bright yellow jacket came running after the dog.

"Stop right there," he called to Harvey.

The dog turned its head to its master, then returned its attention to Harvey.

"Bruno, attack."

But the dog remained still even as the policeman approached.

"Oh for god's sake, Harvey," Melody muttered under her breath. "That's it now."

"Do you mind telling me why you're running, sir?" asked the policeman, panting as he approached.

Harvey didn't reply.

The policeman raised his hand to operate his shoulder-mounted radio.

"I wouldn't do that," said Harvey.

The policeman stopped.

"Is that right? And why is that?" he asked.

"Let go of the radio, officer."

"I'm going to need to take your name, sir," he continued. He spoke into his radio. "Control three two four. Control three two four. I have the suspect."

"I said let go of the radio."

"Right, sir, you leave me no option. Put your hands behind your back. You too, miss." The officer reached for his handcuffs but the sudden action triggered the dog's defensive nature; he turned and growled at his owner.

"Why don't you put your hands where I can see them?" said Harvey.

"Bruno?"

The dog continued to growl. His upper lip upturned and the hackles raised on his nape.

"Hands," said Harvey.

In a smooth, slow motion, the officer brought his hands to his front. In one hand was a pair of matte black handcuffs.

"Why don't you put them on?" said Harvey.

"Oh my god," said Melody from behind him. "You can't be doing this."

The houses at the end of the dark street lit up with the flashing blues of an approaching squad car.

"Do it fast," said Harvey.

The dog continued to growl at its handler as the cuffs clicked into place.

Harvey reached out, with one eye on the dog, and unclipped the radio from the policeman's belt. Then he pulled the push-to-talk unit from the man's shoulder.

"Let's go," said Melody. She knew not to mention Harvey's name.

But Harvey didn't move. The flashing blues drew closer behind the line of trees that bordered the park.

"You won't get away with this," said the officer.

As Harvey checked to see how close the car was, the officer pulled his telescopic cosh from his belt. In an instant, the dog leapt up at the man, biting down hard on his arm and using all of his weight to pull the man to the ground.

"Now let's move," said Harvey, taking Melody's wrist.

He turned and walked away into Moorgate with Melody

behind him. They slipped into a late night pub as the blue lights lit the street behind them.

A rowdy crowd of four men in jeans and construction boots were standing at the far end of the bar and eyed them both as they bustled in. Their eyes hovered on Melody's tight jacket and her red, swollen eyes until Harvey pulled her past them towards the rear exit.

Four heads turned. Harvey ignored them.

The door to the washroom opened, blocking his way. A large man in light blue jeans, a white t-shirt and tan steel-toed boots stepped out. He was taller than Harvey by a clear four inches. At first, he apologised and moved to one side to allow the pair through, but when he caught sight of Melody's swollen eyes, his arm reached across the narrow hallway and blocked Harvey once more.

"Are you okay there, sweetheart?" he asked Melody, his Irish accent thick and fast.

"She's fine, mate. Move out the way, eh?" said Harvey, aware of the flashing blues that shone through the windows, rhythmically lighting the inside of the bar.

"I didn't ask you, sunshine. I was talking to the lady." He turned back to Melody. "Is he giving you bother?"

With a roll of her eyes and a glance at the blue lights in the mirrors behind the bar, Melody shook her head.

"No," she said. "It's fine. We need to go."

But the man caught the flash of blue, then studied them both, putting two and two together.

"Are they for you?" he asked, and gestured at the lights. "Have you got yourselves into a spot of bother, eh?"

"Mate, do yourself a favour," began Harvey, "move out the way. Sit down with your mates and forget you ever saw us. It'll be better for everyone."

The man laughed in Harvey's face. A few hours of drinking beer had soured his breath and the stench of his body odour added to the mix.

"Or what?"

He turned to block their path.

CHAPTER TWENTY-ONE

"What the bloody hell just happened?" shouted Dumas. His voice seemed to run along the tiled tunnel and return to Lola in a haunted whisper.

Nobody spoke.

"Somebody answer me," Dumas shouted.

"They got away, boss," said Antonio.

"They got away?" repeated Dumas. "How did they get away? I thought you were the one controlling the doors?"

"I am, but they must have access too."

"So how can they open the doors if you are the one controlling them?"

"I-I-," Antonio began to stammer.

"It's rhetorical, Antonio. Now tell me where they went."

"I-I-," Antonio began to stammer again.

"Find them," shouted Dumas. Then he turned to Lola. "Who are they? You know them. You must do. Of course, you do. Tell me who they are."

But before Lola could answer, Dumas returned his attention to Antonio, whose hands shook as they hammered the keyboard. Various windows popped up on the screen.

"You have found them?" spat Dumas, his Spanish accent strengthening with his anger.

"I'm trying to access the security cameras in the area," replied Antonio.

"Try harder," said Dumas.

Then once more, he shifted to Lola.

"Do you think it really matters?" he asked. "You think that just because your friends escaped that they will find us here and stop us?" He shook his head. "No. Because, like I said, your father is very short-sighted. It would have been nice if your friends would have been trapped, and your father would have been implicated. He should have gone to prison a long time ago, Lola, but with his silver tongue and his money, he has managed to avoid it. Like the snake, he basks in the sunlight then slivers away under his rock when the heat gets too much."

"You're wrong if you think I'm going to stand here and defend him, Dumas," said Lola. "And you're wrong if you think I know anything about any of this. What my father does is his business. What I do is my business. We're two people. Two minds. Do not paint me with the same poisoned brush you use on my father."

Dumas considered Lola's statement. He turned and strode away in five slow, methodical steps. He swivelled on his feet, took the same five slow, methodical steps back to Lola and slapped her hard across the face.

"You're right. You are two people. But inside you runs your father's blood. It courses through your veins, Lola. Your father taught you well. I know he did. I have been watching from afar. A spectator of your career. Do you wonder why I have brought you here to this place, so far underground?"

"Because you're insane?"

Dumas laughed.

"No, Lola. It is because your father's blood runs through

your veins. You saw the lengths your father would go to protect The Defeat of the Floating Batteries at Gibraltar. I imagine your friends would require fake security, they would have floor-plans of the gallery, and they clearly had access to the security cameras. All of these things require resources, Lola. Your father's resources."

"So?" said Lola, still licking the blood from her lip.

"So, imagine if your father had a choice. Where would his loyalty lie? With the arts? Or with his beloved daughter?"

Lola remained quiet. It was a question she'd asked herself before, but she'd never found an answer. A swell of tears, anger and frustration grew behind her eyes, hot and pulsing with the beat of her heart.

"Mark my words, Lola, before the night is out, your father will show his face." He stepped closer to Lola and held a strand of her hair between two fingers. He sniffed at it, his eyes closed to savour the smell. Then he let go of her hair and let his face take on a cold, remorseless stare. "Or he will lose his daughter."

"I have found them," announced Antonio. "They are inside this bar here. Look."

Dumas glanced across at the laptop that Antonio was presenting.

"Good work," he said. "Are you sure it's them?"

"Positive. I will never forget that man's eyes," said Antonio.

"Good. Tip the police off. Let's make sure they do not scupper our plans."

CHAPTER TWENTY-TWO

Four wooden stools scraped across the old, wooden floor. Four large shapes closed the way behind Harvey and Melody. The large man in front smiled.

"I don't like bullies," he said. His eyes flicked to Melody and back to Harvey.

"This is your last chance," Harvey replied. "Sit down with your mates. Forget you ever saw me." But the sentiment was lost on the man, who looked down on Harvey with disgust. "Melody, go take a seat at the bar. Keep an eye on the door. Order these men five large whiskeys and five bags of ice."

Melody edged past the men as the man in front of Harvey erupted.

"You can't buy your way out of this, sunshine. The way I see it, you have two choices. You can lay on the floor and let us kick the living hell out of you. Or, I'll knock you down, and then we'll kick the living hell out of you."

Harvey was standing in a narrow hallway. If he stretched his arms out, he could touch both walls. Photographs of London from the early nineteen hundreds lined the walls to the washrooms in cheap frames that each shielded their own square of clean paintwork in the surrounding walls stained with a hundred-year-old layer of dirt and tobacco.

Harvey rolled his neck, waiting for the satisfying click each side.

Behind the man in front was the rear exit, which Harvey guessed would lead to an alleyway or beer garden. Either way, it would be a route out of there that wouldn't be covered by City of London security cameras. The wooden door had nine small opaque windows arranged three by three. The reflection of the men behind Harvey was distorted but clear enough. The men were standing two by two like ranks waiting for the command to step into battle.

"Who's first?" asked Harvey.

He hadn't finished his sentence when the big man jabbed out at Harvey's face. It was a move Harvey was ready for. He cocked his head to one side, reached up with his right hand and twisted the man's arm back. Using the momentum of the punch, Harvey pulled his attacker towards him, kicked down sideways on his knee and delivered a finishing blow to the man's throat.

Harvey dropped the big man to the floor wheezing for breath and clutching his ruined leg with gritted teeth. Then he turned to face the four behind him.

He studied the men for a second.

"You're a lefty, you're a righty," he said to the front two. "You're fat, and you're ugly," he finished, addressing the rear two with his last comments.

The two men in front were shorter than the two behind but stocky from a life of construction work. Before either man could react, Harvey took a stride forwards and slammed his forehead into lefty's nose. As if on cue, righty took a wild untrained swing at Harvey who pulled the still-stunned lefty into the line of fire. The man's punch connected with his friend and Harvey shoved the limp body towards righty, who instinctively caught him then, realising his mistake, dropped him. But it was too late. The second it had taken for him to catch his friend had been long enough for Harvey to grab his throat, pinch his windpipe and deliver three hard jabs to his stomach, the last of which cracked a rib.

Righty fell to his knees alongside his two friends, fighting for breath.

Harvey turned to face the remaining two Irishmen.

Ugly took a step forwards, ducking through the doorway into the narrow hall, but all Harvey had to do was to stamp on his outstretched leg as he did, and the man was down.

"Just you left, fatty," said Harvey. "Fancy your chances?"

The last man was left standing alone, dumbfounded at what had just taken place. In less than ten-seconds, his friends had all been floored. A forced look of feigned anger appeared on his face as if he might scare Harvey into reconsidering his position. But Harvey remained firm.

Then, from nowhere, the sound of glass shattering broke the silence. A boot swung up from behind and crunched between the fat man's legs. Fatty fell to his knees, revealing Melody who was standing behind him. She kicked him out of the way and ran past Harvey to the rear door.

"Let's go, Harvey. I couldn't let you have all the fun, could I?" she said with a smile. Then she pulled the door open and checked outside just as the front door to the bar crashed open.

CHAPTER TWENTY-THREE

There was no time to be selective. The inside of the pub had hushed when Harvey and the men had fought, but when the front doors were kicked open and armed police stormed inside, the place erupted. Melody scrambled over the outside side wall with Harvey on her heels. Shouts boomed from behind them as they sought an exit through the neighbouring property.

"Reg, we're going to need your help here," said Melody, pushing the button on her earpiece.

As faithful as a hound, Reg swung into action.

"Let's see where you are," he began. Melody pictured him staring at his screen and working with his homemade software, LUCY, a program designed to track people, phones and tap into satellites to provide live views anywhere in the world.

"No time for fancy games, Reg. We just need an out and fast," said Harvey.

"Okay, I found you. There's a courtyard to the rear of the next property, and behind that is an alleyway that'll take you back onto the main street. I'm on the live satellite now and you have a clear run out. I'd suggest heading north and getting out of there. The place is heating up fast."

Both Harvey and Melody scaled the wall and dropped into the courtyard of an office building. They saw the narrow pass between the two buildings and slipped onto Queen Victoria Street.

"Hey guys," said Reg, "I said to head north. You're going south-east."

Harvey grabbed Melody's hand and walked casually across the road into a smaller lane as if they were just an ordinary couple strolling home from work.

"No time, Reg," said Harvey. "We need to find Lola. We're heading for Cannon Street Station. Have you found Dumas' target?"

"There's so much art in the City. Dumas could be going after any of it. We have no way of knowing," said Reg.

"What does Smokey have to say about it?" asked Melody.

"Not a lot. Now he knows the painting is safe, I think the reality that his daughter has been kidnapped has hit home. He went back up to the main house feeling unwell."

"Reg, we're five minutes from Cannon Street. Find Dumas," said Harvey, then switched off his comms.

Behind them on the main road, a convoy of police cars raced past with their sirens blaring. Melody turned to see the last of them slow, then stop.

It began to turn.

"Harvey," she said, "we've got company."

"Don't look," he replied. He held her hand and crossed the street into another side street. Once out of view of the police, they both ran. The buildings either side of the narrow cobbled street channelled the noise of the engine as the driver gave chase.

Harvey tugged Melody through alleyways, left then right, until they found themselves on the pedestrianised pathway beside the River Thames. London Bridge was ahead. A few drunken office workers stumbled towards them as they ran. Melody didn't need to turn to look; they could hear the pounding of heavy boots behind them.

A ramp leading up to the bridge and Lower Thames Street came up on their right, so they took it then ran with everything they had. Sirens were growing louder as more police were called in to close them off. They reached Lower Thames Street at a set of traffic lights. To their right, coming from the Tower of London, three police cars sped into view. To their left, another set of flashing blues waited for them.

"We're trapped," said Melody, as they reached the road. Behind them, two policemen chasing on foot had just turned the corner.

Before Melody could stop him, Harvey stepped out into the busy road. A taxi swerved to miss him and slammed into the car in the next lane in a hiss of angry steam. The two cars ground to a halt. Two more cars failed to stop in time and smashed into the back end of them, forcing the crash onwards. A motorbike slowed and swerved to avoid the crash, but the rider turned too fast and slid off. The bike came to a halt a few feet in front of Harvey, who picked it up, swung his leg over, revved the engine and shouted to Melody.

"Get on, now."

"What the bloody hell are you doing?" she shouted back at him as she climbed on. Harvey dropped the bike into first gear, revved once more and tore away from the scene.

Harvey didn't reply.

The police car that had been waiting for them roared into life, blocking their way. Harvey mounted the pavement, ducked beneath a traffic sign and took the bike down to the riverside pathway where the cars couldn't follow.

"Reg, we need some help here," said Melody. She switched her comms to open then pulled her arm around Harvey again.

"What the hell are you guys up to?" replied Reg.

"Getting away," said Melody. "Have you found Dumas yet?"

"No," replied Reg, "there's just too many options."

"Where are we heading, Reg?" she shouted above the noise of the motorbike's engine as Harvey slowed to take the bike onto a tiny side street called Swan Lane, back towards the city.

"Cannon Street Station," said Reg. "There's a van parked down a side street, Bush Lane. I'm pretty sure that's where Lola's phone signal came from. Right now, you're four hundred yards away."

"Four hundred yards. Bush Lane down the side of Cannon Street Station," she called to Harvey. Then she returned her attention to Reg. "Hey, Reg, we're coming in hot. Is there anything you can do to help us out here?"

She heard the clatter of keys once more as Reg looked at his options.

"Hold on," he replied. "I've got an idea."

CHAPTER TWENTY-FOUR

"They got away, Dante," said Antonio. "The police haven't found them."

Dumas took three angered steps toward Antonio, stared at the screen and saw the police walking out empty-handed as two EMTs walked into the pub, their ambulance parked a few metres away.

"Are you sure it was them that went inside?" asked Dumas.

"Positive," replied Antonio. "Why else would there be an ambulance on the scene?"

"Can you see where they went?" asked Dumas.

"I'm trying now," replied Antonio, as he flicked between CCTV cameras and began muttering to himself, just as Lola had seen Fingers do whenever he was deep inside a security system. "They could only have gone out the back, which means they could only come out here, here or here."

Each of the various CCTV screens flashed up for a second and were then replaced by the next.

"Here," he cried out. "I have them walking away further down the street. The stupid police are not even looking."

"Well, why don't we hold off phase two of our plan? Maybe we can kill two birds with one stone, if you pardon the pun."

Dumas smiled a cruel smile, which was mirrored by Luca and Marco.

"What's phase two?" asked Lola.

But Dumas just laughed at the question and turned his attention to Antonio.

"See if you can draw them in and make sure we have a good view. I don't want to miss this."

"They're near the river," said Antonio. "How about if I send a little alert to the emergency services?" His fingers played across the keys, and Lola watched with despair as a convoy of police cars cruised Lower Thames Street just moments away from Harvey.

The last car stopped beside the entrance to the side street where Harvey and Melody had disappeared.

It turned.

While Antonio flicked through the metropolitan police CCTV software searching for the right camera, Dumas turned back to Lola to gauge her reaction.

Lola remained impassive.

"Do you gamble, Lola?" he asked.

"Every time I cross the street," she replied.

Dumas dismissed the comment with a smile.

"If I were a gambling man, I would say that your father's friends are in a lot of trouble. But who will get them first? The police?" His mannerisms turned dramatic. "Or me?"

"I would say neither. The police will catch you. At least, you better hope they do."

"And what do you mean by that?"

"Well, Dante, if the police catch you, they might rough you up a little. You'll go to prison, but I imagine you're a fast learner. You'll survive."

"But?" Dumas prompted.

"If he gets you..." Lola nodded at Harvey's form on the screen. "You'll be in a whole world of hurt."

"So you do know him? Do I sense a hint of admiration in your voice?" said Dumas. He flicked his eyes up at Marco who reached from behind her with both hands, pinching her windpipe with one hand and her nose with the other.

Lola fought back, kicking and squirming, but Marco's grip was strong.

Dumas nodded once more at Marco, and his grip loosened but still held her tight.

"Tell me who he is," said Dumas.

Lola sucked in huge lungfuls of air, coughed and composed herself.

"If there's one person in this world who you should be afraid of, it's him. If there's one person who can stop you, it's him."

"I need a name, Lola," said Dumas. Once more, he flicked a nod at Marco and the suffocation began again.

But Lola was ready for the attack. She flung her head back and connected with Marco's nose. Then she spun and kicked out at his legs before landing a hard punch to his throat.

Before Marco had a chance to react, Luca reached across and with one hand grabbed Lola's throat and slammed her into the tiled wall.

Dumas appeared impressed. He smiled his sickening smile and watched as Marco straightened, embarrassed at the blows he'd taken.

"I've got them," said Antonio, disrupting the fight. "They're on a motorbike."

The group all craned to see the action unfold on Antonio's laptop screen. Harvey and Melody were racing from the scene of a crash. A police car blocked their way, but Harvey hopped the bike onto the pavement and tore off towards the river.

"Follow them," demanded Dumas.

"I can do better than that," said Antonio. A fresh window opened on his laptop showing a map of the City of London and icons at each junction.

"What are you doing?" asked Dumas. "I told you to follow them."

"Relax," replied Antonio. "There's only one way out for them." He clicked on one of the icons and another little window opened. "If I click here and here," he said, again muttering to himself, "then the traffic lights will remain red."

Antonio clicked the button to save his changes to the traffic signals. Then he turned to explain. "The City of London is the only city in the UK where the police can override the traffic signals. I can access it from the same console as the security cameras. It's a security feature they built when they created the steel circle."

"You mean the ring of steel?" said Lola.

"Yes, this," said Antonio. "Now, if I give them a green light here," he said, watching on the CCTV screen as Harvey and Melody took Antonio's route, "I can make them dance."

A few moments later, Antonio switched to yet another camera feed and watched as Harvey and Melody's bike stopped in a side street. Parked two hundred yards in front of them was the van that Lola had been thrown into.

Once more, Dumas smiled when he saw her reaction. Her face dropped in horror.

"Before I kill them both," said Dumas, "won't you tell me his name? It'll help me sleep at night."

He glanced back at the screen. Harvey hadn't moved. They were both sitting on the bike staring at the van.

"Tell me," shouted Dumas, and slapped Lola across the face.

The strike reopened the wound from his previous slaps.

Lola spat blood on the floor and stared back at him, licking her lip and tasting the iron.

"He's the devil," she said. "And he's coming for you, Dumas."

CHAPTER TWENTY-FIVE

Bush Lane was a typical London side street, narrow, paved with cobblestones and with large buildings on either side. The gaps between the buildings channelled the sounds of London's Metropolitan Police as they searched the surrounding roads.

"Is that it?" asked Harvey. "The silver van?"

"According to the signal," replied Reg. "A word of warning, I've hacked the traffic signals and I'm trying to deflect the police, but it looks like someone else has the same idea."

"You mean Dumas' man?" asked Melody.

"It has to be," said Reg. "The police are closing in. You guys need to move fast."

"Do you think she's inside?" asked Melody.

"Only one way to find out," said Harvey. He made to kick the stand down, but Melody stepped off the bike before him and ran to the side of the building.

"I'll check the van. If the police come around that corner, you take them on a wild goose chase," she called.

Harvey revved the bike once and checked his mirrors while Melody made her way towards the van. She was fifteen metres away when she stopped and glanced back at Harvey, just as the first blue lights rounded the corner.

The driver of the police car slammed the accelerator and the sirens echoed down the lane. Melody stepped back into a doorway as Harvey took off past the van. He rounded a left-hand bend and felt the rear wheel of the bike slip on the uneven surface. But he countered the skid, straightened and took the next right turn into a dead end. The road was blocked with metre-high bollards two metres apart to stop cars using the back street as a shortcut, but the bike skipped through easily.

There was a screech of tyres behind him as the police cars skidded to a stop, but Harvey was already away on Upper Thames Street looking for a way out of the area. Although it was midnight, the street was crammed with cars honking their horns. Cab drivers were standing beside their taxis to see what was going on ahead, but the traffic lights remained red.

"Reg, can you get me a route out of here?" he asked over the comms.

"I'm working on it," Reg replied.

The left-turn traffic light turned green. Harvey made his way along the right side of the road then, at the last minute, he cut in and joined the traffic heading over Southwark Bridge.

A policeman trying to control the volume of waiting traffic at the junction caught Harvey's manoeuvre and immediately hit his radio while running back to his squad car. A few moments later, while Harvey was tearing across the bridge, blue lights lit up his side mirror.

"Okay, Reg, I need two more things," said Harvey, as he slipped between two cars and out of sight of the police.

"What do you need, Harvey?" said Reg. He was clearly enjoying the buzz of the chase.

"I've got police all over me so I'm going to have to ditch this bike and get back to Melody somehow. Find me a basement car park and fix those traffic lights. It's mayhem back there and I don't need to be sitting in traffic."

"Easy," said Reg. "Take the first right after the bridge. A car park is on your right-hand side. I'm on the CCTV there. It looks like there's a nightclub or a bar or something. Lots of people outside. You can lose yourself in there."

"Nice work, Reg."

"Ah, it's good to have you back, Harvey," replied Reg.

Harvey checked his mirrors. There were three police cars twenty cars behind him. He slowed a little, forcing the car behind him to slow and slam his horn. Then Harvey dropped the bike to the right and shot through a tiny gap in the oncoming traffic. Without even looking behind him for the police, he turned again and slipped around the side of a barrier at the entrance to the underground car park.

At the bottom of the ramp, the car park led around to the left with spaces on both sides and a slope to the next lower level. Harvey revved the engine, found second gear, released the clutch then hopped off the back of the bike, letting it roll on and crash into a parked Ford. Without stopping to look, Harvey ran to a set of glass doors. A magnetic lock was fixed to one side, the type that required a programmed key card to release it.

Harvey strode up to the door and slammed his foot through the glass, which shattered but held in place. Three more kicks pushed the shattered window unit out of the frame, and Harvey slipped through.

The commotion disturbed a security guard, who put his head around the corner and, seeing Harvey, reached for his radio. But it was too late. Before he could even hit the button, Harvey had twisted his arm behind his back, pulled his radio from his epaulette and slammed the guard's head into the wall. He dropped the man where he was standing and made towards the stairs, decommissioning the radio as he walked. He tossed the remains into a wastepaper basket beside the guard's desk on the ground floor, pulled off his jacket and slung it over his shoulder, then stepped out to join the crowd of people standing outside the bar at high tables.

Discreetly, Harvey snatched a bottle of beer from a table where a group of four office workers were standing. He stayed between them and another group of girls while the police wrestled with the car park barrier a few metres away. The barrier raised and all three cars raced down the ramp in convoy.

Harvey returned the beer, thanked the bemused man, and walked to the corner where he hailed a passing cab and climbed inside as two more police cars raced to the scene and closed off the little side street.

"Cannon Street," he said to the driver, offering no please or thanks.

The driver gave a questioning look in the mirror as the mayhem began to erupt behind them. But Harvey just leaned back and looked out of the window. He pulled his phone out of his pocket, pretended to dial a number and put it against his ear.

"Reg, are you there?" he asked.

"Copy that, Harvey," replied Reg over the comms.

"Do you see me?" he asked.

"I'm the only one who does," said Reg. "Half of London's police force is on its way there."

"Well, hopefully, that'll buy us some time. How's Melody doing?"

"I'm doing fine," said Melody. "The van hasn't moved. No sign of-"

Her voice was suddenly lost to a stream of static.

"Melody, come back," said Harvey.

No reply.

"Reg, I just lost Melody."

"Me too. I've lost everything," replied Reg.

"Is Lola's phone still alive?"

"It is, but I can't get onto it. There's something blocking the signal."

The taxi pulled out of Southwark Bridge Road and onto Upper Thames Street. The roads were still full, but the traffic was returning to normal.

"Melody, come back," Harvey repeated.

No reply.

"Mate, drop me anywhere here," said Harvey, banging the glass behind the driver, with his other hand on the door handle. He stuffed a twenty-pound note from his pocket through the window. "Keep the change. Open the door."

The door lock clicked open, and Harvey burst from the car. He ran across Upper Thames Street between the slow-moving traffic on the far side of the road and onto the pedestrian footpath.

"Reg, keep trying Melody," he shouted as he ran.

A few moments later, he turned at full speed through the metre-high bollards that he'd taken the bike through a short while before. Then he turned again onto Bush Lane.

In his ear, he heard Reg's attempts at getting through to Melody. But all that came back were waves of static.

"The signal's being blocked, Harvey," said Reg.

Harvey took the bend at full pelt, just in time to see Melody step from the doorway, her finger on her ear as if trying to work her earpiece.

With a final burst of energy, Harvey gave everything he had. He tried to call out, but as he opened his mouth to shout her name, a flash of white light split the dark street. A bone-shattering crack followed a fraction of a second later and a ball of flame erupted from the van, blowing the doors and windows across the cobbled street. Glass and broken bricks rained down from the building beside the ruined vehicle and a mushroom cloud of black smoke rose up from the wall of fire.

The blast stopped Harvey dead in his tracks, knocking him off his feet and hurling him backwards. He landed on his back, rolled and covered his face as shards of glass and debris began to hit the cobbled street.

"Melody?" he called, scrambling back to his feet.

Melody didn't reply.

He hobbled closer, his leg bruised from the fall.

"Melody?"

But Melody didn't reply.

"Reg, are you there?"

At first, Reg too failed to respond.

"Reg? Talk to me. Did you see that? Can you see her? I can't see anything down here."

No reply came from Reg. But Harvey could hear the rasp of his breathing, faint and in shock.

"Reg, I need you, mate. Do you have eyes on Melody?"

While Reg composed himself, Harvey limped towards the ruined van. More sirens filled the night and people had started to emerge at the end of the road, like zombies drawn to the burning light. Even from a distance, Harvey could see that two girls had their phones out, recording what they saw.

Thick smoke emanated from the carcass of the van, and as Harvey got closer, a police car pulled in from Cannon Street. Harvey searched the smoke for Melody. He pulled his t-shirt up to his face, squinting his eyes.

"Melody?" he called. But there was no answer.

To his left, the blast had blown through a set of fire doors. One now hung from broken hinges. The other had been completely torn off and lay on the ground. An ambulance followed the police car, and behind that, more police arrived.

Using the smoke for cover, Harvey ducked into the destroyed fire exit. But as he stepped through, something caught his eye.

Through the haze of the roaring fire and billowing smoke, behind the silver van lying unmoving on the cold cobbled road, was a body. A police car screeched to a stop beside it.

Harvey lingered, slipping further into the building but with his eyes fixed on the body. The world about him began to swirl. He reached out, holding onto the wall for balance. Two men in green uniforms crouched either side of the body as firefighters ran by shouting orders.

A stretcher was laid out and the two EMTs coordinated rolling the lifeless body onto it.

Thick wavy hair lay across a bloodied face. The jacket was torn and more blood soaked through from a deep wound in her side. But despite the wounds. Despite the blood.

It was her.

CHAPTER TWENTY-SIX

The CCTV feed showed a black screen. Antonio searched for another camera further from the blast. The silence was broken by Dumas.

"That, my girl, was phase two."

"You're a monster."

"And he was the devil, so you say," said Dumas. "But as you just saw, he was just a man, as mortal as you and I."

Dumas turned and began to walk along the tunnel with renewed energy.

"Let's go," he called. "Phase three."

Antonio quickly disconnected the cable from the laptop, and Marco shoved Lola forwards a little harder than necessary. She glared at him and the two shared a silent game of dare.

"Now. Move," called Dumas from around the long sweeping bend in the tunnel.

They came to a fork. A smaller tunnel branched off left and the larger service tunnel branched off right. Dumas waited for them all to walk into view then began along the left-hand tunnel.

Lola reached up and let her hair down, feigning fatigue. She massaged her head with her fingers, then rolled and rubbed her neck.

"What is this?" she asked. "Where are you taking me?"

"My dear, Lola, do you understand the City of London at all? The security measures that are in place? It's one of the safest and well-equipped cities in Europe, you know. The world, more likely."

"I know enough," replied Lola, leaving room for Dumas to embellish on what he knew along with a clue as to his plans.

"So, you know about the ring of steel. But there's so much more to it than a few policemen at strategic places on the City boundary. The City of London has been a target for terrorists for many years. Throughout history, many organisations have put their mark on the City, some more successfully than others."

"So you're a terrorist now?" said Lola. "I thought you were just a greedy art thief like my father?"

"No, Lola, I am no terrorist. But I am a smart man, if I do say so myself. If you know a system well enough, you can manipulate it. You can use it to your advantage. That's all we're doing, using the system to our advantage."

"How do you plan on doing that?"

"Keep walking," said Dumas. "We have a way to go yet."

The tunnel was well lit, an endless length of featureless, tiled walls sweeping left and right.

"What do you think is kept in the City of London?" asked Dumas.

Lola shrugged.

"The banks, some art, probably some stuff no-one knows about."

"There's more than banks and art here, Lola," said Dumas. "Tell me what you think happens when something triggers the security in the city."

"The police swoop in. They close off the roads, and those

cameras you were looking at track whoever did whatever it was that triggered the alarms."

"You're right, but that's only about five percent of what happens. There's a chain reaction. First, the security, as you rightly say, track the target. While this happens, the ring of steel shuts the city down. Nobody gets in, and if the scenario is bad enough, nobody gets out."

"You mean if they think the perpetrator is still inside the ring?"

A cool breeze began to lift Lola's hair from her shoulder.

"Exactly. Then a communication plan feeds through the ranks, up the ladder one rung at a time. The level of severity determines which rung it stops at. Can you guess who's at the top rung?"

"The prime minister?"

"That's right, Lola. Do you remember the terrible bombs a decade ago? Buses and trains were the targets."

"Yeah, seven seven."

"After that episode, the underground system was incorporated into the plans."

They turned a final bend where the white tiled walls stopped, and before them, running left to right, was a dark and dirty underground tunnel. Below them were three raised tracks that the trains ran on. To their left, a small three-runged ladder reached down onto a small concrete walkway that ran along the side of the dark and gloomy underground.

Luca handed out torches.

"Not far now," said Dumas, offering a tight, satisfied smile. His voice was louder now in the much larger tunnel than before and seemed to roll on and on into the darkness ahead.

"I still can't see how any of that helps you," said Lola.

"Do you hear any trains?" asked Dumas.

"They stop the trains too?"

Dumas smiled.

"Now you're getting there," he said. "This way."

The smell of dust and damp was strong. In the shadows, Lola caught the faint movements of rats scurrying, enjoying the break in train activity and venturing out to scavenge the trash that commuters so often discarded into the tunnel.

"Right about now," Dumas continued, his voice loud in the tunnel and reverberating off the curved walls in a seemingly endless journey, "thousands of passengers are being evacuated from the underground stations. Protocol dictates that each train stops at the next station and shuts down. Teams of security professionals swoop in, and one by one, they search each and every train. Only once they are all cleared will the service resume."

"You're going to steal a train?" asked Lola.

"In a fashion," said Dumas. "Do you know what is above us right now?"

"The city," said Lola, "and probably thousands of screaming passengers all scared to death."

"And?" said Dumas.

He stopped walking and shone his torchlight on a set of three steps that led up to an old, steel door.

"Above us, Lola, is hope. It is our dreams. And it is everything you could ever wish for. It is my legacy. My birth right."

"Why don't you stop being cryptic and tell me what it is?"

Dumas nodded at Luca, who climbed the few steps and opened the heavy steel door. Two rats ran from the tiny room, squeaking in surprise. They jumped down into the tunnel, ran across Lola's boot and disappeared from view.

"They won't hurt you," said Dumas, seeing Lola's expression.

The door opened into a tiny, lightless room that Lola presumed to be a storage space of some sort. Luca's torch cut beams of light through thick, dusty, stale air. In the left-hand corner was a generator along with a pile of power tools: drills, grinders and saws. The right-hand wall was peppered with drill holes to form a circle eighteen inches in diameter.

"You're breaking into somewhere," said Lola.

"All your dreams, Lola," whispered Dumas from behind her. "Hopes and dreams."

CHAPTER TWENTY-SEVEN

A new feeling came over Harvey as Melody was lifted onto the stretcher. He stumbled backwards over loose bricks on the ground, clutching at the wall, shrouded in disbelief.

"Harvey, are you there?" said Reg, his voice quiet in the haze of Harvey's mind. "Harvey, you need to get out of there."

But Harvey didn't reply. He couldn't reply. He was incapable of anything but watching Melody. Her body rocked from side to side as she was loaded into the ambulance.

"Harvey, I've got a fix on Dumas. Are you with me?"

It was Reg's voice, somewhere far away.

Something stirred inside Harvey as the ambulance doors slammed.

The light that spilt through the demolished doorway fell into shadow as a group of armed police approached. Their verbal commands were loud as they took control of the scene. Harvey slipped further into the shadows. Behind him was a set of wooden double doors, each with a small reinforced glass window at head height. Harvey peered through one.

"Where am I, Reg?" he asked.

"You're in the loading bay of Cannon Street Station," replied

Reg. "To your left are the retail outlets, to your right, the offices. And directly in front of you is the main concourse."

"She's gone, Reg."

Reg paused before replying. It was clear he was fighting his own battle.

"Harvey, we need to focus. Do you want Dumas?"

Harvey didn't reply.

"He's in the station, Harvey. If we're going to get him, now's our chance. Are you with me?"

Harvey didn't reply.

"Harvey? Are you with me? Come on, I need you. Let's do this for Melody."

"For Melody," said Harvey.

He took a deep breath, rolled his neck and checked the small window in the door again. Crowds of confused and scared people were being ushered from the station.

"Harvey, I need you down at platform level in the underground. Can you get there?"

Outside, a heavy boot dislodged a loose brick on the floor. Harvey edged along, further down the corridor to his left out of sight.

"Guide me, Reg," he whispered.

"I've got you, Harvey. Keep going all the way to the end of the corridor and turn right."

Harvey followed Reg's instructions. The corridor was lit by emergency lighting, which cast an eerie green haze across the walls.

"We need to move fast, Harvey. I traced the signal that triggered the blast to a service tunnel one floor below you. There's been no signal since but they can't be far away."

Harvey peered through the doors. "Everyone's being evacuated, Reg. Do you think he'll mingle with the crowd?"

"No," Reg replied with confidence. "He's down there for a

reason. That station will be cordoned off for the next few hours. The trains have all stopped, and the whole city is on lockdown. I'm sorry to say this, Harvey, but you're trapped in the city until further notice."

"No, Reg," said Harvey. "Dumas is trapped with me. Guide me to him."

"Okay, but your signal is getting weak. Any further underground and the GPS will give up."

"Where do I need to go?" asked Harvey.

"When you turn right, head through into the main concourse. The entrance to the underground is at the back of the building. Go down one set of escalators and there'll be a door right in front of you. That's where the signal came from. But after that, I don't know where they went."

"Got it," said Harvey. "See if you can take care of Melody. Find the hospital and get Smokey to call in a favour. Get her body out of there. I do not want her being pulled apart as evidence."

"Copy that, Harvey," said Reg, sounding strong, but his voice cracked, betraying his inner feelings.

The two doors thundered open with Harvey's kick. The noise was lost in the chaos of evacuating passengers but seemed to agitate the beast inside Harvey; it raised its head and cast a focused shroud over Harvey's vision.

The main concourse of the station was a one-way flow of tired and scared passengers, keen to get home, but forced back up onto the streets by police and emergency services. It was hard to blend in when everybody Harvey saw was walking in the opposite direction. A lone policeman was standing at the foot of the escalators directing people up onto the belt of stairs where many kept to one side, but most climbed up as fast as they could, eager to escape the confines of the station. A few people chose to walk up the stairs that ran beside the crammed escalators. Each of them gave Harvey a quizzical look as he strode past.

"Mate, we're being evacuated. You need to get out. There's a bomb," said one man.

But Harvey didn't reply. As he descended lower on the huge two-hundred-foot-long stairway, the doors to the service tunnel came into view exactly as Reg said they would.

The policeman did a double take when he saw Harvey coming down.

"No, mate, the station's closed. You'll need to go back up," he said. With one hand, he reached across Harvey and tried to steer him to join the masses of people boarding the escalator. With his other, he pointed back up the way Harvey had come.

Harvey continued forwards, pushing the officer's arm out of his way.

"Hey," said the policeman, suddenly turning his full attention to Harvey and gripping his leather jacket.

It took less than a second for Harvey to snap the man's arm back, twist his body around and pull the gun from his waistband. Harvey fired into the air three times and exactly as predicted, the slow-moving herd of people turned into a stampede.

Harvey shoved the policeman into the crowd, where he fell beneath trampling feet, and slipped through the double doors in the midst of the chaos.

CHAPTER TWENTY-EIGHT

A circular slab of concrete eighteen inches in diameter was pulled from the wall by thick, heavy eye bolts. Luca dropped it to the ground, rolled it out of the way and stepped back for Dumas to inspect the hole.

Dim light spilt through into the dark space from the room next door. Dante Dumas stepped aside and offered Lola a look with a sweep of his hand.

"And what will I see?" she asked, blinded by Luca's torch-light in her face.

"Freedom," he offered. "Or death. You choose."

Lola crouched, shone her own torch through the round hole and saw row after row of cages. Each cage looked to be ten feet square, with floor to ceiling reinforced mesh along each side and a thick steel gate at the front. The mesh obscured any view of the contents of each cage.

"What is it?" she asked.

"What do you want it to be?" replied Dumas, as if he was ready for the question.

"Okay, so what now?" said Lola. "I mean, I presume you have a plan?"

"Ladies first," said Dumas.

"Oh no," she replied, holding her hands up and standing away from the hole. "I'm not going in there. No chance."

Luca pulled a gun.

"So you chose death after all," said Dumas.

"Why don't you go in there? Or send one of your goons?" asked Lola. She flicked her head at Luca who stared back with cold, hard eyes.

"Oh, I'll be with you," said Dumas. "But it's a bit of a squeeze for these two."

"Why me?"

"Do you think we brought you for a picnic, or for your company? As nice as it is, no. You have a use."

"So it's a job and you need my expertise?"

"It's a vault, Lola. Your speciality," said Dumas, sounding slightly bored with the discussion and anxious to get inside. "So we do it my way, or not at all."

Luca's gun came back up and aimed at her head.

"We do it my way, Lola. Or not at all," repeated Dumas.

Lola took a look through the hole once more.

"Security?" she asked.

Dumas checked his watch, which sparkled in the torchlight.

"We have a forty minute window, so if you don't mind, Lola," said Dumas. "Marco, head back to the tunnel. Stop anyone who tries to get down here. Luca, get the transport."

Lola lay on her back in the hole and pulled herself through, dropping the few feet onto the dusty floor, then stood up and surveyed the cavernous room. The temptation to smash Dumas' head with the heavy Maglite as he came through was strong. But as pleasing as it would be, it would leave few options for escape with Luca on the other side of the wall and presumably guards, locks and cameras blocking the other exits.

For his age, Dumas was sprightly. He pulled himself

through with ease, straightened and walked deeper into the room as if it were all one practised movement.

"Is it art?" asked Lola, as she washed her light across the locks of the cages and peered into one of them. Inside were rows of lockers, each marked with a five-digit number and a large keyhole top centre.

The next cage along was identical, and the next was similar but with larger lockers.

"It's here," called Dumas. He was in the next row of cages waiting patiently beside the lock. Lola joined him, glanced through the cage and saw exactly what she thought she would see.

"That's a Harris safe," she said.

Dumas held the bag out for her.

"Your tools," he said. "You have precisely twenty-five minutes."

"And if I fail?"

He raised his own gun and pointed it at her forehead.

"I believe in you. Failure is not an option, Lola."

"And the gate?" she asked. "Or do I have to open this as well?"

Dumas checked his watch, just as a metallic click announced that the magnetic lock had disengaged.

"Antonio?" she asked.

"He has his uses," replied Dumas. "No more talk. Open the damn safe."

Lola set to work, encouraged by sporadic reminders of the gun at the back of her head. Inside the bag was a calliper measuring tool, some chalk, a battery-powered magnetic drill, a diamond tip twelve-millimetre drill bit, a roll of electrical wire, and a fibre optic camera on a gooseneck, which connected to a tablet.

"It's all there," Dumas assured her. "Twenty-one minutes."

The centre of the lock was one hundred and twenty millimetres from the edge of the safe door, which was itself more than a metre wide by two metres tall. It was a safe designed for large objects and would weigh eight hundred kilos when empty.

Lola marked a vertical line with the chalk one hundred and twenty millimetres in from the door. Then she marked a small horizontal line one hundred and six millimetres above the centre of the locking spindle.

"What's that for?" asked Dumas. "You're not stalling for time, are you?"

"It's a Harris safe. It'll have a barrel inside one hundred millimetres in diameter. Surrounding that is a fifty-millimetre glass shield, which, if broken, will leak acid onto the porous moving parts. The heat of the chemical reaction will weld them together and render them useless. The safe would need to be burned open. We have a twelve-millimetre drill bit, so my hole will be precisely one hundred and six millimetres above the centre of the spindle. Then I'll mark one below for the camera, while I feed the electrical wire inside the top hole. If I can do that without breaking the glass, I can release the mechanism in a few seconds."

"You've worked with this safe before?" asked Dumas, impressed at Lola's knowledge and happy with his own choice of hires.

"Not this model, but it's a Harris. They went out of business a few years ago when Hamilton won the contracts for the major banks. There's still a few of these around, but not many."

"One less after tonight," said Dumas, as Lola centred the magnetic drill and engaged the magnet.

"How long?" Lola asked.

Dumas checked his watch once more.

"Nineteen minutes," he replied, just as Lola hit the power button on the drill and drowned out his voice.

CHAPTER TWENTY-NINE

The doors hadn't yet closed on the stampede behind Harvey when a large fist came from nowhere and caught him in the face. He stumbled backwards, his weight forcing the doors shut, and barely managed to stay on his feet.

A large man in coveralls with tattoos on his neck and his hands was lining up for a follow-up attack. But he'd hit Harvey once. There wouldn't be a second time.

Harvey stood up straight, licked the blood from his lip and smiled as the man came at him with a wild untrained attack, which in Harvey's experience was based on sheer power and fear. He'd seen it too many times before; men had won fights by using the same approach and began believing that they could fight, thinking they were tougher than the rest of society.

It was also typical of these types of men to concentrate on head blows. While it was true that a well-delivered punch to the head could end a fight in seconds, the style of fighting had many flaws. Harvey thought back to his training with his mentor, Julios, and the words of wisdom that had kept Harvey alive for so many years. When you punch a man's head, you have more chances of breaking your own hand than his head. If the punch is not accurate, the man will not go down and you leave yourself open.

In true form, the man in the coveralls took a wild swing at Harvey's head, who simply leaned to one side and let the punch fly by, then delivered a lightning-fast jab to his gut. The man folded in two, shock widening his eyes. Harvey brought his knee up and connected with his opponent's nose. Then he held the sides of the man's head and followed up with his knee four more times, before slamming him down to the floor face first and pulling his arms behind his back.

Within a few moments, Harvey had removed the man's boot lace and hog-tied him with the lace running around the man's wrists and ankles with his legs bent up behind him. It was an efficient means of restraining a strong man that Harvey had used often in the past. The constant pressure from the legs trying to straighten tightened the knots and prevented move-ment in his hands. The man's sock was stuffed inside his mouth to stop him calling out if he came around.

The smooth tiled floor made sliding the man easy. Harvey pulled him around the first bend until he was out of sight of the entrance, in case some nosey policeman decided to peer through the doors.

Harvey rummaged through the man's pockets. A screw-driver, a pair of pliers, a Glock nineteen handgun, and a folding knife. It was useful. Wherever Dumas and the rest of his team were, it would be likely they would have Glocks too.

Harvey selected the pliers and pocketed the weapons as the man began to struggle against the restraints. He crouched down beside his face, which had turned bright red. His eyes flicked between anger and fear. Harvey watched him for a while in silence, until the man's anger had all but dissipated and fear flowed freely, bringing with it tears.

It had always intrigued Harvey how even the biggest and

angriest of men cried. Many of them had cried from Harvey's presence, along with their own helplessness. Others required a few well thought-out questions to set them off, minimal words but carefully placed. Rarely did a man hold out so long that Harvey had to resort to violence. But when he did, the words flowed, free as a stream.

Being reduced to silent tears did not bring a man down in Harvey's estimation. It was natural, and he'd induced the emotions from so many men in the past that it no longer played any part in his judgement. Sobbing, the next phase of a man's breakdown, was irritating and border lined begging, which Harvey could not condone. Many men had begged for their lives between child-like sobs. At that point, Harvey always knew it was over for them. They were broken men.

Harvey opened the pliers.

It was confession time.

"I'm going to ask you a series of questions. You are going to tell me the answers," said Harvey.

The man neither nodded in agreement nor demonstrated any hostility. He just looked up fearfully as Harvey ripped the sock from his mouth.

"What's your name?" asked Harvey.

The man did not reply.

Harvey hit him on the head with the pliers. It wasn't a hard blow, but it was enough to coax the man into talking.

"Who are you?" Harvey asked again.

"Marco," he replied, his face twisted in pain from the blow.

"Good. Marco, the more you talk, the less you suffer. Understood?"

After a few seconds' hesitation, more for a show of spirit than anything else, Marco nodded.

"Where is Dumas?" asked Harvey.

Only the sound of Marco's breathing came in reply. He

dropped his face to the floor, fighting the urge to give up the information.

Without warning, Harvey grabbed a handful of his hair and shoved the nose of the pliers into Marco's mouth. He fixed on an incisor, then paused and watched as the realisation hit Marco. His eyes widened even further.

Harvey cracked the tooth back and forward, holding the struggling Marco still with his knee until the root finally gave in and the tooth came out. Harvey let it fall to the floor beside Marco's face, which was twisted with agony.

"Where's Dumas?" he asked once more.

Marco spat out a mouth full of blood.

"You've got thirty-one teeth left, Marco," said Harvey.

Marco shut his mouth and turned his head away, but Harvey's finger deep inside his eye socket was enough to force his mouth open and let out a scream. Harvey had to kneel on the side of his head to crack out the next tooth. A rear molar from Marco's lower jaw.

He dropped it beside the first. Tiny spatters of blood glowed red on the small white floor tiles.

Without waiting for answers, Harvey began to pull a third.

"Okay," said Marco. His tongue massaged his damaged gums as he spoke. He nodded with his head and gestured that Dumas had headed in that direction. "There. He's up there somewhere."

Harvey forced the pliers into his mouth once more. He latched onto a tooth and paused.

"Tell me where exactly," said Harvey. "Left or right. Show me with your hands."

With the pliers in his mouth and two bleeding gums, Marco could barely pronounce the words but waved his left hand, indicating that Dumas had taken the left tunnel.

Harvey wiped his hands on Marco's coveralls, straightened, and then bent to stuff the sock back into his mouth. He had just bent to wipe the pliers of his prints when movement caught his eye. In an instant, Harvey snatched his weapon from his waistband and stepped into a wide stance, aiming at the shadow in his peripheral vision.

The figure stopped still and raised his hands.

"How long have you been there?" asked Harvey, lowering his gun.

But the man, as small and slight as he was, remained silent. Only an expression of awe was etched on his face.

"What are you doing here?" asked Harvey.

"I tracked her," said Fingers. "I'm here for Lola."

CHAPTER THIRTY

The diamond-tip drill bit took a while to break the steel surface, but once the outer skin had been chewed away, progress increased.

"How much longer?" asked Dumas.

Lola ignored him. One slip of concentration could break the drill bit and there was no spare in the bag. Dumas apparently took the hint. Lola felt him walk away, and from the corner of her eye, she saw him wander outside the cage to check on the main entrance to the vault.

Counting down the minutes in her head, Lola focused on the job at hand. Whilst maintaining consistent pressure on the handle with one hand, and squirting coolant onto the bit with the other, she ran through the motions of unlocking the safe once the holes had been drilled.

The electrical wire was thick. It would easily be sturdy enough to form a small loop in one end then feed it through the trigger. Once in place, another small length of wire would be used to pass through the loop and back out of the hole she had drilled. All that would be required then would be to pull on the two wires hard enough to raise the trigger, but not too hard that the loop would unwind. She would know when enough pressure had been applied as the spindle would spin without the clicks. She'd used the method before a few times but under less arduous circumstances.

Each manufacturer of a safe had a weakness that ran throughout their models. Harris safes were known to be almost unbreakable, save for the method that Lola was using.

A spindly burr of steel suddenly grew in length as the teeth of the drill bit reached the far side. Lola eased off the pressure to ensure the bit didn't shoot through the hole and break the glass vessel.

She powered off the drill and disengaged the magnet. Then, holding the weight of the device with one hand, she manoeuvred the drill into place for the second hole.

"Fourteen minutes," called Dumas from the far side of the room. He'd heard the drill power down.

"That's five minutes for one hole," she replied. "Leaves me nine minutes to crack the lock once I've drilled the second hole."

"No, that leaves you four minutes to crack the lock," said Dumas. He stepped into view on the other side of the cage's mesh siding. Just his form was outlined in the low light. "We'll need five minutes to unload it."

"What's inside?" asked Lola, as she locked the magnet into place and collected the coolant in her spare hand.

"Dreams, Lola. I keep telling you."

Lola hit the power button again, bored with Dumas' vague responses. Drilling was fairly easy. Lola had learned when she was very young how to handle a drill. She had been taught by one of her father's friends, back in the days when Lola had been small enough to fit where most adults couldn't. The initial ten to twenty seconds were spent just warming up the steel and removing the outer skin to reveal the shiny, silver-coloured material below. Once the hole was outlined, and tiny strands of silvery steel curled from the drill, it was safe to increase the pressure a little. Keeping the bit cool was the trick. A broken drill bit cost time and added risk.

Dumas' shadow fell over her. He was back inside the cage.

"I need light," she said, without turning.

"You'll manage," he replied, without moving.

The battery in the drill began to wane as Lola reached two thirds of the thickness. The sound of the dying motor was lower in pitch. Lola remained quiet but glanced up at Dumas to see if he had noticed. He had. He smiled back at her and nodded slightly as if to convey his confidence in her ability to get the job done.

A long, curly burr of steel began to form at the base of the drill bit. The motor slowed some more. It was down to half speed. Lola eased off the pressure, removing all resistance from the drill. In a series of short bursts, she applied pressure for one second, then removed it. Another second, then removed it. The speed slowed to almost nothing with the familiar sound that accompanied a dying electric motor.

It stopped.

"Are you through?" asked Dumas.

Lola closed her eyes and let out a long breath.

"No," she replied. "Close, but no."

She didn't have to turn to know that Dumas had raised his gun and had it aimed at the back of her head. Thinking fast, she removed the battery pack from the drill, then wrapped it in her t-shirt. She rubbed as hard as she could for a few seconds to generate heat. The socket where the battery connected to the drill was dusty, so Lola blew on it and wiped the inside. Then she pulled the trigger without the battery to discharge the surplus energy.

She reconnected the battery, closed her eyes once more, and hit the power button. A surge of power turned the drill bit as

Lola applied the pressure. Then she released it and shone her torch onto the hole.

"One more burst," she said to herself, willing the drill to turn. She hit the power button again and leaned into the handle.

The torque of the drill with her weight tore through the remains of the steel sheet. Lola felt the give of the material in time to release the pressure and bring the drill back out. She switched the magnet off, dropped to the floor, and peered through the holes.

Dumas glanced at his watch, then peered past his wrist at Lola.

"You just bought yourself nine minutes of life."

CHAPTER THIRTY-ONE

"Where is she?" asked Fingers.

Harvey nodded behind him, further into the tunnel.

"It's Dumas?" asked Fingers.

Harvey didn't reply.

"So the robbery was a setup?" continued Fingers. "He wanted Lola all along?"

"Why would he want Lola?"

Fingers shrugged. "Maybe he needs her skills."

"Her skills?" asked Harvey.

"She's a thief, Harvey. The best there is."

"Why would Dumas need her? He's a thief too, right?"

"Maybe there's something he can't do," said Fingers. "She's excellent at diamonds and art, but she's really known for her ability to crack safes."

"Safes? Down here?" asked Harvey. "How did you find me anyway?"

"When Dumas took Lola, they hit me over the head. I've been stumbling around London looking for her." He held up his laptop satchel. "I managed to find an internet cafe and track her to the van."

Harvey didn't reply.

"I'm sorry, Harvey. I saw the explosion," said Fingers. "I saw them take your friend away. Melody."

The mention of Melody's name stabbed at Harvey's chest.

"I followed you into the building," continued Fingers. "I got caught up in the chaos outside, or I would have been here sooner."

But Harvey was deep in thought.

"Harvey?"

A familiar feeling began to push the grief to one side. It was a feeling Harvey had restrained for too long. A restless tingling began to creep into his fingers. His arms twitched as electricity seemed to course through his body.

Like a cage door had been opened inside him, exposing his innermost feelings while releasing the beast that had stayed dormant for a long time, curious rage took a step into the wild once more.

The sensation of the beast within him roaming free triggered snapshots of his past. His first kill, deep inside Epping Forest. Back then, his rage was untamed, untrained and ferocious, enticed by the emotions of his dead sister, fuelled by the fear of his captive, and satiated by blood.

But the rage that now prowled Harvey's mind closed doors to reason. It quietened consequence with a slash of its sharp claws, and like a dog might guard its owner, the beast sought retribution for the pain in Harvey's heart.

"Harvey?" said Fingers. "Are you okay?"

But Harvey was enjoying the feeling of the beast now surging through his veins. Too long had he maintained control. A rhythmic pulse behind Harvey's dilated eyes kept time to the beating heart of the monster.

"Stop right there," came a voice, loud, clear and authoritative. It reverberated off the walls, obscuring any sense of distance.

But Harvey was trance-like. With his palms open outward, his head tilted back and his eyes closed in a state of semi-meditation, anger and rage boiled inside him.

A hum of activity somewhere far off to Harvey's right. Fingers' voice. Panic.

The beast relinquished control of Harvey enough for him to assess the situation.

Fingers was on the floor, his hands cuffed behind his back just a few feet from Marco.

The police officer approached Harvey with a can of CS gas.

"Get down on the floor, or I'll be forced to-"

It took a fraction of a second for Harvey to break the man's arm, then another two seconds to slam him into the hard tiled wall. He let the officer fall to the floor beside Marco who lay with his face in a pool of congealing blood.

Harvey turned away and faced the empty tunnel in front of him, the beast by his side, angry and hungry for blood.

CHAPTER THIRTY-TWO

"I can't do this with a gun to my head, Dante," said Lola.

She had the first of the two lengths of wire threaded through the trigger mechanism. The tiny fibre optic camera had the loop in view and provided enough light.

The gun's hard barrel was removed from her head.

"No tricks, Lola," said Dumas.

She ignored the comment and continued to thread the second length of wire. The tiny LCD screen provided a magnified visual of what she was doing inside the safe door. The tiniest movement on the outside of the safe caused the end of the wire to shoot off the screen out of view.

She hooked the loop and slowly began to pull the excess wire back through the hole. The delicate work was complete. So she removed the camera and tossed it to one side. With two wires poking from a single hole in the safe door, she slowly increased the tension while feeling the spindle of the safe. When it spun without clicking, the lock would be free.

And there it was.

It didn't matter how many safes Lola had cracked before, the feeling was always the same. A sense of disbelief. Logic told her that the job was done, and all she had to do was turn the handle and the door would be unlocked. But a sense of dread loomed each time.

She reached for the handle.

"How long do I have?"

"Less than a minute," said Dumas.

She applied pressure to the handle, feeling the initial resistance of the locking mechanism search for the lock, but with the trigger free, the two plates that clamped down on the barrel spun with the handle.

The door opened.

Lola crouched down onto her heels and sucked in a lungful of air. The huge steel door swung past her face as Dumas opened it fully. The dim light of the room seemed to darken even deeper and the contents of the safe glowed a yellowish hue that framed Dumas in an almost godlike form.

"Gold?" she asked.

But Dumas was frozen in what seemed like a state of sheer adoration.

"This is my father's gold. It's beautiful, isn't it?" he said after a while.

Inside the safe, sitting in three rows of eight and piled four high, were ninety-six gold bars. Each one of them seemed to sing at Lola.

"Are we going to stand here looking at it?" asked Lola.

"Four minutes," said Dante, snapping to life. "One at a time, walk them to the hole." He reached down for the first one.

Lola watched him leave, carrying the bar in both hands, then stood up and gazed into the safe. Each bar bore a symbol of two crossed swords. She ran a finger over one, cursed at her situation, then picked it up.

She passed Dumas on her way to the hole and felt Luca's rough hands snatch the bar away from her. She bent to see where he was putting them, and to her surprise, beside the set of three steps was a train. Its doors were open and the carriage was empty.

As Lola and Dumas passed the bars through the hole, Luca and Antonio ferried them to the train, until Dumas emerged from the cage with the last bar, grinning from ear to ear.

But his delight was short lived. From behind him came a voice, loud and clear.

"Stop right there."

For a fraction of a second, Lola delighted in the look of failure that spread across Dumas' face. He turned to face the guard, who was standing poised with his radio.

"Put the bar down," the guard said. His taser was aimed at Dumas' chest.

Dumas took a step backwards in front of Lola.

"This is your last warning," said the guard. He glanced into the cage and saw the empty safe. "Where's the rest of the gold?"

Dumas remained silent. The atmosphere was electric. Lola was overcome with the urge to hit Dumas over the head with something. Maybe the judges would go lightly on her. Maybe her father could help.

But sticking out from Dumas' waistband was his Glock.

She weighed up the odds of getting away with the heist. Given her record, she'd likely be an old lady by the time she'd be released from prison.

"Down," the guard shouted, and he re-aimed the taser.

Lola snatched the weapon from Dumas' belt and moved into an open space.

The guard froze.

"Drop it," said Lola.

"Good girl," said Dumas.

Slowly, the guard lowered the taser. His confidence was replaced by fear and the unknown.

"Drop the taser, sir," said Lola. "I don't want to have to do this."

The taser clattered to the floor.

"Kick it to me."

The guard did as he was told.

"Now get on your knees," said Lola, "and put your hands behind your head."

"I like your style, Lola," said Dumas.

But Lola switched her aim and pointed the gun at him instead. "It's gone far enough, Dante."

"Lola, think about what you're doing."

"I can end all this right now," said Lola. "You lose."

"And what about you?" asked Dumas. "So you shoot me and then what? You can't walk out that door. The only way out for you is the hole. Marco and Luca might have something to say about that. I know Luca wouldn't mind seeing you suffer. He's been in prison for some time. I dread to think of the things he'd do to you."

Lola felt the gun waiver in her hand. The weight of the weapon, along with the shot of adrenaline that was releasing into her body, did little to help keep the gun held high.

Dumas took one step forward.

"I can make you rich, Lola, or I can make you dead."

Lola felt her face drop. Her hands locked. She was too frightened to move. The trigger was right there beneath her finger, but the command to move it was lost somewhere in the flow of adrenaline. A tiny bead of sweat ran down her forehead. It caught Dumas' eye.

He took another step.

"You did a good job, Lola, but it doesn't end here," said Dumas. "Now give me the weapon."

As he reached up and placed his hand around the barrel of the gun, Lola's brain issued the command to pull the trigger. But her body resisted. It was as if her survival instinct had taken over and understood that the only way out was through the hole, and the only chance of surviving that was with Dumas alive.

He tugged the weapon from her hands; they relinquished the gun easier than she thought. She let her arms drop to her sides. Dumas passed her the last gold bar.

"This one's for you."

At twelve kilos, the bar was heavier than the gun but felt weightless in the complex blend of emotions that fixed Lola in her stupor.

"Good girl," said Dumas once more.

Then he aimed the weapon at the guard, whose face contorted in a momentary expression of horror as Dumas pulled the trigger and ended the man's life.

CHAPTER THIRTY-THREE

Disabling the policeman barely touched the hunger of Harvey's beast. Instead, it aggravated his rage like an unreachable itch somewhere deep inside. Harvey's eyes streamed with adrenaline. His clammy hands hung by his side and the white, tiled walls of the tunnel slid past in an endless haze of memories, regret and pain.

He approached a fork in the tunnel. The left turn was smaller than the right but brighter and cleaner, perhaps because it was used more often. Harvey turned left, but as he did, his senses pricked. The hair on his nape was standing like men at arms and the beast inside him prepared itself.

With an almost imperceptible movement, Harvey slipped the gun from his jacket. He waited until he'd rounded enough of the bend to be out of sight for a second. One second was all he needed to turn and aim.

Footsteps approached, but not the steady drum-like rhythm of heavy boots, nor was the pace fast enough for it to be someone giving chase. Fingers walked into view then froze at having the gun pointed at him for the second time.

Neither man spoke, but Harvey lowered the gun and eyed

him with caution. Fingers seemed to return the stare with his own weak blend of wonder and fear.

"How did you get free?" asked Harvey.

"The police officer," said Fingers. "I took his keys."

"And Marco?"

"Unconscious."

Harvey glanced back up the tunnel and listened for footsteps.

"I know you want to help her, but I can't protect you," said Harvey.

"I just want to get Lola somewhere safe," replied Fingers. His hands fumbled at nothing as if they should be doing something useful.

"Stay behind me. Stay quiet," said Harvey.

Fingers nodded.

Further underground, the air grew colder and the breeze brought with it the scent of dust and damp. There was no light at the end of the tunnel. No shining beacon of safety. And no Lola. Instead, in the distance, twenty metres from the final bend in the tunnel, a dark foreboding circle marked the end of the line.

"It's an underground tunnel," said Fingers. "Do you think the trains are running?"

Harvey didn't reply.

Two rats scurried along beneath the elevated rails a few feet below where Harvey was standing. To the right, the tunnel veered off around another bend. Only the whistling wind and its breath on Harvey's face indicated that the exit was further that way.

To his left, Harvey was surprised to see a train parked two hundred metres along the dark tunnel. A tiny concrete ledge ran along the side, presumably for workers to use to avoid the rails when they maintained the tracks.

A dull thud boomed from the train.

Harvey closed his eyes. There was a faint grumble of a man's voice.

He took a step closer. The voices came in waves as if the men were walking or moving.

Then a gunshot rang out. It was distant but definitely a gunshot.

Harvey's chest rose and fell as the beast inside him grew impatient. He let his eyes adjust to the poor light, rolled his neck from side to side, and took a step down onto the ledge.

Then, like a train hitting him from behind, the weight of a man slammed into Harvey. Thick arms wrapped around him and the momentum of the tackle sent both men over the ledge. Harvey landed with his stomach bent over a heavy rail. His gun clattered to the dark ground.

His attacker issued a growl from his place between the rails. The large shape of the man was swathed in the black of the tunnel. Only the sheer size of the man and the glistening of blood on his face betrayed his identity.

Without warning, Marco came at Harvey again, but his moves were slow. Harvey dodged the first blow and they squared off with the live rail between them, Harvey with his back to the service tunnel, Marco between the tracks. His blood-stained face, scarcely lit by the tunnel behind Harvey, accentuated the flaws in his skin. He grinned, bearing his missing teeth and spat blood to the ground, urging Harvey to come closer with two quick flicks of his hands.

"So you're the devil?" said Marco.

Harvey didn't reply.

Movement to his side, as Fingers began to walk along the ledge, caught his eye. But Harvey remained fixed on Marco. The beast needed feeding.

Marco stretched his leg out to the gun on the floor, but

Harvey saw the move and stamped down on his foot. With the rail between them, the blows commenced.

A well-practised series of punches from Marco sent Harvey ducking, weaving and dodging, but the last, a right hook, caught his eye and knocked him off balance enough to step off Marco's foot. The bigger man was too slow to reach down for the gun before Harvey had recovered and returned with his own series of blows.

Fingers called out from further along the dark tunnel as Harvey rained blows to Marco's kidneys, ribs and stomach. As Marco turned to block Harvey's lightning-fast jabs to his left side, his right side opened up, allowing Harvey to deliver a powerful hook that broke at least one rib.

Inside Harvey, the restless beast began to settle into the fight. Each blow delivered was an appetiser for the main course. Each blow received was absorbed with guilty pleasure; it was punishment for his failure.

With both hands holding his ribcage, and his face contorted with pain, Marco straightened.

"Hit me," said Harvey.

But Marco made a poor attempt for the gun. With a smooth step across his side of the rail, Harvey kicked it deep into the darkness.

"Hit me," he shouted.

So Marco did. A straight jab to Harvey's face that bloodied his nose. But Marco retracted and adopted a defensive stance.

"More," screamed Harvey.

A hook slammed into his face. Harvey returned with a hook of his own.

"Again."

Once more, the blow caught him square and hard, and once more, he returned with a blow of his own. The rally of punches continued. Harvey roared with each delivery. Marco roared in defence. With each punch he received, Harvey's beast grew in strength, dispatching blows of his own, each harder than the punch before until both men wore a blood-red mask, their features obscured and swollen.

But from nowhere, maybe sensing Harvey's growing thirst for pain and strengthening retaliations, Marco broke the rally. He thrust out at Harvey and grabbed his throat with one hand, blocking Harvey's punches with the other. He dragged Harvey across the rail and slammed his forehead into Harvey's face. A wild, carnal roar emerged from Harvey's gut.

"More," he shouted and spat stringy blood at Marco.

Another head butt. Then, as the lights to Harvey's left grew brighter and the whining of the train's motors hummed loudly in the tunnel, the rails shuddered as if woken from their slumber.

Marco pinned Harvey to the single rail. The vibrations as one thousand tons of steel rolled towards them kicked at Harvey's back.

"You want to die?" Harvey screamed.

But Marco just grimaced from the effort it took to hold Harvey in place.

"Yeah?" continued Harvey. "Do you want it as much as me? Let's do it together."

Spittle flew from Marco's lip as the pressure on Harvey's neck increased. Harvey reached up and returned the move, pushing Marco away. The two men held each other's necks, but Harvey was pinned to the rail.

Harvey's eyes flicked to the train and back. Thirty metres and closing fast.

"You want to do this?" he shouted.

But before Marco could react, Harvey reversed the pressure. He pulled Marco towards him, knocking the bigger man off balance and turning him around so that Harvey was now pinning down Marco.

Twenty metres.

Harvey slammed his forehead into Marco's face.

Once.

Twice.

Three times.

Then, as the shadow of the underground train loomed above them, Harvey dropped to the floor.

The train rolled slowly overhead, sending a whirlwind of dust and grit into the air all around him. Loud deafening booms of straining steel rails and wheels filled the tiny space. A shower of yellow sparks rained down on Harvey as electrical contacts brushed their steel counterparts.

The two halves of Marco's body slumped at Harvey's feet.

CHAPTER THIRTY-FOUR

Two big strong hands pulled Lola through the hole and slammed her up against the dirty wall. Luca's big head, silhouetted against the interior lights of the train behind him, leaned into Lola. The big man sniffed along her neck, savouring her scent, then issued a satisfied moan of delight as if he'd tasted a fine wine or a morsel of exquisite flavour in an excellent restaurant.

Behind him, Dumas scrambled through the hole. His coveralls stretched out onto the loose grit and dust, which showered to the floor when he stood up.

"No time for that, Luca," he said. "We've got a train to catch. Get ready to go."

Dumas stepped down behind them and onto the train, readying himself for the next part of his plan.

Luca lingered for a moment and although his face was shrouded in shadow, it wasn't hard for Lola to imagine his lustful leer.

"Get away from her," came a voice, familiar but weak. "Get away from her or I'll shoot you right now."

Luca took a single step back and turned sideways to reveal a man, slight, small, and holding a gun in two shaky hands.

"Fingers," said Lola. "No, run."

"And what are you going to do with that?" said Luca.

"He'll do nothing," said Dumas, stepping off the train with a gun to Fingers' head. "Nice try. Brave but stupid. Get on the damn train." Dumas waved his gun at the waiting train. "Both of you."

Fingers' face dropped from a tight but fearful expression of bravado to sudden panic and helplessness as it dawned on him the mistake he'd made.

Lola met his stare, but could only offer a sympathetic smile.

Both their lives were at risk, and Fingers had been her only chance of rescue.

"Let's go," called Dumas.

The tiny clicks of electrical switches sparked more lights into life as relays engaged, and capacitors hummed as energy built inside their wound copper bodies.

Lola stepped past Dumas and into the carriage. To her right, the door to the next carriage was open. At the far end was the driver's cab with Luca at the controls. To her left was a closed door and beyond that, the dark tunnel. Two large military cases on heavy casters were sitting by the doors.

"Into the first carriage," said Dumas. He followed them through, closing the door behind him.

"I'm connected," announced Antonio. When he saw Dumas enter, his voice changed, adopting a hint of apprehension. "I've cleared us a route out of the city, but we need to move fast. I don't know how long I can control the switches."

"Luca, go get Marco then get us out of here," said Dumas. "You two, sit." He gestured for Lola and Fingers to take two seats opposite each other.

The doors hissed closed and Lola's head rocked to one side

as the initial burst of energy from the capacitors set the train in motion.

"Dante," called Luca from in front. "We have a problem."

"What is it?" called Dumas, then gestured for Lola to move ahead of him to the driver's cab. "Move."

"Dante?" said Luca again.

By the time Lola reached the door of the cab, Luca had slowed the train to a walk.

"What are you waiting for?" said Dumas, as he fought his way past Lola into the cab.

"It's Marco," said Luca. "He's on the tracks. But who's that he's fighting?"

A cruel smile spread cross Dumas' face.

"That's the devil," he said. "What are you waiting for? Run him down."

"But Marco-"

In an instant, Dumas had the gun raised and held it against Luca's temple.

"I said, run him down. He will move. He's not as stupid as he looks."

For a fraction of a second, a sense of hope quenched the butterflies that ran riot inside Lola's stomach. The two men stared each other down in a silent battle of power.

Luca eased the train forwards. He cracked the window as far as it would open and called out for his brother to move and get on the train. But they were too far away and the deep grumble of the train as it rolled over the steel rails was too loud in the confines of the tunnel.

"I said forwards," said Dumas.

He slammed Luca's throttle hand forwards. Immediately, the train picked up speed, forcing Lola to reach for a handle that hung from the ceiling. She could see the battle ahead. Luca tried to pull the handle back and slow the train. But Marco and

Harvey grew closer in the front windscreen. In the midst of their fight, Harvey had switched positions and had Marco pinned to the rail.

"No," cried Luca.

Time appeared to slow to a stop and the two men disappeared from view.

The bump of the wheels on the men's bodies was barely discernible as seventy tons of steel, glass and wood tore over them and ripped them to pieces.

Lola stood up, stunned.

Dumas released his grip on Luca's hand and rearmed his gun.

"You just doubled your pay. Now drive," he commanded, and stepped back into the carriage, pushing Lola with him. "Sit."

Lola sat down. She folded her arms across her stomach as her insides sought to spew anything and everything lose from her bowels and mouth.

A tear ran down Fingers' face opposite her.

Lola shook her head.

But Fingers lost control. He sniffed and sucked in a lungful of air and began to pant.

Dumas looked down at him.

"Don't worry. In fifteen minutes, it'll all be over," he said.

The statement did little to reassure Fingers, but his reaction served to amuse Dumas.

"Leave him alone," said Lola, having to raise her voice above the thundering train. "Can't you see he's scared?"

But Dumas ignored her, choosing instead to peer through the windscreen in the driver's cab.

Lola followed his eyes. Flashes of empty stations rushed past. There was a burst of activity from one station as the authorities examined an empty carriage for more explosives. They reacted to Dumas' stolen train.

"I'm getting blocked out," called Antonio. "I think they're onto us."

"Can they shut the train down?" asked Dumas.

"No, I still have control of the power."

"Good. Keep control. It's not like they can put up a road-block now, is it?" Dumas laughed.

He turned back to Lola, cast his eyes on the carriage behind with the gold, and then glanced at his watch.

However much Lola loathed Dumas, she couldn't help but admire his ability to retain his composure. The train hurtled past the authorities, police, the army and likely the special forces with more than half a ton of stolen gold on board, and at least four dead bodies in its wake. Dumas seemed to absorb it all as if he was untouchable.

But behind Dumas, through the windscreen at the front of the train, a bloodied hand rose up from below and slammed onto the glass.

CHAPTER THIRTY-FIVE

Fighting for purchase on the front of the train, Harvey held fast to the shunting ram with one hand and reached up with the other. He took hold of a small ridge in the train's steel body then stretched his leg out to the other ram.

With no weight to pull, the single carriage picked up speed quickly. The motion pinned Harvey to the train, and the tunnel sides flashed past in snapshot images of morphed pipes, cables and track. Then a bright station lit Harvey's world, revealing the next handhold.

The train accelerated. The wind that held him to the train was cold, stinging and full of grit, which stung his face and eyes, and the steel he clung to was hard and sharp.

With his left hand, he reached for the handhold, and with the other, he reached up and slammed his hand onto the glass.

No change in speed indicated that he'd been heard.

He pulled himself up.

Arranging his feet across both the shunting rams, Harvey straightened to full height and peered through the windscreen at the wide-eyed driver, who was dressed in coveralls, the same as Marco.

They passed another train. With just inches between the carriages, the force of the two huge, steel structures passing each other sucked Harvey to one side. But his feet were planted and his hands were strong.

The driver pushed forwards on the controls, accelerating the train even faster. Then, with a fresh blast of cold and a rush of wind that tried to suck Harvey from his position, the train broke free of the tunnel and into the night.

Exposed to the elements, he clung harder to his holds. Searching for a way into the train from the front, Harvey felt around for his next move and began to climb. But as he pulled himself up to the roof, shots tore through the reinforced glass. The last bullet of three ripped a chunk of rubber from his boot as he pulled himself out of view.

The train top was smooth with barely a crevice or crack to cling to, only a narrow channel on either side for the rain to drain off. A film of dirt and grime clung to the dried blood on his skin and the rushing wind pulled at every loose part of his clothing. Keeping as much of his body flat against the steel roof as possible, Harvey made his way along it inch by inch.

Several wild gunshots penetrated the roof, forcing Harvey to one side. He lost his grip on the right-hand gutter and slid down to the left, his fingers only just catching the narrow channel. It took all of his core strength to keep his legs from swinging down to the window and into view.

But from one side, five metres in front of him, he saw the passenger doors being forced open. The driver leaned out and peered up, looking for Harvey.

Harvey swung back onto the roof, opening his legs as far as he could, and watched helplessly as the man's arm swung onto the roof and fumbled for the rain gutter. With help from below, he pulled himself up to lay flat opposite Harvey.

At first, the man didn't move. Fear gripped him and his knuckles turned white with terror as he clung on for his life.

He began to slide closer to Harvey.

Sensing the oncoming danger, Harvey raised himself up to one foot, testing the train as a surfer might feel the movement of the board. Braving the wind that threatened to shear him from the roof, the man let go with one hand and reached behind him for his gun.

Harvey rose up onto both feet, bracing against the wind with his legs wide apart. He took a step forwards, coaxed further by the force of the moving train.

The man pulled his weapon and pushed up onto one knee. Holding fast with one hand, he raised the gun at Harvey.

Another step pushed Harvey forwards to within reach of the man, and as both men fought to balance, he reached out and grabbed the man's gun hand. With his foot, Harvey stamped down on the man's hand clinging to the train, sending them both reeling backwards along the train top. The gun fell between them. Both men eyed it, but only the bigger man made a move for it, which Harvey was counting on. The move opened up the man's defences.

Harvey began to get a feel for the moving train. He pinned the man's arm to the roof and, with his knee in the small of the man's back, Harvey delivered three blows to the back of his head. Each one slammed his face into the hard surface below.

But the man was wily and strong. He let go of the gun, spun beneath Harvey then rolled on top of him, pinning Harvey's shoulders down with his knees.

The gun slid along beside them, but neither man attempted to go for it.

With both fists, the man dealt a series of blows to Harvey's face, who was unable to move and unable to defend himself. Countless punches rocked Harvey's head until there was no longer any pain, just violent blows that snapped his head from side to side.

The loud horn of another train passing in the opposite direction shook them both and seemed to disrupt the flow of the man's punches. He threw one last hook, which Harvey absorbed. He sucked in the power of the blow and with every piece of the animal fight inside him, Harvey fought to pull his arms free.

But the man on top of him was bigger and heavier. With a desperate kick of his right leg, Harvey hooked the man's neck and forced him backwards off his shoulders, then slid out from beneath him and rolled on top. As if a practised choreography, the man rolled with Harvey, reversing his move. He then stood up and backed away.

The reprise gave Harvey time to find his feet. Once more, the gun was between them. Once more, neither man made any attempt to reach it; both were content with the physical fight.

The train continued to roll over the rails. The surroundings had long since turned from the brick buildings of the city to the rows of apartments and old houses in the East End of London. The scene was slowly beginning to show more signs of green as the train cut through East London and into Essex.

It was as they passed through the town of Dagenham that, over the man's shoulder, Harvey saw a bridge approaching; one mile away, maybe more.

With a roll of his neck, Harvey felt the satisfying clicks. He turned side on to Luca and adopted a judo stance he'd learned from his mentor, way back when the beast was born.

Luca moved with little grace into a street fighter's stance. It was the posture of a man who had learned how to fight by watching films, getting drunk in bars, and fighting men smaller than himself.

Luca dropped his arms and ran at Harvey.

Harvey held his ground, unmoving while facing the oncoming two-hundred-and-fifty-pound man until the very last moment, when Harvey dropped backwards, reached out, grabbed Luca's coveralls and raised his foot into the big man's stomach. The move was timed perfectly.

The bridge ripped Luca from Harvey's hands and left a fine mist of red spray in the air.

As the train rolled on under the night sky, Harvey lay back on the roof, allowing his heart to settle and his breath to return.

And the beast to savour its kill.

He searched for a way off the roof, deciding that the rear of the carriage would be safer to enter. But it was as he did so that a jolt rocked his balance, sending him to his knees. The train felt as if it was accelerating. Then Harvey realised that the rear carriage had broken free.

CHAPTER THIRTY-SIX

"You, inside. Drive the train," said Dumas. He pointed with his gun to the empty driver's cab.

"I can't drive the train," said Fingers. "I don't know how."

"Antonio, make sure she doesn't move," said Dumas. Then he pulled Fingers up by his hair and pushed him along the carriage into the cab. Dumas fumbled in Antonio's bag and pulled out a roll of duct tape, then disappeared into the cab.

"Why do you let him push you around like that?" asked Lola, keeping her voice low.

"I am a rich man," replied Antonio. He gestured at the second carriage with the two cases of gold.

A loud thud came from the roof, followed by a series of lighter thuds as the two men up top fought it out.

"Do you honestly think he's going to pay you? Do you honestly think that he has any loyalty to anyone but himself?" asked Lola. "Look at Marco. You saw what happened to him. And now Luca." She flicked her eyes up, but Antonio's remained fixed on hers. He was smart enough not to fall for the distraction.

He leaned in close to Lola, keeping the gun away from her reach.

"What makes you think I won't just take the gold myself?" said Antonio, his voice suddenly mature and confident.

He winked at her then moved away as Dumas emerged from the cab.

"Antonio, rig the last of the explosives to the accelerator," he said, without removing his eyes from Lola. Then he stepped closer to her. More loud thuds from above caused him to flick his eyes up. It was as if he was picturing the fight that was taking place on his behalf.

"You can't get away with this, Dante. They'll find you eventually. And if the police don't, my father will."

"Au contraire, my dear Lola. You see, we are coming to the end of the line. Soon we will go our separate ways. I will seek a place in Spain so beautiful that even the most exquisite art, such as the Defeat of the Floating Batteries at Gibraltar, would not compare. And you? Well, there was a moment while you were cracking the safe that I thought you could be useful. I could get used to having a pretty woman like you around."

"Don't push your luck, Dumas."

"But alas, you have shown your true colours." He paused for a moment to let Lola digest his hideous, smug words. "They will find you and your friend in pieces, spread out as far as the eye can see." He spread his arms wide to accentuate the statement.

"And how do you plan on getting the gold to Spain? There'll be a manhunt out for that."

"Dear, when you have that amount of gold, you will be surprised, I think, at the levels to which people will go to please you. Blind eyes will be turned, palms will be crossed, and the sun will shine down on those bars as it did so many years ago. Its golden rays will kiss those golden bars, and the world will light up in glory."

588 J. D. WESTON

Lola remained silent. No words could remove the madman from his dream. She'd seen that enough times with her own father.

"It is a day I have been waiting for all of my life, Lola. And I'd like to thank you for your help."

"You can thank me by letting us go."

"Sadly, no," he replied.

"The accelerator is rigged, Dante," said Antonio, as he stepped out of the cab. "We are getting close to the pickup."

"Good work, Antonio," replied Dumas. "Prepare to split the carriages."

He turned back to Lola, offering a weak expression of sorrow that conveyed more of his smug arrogance.

"Well, this is goodbye, Lola," he said. "I'll be sure to drop your father a line and tell him how brave you were." He finished by blowing her a kiss and moved towards the rear of the train. He opened the doors between the carriages, stepped across the small gap and winked at Lola once more.

"Antonio, let's move," he called.

Gathering his things, Antonio scrambled past Lola, hurrying to reach the second carriage before it was too late.

"You don't have to do this, Antonio," said Lola. "You're better than that."

Antonio stopped running and turned, but continued to walk backwards.

"You're a poor judge of character if you believe that, Lola."

He held her gaze for a moment, then turned and ran to the rear doors.

A jolt ran through the train as the carriages split just as they passed beneath a bridge. The few moments of the black outside made her feel as if she'd entered a new world. Above her, the roof rumbled as if something heavy was dragged at speed along the length of the train. A dark, twisted and ruined human form fell from the back of the carriage to the tracks below.

It was a world where the ticking clock of life ticked faster than ever before. And for a just a short time.

The second carriage was already far behind, slowed by friction, alone in a place where either side of the train tracks, open green, large lakes and clumps of trees spread far and wide as if they held the houses and office blocks at bay. It was a final stand for the environment in its war against urban sprawl.

"How are you doing in there, Fingers?" she called out.

A few seconds of silence passed before his timid voice returned, cracked and afraid.

"I need help," he replied. "I can't let go of the accelerator. I'm taped to it and they rigged it to blow if I move it. I'm bloody stuck, Lola. Help me."

"I'm cuffed to the seat, Fingers. I think we need to accept it."

"Do you know where we are?" asked Fingers.

"This is the District Line. There's about five more stations to pass through until we reach Upminster."

"What's at Upminster?"

"It's the end of the line, Fingers," called Lola. "It's the end of everything," she whispered to herself.

"No," screamed Fingers. "Not like this. This wasn't how it was meant to be."

Lola squeezed her eyes closed, restraining the tears that had begun to pool behind them.

"You've been a good friend, Fingers," she said, trying to convey strength in her voice. "The best I could have asked for."

The train hurtled through the town of Hornchurch. The houses that backed onto the tracks blurred with tears and fog as memories swirled inside Lola's mind. With just minutes to live, she sought the memories she cherished most, for one last glance at them, to enjoy them one more time. But each time the

590   J. D. WESTON

memory of her mother and father swinging Lola by her arms as they walked through a long forgotten forest, or the memory of her mother's beaming face, bathed in sunlight as she handed Lola an ice-cream came to the front of her mind, the image of Harvey Stone torturing Cordero and her father's cold expression pushed them out the way.

It wasn't the memory Lola wanted to be thinking moments before she died. It wasn't how it was meant to be.

"Lola?" Fingers called out.

"I'm right here, Fingers. You and me together. Don't be afraid."

"That's just it, Lola," he replied. "I'm not afraid."

He stopped as if there was more to come. Lola pictured his face. He'd see the end before she would. It would be Fingers that saw the end coming. For her, it would be sudden, quick, and over before her brain registered the crash.

"I love you, Lola," he said. "I always have. Since we were young, all I ever wanted was to be close to you. To be the one you came to. To be the one who held you."

Words escaped Lola. His words hit her hard. They sucked the breath from her chest as if some unseen hand squeezed her heart tight.

"I'm sorry," Fingers continued. "I'm sorry I never told you. I'm sorry it had to be now. I'm sorry."

"No," said Lola, "don't be sorry. I'm here with you right now, and if there was anyone I'd want to be with in all this, it's you. I wish I could hold your hand, Fingers. I wish I could see your face."

"How long do we have?" Fingers called out.

"About three minutes would be my guess," Lola replied. She pulled at her handcuffs once more. But the effort was futile.

The rear door of the carriage banged hard against the train

as it swung open. A river of tracks rushed past and disappeared into the darkness.

But there was a movement. A leg lowered into view. A black boot found a handrail. Then another.

Harvey Stone swung into the carriage and dropped to his knees. Then slowly, as if he was savouring the safety of the carriage, he raised his head and stared up at Lola.

CHAPTER THIRTY-SEVEN

"Reg, are you with me?" said Harvey as he stood up. He ran his forearm across his forehead, smearing Luca's blood across his face.

"Loud and clear, Harvey," replied Reg over the earpiece.

"Are you tracking me?" asked Harvey, as he strode through the carriage. He eyed Lola's cuffs and stepped into the driver's cab.

"I don't have a visual, but GPS tells me you're travelling at seventy miles an hour towards Upminster."

"Dumas is behind us somewhere. Get a visual on him. He's in a single carriage with two cases of gold somewhere near Dagenham. My guess is that he's got some kind of escape planned by road."

"What about you?" asked Reg.

Harvey's eyes flicked from Fingers' frightened face to his bound hands and then followed the three thin wires that trailed from the driver's console down and into a small bag.

"Can you stop the train?"

"You're on a train?"

"Can you stop it, Reg? It's rigged to blow."

"How long do you have?"

"Look at the GPS."

"I'm looking now."

"Upminster is the end of the line."

"At seventy miles an hour you've got about two minutes, Harvey. It would take longer than that to hack the main system, let alone isolate a train."

"Can you do it, Reg?"

"No, Harvey. I'm sorry," said Reg.

It was the first time Harvey had ever heard Reg say that he couldn't do something. The news came like a breath of cold air.

"Find Dumas and stop him," said Harvey.

"What about you?" asked Reg.

Harvey searched for the words, seeking a plan, but nothing sprang to mind.

"I'll figure something out," said Harvey.

Reg seemed to hang on Harvey's words.

"Is that Reg?" asked Fingers.

Harvey nodded.

"Have him hack the Transport for London system. There's a chance he can access the switches to take us onto the British Rail line. It means we'll shoot through Upminster instead of slamming into the barriers. That should give us another thirty minutes as long as we don't hit something coming the other way."

"Reg, did you hear that?" asked Harvey.

"Already on it," said Reg. "Is that Fingers?"

"Yeah, he's tied to the accelerator. If he moves, it'll blow."

"Put him on the line," said Reg.

Harvey pulled the earpiece from his ear and placed it into Fingers', whose face was screwed up with thought, but he immediately began talking to Reg.

Harvey slipped from the cab and set to work on Lola's cuffs.

"We may have bought more time," he said, as he released her.

"How did you do that?" she asked, rubbing her wrist and flexing her arm.

"Someone taught me once," replied Harvey.

"A criminal?" asked Lola.

"No. A policewoman. Help me get the doors open in case we have to jump."

"Jump?" cried Lola. "I'm not-"

"Fair enough, but if Reg and Fingers can't work their magic, you'll be blown to kingdom come and I'll have a few broken bones. Your choice."

A few moments later, Lola was standing by Harvey's side as he worked his fingers between the sliding doors. A tiny slither of a gap grew to a finger space, enough for Lola's hands to reach in. She pulled on one door while Harvey pulled on the other until they were far enough apart for each of them to jump down onto the embankment below.

Finding the knife he'd taken from Marco, Harvey handed it to Lola.

"Cut Fingers free," he said.

"But what about the-"

"Just don't let him ease off the accelerator. Keep the pressure on."

Lola took the knife and moved away from Harvey, who was standing and looking out at the night, the rooftops of sleeping houses and the rushing trees. The air felt good and clean, cool and refreshing, but the cleanse failed to quieten the beast that grew restless inside his body.

"They did it," cried Lola from the driver's cab. She leaned through the single door. "Harvey, they did it. They changed the switches."

He glanced back at her, nodded and then returned his attention to more pressing matters.

The final station before Upminster flashed past in a blur of lights, then vanished, leaving only fluid memories of Melody in its wake. They played out like a reel of mismatched films, spliced with sadistic hands to form a looping nightmare of hellish design.

Like a lava bubble bursting, Harvey's eyes pulsed once. The throb of blood surged through him, seeking adrenaline, seeking...

Redemption.

A cool, familiar sweat formed on Harvey's nape. He found himself rolling his neck once more from side to side, delighting in the satisfying click with guilty pleasure.

"You die with me tonight," said Harvey to no-one but the beast.

CHAPTER THIRTY-EIGHT

"I'm sorry for what I said," said Fingers, as Lola pulled the tape from his hands and cut the excess off.

"Keep the pressure on," replied Lola. Then she let out a long breath. "It's okay. I knew. I always knew."

"You knew?" said Fingers. "And you let me-"

"You're my friend. You're a good friend. I don't want to lose that. I figured maybe one day, but-"

"But?" said Fingers, his voiced twinged with hope.

"But that day never came," said Lola.

"And it nearly never did," said Fingers. "What about now?"

Lola's eyes widened at the comment, but then she frowned and hushed her voice.

"You do realise we're standing beside a bomb, and I just had to cut your hands free? We nearly just died, Fingers, and you're asking me-"

"I'm asking if you feel any different now," said Fingers. "We bought ourselves more time, but we're still standing beside the bomb. So how about it?"

"You've put me on the spot a little, Fingers. Can I mull it over?"

"I'm not going anywhere," he said with a smile. "Can't we just wedge this accelerator open and jump? I feel so trapped."

"And send a seventy mile an hour bomb hurtling through the countryside?" said Lola. "Why don't you ask Reg if he knows anything about disarming a bag full of explosives?"

"Hey, Reg," said Fingers. "Are you there?"

There was a silence before Reg replied. Lola saw Fingers' face crease as he strived to hear Reg speak over the earpiece.

"Sorry you had to hear that," he said.

A blush of red filtered across Lola's face.

"Do you know how?" asked Fingers. His voice rose with excitement. Lola straightened. A glimmer of hope had shown its face.

Another silence.

"He needs photos," said Fingers. "Expose the wiring and use my phone, and don't miss anything out. He needs the full circuit."

Lola set to work pulling the bag away from the white bricks of explosives, being careful not to disrupt any of the cabling. She snapped five photos, found Reg's contact on Fingers' phone and sent them across.

"I didn't know you had his number on here," said Lola.

"He's one of the most talented technologists I've ever seen, Lola. It would be like you meeting Catwoman."

"Catwoman?" replied Lola. "Is that who you liken me to?"

Fingers seemed to ponder his answer with pursed lips and an amusing thoughtful upward gaze.

"Once or twice," he said, "but it was mainly about the outfit." He smiled a confident smile. But it flattened as his eyes fell back on his own hands, which held the accelerator lever away from the pair of wires.

"Hold on, he's back," said Fingers. Then he quietened as Reg relayed some instructions for Fingers to convey to Lola. "The circuit is using the train as the earth. There's a copper strap somewhere beneath the console that grounds the connections. We need to short the black wire against the copper strap, then cut the red wire. The explosives won't be disarmed but it'll mean we can ease off the throttle and wait for the bomb squad."

"Wait for the bomb squad?" said Lola. "You do realise I just helped rob a vault in the City of London, stole a bunch of gold, and aided and abetted a known criminal? Not to mention the murders that happened in between all that."

"Reg says we need to hurry because there's a train fifteen miles away and we're in its way," said Fingers.

Lola stared at the explosives, a small mass of wires sitting atop a few white bricks connected by a few random electrical components.

"We need some cable to create the short," said Fingers.

Lola turned the knife upside down and used the handle to smash through a few of the instruments on the driver's console. Once the glass was broken, she forced the dials through to reveal several bunches of cables below. One of them was as thick as a man's arm.

"Can I cut any of these?" she asked.

"How would I know?" said Fingers, peering into the hole.

Lola isolated a single, green cable. She pulled enough slack to give her a one-metre length, then closed her eyes, put the blade of the knife on the plastic coating, and sucked in a deep breath.

Then cut.

There was no explosion. No flash of light as the detonator sparked into life.

She pulled the cable out and twisted one end around the copper strap that grounded the console as Fingers relayed her actions to Reg for confirmation. She was standing poised with the other end of the cable in her hand and hovered above a small connector block on top of the brick of explosives, from which, the black cable ran to the accelerator.

"It needs to be a good solid connection, Lola. Twist it on as tight as you can," said Fingers.

She touched the wire in her hand to the black wire.

Nothing happened.

A few twists later and the circuit was complete.

"Now we can remove the black cable from the accelerator," said Fingers, repeating everything he heard Reg say as if he himself were the bomb disposal expert.

With barely a hint of hesitation, Lola ripped the black cable from the dashboard. Fingers pulled the accelerator back towards him.

The train began to slow.

Fingers pushed himself from the chair, and with unsolicited elation, Lola wrapped her arms around him. They hugged for longer than they cared. Fingers was the first to pull away, a little at first, but then he brought his hands up to Lola's face and held her, watching her as if it were for the first time.

Their kiss felt warm, natural and needed. Tension fell from Lola's muscles as water falls from rocks, as the two embraced and searched each other's bodies with elated hands, and the train rolled to a stop in the Essex countryside.

But the pleasure was short lived. A light grew brighter in the driver's cab. A rumbling grew deeper and heavier.

Then the blast of an oncoming train sounding its horn fixed them to the spot in fright. Lola clung to Fingers, who held her tight and in the few seconds left, he stared in the face of the oncoming train, his whitening face a picture of resolve.

But when Lola opened her eyes again, the rumbling of the train, which had thundered past on the other tracks, began to fade away. Only the sound of a helicopter overhead remained. Its spotlight searched the ground around the train.

Fingers began to laugh, quietly at first, but then as Lola joined in, the laughter increased. They kissed once more in pleasure, thankfulness and gratitude.

Lola stepped from the driver's cab into the carriage.

"Harvey?" she called out.

"What's wrong?" asked Fingers, joining Lola at her side.

"He's gone."

CHAPTER THIRTY-NINE

For many years, Lola had shunned the wealth and power her father had accumulated, choosing to remain on the path her father had set her on when she had been a child. A thief of the highest order. But when the police officer had unlocked her cell door and ordered her outside, her father's wealth and power had come to fruition.

Shame embraced her as Samuel drove them through the magnificent iron gates of her father's estate. At the very worst, she thought, he would convey his outrage at her lack of trust in him, at her ability to break the family in two so easily, and then hug her as a father should. At the very best, he wouldn't acknowledge her insolence at all and start with a hug, choosing to save the discussion on trust for another day. Either way, she knew he would hug her, and she knew everything would be okay.

The grounds of her father's estate always carried within it a sense of peace and calm. The trees rocked with the gentle wind, but the movement was slight as if losing a leaf to the ground would disrupt the balance and order of the pristine landscaping.

The house itself bore a very different ambience. The

hallway felt, and to Lola always had, as if it wallowed joyously in shadow. Dark wooden panels formed foreboding vertical lines that met with the intricate, looping designs of the mouldings, which ran across the walls. They formed frames of dark space filled with the heavy oil paintings that perhaps had once shone and glowed in the morning sun. But now they had succumbed to the bleak, hostile and unwelcoming entrance of the great house.

A few rooms in her father's house pleased her enough to raise her spirits. The greenhouse and pool room with their glazed roofs trapped the sun as a troll might trap a passer-by, by reaching out from its cave and pulling inside its captive, leaving them with a view of the bright outside but surrounded by darkness.

The room Lola had called her own since as long as she could remember was south facing with a large balcony and floor-to-ceiling windows across two aspects. Thick curtains hung either side of the stone mullions but they were rarely closed. Her permanent reprise from the sombre house was adorned with bright, colourful pieces of art she had collected using her specialist skillset across close to two decades. Most of them were unknown paintings by unknown artists. But a favourite of hers that hung in front of her bed was a Dali, obscure, uncatalogued and full of intrigue without the need for shadows. The room was full of life, with fresh flowers each day, and walls as white as white could be. It was a stark contrast to the unsmiling perverse Caravaggios that stalked her journey to and from her room.

There was a gentle knock at her door.

"Come in, Samuel," she called out. She was standing at her balcony doors dressed in only a soft towel, looking out over the gardens to the world beyond.

"Ma'am," said Samuel, his usual precursor to a much more

ornate and well-crafted sentence. He sucked in a lungful of air, but before he could speak, Lola interjected.

"My father wants to see me," she said. "You have prepared dinner, and he is seated."

Samuel gave a look of dejection at his own predictability.

"I'll be down in five minutes," she replied to his silence. "When I'm dressed."

She let her towel drop to the floor and padded to the six huge wardrobe doors.

"Is it a formal occasion?" she asked, as Samuel began to pull the door closed to leave.

He stopped, averting his eyes to the gardens.

"No, ma'am. Your father is in his robe. But we do have guests."

"Guests?"

"Three to be precise, ma'am."

"I see," said Lola, pulling her baggy pants from their hanger. "And father hasn't dressed for the occasion?"

"No. In fact, he's been in his robe since you were taken."

"Samuel?"

He turned to look at Lola, holding her eyes in his own in a conscious effort to prevent them from wandering where they shouldn't.

"Is he well?"

"I'm afraid he took a turn for the worse, ma'am. The whole episode has taken its toll on him. Mr Tenant has been a great help of course. But..."

"But?" said Lola. She pulled a fresh t-shirt from the shelf. "Oh, come on, Samuel, you've seen me naked a thousand times already."

"I'm afraid it never gets any easier, ma'am."

"And my father?"

"He needs his daughter. I'll confirm that you'll be down shortly."

Samuel left the room, but before the door closed fully, it reopened and he stepped back inside as Lola pulled her T-shirt down and flicked her hair out.

"Ma'am?" he said.

"Samuel?"

He seemed at ease now that she was dressed.

"I just wanted to say welcome home, ma'am." He bit his lower lip as if he thought he may have overstepped his mark. "I'm glad you're safe."

They shared a silent moment of appreciation for each other. Then Lola watched as Samuel closed the door fully, leaving her to finish dressing.

Her bare feet slapped on the parquet flooring a few moments later. The voyeuristic eyes of an eighteenth-century hooker sprawled across a chaise longue followed her to the staircase, where Angels Appearing to Shepherds and other Benjamin West pieces continued the accompaniment.

The conservatory was perhaps Lola's favourite room in the house. The light and airy feel with clean white surfaces appealed to her, along with the same view of the gardens that her balcony enjoyed.

Voices travelled along the long corridor like whispers of the paintings in the night. A deep grumble ceased all others. Her father's voice.

A light and self-conscious laugh, which was Fingers', was followed by a monotone, more confident inflection, Reg Tenant.

A silence fell, or so Lola thought. She stepped through the double doors to find all three men sitting around the large formal dining table that her father had relocated when he lost his leg. Each of the men was quiet, their attention captivated by the quiet words of a woman who was sitting beside Reg Tenant.

"Lola, come, dear. Join us," said her father. "We've been waiting for you."

Lola approached the table, hugged her father, and felt his gratitude through his strong arms. He wouldn't mention his emotions in front of guests. He didn't need to. Lola felt it.

She glanced around the room, nodded at Reg and grinned at Fingers. The woman eyed her with a curious friendly smile, flavoured with humility.

"I thought you were dead," said Lola.

CHAPTER FORTY

"It was close," said Melody. "I wasn't close enough for the blast to burn me, but the force threw me against the wall. The CCTV footage shows me bouncing off the brickwork. My head took the brunt of the impact and sent my body into shock."

"They released you so early?" said Lola. "It's been one week."

"No, your father had my recovery redirected here. I'm grounded until I get the all clear."

"I thought she'd stand a better chance of a full recovery here, rather than the four gloomy walls of a hospital," said Smokey.

"It's a very kind gesture," replied Melody.

"The least I can do. My physician is one of the best in the country, and well, he visits me daily so it's really no bother at all."

Smokey picked up his wine glass.

"I'd like to raise a toast," he began. "We set out to save the Defeat of the Floating Batteries at Gibraltar, and we did so with gusto. Along the way though, I learned a most valuable lesson. Lola dear..." He reached out and held her hand on the table. "Please forgive me. I lost sight of what is truly important, and for that, I can only apologise."

"You don't need to-"

"But I am, and I will," Smokey interrupted. "It is the job of the living to preserve the art on the walls of this house and in the homes and galleries around the world, so that generations to come may enjoy them as we have. But not at the cost of lives. How can we enjoy, admire or question art when the very essence of ourselves lies in fragments? Dumas may still be out there with the gold, but I feel it will be a long time before he returns to darken our days."

"Father, you're forgiven," said Lola. "Let's eat."

With a tear in his eye, Smokey raised his glass.

"What are we toasting?" asked Reg.

All eyes fell on Smokey as he sought a suitable choice of words. Melody tried to guess what he'd say during the tiny moment of silence. Perhaps a few words for Harvey or for the risk everybody took. But once more, Smokey surprised her.

"Life," he said.

"'To life," everybody repeated.

But Fingers still held his glass high as others sipped at their wine, and Melody placed her water on the table.

"And love," said Fingers. His eyes locked with Lola's and the two shared a moment.

"Are you okay, Melody? Are you comfortable?" said Lola.

"There's still one of us missing," she replied.

The room hushed.

"I'm sorry, Smokey. I can't enjoy this meal knowing that he's still out there risking his life while we toast to life and love. If it wasn't for him, some of us wouldn't be here at all today."

"And how do you suggest we make amends?" asked Smokey.

Melody turned to Reg.

"Can we track him?" she asked.

But Reg shook his head.

"He has no phone and no tracker. He's untraceable."

"But there must be something we can do," said Lola. "I feel simply awful." She returned her cutlery to the table.

"Where will he go?" asked Smokey. "I understand he has a house in France?"

"No, he won't go there. He won't stop until he finishes the job."

"Do you think he'll carry on after the gold?" asked Fingers. "Dumas will be long gone by now."

"No, Harvey won't care about the gold. He thinks I'm dead. He'll be on Dumas' heels and won't stop until..."

She stopped before the sentence became inappropriate for the dinner table.

"Until what, Melody?" asked Smokey.

It was Melody's turn to feel the burn of everybody's eyes as she sought the right words. She looked up at Reg, the one person in the room who understood Harvey as Melody did.

"Until he's broken Dumas," said Reg. "Until he's found him, hung him up and torn every piece of his flesh from his still-breathing body. Even then he won't stop."

Reg held Melody's gaze and spoke the words as if they were his own. As if he himself was capable of the things of which he spoke. The punishment.

"Retribution?" asked Smokey.

"We need to find Dumas," said Lola. "If we can track Dumas, we'll find Harvey."

"Yeah, but how do we find Dumas?" asked Fingers. "If we could find Dumas, then surely we could get the gold back."

"We lure him out," said Smokey.

"And how do you suppose we do that?" asked Fingers. He folded his arms across his chest and leaned on the dining table.

"What's the one thing Dumas wants but can't have?"

Melody saw it coming. But by the looks on the faces of the others, nobody else had fallen in yet.

"Me," said Smokey. "He wants me dead."

"No, father," cried Lola.

"Samuel?" Smokey interrupted with a hand raised to quieten his daughter.

Samuel stepped forwards, his raised eyebrows inviting his employer's order.

"Prepare the jet. We're going to Spain."

CHAPTER FORTY-ONE

"You have to understand, Lola," said Smokey. "How can I go on not knowing if Harvey is alive or dead? If he is dead, then it's my fault and I should pay the price."

"There has to be another way," said Lola.

The light above her seat pinged on, illuminating the outline of a seat belt.

"If Harvey is alive, we can stop him. He doesn't know Melody is alive. Perhaps if he knew, he would stop."

"And you would stop too? We can call the whole thing off?" asked Lola.

Smokey's private Learjet jolted into life. The tarmac began to roll past the window as the pilot positioned the plane at the end of the runway.

"Maybe," said Smokey. "The truth is, Lola, that I do not know what will happen until we draw Dumas from his hiding place."

"And how do you know he'll be in Punta Secreta?"

"Do you remember the painting, the Defeat of the Floating Batteries at Gibraltar?"

"How could I ever forget?"

"Punta Secreta is directly opposite Gibraltar on the Spanish coast. It is a small town, overshadowed by Algericas, but its history is strong."

"And that's what makes you think Dumas will be there?"

"No, my dear. Dante Dumas' family used to rule the area, many years ago, before even my grandfather's grandfather was born. It was a time when the Spanish were a force to be reckoned with. But when the British spread their wings, the Spanish were pushed to one side. The war that had been fought for so many years at sea finally came to the land. Entire towns were wiped out. Families were erased from history as if they never existed."

"The Defeat of the Floating Batteries at Gibraltar," said Lola.

"A tiny moment in such a tragic time, but poignant nonetheless," replied her father. "If Dumas is settling down in Spain with his new-found wealth, that's where he'll be."

"So how do we find him?" asked Lola.

"We don't. He'll find us."

"You are going to walk into the lion's den? He will have men there."

"Yes, I imagine he will have loyalty. His family's name lies at the very root of the town."

"And how do you expect to stop him?"

"I don't Lola," said her father. "If Harvey is there, he will stop Dumas."

"And if Harvey isn't there?" said Lola. "Have you even considered that?"

"Then, my dear, you have to prepare yourself for the worst."

"No, Dad. No. You can't do this. I won't let you."

"Lola, Lola, please."

He rested his hand on hers and squeezed it tight. But his hands were fragile. The squeeze was nothing compared to what it used to be. She hadn't seen before, but now it was clear. Her father's frailty had crept in like a weed might infiltrate a flower bed, growing and taking root under the cover of darkness, deep within the soil. And then one day, when it is all but too late for the plant, the weed reveals its finest work.

"If we cannot stop Dumas, then he must stop me, Lola. It is the only way that you will live a quiet life without me."

A single tear fell from Lola's eye. It dripped onto her face and ran along her cheek, unhindered by flaws to her lip, where it hung and fell.

"I've made all the arrangements, Lola. The estate-"

"Stop," she said. "Just stop. Harvey will be there. I'm not coming back without you."

"I don't expect you to come back without me, Lola." He reached across, held her hand in his and gave it a soft squeeze. Then he smiled his trademark childish smile. "I just might be in a box is all."

CHAPTER FORTY-TWO

"Okay, listen up everyone," said Melody, as the plane taxied off the runway at a small airstrip outside Punta Carnero.

Melody was standing at the bulkhead addressing Smokey, Lola, Samuel, Reg and Fingers as if she was briefing a team of black ops specialists about to go behind enemy lines.

"We have one objective, and that is to bring back Harvey. The current status is that he thinks I'm dead, and due to his nature, he'll be seeking revenge. We're all aware of the type of revenge that Harvey is capable of. If we can avoid that and get out before Dumas knows we're even here, we'll be fine. But if Dumas gets wind of us, things could go south very fast. This is his hometown. He has allies here. We do not."

The team looked back at her with nothing short of admiration. Her confidence and the general manner in which she carried herself gave weight to the speech she was making. Not a soul disrupted her.

"We know that Harvey is after Dumas. We also know that Dumas and Smokey are old enemies." She paused before continuing. The statement needed to be made but she selected her words as a surgeon might select a scalpel. "We know that Dumas would go to lengths to have Smokey killed. We're going to avoid that at all costs."

She held Smokey's appreciative stare and ignored Lola's tearful expression in her peripheral.

"Smokey and Lola will venture through the town as tourists. There are a few hotels, restaurants and beaches. Tourists aren't out of place. I will be shadowing them. The moment Dumas makes an appearance, we need to be on the ball. If Harvey is here, you can bet your life that he'll be close by."

"And us?" asked Reg. He was sitting beside Fingers. Both men had their laptops out in front of them and had spent the flight comparing codes for software that they had designed.

"Samuel has made the arrangements for a hotel. You'll be comfortable. It has internet and coffee. Do you need anything else?"

Both Fingers and Reg shook their heads.

"We will all be wearing GPS trackers. We will all stay in communication. And we will all be leaving here in one piece."

"How do you plan on getting Harvey to come with us?" asked Lola.

"Leave Harvey Stone to me, Lola. He thinks I'm dead. He'll slaughter anyone he thinks played a part in that. When he sees I'm alive, he'll stop."

"And you get to fly off into the sunset with your man?" said Lola.

"And we get to stop any more bloodshed, Lola," replied Melody. "Enough people have died."

"And the gold?" asked Smokey.

The statement was out of place. Melody mulled it over before replying.

"The gold is not our concern, Smokey."

"But if we can save it?"

"The gold is not our concern, Smokey." She let her answer

hang for a moment. "Is everyone clear on what we're doing?"

Everyone nodded and began to stand from their seats.

"Samuel," said Melody, "how about being the designated driver?"

"Thought you'd never ask," Samuel replied.

At the foot of the steps, two officials checked their passports for the EU symbol, confirmed the photo was an accurate reflection of the passport holder, and then guided them to a waiting mini-van.

Melody slammed the side door, then moved to the passenger seat. She leaned inside.

"Mind if I ride shotgun?" she asked.

"Not at all," replied Samuel. "Do you know where you're going?"

"It's a small town. I did some research on the flight. We'll drop the boys off at the hotel, then head into town. Drop me off somewhere out of sight and take Smokey and Lola to a restaurant."

"Copy that," said Samuel. For the first time, his voice lost its submissive edge.

"Were you always a butler, Samuel?"

"Not always."

He pulled away from the airport onto a narrow lane. In the distance, irregular rows of white-washed houses, dotted with pastel blues and hues of yellow, built within small plots of land across the hillside. The sea lay beyond the town, blue and sparkling. Samuel settled into the drive, maintaining the forty kilometres per hour speed limit.

On the left, atop a green hill, was a castle.

"Two hundred years old," said Samuel, catching Melody's gaze. "Built to stop the English encroaching any further."

"You've been here before?" asked Melody.

"It's a small town. I did some research on the flight," replied

Samuel.

Melody fought to restrain her grin.

"Have you worked for Smokey for long?" she asked.

"Long enough to know better, and too long to change things now," he replied. "Besides, who'd look after them if I left?"

"So you're part of the family? That's nice."

"I'm their butler. They pay me to serve them."

"But surely, over the years-"

"Over the years, Melody, I've seen Lola grow up. I've seen my employer lose his wife. And I've seen more than any man should have to keep quiet about in ten lifetimes."

"So it's a mutual understanding then?"

"They need me, and I need them."

"No," said Melody. "You're family. You just don't like to admit it."

The gentle ribbing brought a smile to Melody's face. She wondered when was the last time she smiled.

"He's special to you, isn't he?" asked Samuel.

Melody didn't reply.

"Come on. I showed you mine," said Samuel. "Give a little."

Melody nodded softly. The smile faded.

"He's nothing to me. He's everything to me. He's a part of me."

Samuel let out a soft whistle of air between pursed lips.

"Deep," he said.

"You asked."

"And you can control him?" asked Samuel. "I mean, you really think you can bring him in and stop him?"

"You know what, Samuel? I'm the only one on this planet that stands a chance."

She looked back out of the window.

"If I fail, I wouldn't be surprised if he slaughtered the whole town trying to find Dumas."

CHAPTER FORTY-THREE

"Comms check everyone," said Melody. "Let me know you're online."

"Copy," said Reg and Fingers.

Melody turned to face the rear of the van and slid the glass window open.

"I hear you," said Smokey.

"Copy," said Lola.

"Samuel?" asked Melody.

"I hear you," he replied.

"Okay, good. We're all here. Remember to keep the channel open. Tell us everything that's going on no matter how trivial. Reg, Fingers, do you have the satellite link yet?"

"Yes, we've borrowed access to an international satellite," said Reg.

"Good. Keep your eyes and ears open." She turned around to face the rear of the van again. "Okay, let's do this."

The sliding side door of the mini-van slid open, and Samuel reached in to set the ramps for the wheelchair. Between them, Samuel and Lola eased Smokey from the van.

"Pass me my crutches, Samuel."

"But, Father-"

"Just pass me the crutches. I'm not being stuck in this damn thing all day. It's hotter than the sun here and there are more potholes than road."

Samuel held the crutches steady while Lola helped her father from the chair. Then she collapsed the chair and slid it back into the van.

"There," said her father, "I'm just as tall as the rest of you for once. How about lunch, Lola?"

Samuel climbed back into the van as Lola leaned into the side door to talk to Melody.

"We'll be here an hour or so, maybe a little more. Then we'll move on to somewhere else."

"Okay. I'll have Samuel drop me somewhere close by. You won't see me, but I'll be with you every step of the way."

She slammed the door, then put her hand on her father's arm to help him cross the road. Behind them, a few houses were sitting like stepping stones before the Mediterranean. In front of them, the Blue Lagoon restaurant was perched on a small, rocky knoll.

"How wonderfully Mediterranean," said her father, as Lola urged him across the road between the sparse traffic. A set of steep stairs led to the restaurant from the roadside, but to the side of the building, a ramp for cars to access the car park proved to be more suitable for Smokey's crutches.

The effort took ten minutes, but soon, they were both being seated on the veranda with an open view of the sea. Terracotta rooftops and bougainvillaea struck colour to the whitewashed foreground while grassy patches adorned the limestone ground below.

"So beautiful," said her father. "It's only when you come to a place like this that you wonder what on earth you've been doing with your life."

The statement required no answer. Lola allowed her father to muse. The fresh sea air would do him good.

She caught the attention of a waiter and ordered a sparkling water and a salad. Her father ordered the fish with a crisp white wine, then leaned back and sucked in the air.

"We needed this, Lola," he said. "After what we've been through these past few weeks, we really did need this. Yes, we did."

"You're not forgetting why we're here, are you?" she asked. "It's not a holiday."

"Oh, but it should be," he replied, his voice full of dejection. "It weighs heavy on my heart, my dear. We force ourselves into stressful lives allowing for a few weeks a year to come and relax in a place like this. We've got it all wrong, haven't we?"

"I imagine that a life here would come with its own challenges, Father. It's not exactly booming, is it?"

"Given the choice, Lola, would you have the financial assurance we enjoy and the associated luxuries, or would you trade it all for a life somewhere like this, not knowing if you'll have money for food next month?"

"Is that a loaded question, Father?" She smiled. "Are you trying to tell me something?"

"No, of course not. But you've never had to go without. You haven't experienced it, and that's what I always wanted, for my family to be looked after."

The waiter slipped between them with his tray. He cracked the sparkling water bottle open and poured a glass for Lola over ice and lemon, then poured a little wine for Smokey. Smokey collected the glass between his finger and thumb then swirled the wine. The thin layer of residue emitted a scent that Smokey inhaled. He took a small sip of the wine, let the flavours separate in his mouth and then placed the glass on the table with a nod to the waiter, who poured half a glass for him.

"Please," said Smokey, "leave the bottle."

"As you wish, sir," the waiter replied in his thick Spanish accent. "I will bring your food in a little while, but please, I will be here if you would like something else."

"Thank you," said Smokey, as the waiter left them alone.

"Samuel could get some tips from him," said Smokey.

"Do you think Dumas will show?" asked Lola. "I mean, do you think our arrival has been noticed?"

"Something tells me yes," her father replied. "He will have his spies out for sure. I imagine that the villagers would be more than willing to feed him information for a slice of his pie."

A short while later, when Smokey had folded his serviette and placed it over his half-finished fish and Lola had finished her salad, the two relaxed back in peace and stared up at the castle that was sitting atop the hill overlooking the Mediterranean and Gibraltar.

"It's hard to think that two hundred years ago this place was ravaged by the atrocities of war, isn't it?" said Lola's father.

"I can't see them moving any faster than they do now," replied Lola. "There's hardly a lunchtime rush, is there?"

"Shall we get the bill and venture elsewhere?" suggested Smokey.

Lola flagged down the waiter, who approached with a smile from loitering on the next table, which Lola had guessed was just a display to be on hand when the rich tourists wanted something, a ploy to increase the generosity of the tip.

"Could we get the bill, por favor?" she asked.

"The bill?" he replied. "No, your meal is on the house. I do hope you enjoyed it?"

"It was fantastic, thank you. But why is it on the house?"

"Please," replied the waiter, and with an open hand, he guided their eyes to the man who was sitting in the corner beneath a cream hat in a black shirt and white pants.

"Señor Dumas will see you now."

CHAPTER FORTY-FOUR

Opposite the Blue Lagoon restaurant in a derelict house, Melody was standing in the shadows with a one-hundred-and-eighty-degree view of the street and the rooftops above. The doors of the house had long since fallen off or been removed to service another house nearby. The windows were mostly intact, but the collapsed ceiling offered ample accommodation for local birds to nest.

A few cars passed by, and while Reg and Fingers ran the plates, Melody scanned the drivers, judging them to be safe, potential or a direct threat based on appearances. The three drivers, two of which were elderly and one of which was a local man in his pickup with a goat in the back, had all been marked as safe. Their number plates supported their innocence.

"Looks like they're finishing up eating," said Melody. "They'll be moving soon. Can you guys run a check on the street? Make sure there's no parked cars, vans or loitering people. Identify the potential threats, Reg."

"We're on it," came Reg's reply. "We have a blue Nissan two hundred yards to your right, and a silver Mercedes to your left, and half a dozen motorcycles within a five hundred yard radius of the restaurant. The only thing we've seen move is the three cars that passed and Samuel's van, which is parked two hundred yards away on the coast. Everything else has been foot traffic."

"Only three cars moved in the thirty minutes we've been here?" said Melody. "Is this place asleep, or what?"

"The entire village would fit on a few football pitches. I guess they don't need cars to get around."

"Well, it should make spotting Dumas easier," said Melody. "Sit tight. Smokey and Lola are moving. Do you have eyes on them?"

"We do. It looks like they're talking to someone," said Fingers.

"Can you get a look at his face?"

"Negative," said Fingers. "He's wearing a hat."

"Okay, I've got him," replied Melody. "White hat, black shirt, and white pants?"

"That's him," said Fingers. "They're sitting down with him. Do you think it's Dumas?"

"You tell me, Fingers. You're the only one here who's seen him."

"I can't see a thing with that hat."

"Okay," said Melody. "Scan the area and watch for Harvey. He may be close. I'll see if I can find a different angle and send you a photo. Do you guys have facial recognition?"

"Yes," said Reg. "I have access to LUCY."

"Give me two minutes," said Melody, and she slipped back into the shadows.

"They're moving, Melody. Do you have a visual?"

"No, I'm at the back of the house. Talk me through it."

"Smokey's on crutches in front. Lola and the guy in white are walking behind. They're heading to the car park."

"Any sign of Harvey?" she asked.

"Negative, Melody. It's dead down there."

"I need to get a visual on this guy. If it is Dumas, Harvey won't be far away."

In true Mediterranean style, the ground floor of the tiny house was divided into a reception room and a south-facing kitchen with a back door to a rocky and barren yard. A few old chairs were scattered around the plot as if someday, a long time ago, the view across the Med was enjoyed with a sangria or two.

The neighbouring house, in all its glory with the terracotta roof, bougainvillea-lined yard and immaculate lawn furniture beamed with life, in stark contrast to where Melody was standing. She eyed the property for movement. There were no open windows, despite the heat of the day. There was no car parked outside in the rocky driveway.

"Reg, am I clear to move? The house next door looks empty. Tell me what you see."

"I see no movement. No heat signal. And the roads are clear. Go."

She glanced around one last time then shoved off the wall to make a run for it. But a hand swept across her face from behind. She sucked in a lungful of thick chemical fumes. She knew the smell, but the fog overcame her regardless. Darkness crept into her vision from all sides, leaving a diminishing circle of light.

Then black.

CHAPTER FORTY-FIVE

"Nice of you to pop by my little town," said Dumas. "How do you like it so far?"

He was sitting with his legs crossed and his hat pulled down across the top half of his face. A slither of eyes stared out at Lola and Smokey.

"We've only seen this place so far," said Lola. "But it's not bad. The salad was limp, but I can't complain."

"I watched you arrive. That's a nice van you have there, Smokey. Times are good for you right now, I see."

"I could say the same for your yacht," replied Smokey. "I can only assume it's yours. There doesn't seem to be any other money in this hole."

"Beautiful, isn't she?" replied Dumas. "It gets me around at a pace I enjoy."

"I'm sure it does, Dante," said Smokey.

"I'd like to show you something. Would you join me?"

"And if we said no?"

Dumas raised an eyebrow. His eyes flicked across at two men who were sitting at a nearby table. They were both dressed casually with dark hair, weathered skin and lean muscular arms from a life on the sea.

"It's amazing how the spirits of the local people are uplifted when prosperity docks in their bay," said Dumas.

Lola glanced out to sea at the yacht that was moored inside the breakwater.

"Prosperity?" she asked.

"I named her myself," replied Dumas. "Fitting, isn't it?"

"That depends on your definition of prosperity, Dante," said Lola.

"Before we leave," said Dumas, ignoring Lola's comment, "you haven't told me what you're doing here."

"It's a nice place. The sun is shining."

"What a coincidence that you should run into me then, Smokey. Of all the coastal paradises in all the world."

"How long before you ruin it, Dante?"

"You've come for me, haven't you? Well before you get carried away, you should know that beneath the sleepy façade, this town is my home. These are my people. All I have to do is say the word and poof." Dumas animated his threat with jazz hands, then let them fall to his lap. "We've known each other a very long time, Smokey. Did you know, Lola, your father and I used to be in competition? I'm sure he's told you the stories. You see, we both had similar backgrounds. Our families both lost their wealth but your father and I managed to find it again. Aside from the obvious physical differences, we are but the same man inside."

"You couldn't be more wrong, Dumas," said Lola.

"Tell me about Cordero. Was it fun to watch him suffer?" asked Dumas. His eyes flicked to Lola's chest then returned, unashamed. "Where we will go was once my family home. For the time being, I am but a caretaker, but soon it will be in my family once more, and everything that was shall be again. I think it's rather poetic. Don't you, Lola dear?"

Lola bit her tongue.

"You keep looking around, Lola. Are you expecting company?" Dumas' head cocked to one side, ready to contemplate her next words. But Lola remained silent.

"Well, folks, if that is all we have to say, I suggest we take a short drive."

"And where is it we're going?"

Dumas rose from his chair, leaned over the table and seemed to inspect Lola's hair.

"Remove it," he said.

"Remove what?" Lola protested.

"The earpieces. Remove them. Both of you." His voice had grown abrupt and his eyes narrowed as both Lola and Smokey removed the earpieces and placed them on the table.

"If I ask you how many, you will only insult me with lies. So I will leave it there. But know this, there is no escape for you both, and if anybody tries to stop me now, they will be fish food before the morning."

CHAPTER FORTY-SIX

Water dripped close by in an unending monotonous rhythm that echoed off dark but shiny stone walls and seemed to fall into step with the racing beat of Melody's heart like an accompaniment; one drip, two beats, one drip, two beats.

No searing pain stabbed at her forehead when she opened her eyes. Yet the deep shadows that held the light at bay turned her around in dizzying waves of nausea as she fought to sit upright. But with no visual reference, the best she could do was allow her mind to decide.

She slumped to the floor again with her head in her hands.

Beside her, fixed to the cold, stone wall by four rusty bolts, was a tarnished surface, an iron bracket and a thick chain. Her heart dropped. Sensing the inevitable, she grabbed the chain in the dark and ran her hands along its coarse surface until she felt the tug on her leg.

She dropped the excess chain to the stone floor, leaned back against the wall and ran her hands through her hair, realising then that her earpiece was missing. She searched the floor around her, wondering all the while if she had dropped it, or if her assailant had removed it, knowing that Reg and Fingers could hear her plight. There was no sign of the device on the floor or in her clothing, and once more, the reality of her situation found a fresh wound to dig its claws.

A slice of dim light shone from one corner. At least fifteen feet high, its dismal effect on Melody's prison reached the floor with enough power to light the fur of a rat, but not enough to illuminate a door.

Five steps in each direction were the limit of the chain, with each adjoining wall being six of Melody's steps from the iron bracket. She stretched to allow the trickling water to run across her fingertips then wet her lips. At the limit of the chain, she checked every possible inch of each wall. But she found no door and no window.

She resorted to scrambling on the floor for a trapdoor, but all she found was dirt, small animal bones and the droppings of the rats that circled the edges of the cell, sensing that feeding time had come. Infrequent chirps and squeaks from the rats were the only accompaniment to the incessant teasing of the water.

Having ruled out each of the walls as the exit, and having examined as much of the floor as she could, Melody leaned back and stared up at the light. There was a hole, three feet wide and as tall as a man, but there were no steps.

"It's an oubliette," she said to herself, hearing her whisper die in the damp, stale air. "I must be in the castle."

The stone walls and floor, and the ancient smell of years of debauchery, suffering and neglect that seemed to cling to the walls, all supported her theory. But nothing helped her escape. The only clue to her future lay in the bones of dead animals.

Once more, she examined the ankle cuff, fumbling in the dark to understand the ancient mechanism. But with no tools and no light, it was guesswork at best. She considered using animal bones to work the lock, but there was no keyhole that she could feel.

As a last resort, Melody got to her feet, wrapped the chain around her hands and, by snapping the chain tight, tried to work the bracket loose.

She stopped after two minutes, having come to the conclusion that in the few hundred years the castle had been there, she would not have been the first person to try this technique. The exertion and the chloroform combined in a dizzying rush of poisoned blood to her head and sent her to her knees. Burning waves of nausea washed over her, forming a layer of cool sweat on her brow and nape until she lay flat on the cool floor.

A rat, emboldened by Melody's stillness tested the sole of her boot with three tugs. A swift kick sent it scurrying to the safety of the wall opposite, but more ventured in, each of them with their beady eyes set on Melody's body. She allowed the small pack to get close. Six small shapes darker than the floor twitched at her feet and legs. But only when they had all crept close did Melody attack, fighting them off with frantic violent kicks. She connected with one, and as it recovered from slamming into the wall, she stood up and stepped on its head, feeling the tiny skull crush beneath her foot.

She picked it up by its tail, and threw it to the far side of the room, then listened to the pack venture over and begin their meal. The reprise in their attack gave Melody time to think. But the dark walls and shadow induced no useful thoughts. She was sitting with her legs drawn up to her chin, cradled her head between her knees and wrapped her arms around her ankles.

Sleep came in fitful bursts. Undisturbed by the rats, her mind took her on short trips to the past. In every dream, regardless how inaccurate the scene, Harvey was by her side. Each time she woke, she checked for rats. But they were busy eating the remains of their friend. Then she checked the dim slither of light up high in the corner. But each time there was no change.

Until the last time she woke.

In the overwhelming darkness, she sensed more than saw, darker and heavier than the walls of her cell, the unmistakable shape of a man standing over her.

CHAPTER FORTY-SEVEN

The castle had long since lost its menacing drawbridge and portcullis. The moat was home to wildflowers that were rooted deep in the rocky ground, and high on the walls above potted trees hung from the walkways in the place of cannons and soldiers.

The entrance welcomed visitors with ornate carvings on two huge front doors that filled a giant archway. A symbol of what looked like two crossed swords had been carved into the keystone. But years of weathering had reduced the image to two unnatural grooves, wider than the natural cracks that adorned the old stone walls.

Where once there may have been torches sitting in iron brackets to light the impressive hallway, electric lights had been fitted. Although sympathetic in design to the origins of the castle, they stole a slice of the medieval feel that manifested in the castle's very core.

The rug beneath Lola's feet stretched the length of the hallway, guiding visitors to two more doors, which Dumas opened and was standing beside, while waiting for her to help her father through them. The walls were home to old oil paintings, none of which Lola recognised as revered artists. But they were of impeccable quality nonetheless.

Each frame had been hung with precision and taste, equally spaced between the uprights so that each portrait was equally lit on either side. Dumas waited with a devilish smile on his face as if all his dreams had come true. He was standing beside an area of original bare stonework, cold to the eyes and out of place.

Dumas followed Lola's eyes and his smile weakened.

"One day," he said.

Lola stopped with her father and stared up at the space.

"Imagine how impressive it would look there," Dumas continued. "It's almost as if it was meant to be."

"You'll never get it," said Smokey. "Not in our lifetime. The Guildhall Gallery was built around it. All the gold in the world couldn't convince the Society for the Protection of Sacred Arts to give it up."

"Not while the director is alive," said Dumas. "But who knows? Maybe the society would benefit from some fresh blood."

"And stolen gold?" said Lola.

"The gold belongs to me," he snapped. "It was stolen, and all you did was steal it back for me."

"Is that why we're here?" asked Lola. "I mean, I'm grateful for the tour, but if all you want to do is boast about your new found wealth, I'm sure there are other sights to see."

"I think we both know why you're here." Dumas spoke softly, his voice twinged with a sadness that even his arrogance could not belie. "Follow me," he said, then turned and disappeared through the doors. "And don't think about running. I'm sure even I can catch a one-legged man and his bitch daughter."

"Do you think Melody followed us?" whispered Lola.

"Of course. Don't worry, dear. Reg and Fingers will be

watching this place from above, and Melody is probably scaling the walls as we speak."

They followed Dumas through the double doors and entered into a large room that had been decorated in a similar way to the hallway. Eight large windows cast eight bright shafts of sunlight onto the floor. A dining table was positioned at one end of the room in the shadow of a huge, dark oil painting. At the other end, two red, leather couches were positioned opposite each other with an ornate wooden coffee table placed in the middle. No paintings adorned the walls, just two simple and original torch holders from which hung chains and shackles. A pair of jewel encrusted daggers were mounted on the wall to one side.

"Do you know what those are for?" asked Dumas gesturing at the chains and shackles.

Lola didn't reply.

"When a man offended the Don of the castle, he would be stripped and hung there, humiliated until the Don grew bored or until he was replaced by another offender."

"And then he'd be killed?" asked Lola.

"No," her father cut in. "He'd be cast into the oubliette and left to die."

"What's an oubliette?"

Smokey and Dumas shared a moment of respect for each other's knowledge with a glance.

"It's French," said Dumas. "It's somewhere you put someone to forget them."

"To die?" asked Lola.

"To die," confirmed Dumas.

Lola tore her eyes from the chains and continued to take in the room.

On the coffee table was a silver tray. It was rectangular in shape with solid, gold-coloured handles at either end and finished with ornate patterns that ran across its surface. Three coffee cups had been placed on the tray along with a pot of fresh coffee.

It was only when Lola saw the pot that she smelled the coffee. The smell seemed to accentuate and complement the musky odour of the ancient room.

"I haven't finished in here yet," said Dumas. He appeared to have calmed down from his little outburst, and had returned to his boastful character. "I have great plans for this room."

Through a window beside the couches, Prosperity could be seen in the shallow cove.

"I'm sure you'll be very happy here, Dante," said Lola.

"Sit, please." Dumas offered them both a couch, took a seat himself and began to pour coffee. "We may as well be civilised."

Lola helped her father to one end of the couch, then took her place beside him. Her eyes darted across the room, taking in the small decorative flourishes that, at a glance, could easily be missed.

Central to the dining table, mounted with prominence, was the large oil painting framed in heavy brass. The painting depicted the Spanish army fleeing Gibraltar following their failed attack on the British. In the foreground, a Spaniard lay dying and refusing help from the English officers who were beside him.

"Don Jose de Barboza. It's about dying with honour," said Dumas. "Fascinating, isn't it? But we're not here to talk about my collection or my castle, are we? No? In that case, let's talk about why you're both here."

Both Lola and Smokey remained silent, choosing to see where Dumas led the conversation. Dumas placed his hat on the coffee table, ran his fingers through his silvery hair, and then leaned forwards to sip at his coffee.

"I'll start then, shall I? You've come to stop me and to get the gold. Maybe you'll return it. Maybe you won't."

"You're wrong," said Lola.

"Am I? So enlighten me."

The pause as Lola searched for the words was too long. Dumas read between the lines.

"So you've come to kill me? You see, I can't help but notice how pale you are, Smokey. How weak you've become. You've been bedridden for some time, I know, and confined to your wheelchair, which must have been dreadful for you. So you thought that coming here would draw me out of hiding. But as you can see, Smokey, I am not hiding."

"What makes you think-" began Lola. But Dumas raised his hand to stop her.

"The time for little girls to give their opinion is over, Lola. It is time for the adults to talk."

He snapped his fingers over his head and, from nowhere, a hand reached out from behind the couch and smothered Lola's face with a white cloth laced with chemicals.

Lola fought back. She kicked out, sending the table across the room and the coffee to the floor. But the man was strong and the chemicals were powerful. The fight drained from her like blood from a wound. She felt her father beside her, defending her with his crutch. But her vision faded to black, and dreams of Spanish soldiers fleeing Gibraltar on the burning batteries, while the English sent cannon fire over their heads, filled her mind. The scene played over and over, looping time and again. And then nothing but darkness.

CHAPTER FORTY-EIGHT

"So how are you going to do it?" asked Smokey. The words of her father were the first Lola heard when consciousness found its way back to her. "I don't want Lola to see."

At first, the words formed part of a dream. They were a strange narration to an even stranger story where men on horseback appeared through the cannon smoke and formed a circle around Lola, who had been tied to a post.

"But she should see, Smokey. It will be a lesson to her. To watch her father die because of his actions will be her greatest lesson. And one, I'm sure, she'll never forget."

Men on horseback faded, replaced by stone walls, paintings and two old men who were sitting opposite each other on red, leather couches. She gagged as she bit down on the cloth that had been tied around her head. A dull ache ran through her arms and hard steel restraints dug into her wrists with chains that were fixed to the wrought iron brackets where, a long time ago, those who had offended the Don were chained and humiliated before being cast into the oubliette to die.

"How," continued Dumas, "is your choice. To fall from these walls onto the rocks below would be quick and certain, but would leave little of you for Lola to take home. I know that's something you're keen on."

"You're sick, Dante. I thought after all these years, you'd allow me the decency of an honourable death."

"But do you deserve honour, Smokey?" said Dumas. "It will be by your own hand that you die, not mine. There's no honour in suicide."

Dumas leaned forwards and placed a small white tablet on the silver tray. Then he reclined back, crossed one leg over the other, and waited for Smokey to speak.

"This is my alternative?" asked Smokey.

"You always were a smart man, Smokey. But don't be fooled by its appearance. Taking the pill will allow Lola here to mourn your body. It'll give her something to carry home and bury in those fine gardens of yours. But your death will be slow. The chemicals inside that pill will enter your bloodstream, sending its fire coursing through your body and eating its way through each one of your organs. The manner of your death will depend on which organ gives up first. You will suffer incredible internal bleeding and a pain unfathomed even by medieval standards. And, of course, Lola there will be watching, helpless while you squirm on the floor trying to rip your skin off to get to the source of the pain."

Lola gave a muffled outburst, incomprehensible even to herself.

"Ah, she's awake," said Dumas, standing to admire her with roaming eyes. "I apologise for your discomfort, Lola. But I didn't want you to miss the show. I understand that plans have already been made. You're rich, Lola. What will you do with all that wealth?"

Lola fought against her restraints, but her efforts were futile. She inhaled through her nose and felt her eyes wide with anger but wet with helpless tears.

"How do I know she'll be okay?" asked Smokey. "How do I know you'll let her go?"

"Oh, I won't be letting her go," said Dumas, his eyes fixed on Lola's. "She'll be my first mate, at least until she's proved to be trustworthy enough. Then perhaps I'll find some corner of the world to set her free. I have no argument with Lola."

He spun on his heels to face Smokey, who was staring at the pill.

"So what will it be, Smokey? The easy way or the hard way?"

"And what if I said neither?" said Smokey. The strength had gone from his voice, leaving behind the cracked and broken remnants of a once powerful man.

"That's easy," replied Dumas. "I'll force feed Lola the pill and it'll be you who will watch your daughter die. It will be a very slow and painful death. It's an easy choice you are faced with I'm sure, Smokey."

With all reasoning gone, Lola snatched at the chains that held her against the wall. She screamed within the confines of her gag. But all her efforts did were raise a smile on Dumas' face and cause her father to crumble further.

Smokey reached forwards and took hold of the pill, staring at it in the palm of his hand with the curiosity of a child observing a captured poisonous insect before it sank its teeth into his soft skin.

It was with clear regret that her father tore his eyes from the pill and stared up at Lola.

"Close your eyes," he said.

She wanted to scream at him, to tell him no, to wait for Melody. But his eyes told her that it was too late. He nodded once with his lips pursed and his face gaunt as he fought to hold himself together. For her sake.

"Do it," he said.

A tear rolled from his eye, but he didn't wipe it away or hide his face. For the first time that Lola could remember, her father allowed his emotions to run free. It was written in his eyes, in his face, in his slumped posture.

"Do it now, Smokey," shouted Dumas, sensing the tension between father and daughter. "Or it's the high jump for you. I'll throw you off myself if I have to."

Lola held her father's sorrowful gaze one last time. In her mind and heart, she spoke volumes, telling him everything she should have said before. She told him how sorry she was, how he was a good father, but most of all, how much she loved him. She left him with a look that conveyed her open and broken heart.

The edges of her father's mouth curled briefly, revealing the faintest of smiles as if he'd understood everything from his daughter's look.

"Do it," screamed Dumas.

Her father nodded at Lola, who closed her eyes, letting the flood of hot tears that she'd fought so hard to hold back cascade across her skin. The urge to open her eyes and scream at her father was overwhelming. But to see him die in pain at his own hand was not the last image she would hold in her heart. Her mind scrambled to find an image of him to adore, to cherish. Anything but the shell of a man who was sitting ten feet away with a fatal pill in his hand.

The room fell silent.

Lola squeezed her eyes closed, searching for the sound of her dying father fighting the pain of his organs being eaten away by chemicals. But when the noise came, she abhorred the thud of her father's body hitting the stone floor, the sound of his struggles against the sparse antique furniture, and his final dying breaths. There were two loud thuds followed by a wild scream.

Then the room fell silent.

Lola's heart thumped. Her breath came in short irregular waves leaving her breathless. Images of what might confront her played across her mind, but her eyes would not open. Before she had fought to squeeze them closed; now she fought to open them.

Just a crack.

A slice of blurred light magnified by tears.

A little more.

A dark shape, familiar yet fearful.

She forced them open, blinking away the tears.

Harvey Stone.

CHAPTER FORTY-NINE

A scream echoed off the cold, stone walls, shrill and sharp in the thick, stale air. But just like the dim light, the noise had faded to a haunting whisper by the time it entered Melody's oubliette.

"Sounds like the fun has started without us," said Samuel, his perfect English articulated with its usual clarity. "We can have some fun of our own."

"Samuel?" she said. "What are you doing here? Help me get these chains off."

"I think we both know that's not going to happen, Melody."

The truth struck her like a brick to the head.

"You snake. Of all the people I thought-"

"You thought wrong."

"Why? At least tell me why."

"I thought that would be obvious. Dante is a winner. Smokey was destined to lose."

"With you by his side, he was bound to lose, Samuel."

Samuel laughed and paced away from her, his dark shape succumbing to the shadows until only his voice gave away his whereabouts.

"How long has it been? When did Dumas buy you?"

"Oh, a long time ago," said Samuel. "Years, in fact. It was perfect. I sent Smokey chasing shadows all across the country while Dante made us rich. In the meantime, I enjoyed the fruits of Smokey's labour."

"So this was planned?" asked Melody.

"No, but plans change. To be a winner, you need to roll with the punches, Melody. We knew Smokey would go after the painting. We knew he would try and stop us."

"You didn't count on me."

"And look how that worked out."

Melody searched the darkness for his shape, but her eyes landed on the ladder he'd used to climb down into the oubliette.

A chance.

"What's happening up there?" she asked.

"Death."

He spat the word as if verbalising it had left a bad taste in his mouth. He let it hang in the air, clear and sustained with his breath.

"And me?" asked Melody.

Even Samuel's smile was audible. He inhaled, long and slow.

"Life," he said, but cut the word short. "If this is what you call living."

"With the rats? That's not my style, Samuel."

His face appeared beside hers, close enough that she could feel his breath on her skin.

"Like I said, Melody, to be a winner, you need to roll with the punches. How comfortable your life is all depends on how well you adapt to your new life."

She felt his finger brush her forehead, cold to the touch, yet soft like a lover. Melody braced herself against the wall. Her back became rigid with anger and fear, the muscles taught and hard. Her senses woke with pulsing stabs at his smell, his shape and his presence.

Samuel's finger traced the outline of Melody's forehead, sweeping the loose hairs to one side. He moved closer to crouch before her. The softest light from above lit the side of his profile to reveal a handsome man. But his dark, cruel eyes sunk into the shadow, allowing only a glint of light to shine through.

He blinked once, then let his finger trace Melody's nose. He let it fall to her lips then traced the outline of her mouth. Then it was gone. His hand hovered in front of her, teasing her, then dropped to her chest, removed of any tenderness. In the darkness, his breathing grew in intensity as he felt his way to excitement, leaving Melody clenched and waiting for her chance. Waiting for him to commit.

But instead he moved away.

He stepped back into the shadows.

"Are you going to play nicely?"

CHAPTER FIFTY

Three feet in front of where Lola was fixed to the wall, Harvey stared back at her. But it wasn't with the cruel, hard eyes she'd seen before. He had a look of compassion and for the first time, Lola attributed the man with human emotion.

There was a choking sound from behind him. Her father was on his front. Mucus hung from his mouth to the floor in a long, pink string. The only occasional jolt of life came as the chemicals broke through another part of his insides and teased a nerve with its acidic touch.

Any remaining strength washed from Lola's body at the sight of her father fighting for his last breath. Her legs buckled and the chains rattled against the stone as they caught her weight and buried into her flesh. But she felt no pain. The man who had raised her, who had taught her everything she knew and who had allowed her free rein to become who she was, was lying in a pool of his own vomit and blood.

It was not the memory she would treasure. But she feared it would be an image that would come to haunt her.

Beside her father, on the other side of the coffee table, Dumas stared down at his hands, which had been laid flat on the table's surface and pinned with the two long daggers that had hung on the wall in the hallway. His face was twisted in a blend of agony and anger as he sucked air through his gritted teeth and cursed in a long string of incomprehensible Spanish.

"There was nothing I could do," said Harvey.

Lola averted her gaze, letting her eyes roam the room for a mental distraction, fighting the urge to scream and shout and let the tears flow.

But Harvey's presence lured her back.

"You might want to close your eyes again," said Harvey.

A transformation took place in front of her. His eyes glazed over, returning once more to the cold hard stare that Lola recognised. A chill ran the length of her spine as Harvey turned away to stand behind Dumas.

Lola looked on with incredulity at Harvey's calm composure. He rolled his head from side to side, feeling the click at each extreme. Every part of her wanted Harvey to end Dumas, to make him suffer. The fight inside her was back, and her feet found the floor. Like a wild animal, she tore at the chains.

But Harvey remained calm. His control somehow overshadowed Lola's physical desire to tear Dumas apart.

"You want the gold?" said Dumas, striving to turn his head to see Harvey, but restrained by his pinned hands. "I'll give you gold. How much do you want?"

"You can't give me what I want," replied Harvey. "All you can do is ease the pain."

"What are you doing?" said Dumas. The authority his voice had carried just five minutes before had been replaced by a high-pitched childlike tone, full of fear and emotion.

Quiet as can be, Harvey stepped away and began to browse the wall decorations.

Lola screamed against the gag for him to kill Dumas who,

seeing Harvey's back was turned, fought against the knives that pinned him down.

But Lola's plight went unanswered. And Dumas' hands remained fastened to the table.

A pair of pikes, six feet long, lay crossed above a wooden shield that bore the same cross-swords symbol as the keystone above the two front doors of the castle. A fine sword, sheathed in leather and decorated with animal bone, took pride of place between two of the huge windows.

But it was a mace that caught Harvey's attention, a ball of sharp iron spikes fixed to an eight-inch handle by a chain three-feet long. It would have taken a strong man to wield the weapon in combat. But the damage it would have caused as he swung the ball on the battlefield in deadly arcs would have been phenomenal.

With little effort, Harvey lifted it from its iron hook. He swung the ball back and forth, gauging its weight as he made his way to stand in front of Dumas.

Dumas' eyes rocked back and forth with the pendulum motion of the mace. He pulled against the knives. His body juddered as nerve endings tore against the ancient blades.

"What?" he said. "Anything you want. We all have a price. Just name it, and it's yours."

Without warning, Harvey swung the mace high over his head and slammed the spiked ball down onto the fingers of Dumas' right hand. Dumas dropped to his knees, growling in pain and letting his forehead rest on the table as if he was praying. Three of his crushed digits hung from his hand by thin strands of sinew. Shards of broken bone protruded from his skin and blood pooled into the deep grooves in the wood made by the sharp spikes.

Harvey raised the mace once more. The movement made Dumas too frightened to look up.

"I'm sorry," said Dumas, cowering his head into his shoulder. "He had it coming. If you only knew the things he'd done."

Harvey lowered the mace and peered over his shoulder at the corpse of Lola's father lying on the floor behind him. Blood had leaked from the old man's mouth and found channels in the old flagstone floor.

Bringing the mace high above him, Harvey forced the ball and chain to the table, destroying Dumas' other hand.

"It's not the first time I've removed someone's hand, Dumas," said Harvey. "I know what's going through your mind."

But Dumas was incapable of replying. Instead, a whimper of sound emerged from the back of his throat. He bit into his own arm as if he was restraining an outburst. But his agony was clear.

Lola savoured the moment. A run of saliva hung from her lips like a crazed savage, steering Harvey with evil thoughts of brutality.

"I know the torment," continued Harvey. "Hands are a crucial part of our existence. Without them, we're useless. There's a part of your brain now adjusting to that. It's thinking of all the things you can no longer do without help."

At the sound of Harvey's words, Dumas' face dropped. The fight had vanished.

"You're powerless, Dante. Everything you've worked for, the power you fought so hard to obtain, it's gone."

Harvey took slow purposeful steps while he spoke. It was as if he was immune to Lola's thoughts. But when he turned and walked towards Dumas, her heart began to race once again.

"But another part of your mind can see past your ruined fingers and hands, can't it?"

With a violent snatch, Harvey grabbed a handful of Dumas' hair and wrenched his head back. Leaving the mace to fall to the floor, Harvey then picked up a ruined finger. He twisted it around, ripping what skin and sinew remained until it was free. An inanimate object held in front of Dumas' face. Tantalising but useless. Until it was forced into Dumas' mouth. Harvey held the man's mouth closed as he squirmed and tried to spit and stop the inevitable, involuntary swallow.

And then it happened.

Dumas convulsed, dry heaving as his own ruined forefinger made its way down his gullet.

"Was that the finger that pushed the button?" asked Harvey. "Tell me. Was it that finger? Or was it this one?" He picked up another and forced it into Dumas' mouth. The swallow came a lot faster than the first. Dumas shook his head to remove the bitter taste of irony blood and flesh, then spat blood to the floor, panting.

"What button?" said Dumas, once he'd caught his breath.

Harvey collected the mace from the floor and rose up high behind Dumas, ready to deliver the final blow to Dumas' head.

Lola watched, willing him with muffled pleas.

"The van," said Harvey. "You know what I'm talking about."

An understanding seemed to iron the agonised creases from Dumas' face. A smile grew, faint at first, but as the realisation dawned on Dumas, his head fell back, his body tensed, and a laugh, cruel and sickening, bellowed from the pit of his twisted stomach.

"The girl?" said Dumas. "It's the girl."

Harvey raised the mace.

But Dumas continued to laugh, fighting himself for a chance to speak and breath.

"You mean the little bitch who died in the blast?"

Two clicks of Harvey's neck, one to each side.

"The little tart you carried away from the museum? That's right, Harvey Stone, I saw you. I watched it all."

Harvey didn't reply.

"I told you before that I can give you anything you want."

"You can't give me what I want. You took her from me," said Harvey. He tensed his body in a powerful curve, gripping the mace with two hands over his head, and sucked in a deep breath, ready to smash Dumas' skull apart with a single blow.

Lola was frozen, torn between horror and delight. Her hot, gagged breath and endless tears had swollen and reddened her face. Her shackles had ripped her skin apart, leaving blood to run freely down her arms. But at that moment, she was free, flying high above the scene like a vulture relishing in the brutal act of life and death.

Dumas laughed once more, then cut it off in one short, sharp stab of laughter that caught Harvey's attention.

"She isn't dead, you fool."

CHAPTER FIFTY-ONE

With her back against the wall and the slack chain in her hand, Melody rose into a defensive posture. She held the chain behind her, ready to whip out at Samuel if and when he showed himself. Her head darted from left to right, seeking the shadows for subtle changes. But there was no sign of him. She strived to hear his polished brogues on the dirty floor, but her short breaths were loud in the tiny oubliette.

"You want me?" she said. "You come and get me."

A flash of hot breath against her skin to her right. Melody whipped the chain around; it found nothing but the hard, stone wall and clattered to the floor. Rats scurried to the corner, squealing at the excitement as she dragged the chain back and prepared herself for another attack.

"You're scared," said Samuel.

But Melody couldn't place his voice. The rats, her pulse and her breath filled the room with an incessant hum.

"You should be," he whispered, just inches from her ear, sending her reeling and backing away as far as the chain would allow. But at the limit of the chain, there was no excess to use as a weapon. So Melody dropped it, closed her eyes and inhaled deeply to calm her breathing.

The squealing of the rats was a pitch high in the spectrum of sound. The dull thud of her heart in her ears with its bass tone was low. Although the walls to her sides were hidden by shadow, she pictured them in the light, as they once must have been, even for just a short time. Years of damp had stained the large stones with shades of greens and browns, and they glistened as an ever-moving layer of moisture flowed across them. The floor, bearing hundreds of years of dirt, grime and filth, was bare, save for the length of chain that held her captive.

The image formed in her mind clearly. Between the sounds of the rats and her heart was a void, in which tiny sounds took their place, pin pointing Samuel to the wall on her right.

Keeping her eyes closed, she stepped forwards. The chain dragged behind, metallic against the stone.

Samuel moved past her; the change in the air was apparent.

But Melody remained still. She pictured him walking around her, lustful thoughts stirring his loins.

Melody pictured breaking his neck.

She stepped forwards once more. Again, the chain dragged behind, forming a loop of excess, not quite enough to use as a weapon. But her position in the room was clear. He was behind her now, darker than the shadows, and hard as only a man can be.

Melody felt the temperature raise maybe half a degree. It was subtle, almost indiscernible, but it was there.

And then he was in front of her.

"Found you," he whispered.

His words brought only a smile to Melody's face. She had lured him close.

"Don't fight me," he said. It was as if he had only mouthed the words and allowed his breath to form the sound.

A long exhale was followed by a wandering hand, as it explored Melody's body with a tender, childlike touch. Samuel's breathing quickened. Though Melody kept her eyes closed, his rhythmic movements needed no explanation. The sounds of his torment grew in intensity with his groping hands and the waves of his stale breath on her neck as he leaned into her. He gave a final shudder and exhaled. His hard grip on her chest released, returning to his soft inquisitive touch, then he slid from her to the floor.

Her vision of the room became confused, a swirl of imagery. The walls were no longer on the sides. The rats were no longer behind her. Now a shadow loomed over her, as if its presence fed off the diminishing darkness to become greater than ever before.

She opened her eyes and dizzied at the sudden intake of the dim light in the corner of the room, which framed a human form like the devil himself.

"Harvey."

CHAPTER FIFTY-TWO

The blade of the sword sucked at Samuel's flesh as Harvey pulled it from his body and hoisted Melody off her feet. Never before had he longed for a single kiss. Never before had he wanted Melody in his arms so much. Her legs wrapped around his waist, squeezing him tight. Her arms pulled him closer and her hands felt his face, his neck and chest as if searching for some flaw like she doubted it was really him.

They paused for breath with Melody held high, but neither spoke. There were no words. There was no light. Only two people, once lost and now found.

The kiss lasted an age, but not long enough. When Melody relaxed her legs and slipped along his body to the ground, she still clung to him, running her hands across his chest.

"Do you know how long I've waited for that?" she asked, resting her head on his shoulder.

"Are you hurt?" he replied.

"Physically?"

Harvey didn't reply.

"Where's Dumas?" said Melody. The urgency returned with her senses.

"Smokey's dead."

"Was it-"

"Dumas?" Harvey interrupted. "Yes. I was too late."

"And he's here?"

Harvey nodded.

"I haven't finished with him yet."

The iron shackle on Melody's ankle was no match for the hard, steel blade, which prized the two halves apart and clanged to the floor beside Samuel's naked body. With a glance around the room, and seeing the dark form of the corpse, black against the charcoal floor, Harvey took Melody's hand and led her to the ladder. Once Harvey had climbed up behind her, he pulled the ladder up and tossed it to the floor.

"Is he dead?" asked Melody.

"He will be," replied Harvey. Then he took her hand again and made his way to the hallway, where he replaced the blood and filth stained sword to reform the wall-mounted cross.

Melody was already at the two wooden doors. She stopped to take in the scene with two slow movements of her head, then rushed inside. Harvey was standing at the entrance as Melody silently untied Lola.

Gasping for breath and erupting in tears, Lola fell onto her father's body, smothering him and willing him to reply, to move, to react in some way.

Harvey made his way over to the coffee table, where two sharp daggers remained, stuck in the bloodstained wood. Three fingers remained atop the table's surface, arranged like cutlery in a neat line, but crushed and destroyed.

Small chunks of flesh garnished the bloodied blades.

"Where is he?" asked Harvey.

But Lola had buried her head into Smokey's chest, savouring the last time she would ever touch and feel her father's skin.

Melody looked from Harvey to the blades. Her eyes

narrowed as she pieced the scene together and came to the right conclusion.

"Lola," she said, "where's Dumas? Where did he go?"

Sobbing, Lola raised her head and held Harvey's stare.

"He ran," she said. "He pulled himself free and ran, like the coward he is."

It was all Harvey needed to know. As Lola returned to grieve, Melody came to Harvey's side.

"We need to go after him," she whispered. "Do we leave her here?"

Harvey didn't reply.

He stepped away from Melody and opened the doors to the ancient battlement. A plant pot had been placed at one end, and a small table and chairs offered a view across the Mediterranean like no other.

"Melody," he called.

Then he waited to hear her boots on the flagstone floor. She sidled up beside him, working her way beneath his arm. Her body was warm in the cool, late afternoon air.

He pulled her closer to plant a kiss on the top of her head.

"Do you see that?" he asked.

"See what?"

"The view."

"I see it," she replied.

"Look closer."

Harvey followed Melody's eyes as they withdrew from the breathtaking horizon, across the glimmering shades of blue, and found Dumas' yacht moored in the bay.

A sudden intake of air told Harvey that she saw what he saw. Between the yacht and the dock at the foot of the cliffs, a tiny speeding dot made its way across the ocean, leaving a wake, white against the darkening water.

"Do you think that's where the gold is?" she asked.

Harvey didn't reply.

"We can't let him get-"

"Go and get Lola," said Harvey.

"No, Harvey. She doesn't need to see him get away."

"Do you trust me?" asked Harvey.

Melody hesitated, searching his eyes.

"With my life."

A soft kiss followed as if the words were not enough unaccompanied.

"Get Lola."

Melody loitered at the door, looked back, and then stepped inside.

"Reg, come back," said Harvey.

"Loud and clear, Harvey. It's good to hear your voice."

"Likewise, Reg. Sixty seconds."

"Copy that," came the reply, as Melody stepped through the doors with Lola in tow, her head lowered. She eyed Harvey with a shadow of distrust, but Melody shook her head, a subtle movement that seemed to ease Lola's fear.

"I want you to see something, Lola," said Harvey.

She looked up at him, but her mind was elsewhere.

"Sometimes, Lola, people take things from us. Things they can never return."

Harvey felt the sting of Melody's stare as she too listened to what he had to say.

"I know what you're feeling. I lost everything and I spent my life finding out why. It's why I am who I am. Believe me, Lola, I know you're hurting. I know it's hard. And I know that no matter how wrong it is, no matter how much you don't want to believe it, the only thing that will help you right now is revenge. The feeling will pass. No doubt, you'll be sickened by your own thoughts. But the thoughts will return. You'll always have this unsettling feeling in your stomach. A need to know."

"Harvey, stop," said Melody.

But Harvey didn't reply.

"I won't stop, Harvey," said Lola. Her voice was monotone.

She stared at him, and for the first time, Harvey saw no fear in her eyes, just the shine of her tears, and the swell of her pride.

"Come and stand beside me," said Harvey. He held her hand, and Melody moved across for her to stand between them.

"I want you to look out to that yacht," said Harvey.

Lola's breathing quickened. Her grip on Harvey's hand tightened, then relaxed.

"Prosperity," she said.

"Do you see him?" asked Harvey.

The grip on Harvey's hand tightened once more. Lola's chest rose and fell like the waves and troughs of an ocean storm.

"Use that, Lola. Feel it."

She stuttered an exhale, too violent to retain. Her eyes narrowed on the tiny dot that climbed from the boat into the yacht, helped by a younger man, slight in build and subservient even from afar.

Through Lola's clammy hand, Harvey felt her racing pulse, which matched her violent, rasping breath.

"Use it, Lola. Think of him. This is your one chance. Hold your father in your mind. Do you see him?"

Lola began to hyperventilate. Her swollen eyes bulged and she clung to Melody and Harvey, swaying with the power that coursed through her.

"I said do you see him, Lola?"

"Yes," she shouted.

"Louder, Lola. Do you see the man that killed your father? Can you see your father's face in your mind?"

"Yes," she called, then quietened. Her breathing slowed and a look of clarity washed across her tortured face.

Her eyes hadn't left the yacht once.

In the second of silence that followed, Harvey glanced across at her and smiled as a fireball erupted into the evening sky. The flames billowed, searching for oxygen and stretching with fiery fingers far across the water, then high into the air. A moment later, the dull thud of the explosion ricocheted off the castle walls. A black cloud of smoke mushroomed high into the sky, filling the small cove with black, fiery fog.

Fragments of Prosperity fluttered back into the ocean, diving and spinning in and out of the smoke that hung across the surface of the waves like a blanket. Lights from nearby boats flicked on one by one and swept across the water, searching the fog that had settled, and began to roll with the wind to reveal a final glimpse of the burning yacht. All that was left was a shard of white, brilliant against the darkening blue, as it slipped from sight and into the deep.

CHAPTER FIFTY-THREE

The service was held in Kent, God's Garden, as the signs by the roadside claimed. From there, the congregation moved to Smokey's estate for the celebration of life. On the grand terrace, hostesses in black dresses offered canapés and refreshments to guests, and a four-piece quartet lifted the spirits with the work of Pachelbel, Mozart and other tasteful compositions.

In attendance were members of various art organisations and politicians that were acquainted with Smokey with varying degrees of trust, like layers of an onion. The surface acquaintances, mostly politicians, provided anecdotal accounts of Smokey's projects, programmes and escapades in the hunt for the protection of art. The deeper layers of acquaintances, who had known Smokey when he was a struggling art thief, spoke loosely of his adventures with the tale focused on Smokey's passion for a particular painting.

The congregation was held on the grand terrace that overlooked the impeccable gardens. At the foot of the stone stairs, Harvey was standing looking out at the rows of hedges, the lake and the perfect lawns as the quartet entered into the opening bars of Samuel Barber's Adagio for Strings. A single haunting violin hung in the air with a single sustained note until, as if rising from the depths of sound, the remaining three emerged to support the lead.

Heads turned and the group parted as Melody cut a path through the congregation and stopped at the top of the stairs. She was dressed in a long, figure-hugging black dress and delicate black heels. A small, half-veiled hat was positioned with style at an angle that balanced the wave of fine hair she had allowed to hang from one side.

She held the balustrade as she descended the steps with an elegance Harvey had not seen in her before. A flash of light from her left hand caught Harvey's eye.

"You're not joining the party?" she asked, as she moved closer to him.

"I'm not the partying type."

"What type are you?"

"The type of guy that prefers quiet walks to idle chatter with strangers."

"Do you walk alone?"

"Sometimes, recently."

"Can I join you?"

Harvey didn't reply. Instead, he took Melody's hand and walked towards the bridge.

"You still wear the ring."

"I'm still engaged to be married, Harvey. Until somebody tells me otherwise."

Harvey didn't reply.

"So what are your plans?" asked Melody. "Do you still have the house in France?"

"Of course. Although I haven't been there for a few months. I've been a little occupied. I'll head back there for the winter."

They stopped on the stone bridge, which spanned the narrowest part of the brook that fed the lake.

"How about you? Do you still have the dog?" asked Harvey.

"Boon? Yes. Well, Reg and Jess have been taking care of him for the past few months. I've also been a little occupied."

"I actually miss that dog," said Harvey.

"I actually miss that house. I miss France, our beach, the garden."

She stopped, as if sensing that she was pressing too hard.

Harvey stood up straight, pulling Melody into him but holding her arms tight against her side.

He kissed her and let his hands slide up her bare arms, then across her shoulders to her neck, where his fingers traced the outline of her face. Harvey pulled away, letting his fingers wander across her lips.

"I miss us," said Melody.

Her white teeth bit into her lower lip in anticipation of his answer.

Harvey didn't reply.

The End

Also by J.D. Weston

Award-winning author and creator of Harvey Stone and Frankie Black, J.D.Weston was born in London, England, and after more than a decade in the Middle East, now enjoys a tranquil life in Lincolnshire with his wife.

The Harvey Stone series is the prequel series set ten years before The Stone Cold Thriller series.

With more than twenty novels to J.D. Weston's name, the Harvey Stone series is the result of many years of storytelling, and is his finest work to date. You can find more about J.D. Weston at www.jdweston.com.

Turn the page to see his other books.

THE HARVEY STONE SERIES

Free Novella

The game is death. The winners takes all...

See www.jdweston.com for details.

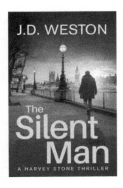

The Silent Man

To find the killer, he must lose his mind...

See www.jdweston.com for details.

The Spider's Web

To catch the killer, he must become the fly...

See www.jdweston.com for details.

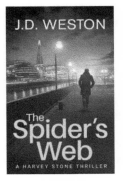

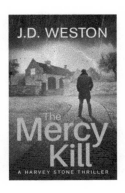

The Mercy Kill

To light the way, he must burn his past...

See www.jdweston.com for details.

The Savage Few

Coming 2021

Join the J.D. Weston Reader Group to stay up to date on new releases, receive discounts, and get three free eBooks.

See www.jdweston.com for details.

THE STONE COLD THRILLER SERIES

The Stone Cold Thriller Series

Stone Cold

Stone Fury

Stone Fall

Stone Rage

Stone Free

Stone Rush

Stone Game

Stone Raid

Stone Deep

Stone Fist

Stone Army

Stone Face

The Stone Cold Box Sets

Boxset One

Boxset Two

Boxset Three

Boxset Four

Visit www.jdweston.com for details.

THE FRANKIE BLACK FILES

The Frankie Black Files

Torn in Two

Her Only Hope

Black Blood

The Frankie Black Files Boxset

Visit www.jdweston.com for details.

A NOTE FROM THE AUTHOR

The Stone Cold Thriller series is set in East London and Essex and features places from my own childhood.

The headquarters building was just a few streets away from my first flat in Silvertown. The farm where the girls were kept is fictitious but Pudding Lane was a favorite haunt of mine, a place to park our cars and do all the things that teenagers like to do.

The big house is real. My parents lived there for a while before I was born and I have vague memories of visiting the owner as a child. Sadly, the image of the house and rabbits in the surrounding fields are all I can recall thirty-something years later.

Epping Forest is real as many of you know. I have many memories of long walks with my family in there. When I became old enough to drive, the forest was a cool place to hang out, camp and just escape the urban life.

If you know the area, and recognize places from the stories, please do reach out to me. Theydon Bois will always be a special place to me and I'm sure if you've been there, you'll feel the same.

Thank you for reading.

J.D.Weston

To learn more about J.D.Weston
www.jdweston.com
john@jdweston.com

ACKNOWLEDGEMENTS

Authors are often portrayed as having very lonely work lives. There breeds a stereotypical image of reclusive authors talking only to their cat or dog and their editor, and living off cereal and brandy.

I beg to differ.

There is absolutely no way on the planet that this book could have been created to the standard it is without the help and support of Erica Bawden, Paul Weston, Danny Maguire, and Heather Draper. All of whom offered vital feedback during various drafts and supported me while I locked myself away and spoke to my imaginary dog, ate cereal and drank brandy.

The book was painstakingly edited by Ceri Savage, who continues to sit with me on Skype every week as we flesh out the series, and also throws in some amazing ideas.

To those named above, I am truly grateful.

J.D.Weston.

Lightning Source UK Ltd.
Milton Keynes UK
UKHW011901020121
376256UK00013B/221

9 781914 270468